Dedication

To my parents, Frank and Mary Jane, who have always stood by me and supported me.

To Renee Alexander for her great proofreading skills and prompting to keep moving forward.

A special thanks to Shimira Cole, for cultural development editing, and adjusting my perspective on the African American society.

Any remaining errors are mine.

Forward

If you have not read Part One of *The Infinite Jeff,* please do so now. Part two is not a standalone story.

In Part One, Stanley, an out of work technical writer, has been struggling to find a new job and find meaning in life. Of the three areas he feels should give meaning to life—family, work, and religion—he's realized that to find a job, he's going to have to leave the only one that has meaning to him, his family. Resigned, he starts looking for work out of state.

Shortly thereafter, he gets a short-term contract job on the other side the country. Too broke to fly, he has to drive to go be "just a tech writer" at "just another company."

At the beginning of his cross-country road trip, he reluctantly picks up a hitchhiker, Jeff, who surprisingly is going to the same town as Stanley. As they drive, Jeff leads Stanley on a strange, life-changing adventure. Along the way, Jeff introduces Stanley to new concepts of religion and raises many questions about life.

When they arrive at their destination, Stanley drops Jeff off.

Chapter 17

I watched Jeff walk down the block, then around the corner of an old, dirty brick building and out of sight, my mind a cyclone of chaotic thoughts.

After this mind-blowing trip to Bethlehem, the contract job seemed so pointless that I wondered how I could even go tomorrow. I knew I had to, to keep my house and feed my family. But after this trip, a two-month contract job seemed such a petty thing, so petty a goal.

I had to do it. But I didn't want to.

I wanted to keep driving and searching for answers to all the questions Jeff had raised in me.

But that wouldn't feed my wife and kids.

With a disgusted sigh, I pushed the thoughts aside. Jeff was gone and I had a life to get back to.

Giving the shifter a frustrated thrust, I put the car in gear and then pulled back out onto the street. I glanced at the dash clock and it was just after one o'clock.

Guess I'd best get some lunch, I thought with a sigh, find the hotel and take a nap. I could unpack after that.

The good news was, now that I was in town, everything was per diem, so the expenses were taken care of. Plus, since Jeff had paid for all the gas, food and hotels on the trip, I actually had some extra cash.

That happy thought lasted until I realized I could now pay my mortgage, but would then, again, be moneyless.

Oh well. Such is life. Several other such thoughts passed, then I had to chuckle. *It's all part of the experience.*

Feeling somewhat better, I found a place for lunch and ate, but on the way to the hotel my mood sunk again.

This contract job was just a meaningless job I needed to get by, then I'd head home and find another meaningless job, just to get by. Then what? What was next? Would the whole rest of my life be 'just getting by'?

During the trip out here with Jeff, I'd been so caught up in the experience that I felt, for the first time, I was part of something real, something important. And now, the thought of going back to "just getting by" felt awful, especially when he'd left me with so many unanswered questions and no way to answer them.

After I got to the hotel, checked in and found my room, I flopped on the bed and called Beth to let her know I'd made it. Unable to help myself, my self-recriminations poured out and the poor woman had to listen. "You should've been the one on the trip with him. You'd have had the wherewithal to ask him the obvious questions. I blundered through the whole trip with the most incredible person ever, and for Pete's sake, I don't even know his last name. I can't even look him up in the phone book! I don't know where he lives!"

She didn't respond, so I continued, "What am I supposed to do, Beth? After what I just went through, how can I go to a stupid job at some stupid company, doing what I've hated at every other company I've worked for?" I paused as an idea struck. "Maybe I'm here for a different reason. Maybe I shouldn't even go there tomorrow. Maybe I should track Jeff down instead."

"What?" she exclaimed. "Stanley, that's stupid. Getting the house foreclosed on so you can go on a religious quest is *not* an option. Go find a mountain top after work if you must, but while you're at work, focus on the job. Don't get yourself fired because you can't focus." She paused, and then continued more sympathetically. "I'm sure Jeff would want you to take care of your family first."

"Yeah, you're right," I wearily admitted. She never failed to get to the basics of the problem. I needed to take care of my family. "A mountain top, huh?"

"After work, Stanley. Only after work."

I laughed at myself as I tried to remember if there were any mountain ranges within driving distance, but couldn't. Then I wondered where else people went for the mountaintop type of thing.

After we chatted for a bit more, I hung up, reclined back onto the bed for a nap, and while questions whirled in my head, fell asleep.

A couple hours later, I woke, much refreshed, and spent the afternoon settling in. I unloaded the car and got things organized, hit the grocery store for staples, and got my computer up and running. I spent some time on Skype with Beth and the kids, and afterwards, did the best I could to dig up some enthusiasm for work tomorrow.

* * *

That night, I was tired enough from all the driving that, even with the nap, I fell asleep quickly. But I slept restlessly and woke even less excited about going to a trivial short-term contract job after completing the most incredible journey imaginable. Even with Beth's orders in the front of my mind, I had a terrifyingly strong impulse to stay home.

After a long struggle with myself, I finally had to admit that I didn't know who Jeff was, I didn't even have the vaguest notion where to start looking for answers to any of my questions, and I couldn't figure out what else to do other than go to work, so I got out of bed and into the shower.

Standing with my face raised into the stream of hot water, I amused myself by brainstorming wild alternatives to working, but every one turned out the same: I couldn't pay my bills. Well, the bank robbery idea might work, if I could get away with it. But I nixed that one as unfeasible; I had the wrong skill set. Besides, I told myself as I turned off the faucets, it was only for two months. With a sigh, I resigned myself to the inevitable.

The follow-up emails I'd exchanged with the Institute's HR guy had said their dress code was casual—jeans, T-shirts, etc.—but for my first day, I figured business-casual was smarter, so I put on khaki pants and a nicer shirt. I'd wait to see what the culture was like before I brought out the Batman T-shirt.

In the small kitchenette area of the hotel room, I grabbed the cereal and milk—breakfast of champions—and took them to the table. As I ate, I looked around the hotel suite. It was small but nice. There was a small bedroom, with a bed I'd found to be very comfortable last night, a small living area with a nice TV and a kitchenette off of the living area with a fridge, stove and microwave. I liked the color scheme with its earth tone browns and greens. It sounded kind of funny for me to say to myself, but there was an energy to the place. I wasn't even sure what I meant when I thought it, but it seemed that this would be a comfortable place for a couple months. I had to admit that things could be a lot worse.

After I cleaned up, I gathered everything I thought I'd need and headed out the door.

Havens Research Institute was only a five-minute drive, and I got there at eight-thirty, a half hour before they'd told me to arrive. I wanted to be early so I could have time to sit and mentally prepare. Of all the things I truly hated in life, walking into the first day of a job was close to the top of the list, right under brussel sprouts.

As I turned onto the road to HRI's parking lot, I was surprised to see the road had a bicycle lane, and even more surprised that the bike lane was almost as busy as the rest of the road. Then I saw the solar panel arrays and slowed to make sure I didn't flatten any bikes as I gawked. The arrays lined HRI's side of the road and were mounted in fancy designs, like exotic flowers. "Those are extremely cool," I said to myself.

I turned into the parking lot and was surprised how few cars there were; I'd gotten the impression from the HR guy that most folks arrived early. Deciding to be grateful that parking was plentiful, I pulled into a spot between a couple Jettas. Both were newer models than mine and TDIs; one had a biodiesel sticker on it. And the Crown Victoria parked in front of me had a "CNG" bumper sticker—compressed natural gas—which was pretty cool, too.

After turning off my car, I closed my eyes hoping to reduce my anxiety level, but gave up when I was interrupted by the voices of people getting out of a car pulled up nearby. It was a Honda Prius with three men and one woman getting out. I nodded to myself in approval of carpoolers using a hybrid.

After the people had passed me on their way to the building, I opened my door and stood beside my car looking around the parking lot more. Off to my left was an area, with a sign over it saying "EV Recharging Station," which was half-full and shaded by more solar panels. The rest of the parking lot was like a showroom for diesels, hybrids, electric vehicles, and alternative fuels. The two cars in the parking lot which didn't fit were a mid-80's Ford Escort and a 60's vintage Rolls Royce.

Curiosity got the best of me, so after I let a bicyclist pass, I walked over to the Escort. When I was younger, I'd owned an 80's diesel Escort that had averaged over fifty miles-per-gallon, and I'd mourned that car when I'd finally laid it to rest in the auto graveyard. Sure enough, the Escort here was a diesel, too, and in great shape for its age.

Next, I walked over to the Rolls. It was a mid-sixties Silver Cloud; I'd always loved that style, a work of art. I walked around this one, checking it out. Silver top over a dark blue bottom, its paint job was perfection. Its red leather interior looked as pristine as the outside, and the burled wood trim glowed, yet I had the impression it was a well-driven car.

The low roar of a bus caused me to turn as it pulled up to the front sidewalk next to the motorcycle parking, which had more wheels on it than the car parking had. As people got out of the bus, it was like a bus version of the circus clown car, people just kept unloading from it. Flabbergasted because most busses I'd seen had had only one or two people exiting an almost empty bus, I watched as the bus pulled away, then turned to watch the line of people going up the sidewalk toward the building.

Seeing all of this began to ease my first-day butterflies. A company who employed the people represented by this parking lot couldn't be all bad.

With my spirits somewhat lifted, I started up the sidewalk towards the front door, past a full bike rack that was worked beautifully into the landscaping. Beyond that, a couple people in coveralls, with "HRI Grounds Crew" on the back, were crouched working around some flowers. As I passed, they looked up from their work and greeted me with smiles, and we exchanged, "Good mornings." Obviously, they worked hard making the area look natural and wild yet wonderful. Ample shade was provided by a mixture of large old trees and younger ones. Benches and tables were scattered around. There was even a small creek running in front of the building, with a wooden bridge integrated into the sidewalk that led to the front door.

I paused on the bridge for a moment and looked around. It was an incredible place, built to be part of nature instead of trying to subdue and control it.

Two people, chatting amicably, passed me, bringing my attention back to my destination, and I began walking again.

The two-story brick building, with its one-story entry area, had lots of windows and was worked into the landscape so it didn't look like a factory. Over in a corner of the "L" of the building was a huge cedar water tank, raised almost a story off the ground on sturdy stilts and almost another story tall. I figured the tank must be used for rainwater harvesting which was another check in HRI's favor, because I'd never understood letting rain run off your roof and into the sewer, and then actually paying for water to water the lawn.

Looking past the tank I could see a number of wind turbines

peaking above the roofline and turning slowly in the breeze.

I walked under the arched awning that covered the last part of the sidewalk, then through the glass front doors, with "Havens Research Institute" etched into them, and into the reception area. My spirits, having been lifted by the landscaping, were lifted further by the cheerful atmosphere of the sunlight flowing from an impressive arched glass skylight, about fifteen feet wide, that ran the length of the room, about thirty feet. Scattered around the room were an abundance of plants and comfortable-looking furniture.

Everything I'd seen so far made it easier to smile as I approached the white-haired, elegant receptionist, who sat behind the curved highly polished wooden desk, and explained I was there for a contract position.

"Oh, that's great!" she replied with warmth and enthusiasm. "My name is Summer. We've been looking forward to meeting you, Stanley."

"I'm looking forward to it," I responded and was actually feeling more like that was the truth.

Chapter 18

As Summer continued speaking, her good cheer came across as her natural temperament, rather than a façade for the role she filled. "Aaron said he had a nice chat with you on the phone and he had a great feeling about you."

Recalling the brief phone interview with Aaron, who'd been the supposed technical part of the interview process but he'd only asked me about the weather, all I could conclude was that the guy must really like the weather to have told the receptionist about the call.

She shuffled through some paperwork, found my information and looked it over. She made a quick phone call and then informed me, "Tom, from HR, will come get you in about fifteen minutes. That'll give you a little time to fill out this paperwork." She handed me a clipboard with a couple papers on it and a pen.

I sat on a nearby sofa and filled out the all-too-familiar forms required when starting a new job.

When I heard a group of people coming through the door, I glanced over. During my many years of working in corporate America, nothing drove home Thoreau's words of "quiet desperation" more than watching people walk through the doors of their workplace; I'd argue that people walking into a funeral were usually more cheerful. But this group entering HRI's doors wasn't like that; they interacted with energy and good cheer. As I thought back to the rest of the people I'd seen since I'd gotten out of the car, I realized everybody had appeared pleased to be coming to work. How bizarre.

After I completed the paperwork, I gave it back to Summer, then began to wander around the reception area. A large portrait on the wall had a plaque under it stating it was the company's founder,

Clinton Havens. Beside it were rows of smaller pictures of the same guy with various important people. The picture of Havens standing with Buckminster Fuller, next to a geodesic dome, caught my eye. I couldn't help a flash of envy; Fuller had always impressed me, and I'd have liked the chance to meet him.

Beyond the pictures was a fancy set of double wooden doors, standing open, leading into a fairly typical polished wood and glass executive area. Behind Summer on the other side was a matching set of doors, and beyond that was a wide, curved open stairway leading to the second floor. I nodded approvingly. It was all very fancy, nice and welcoming.

I returned to my seat and picked up a brochure about the company off the glass coffee table. The slogan on the brochure read, "Havens Research Institute— Changing the world through technology and caring for people."

As I opened the brochure to read more, a middle-aged man came into the lobby and introduced himself to me. "Stanley, I'm Tom from HR; we talked on the phone. We're glad you accepted our offer. We really need your skill set."

Standing and extending my hand to meet his, I answered in typical first-day-employee fashion, "Thanks. I'm excited to be here and hope to put my experience to work here."

He smiled encouragingly at me. "I have no doubts at all. Now relax, you don't have to impress anybody here but yourself. Did you eat breakfast? I hope not, because I haven't, so I'd like to get something, if you don't mind."

His response was almost shocking. He'd correctly read a lot into my reply and answered in a way that set a relaxed mood for the rest of our meeting. But I commented only on the breakfast part. "I ate a little, but wouldn't mind some more."

"Good, let's go to the cafeteria. They have pretty good food."

As I followed him to the left of Summer's desk and approached the double doors, he pointed to the right. "The other set of doors lead to the executive area, but we don't use that much, except to impress customers."

We entered a large, open room filled with low-walled cubes, maybe fifty of them, but I only saw a few people scattered throughout them. The room was carpeted in one of those dark, multi-colored patterns that didn't show dirt, and it looked new. In fact, the whole place looked clean and in excellent repair.

"How was the trip out here?" Tom asked to break the ice.

I almost laughed. His question was only small talk to him, but how could I really answer with any honesty? How could I explain Jeff to somebody who hadn't met him?

Not knowing what else to say, I fell back on the noncommittal answer. "Oh, it was fine." I guess on some level it was fine, so I'd leave it at that.

"Good. Glad you made it here safe. Let me give you an overview of the company and a little on how it works before I pass you to Jane from finance. Today, you'll be meeting with HR and finance and so on, and then have a tour of the building and some of our projects. We planned a short day for you, and since you're new to town and probably have a lot of logistics stuff that needs to be done during business hours. Tomorrow, you'll be meeting your supervisor and teammates, and given your desk and such."

"Sounds good," I replied, not knowing what else to say to the consideration I'd never experienced in any other company I'd worked for. As we turned into a wide hall that led toward the back of the building, I ventured my own attempt at small talk, "I looked at the company's website and at the brochure in the lobby. It sounds like a really good place to work. I'm looking forward to it."

"It's hard to describe everything about the Institute on the website or in brochures," Tom replied with a shrug. "Every other company's website tells how great they are and what a great place it is to work, true or not. We figure most people wouldn't put much stock in our website, so we keep it pretty generic."

Floored by his honest answer, it took a moment to form a reply. "What you had there sounded pretty good, but I see your point. No company's going to say, 'We're an okay company and a so-so place to work.'"

Tom smiled. "If they did, I'd be tempted to go work for them, simply because they're honest. That's a hard quality to find in a company." He paused a moment, as if gathering his thoughts. "Honesty is something we take very seriously. This is a very different place to work."

That I could believe, and I'd only been here fifteen minutes. "I got that feeling from the parking lot and walk to the front door. I drive a TDI Jetta, and I've always been interested in solar power and rain water harvesting."

Tom looked at me with a pleased expression. "Then you're going to enjoy it here. Not only does that type of technology cover a lot of our research, but the people here have a passion for it. There is very little "work" done here; most of the employees come to play with our cool toys."

As he said that, a group of people in lab coats passed us. Like the people walking in the front door, this group's mood leaned toward excitement, rather than drudgery.

Adding the lab-coat-people's mood to Tom's comment about cool toys, my cynical streak silently replied, "Which is why they needed to hire a contract tech writer, because documenting stuff is the not-fun part of the job." But I was smart enough to only say aloud, "That sounds great."

We walked through the archway that led into the cafeteria and the smell of breakfast greeted me.

It was a busy place, bright and sunny, with colorful artwork illustrating each serving area. The energy level was high and the mood was cheerful. Immediately, I liked it. It seemed more like a destination than a place you'd go to eat in a hurry when you couldn't get off campus.

We walked up to one of the serving areas, and while I looked at the menu, stood back out of the way of people who knew what they wanted.

Thankfully, most of the prices looked reasonable. Some things looked over-priced, but there was enough cheap stuff that I could eat well without spending too much. But some of the items didn't have prices. "How do we find the prices of the things that aren't marked?"

"Those are free," Tom replied. "Our health plan is self-funded, so as a company, we try to promote things that reduce our healthcare costs. Of course, people can bring anything they want to eat from home, but here in the cafeteria, the healthiest foods are free. Then on a sliding scale, the least healthy are the most expensive, which are used to subsidize their healthier counterparts."

"Wow!" I said, looking around astounded. "Talk about thinking outside the box."

"Not many boxes around here, Stanley." Tom patted me on the back, either in comfort or warning, I wasn't sure which. "But I'll tell you more about our health plan later. Or you can talk to Mr. Havens about it when you meet him later today. He might scare you though; he's almost fanatic about it."

Talking about health insurance kind of brought me down, because contractors rarely got insurance, and those who did always had waiting periods much longer than my two-month contract. At home, I hadn't been able to afford the COBRA insurance from my last job, so my family was uninsured right now, which wasn't likely to change anytime soon and was very scary.

But the free food is a great idea, I thought, purposefully pushing the depressing thoughts away. Free food would cut my budget, and I might actually come out of the food per diem making a little money, which was money in my credit card company's pocket. Plus, I needed to lose some weight.

I chose the whole-wheat waffles with no price listed, which looked really good on the plate the guy wearing a tall chef's hat handed to me. After I put the plate on the tray Tom handed me from the stack I hadn't noticed, I looked around for drinks and spotted a fountain drink machine. I walked over and was pleased they had Mt. Dew, until I looked at the menu and cringed; it was clear they didn't know about the health benefits of Mt. Dew. Despite my Mt. Dew addiction, I was impressed; all the soda was expensive but there was a juice bar and they had rainwater. I looked at the juice bar menu but ended up asking the guy what he recommended. I wasn't sure what he handed me but it was very green. I tried to look more pleased than I was when I took it. All in all, it was a great way to get people to change their habits.

With my green drink thing and waffles on the tray, I followed Tom out to the eating area, which was colorful and comfortable, with tables that were easily moved to provide various-sized groups their preferred seating arrangements. The place was pretty full, but we found an empty table.

"This is a nice place," I said as I sat. "I like the concept of the pricing levels. And the cooks' hats are cool, too."

Tom nodded as he dug into his breakfast. "Most of them aren't just cooks; they're full-fledged chefs. Many of the rest of the kitchen staff are in the process of becoming chefs. We're a training ground for a couple of the local culinary schools."

While he was talking, I'd taken a few bites of the waffle—with real maple syrup—and understood why Tom loved to eat here. "That's really cool. And this is an excellent waffle."

His mouth was full, so he nodded in agreement and smiled.

I continued enjoying my free breakfast and looking around at the mixture of people in lab coats and street clothes, business casual to shorts and sandals, all talking cheerfully to coworkers. The only guy in a suit was obviously a salesman, and he was in cheerful conversation with a lab-coated pair. Even the few sitting alone seemed unusually content. This might not be such a bad job after all,

I thought. My Batman shirt would fit right in.

The table next to us was getting into a pretty heated discussion, which I couldn't help but notice. Apparently, someone who wasn't at the table had done something wrong, and a couple people at the table weren't happy. I heard a name come up a couple times, then one of the calmer people said, "Call her." The phone call was made, and the table then focused on their breakfast in relative silence.

Tom noticed me watching. "This isn't by any means a perfect place. People are people, and we all see things differently. And here, because most folks are intensely passionate about their work, things can sometimes get a little heated. If you challenge their ideas, process, project or whatever, you'd better be ready with your facts to back yourself up."

It was good to see a flaw around here, I thought, not realizing before that moment that I'd begun to get an it's-too-good-to-be-true feeling. Those feelings were always a letdown.

Tom and I were almost finished eating when a middle-aged woman approached the table next to us, sat down and the heated discussion resumed.

I was trying not to eavesdrop too obviously and didn't understand all the details of the highly-technical discussion, but after only a few minutes, their disagreement ended with the original unhappy folks apologizing to the woman, at which point they all exchanged polite good-byes and she left.

I looked at Tom. "What was that about?"

"Come on." He stood and motioned for me to follow. "I'll explain on the way out."

I grabbed my tray, followed him to the dish drop off area and set my tray on the conveyor belt to be washed.

As we walked back out to the hallway, Tom explained, "I don't know the details of how it got started, but we have a cultural tradition around here that if someone's name comes up more than a couple times in a conversation, in either a positive or a negative light, then either the conversation has to change or the person mentioned needs to be involved."

"That's interesting," I said, trying to hide my confusion, "but what's the purpose?"

"Clear communication. You'll never have to worry what people are saying behind your back. If someone has a problem with you, they'll either say it to your face or keep it to themselves. You'll also know when people are saying *good* things about you, which helps you understand the true impact of your actions. Plus, it insures that everybody is getting the correct info from the horse's mouth, instead of issues being passed around like gossip, and meanings getting twisted in the process."

"Doesn't that run counter to human nature?" I'd seen some amazing things on the trip out here with Jeff, but this piece of company culture defied centuries upon centuries of normal destructive human behavior, even though it seemed well-absorbed enough to be almost automatic to those at the table next to ours.

"You notice how it ended?" Tom inquired.

I thought about it for a minute as we walked past the open cube area I'd seen on the way in, then down a hall beyond. "I didn't understand much of the conversation, it was too technical for me, but the gist was that the people accusing her had misunderstood what she'd done. Once she explained it, the issue was straightened out and the conversation was over."

Tom nodded. "And the ones who'd misunderstood were open to admitting their mistake. Their ego wasn't attached to being right. It's important to put personal opinions and issues aside and look at things with the end-goal being what's best for the project, instead of stroking individual egos. No one here thinks less of someone who admits they're wrong, but they'll come down hard on someone who lets their ego get in the way of the project."

Wow! Just think of the great things that could be accomplished if people could get their need-to-be-right out of the way. "That's outstanding. That type of behavior could stop wars. But you said you don't know how it started?"

"Let's sit here a second," Tom said and waved me to an area with tables and chairs, that looked out onto a sun-dappled courtyard between two wings of the building. He sat and I did too.

"When Clinton Havens," Tom began, "saw a problem, he made sure it got fixed. The story goes that in the very beginnings of HRI, Clinton brought in a bunch of top psychiatrists, and they worked, studied, and then practiced with the people employed here, to make some specialized people-skills—like you just saw—a part of the culture."

"What other skills?" I asked, intrigued.

"They'll make more sense if you experience them."

"Anything I should watch out for? I mean, if I don't know the culture, it'll be easy to make mistakes."

He shook his head. "The only thing that pops to mind is

language, but you have a degree in English, so you're okay."

I was confused by that. "What do you mean?"

"People here expect a high level of communication. Not necessarily ten-dollar words, but mostly not using one-cent words. Be open and honest, even when you disagree, and you'll be fine. People here expect you to use your higher-brain functions."

His last sentence brought back memories of Jeff and me talking in the gas station about the goofy mobile and how their lack of language skills was holding them back. "Ah, I got it. No, that's not a problem with me."

He smiled. "I didn't figure it would be. Trust me, you'll do fine. The only part you'll hate is leaving." He paused, looked out at the courtyard for a moment and then back at me. "I have to be honest with you, though. It's kind of strange that you were hired on such a short-term contract, especially when we rarely use contractors."

"Why not use contractors?" Most companies used them as short-term help when a project needed an extra hand.

"Mr. Havens feels the company should commit to people right away. But with you, Mr. Havens very specifically said to hire you as a contractor," Tom said a little apologetically.

I wavered between befuddled and insulted for a moment, then swallowed my pride. For a contractor, they were paying me a ridiculous amount of money, and I needed to feed my family. Plus, there was always the hope that they'd turn me permanent, but this was only my first hour on the job, so it was far too early to start talking about things like that. I simply answered, "Okay."

Tom changed the subject. "I wanted to spend some time with you before I passed you off so you could settle in a little. I know how hard the first day is, and you'll be getting an earful from some others, so I wanted to get you started off on the right foot. If you have questions later, feel free to stop by my desk. Ask anybody, and they'll tell you where it is."

I had to smile because he'd succeeded; my first-day butterflies were gone. "I enjoyed talking with you, Tom. You've helped me look forward to working here."

He grinned. "Then my job is done. I'll get you to Jane in finance."

"Great."

We rose and walked down the hall a little more, then turned into another open office area, and I followed him to the back wall which was lined with real offices with doors, the first I'd seen outside my glimpse of the executive area.

"Anybody who wants or needs a doored office can have one," Tom said. "We usually have tons extra, because most people spend too much time in their labs to care where they sit. If you want one, let me know."

"Okay," I said, thinking that was very strange. Usually there was a huge battle for offices with doors.

"Mostly," he continued, "the only people with doors are HR and the lawyers, folks who spend their time on confidential stuff. Anybody else who needs momentary privacy grabs one of the small conference rooms."

"Sounds good," I replied, because I didn't know what else to say.

Chapter 19

Tom knocked on the closed glass door of a partially frosted glass-walled office. The woman behind the desk beckoned us in.

"Stanley, this is Jane. She'll take care of all your HR paperwork. It was very nice meeting you." Tom turned away and was gone before I could thank him.

Jane stood and shook my hand. She was a trim and fit woman in her mid-forties. "Welcome to Havens Research Institute, Stanley. Have a seat right here."

"Thank you." I sat where she indicated.

"Alright, let's get this taken care of." She typed stuff, scanned her computer screen, typed more, and then turned to me. "We pay monthly and there's no direct deposit. You'll have to come to the financial advisor to pick up your check."

I cringed. I hadn't thought about how often they'd pay me. Most contract jobs paid weekly, but if this one didn't, I was in trouble, because it meant I wouldn't get paid for at least a month, and depending on how they did the accounting, maybe two months. My credit cards were about at their limits, and we couldn't hold out two months before a paycheck. Then the second part of her statement registered. They didn't have direct deposit? That was strange. I couldn't imagine why a company wouldn't offer it.

Returning to the present, I looked back at Jane, and realized she must have seen something in my reaction, because she turned back to her computer monitor.

"Looks like you've been out of work for a while," she said. "Let's see what I can do for you. I know a lot of the long-term unemployed end up with heaps of credit card debt trying to get by." She glanced at me. "I hate to ask such a personal question, but is that the case with you? If so, please be honest; we can help."

I didn't want to answer, but if these guys could help, I'd take anything I could get. "Yeah. They're about maxed out, and I'm really worried if I have to wait to get paid."

"Yes, I can see that. Let's get you started with our credit card loan program." Jane gave me a glance that let me know she wasn't blaming me and understood the bind I was in. "Mr. Havens, Sr., was very worried about credit cards' influence on our society. So as soon as this company started making money, he set up a loan program for employees. One-percent loans to pay off credit card debt. In all the years of the program, no one has defaulted."

"Sounds too good to be true," I muttered.

"I know, but Mr. Havens was a visionary. To begin, there are three requirements to qualify for the loan."

That was more like it, I thought, wondering if I'd qualify. With the hit my credit rating had taken, I couldn't refinance the house or cars to cut my payments, so I'd been stuck and angry. It seemed stupid. I was broke because I couldn't get a job, but the banks wouldn't lower my payments so I had a better chance of keeping up, and when I'd gotten behind, they'd raised my fees and rates even more, and then the banks complained about how many borrowers were defaulting on their loans. Duh!

"Number one," Jane said, drawing my attention back to her, "you'll have to sign this form promising that, once we pay off your current cards, you'll have only one credit card and will never have a balance carry over month-to-month while you're on the program." She placed a piece of paper in front of me.

I looked at it and read it. It simply read, "*I promise to have only one credit card and to never have a balance carry over month-to-month while on the program.*" It sounded a little too idealistic, but I wasn't going to look a gift-horse in the mouth.

She pulled out another paper. "Number two is an agreement to meet monthly with one of our financial planners. You can meet with them more often, if you want, but you'll, at least, meet with one of them when you pick up your check. In fact, that's why we don't have direct deposit. It forces everyone to sit with a financial planner."

That cleared up the direct deposit question for me, but I wasn't sure I liked the idea of being forced to meet with a financial planner.

She handed me the paper. Again, that one sentence.

"And number three," she said, "is to go through a financial

planning course."

I looked at her questioningly. "Financial planning course?"

She enthusiastically answered, "Yes. We have a number we can suggest. They usually meet once a week for a couple months. It may sound dull but they end up being very exciting to most people. They really help you start to see a bigger picture with money."

I continued my questioning look. "I'm only here eight weeks."

"Hmmm, that may be an issue." She tapped her fingers on the desk as she thought. "Your wife isn't here, is she?"

"No."

Jane nodded abruptly. "Let's do it this way. There are classes held all over the country. I'll do a little research and sign you up for one in your area after you get home, and you'll still qualify for the loan now."

I was confused but answered, "Okay." It still sounded too good to be true, but at the same time, too good to let pass by.

She pulled a book out of a desk drawer and handed it to me. "Read this in the meantime. You'll like it. It's a good book."

I looked at it, *More Than Enough* by David Ramsey. "Okay, I'll read it. That isn't a problem."

She smiled at me. "Good. That's it," she said. "Take the forms with you, and when you're ready, sign them and bring your credit card information to your financial planner—who is Sam, you're meeting him next—and we'll get the loan done. Repayment of the loan will start after you have completed the finance course."

I did some quick math: two-month contract plus three-month course. "That's over five months from now."

"I know. But don't worry, the interest won't begin until you start repayment."

"No, I wasn't worried about that. I was thinking that it was a long time before I started paying it back."

She grinned. "It's great, isn't it? But that's how Mr. Havens set it all up, and it works."

If it was true, my credit card debt was going to be gone, replaced by a one-percent loan that I didn't even have to start paying on for over five months. The prospect was exciting.

"Take the forms with you and talk to Sam about them. He can give you all the details. Now, on to the next set of paperwork." She briskly turned back to her computer. "After five months out of work, I doubt you can wait for a paycheck." She did some typing on the keyboard. "Okay, I changed it." She gave me a look of satisfaction. "I just love working for a place that handles their own payroll. I can be flexible."

She turned back to her typing. "Normally, our hourly employees get paid on the first of the month, with any hourly adjustments accounted for on the following paycheck, so a month's lag. But there's no way we can do that for you. So, I'll do a little tweaking and the paycheck you get on the first of the month will be for a straight month of time. Two weeks paid in advance, in other words, and we'll straighten out the hourly details next month and your last paycheck after you get home will be reduced by the amount of the advance to balance it all out. That sound good?"

It was so much more than I'd ever expected that I wasn't sure what to say. "Sure."

"Great! And the last piece is that, even though you're a contractor, you're still subject to our one day a week charity requirement."

I gave her a questioning look, realizing I'd been doing that a lot since I walked in HRI's door this morning. "Charity requirement?"

She typed more as she replied, "Something else Mr. Havens, Sr., required. One day a week, during work hours, we volunteer at a charity of our choice. Aaron, your manager, will tell you more about it. If you want to put in more time at your charity, you'll be compensated."

The printer beside her started up, when it spit out a piece of paper, she grabbed it, signed it, and handed it to me.

It was a check, a good-sized check, which I'd done nothing to earn yet. I looked at her mystified.

"I've worked with several people who'd been unemployed for a while, so I know what's up," she said with a kind smile. "This, in essence, comes out of your last paycheck, so plan for that, but this should tide you over until the first of the month. Sam is our lead financial adviser. I'll take you to him for your first meeting."

"Um." I couldn't say anything else as I continued to stare at the check.

She laughed. "Welcome to HRI, Stanley, the strangest company you've ever worked for."

* * *

After I put the check into my wallet and gathered up the book and the forms, Jane took me a couple offices down to another glass-walled office to meet Sam.

He looked to be in his early sixty's, and he sprang out of his chair and shook my hand like a vise. "Welcome, Stanley! Sorry, but we have to rush through this; I've got a racquetball game in a half hour and can't be late for it. So, sit and we'll get this over as painlessly as possible."

Before I could respond or even sit, he spoke again, "It's so great to finally meet you. Great, great, great! Let's crunch some numbers, and we'll get you on the road to freedom. Or you can meet with someone else on my team if you'd rather. They're all super people."

The few seconds I'd been with Sam convinced me of three things: his energy level exhausted me, he was one of those people you immediately knew you could trust, and I had the bizarre sense that I wanted to be just like him when I grew up. Laughing to myself at my own absurdity, I said, "Thanks, Sam. Meeting with you is fine. And financial freedom would be nice." I sat in the visitor's chair and put the book Jane gave me on the corner of his desk.

Quickly, he responded, "Oh, it is, it is. I know it's strange and maybe seems controlling that you have to come visit us every payday, but you'll see that it's actually wonderful."

I couldn't see anything about my finances being "wonderful." "How so?"

"Clinton—Mr. Havens, Sr.—didn't like people being distracted from their jobs. And financial worries are *huge* distractions. So he put me in charge of making sure everybody's finances are in order. That way, real priorities can be focused on."

"Priorities?"

"Like finding out what people love to do, what their strengths are, and helping them figure out how to do what they do best."

"Huh," I managed to get out when he took a breath.

"I've the greatest job in the world!" Sam exclaimed. "Every day, I leave work knowing I've made a difference. Once your money's in order, you'll be able to focus on what's really important, and I get to help you do that. How great is that?" The man was almost giddy with excitement. "How many people can say they make a difference every single day they go to work? Well, I mean outside of this company that is."

"Not me," I grumbled.

"That'll change," he said, shaking his finger emphatically at me. "You'll see, that'll change." Then he turned to his computer and began firing question after question at me about my finances.

As I sheepishly answered, I watched his fingers pound on the keys at an impressive rate, entering my answers into the computer. And amazingly, he managed to ask and have me answer some very pointed and personal questions with only an acknowledgment of the facts and no indication of judgment.

When he asked, I gave him the papers from Jane. He looked at them very quickly and put them aside.

This reminded me of a question I had after I left Jane. "What about emergencies? I mean, not having a balance on credit cards is a great idea, but what about real life? Hospital or car emergencies?"

He leaned toward me, enthusiastically. "Emergency fund, Stanley, emergency fund. You'll have money for emergencies, so you *don't* have to put them on your credit cards." He must have seen something in my expression, because he gave me an understanding look and everything in him softened for a moment. "I won't let you down, Stanley. If something comes up between now and the time you have a financial cushion in place, we'll deal with it together. This loan isn't with a bank, it's with HRI. And I, personally, will make sure that if something comes up, we'll take care of it."

I couldn't help but believe the guy, so I signed the papers.

The minute I set the pen down, he was back to his exuberant self and off onto another financial topic. I didn't have a clue how a guy that old kept it all straight, because my head was spinning.

A bunch of questions and a couple more signatures later, he declared himself done and enthusiastically shook my hand. "Welcome aboard, Stanley, welcome aboard. Where's your next stop?"

It took me a moment to process his question. "They didn't say."

At light-speed, he shot out of the chair and answered, "Let's get you back to Summer; she knows everything. And if you ever want to play racquetball, let me know. Gym's free for employees and family."

Mentally woozy from all the changes being thrown at me so quickly, I stood, grabbed my copies of various forms and folded them into the book. Sam left the office, and I followed, with him walking at a speed I had trouble matching.

As we hurried down the aisle of mostly empty cubes, I realized that being able to play racquetball again sounded great. "I'd love to play racquetball. Although you'll have to go easy on me, I'm a little out of practice."

He laughed. "The first time I might, but only then."

"Sounds good," I answered with my own chuckle.

As we walked we passed a restroom, I heeded nature's call and slowed. "I need to stop here for a minute. Afterwards, I can find my own way back to Summer."

"You sure? I don't mind waiting," Sam replied.

While I suspected he meant it, I figured he'd have the carpet worn out before I got done, so I let him off the hook. "I'm sure. And I'll be talking to you later about a racquetball game."

Again, he gave me a vise-like handshake. "I look forward to playing. It was great meeting you." He turned and left as quickly as we'd come.

Chapter 20

As I pushed the restroom door open, I admitted that I'd mainly wanted a minute to myself to come down from Sam's energy level. The morning had been overwhelming so far, in a good way, but I needed a break.

I walked into the restroom and saw a man—in blue coveralls with "HRI Grounds Crew" on the back and his cleaning supply cart at his side—intently cleaning the mirror over the sinks. I caught the man's reflection and he smiled at me, I smiled politely back.

I set Jane's book on a shelf across from the sinks and walked toward the urinals, then my brain finally caught up with itself, and I stopped dead in my tracks and looked at the polished tile floor for a moment, trying to recover from yet another shock. "A janitor?"

"Groundskeeper, friend," was the reply from the man cleaning the mirror. "I take care of the whole place."

Shaking my head and silently laughing at myself for having assumed I'd really get out of his manipulative clutches so easily, I turned to look at Jeff in the mirror and realized why I almost hadn't recognized him. Yesterday, his bruises had been turning that yucky purplish-green color, but today, his face didn't show the slightest hint of Bear's conversion experience. Without the cuts, bruises and swelling, Jeff almost looked like a different person. But a janitor? No, *groundskeeper*. "Jesus was a carpenter, and you're a 'groundskeeper'?"

"Disappointed?" he asked, turning to face me.

I walked over, leaned my backside against the sink, crossed my arms and looked at him. "I don't know. I guess I didn't even wonder what you did. Like so many other things I didn't ask."

"Well, this has worked out then," he said with his ever-present smile. "We'll be seeing each other around, and you'll be able to ask those questions. That is, if you're okay with me being a janitor."

I had to laugh. I simply had to laugh. "You being a *groundskeeper* seems just about right."

Then I looked down at the floor again, to work up the courage to admit my thoughts. "I'm glad our time isn't over. Yesterday, it didn't make sense that it was."

He smiled his intense smile. "You and I have more to experience, Stanley, never fear."

I snorted disparagingly. "Somehow, after the trip here, that isn't reassuring."

He chuckled. "We'll have to see. But right now, I have a job to do." He hugged me, then efficiently replaced the cleaning supplies on his cart and wheeled the cart out the door without a backward glance.

I leaned against the sink for another couple minutes, shaking my head and laughing softly.

What a jerk he was. He'd known the whole trip that we'd be here together and hadn't said a thing.

And what an idiot I am. On the whole trip, I'd never asked what he did for a living. Then I remembered him saying, when I first picked him up, there were a lot of people with TDI's at the place he worked. I should have guessed he worked here when I saw the parking lot this morning.

After I finished my business, I grabbed my book and headed back to Summer.

On the way, I stopped in a quiet corner, dug my cell phone out of my pocket and called Beth. "You won't guess who works here."

"Really? Jeff is there?"

"Okay, so you guessed," I said, a little disgruntled that she'd so easily picked up something that had completely blindsided me. "But you won't guess what he does here."

She was quiet for a minute. "You got me on that one. He has money doesn't he? So, it must be something high-paying."

She's a brilliant woman. "I didn't think of that, but that's wrong. He's a janitor here. Which comes back to your point. How can he throw hundred-dollar bills around like nothing?"

"A janitor?" she asked, sounding skeptical.

Then it occurred to me. "Oh, his parents were wealthy, and they left him lots of money."

Beth tried to follow the logic. "Then why would he be working as a janitor? I mean, there's nothing wrong with that, but it seems like he'd be doing a job where he could make more of an impact. I guess Jesus was a carpenter though, so..." She trailed off, trying to make the connection.

"I need to go," I said, knowing they probably had more people for me to see and paperwork for me to do. "I just wanted to call and tell you about Jeff. I've a lot more to tell you, too, but I don't have time right now. And it's all good, so don't worry."

We said good-bye and hung up, and with only one wrong turn, I found Summer's desk.

Summer sunnily smiled at my approach. "Did you finish with everyone?"

"I think so. I talked with Tom, Jane and Sam. Sam said to come back here. He said you'd know what I needed to do next."

"Mr. Havens is out of his office at the moment, but I'll let him know you're here. He likes to meet all the new employees."

That made me a little nervous; I never liked dealing with the upper management. After a couple bad experiences, I'd learned I was much better off if they didn't even know who I was. Of course, I didn't say any of this and replied, "Okay."

Summer continued, "He shouldn't be long. You can wait in his office until he gets there." She stood and rounded her desk leading me to the right, past Clinton Havens' portrait, through the set of executive doors and to another pair of massive mahogany doors. She opened one of them, and I followed her into a richly paneled room with tree-shaded windows that overlooked the front parking lot. She motioned for me to sit in the chair in front of the huge antique wooden desk, and as I sat, she asked if I wanted anything to drink.

I didn't, so she shut the door behind her, and there I was, alone, in this exquisitely decorated office, feeling uncomfortable and out of place.

On the wall behind the desk was a different portrait of Clinton Havens standing beside, I assumed, his wife. I stood and leaned over the desk to get a better look at the name plate, *Clinton and Victoria Havens*. They were a very nice, kind-looking couple. The people here at HRI who'd talked about him almost glowed as they did so. Whoever had painted the portrait had captured that aspect of him, which helped lessen my nervousness about meeting him.

As I looked around more, I had to admit that Clinton sure had good taste. It was a beautiful office.

After about five minutes of waiting and looking around, my

nervousness started building back up. Sitting in the CEO's office, on the first day of a two-month contract job, was the last thing I'd expected, and I couldn't imagine any circumstance where this would be a good thing. To distract myself, I opened the book Jane had given me and began to read.

I heard the door open and glanced over.

A yellow cleaning cart was being pushed through the door, followed by Jeff in his coveralls.

"Hey," I said to Jeff.

"Hey back, friend," Jeff replied as he stopped the cart, then went behind the desk to get the trash can. "You seem nervous."

I shrugged as Jeff emptied the trash into the cart. "Supposed to be meeting with Havens, but he's late. And I can't come up with any good reason I'm here, so I'm not looking forward to it."

Jeff put the trash can back into place and flopped into the big leather chair. "Why wouldn't you be looking forward to it?"

I opened my mouth to answer, then something registered about the way he sat in the chair. Confused, I looked to the cleaning cart, which he'd handled with a comfort that came from much practice, and back to his coveralls, then up to his face, and for the first time saw the amusement gleaming in his eyes.

I looked at him for a long silent moment, confusion turning to astonishment as a cascade of puzzle pieces fell into place. I glanced up to the picture of Clinton and Victoria, then back down to Jeff, who was grinning at me unrepentantly. "Your folks." It wasn't even really a question.

Jeff nodded, still grinning. "The greatest parents a kid could have. And sorry to keep you waiting, I had to finish giving another bathroom a quick wipe down."

"You could have told me!" I exclaimed, relief at not having to face an executive inquisition warred with anger over Jeff's seemingly inescapable need to play games with me.

"Where's the fun in that? I like surprises, don't you?"

"Not so much," I muttered, knowing I had nobody to blame but myself. "'I'm Jeff,'" I quoted sarcastically Jeff introducing himself to me after the first call he'd gotten on my phone, "'I guess we never actually introduced ourselves.'" I shook my head. "You couldn't have bothered to say 'I'm Jeff Havens?'"

He looked at me like he was waiting for me to catch onto something important.

Finally, I did. "And I never asked your last name, did I? Did you make sure I didn't ask?" I accused. "So I wouldn't know what was coming up?"

"Didn't have to. But you're right. If you'd asked, the trip would've been different." He shrugged, his expression relaxing into his normal smile. "Far different and not as useful."

Again, he was right. If I'd known I was coming to work for his company, if I'd known I was going to spend the next two months with him, I'd have handled the trip totally differently.

"Did Summer offer you anything to drink?" he asked. "I've some Dew in the fridge."

I gave a sigh that was resignation mixed with irritation at his games. "Yeah. That'd be great. It's been quite the morning, and I can't afford a Dew in the cafeteria."

He snickered as he got out of the chair and walked into a small room off the office, then returned with two cold cans and tossed me one.

I put the book down on the desk in front of me, then popped the can's top and took a drink as I looked back up at the portrait on the wall behind his desk. "Nice painting of your folks. Why aren't there any portraits of you?"

Smiling, he spun his chair around to look up at the portrait. "They were an awesome couple. And this is my father's company, not mine. If I hung portraits of me around here, that'd put me at his level, and I'm not."

That was a cool statement. A very Jeff statement.

"Everything I do here is because of, and for, my father. This isn't about my glory or my place in history. Doing my father's work is what's important." He turned back, facing me.

"Is that a double-entendre?"

He winked at me. "Take it how you want."

As there didn't seem to be any way to answer that, I took another swig from the can.

He continued, "You accepted me as a janitor, too. That's pretty cool and important."

"Groundskeeper," I said, keeping a straight face. "If you'd have been a janitor, that would put a whole different spin on things. I might've had to head back home."

He laughed. "That'd definitely be below the threshold."

I nodded, then said, "Glad you understand my limits." In a more serious tone, I put him on the spot. "So was it just a ploy? The janitor-thing. To see how I'd react?"

His expression changed to one of mild disagreement. "No, I actually clean the bathrooms, take care of the grounds, and whatever else needs to be done around here. But so does everybody else. All our people do rotations on the grounds crew. HRI doesn't have a landscaping or cleaning service."

Having high-priced—given what they were paying me— employees cleaning bathrooms seemed inefficient and more expensive than hiring lower-priced maintenance people. "Why?"

"You'll understand after your first rotation."

Now I was shocked. "You're going to pay me this kind of money to clean bathrooms?"

Jeff mockingly returned my shocked look. "You above cleaning bathrooms?"

Trying to cover my misunderstood question, I hurriedly replied, "No. It's just that..."

Jeff smiled and held up his hand stopping me. "Only playing with you, Stanley. Yes, we're paying you 'this kind of money' to clean bathrooms, when it's your turn on rotation. But enough of that. Has everyone been treating you okay?"

It took me a moment to catch up with the new topic, then I quoted the HRI pamphlet, "'Changing the world through technology and caring for people.' They've definitely got the second part down; I've been treated very well. And I'm looking forward to seeing if they have the first part down as effectively."

"I can guarantee they do." Jeff tipped his head back up toward the portrait. "That motto sums up my father. He was a great man, with a great vision."

"Isn't that also what you said you're here to do? To change the world?"

"Sure, but that was his vision and passion long before I entered my parent's life. Between them, they were the perfect people to raise me. My father's love for learning, his love for growing himself and others, and his love for people and technology gave me a start in life that I couldn't have gotten anywhere else."

I looked up at the portrait and said, "So, your father laid the foundation for your work?"

"Both my parents did. Dad created HRI, which is, as you've already discovered, a different company. The twenty/eighty model—where twenty-percent of the people do eighty-percent of the work—isn't only extinguished at HRI, it's been beaten up and trampled.

"Most of the world," he continued, "seems to be moving toward a ten/ninety model, where ninety-percent of the population is mooching off the ten-percent who are doing the real work, the creative and innovative work."

"I can't argue that point with you." Heaven knew I'd seen plenty of examples of it in my life.

"But here at HRI, the experts that we've brought in say HRI is running between ninety-five- and one-hundred-percent active, creative participation, depending on how exactly the counting is done."

"That's astounding." I thought about the jobs I'd had, and to be honest, in most of them, I probably fell into the eighty-percent who were doing only twenty-percent of the work. Which then made me wonder what a company would be like if practically everyone was mentally vested and working up to their potential. I suspected that would be a pretty cool company to work at.

As I thought that, I looked toward Jeff, who was waiting patiently for me to be ready to continue, and I was almost overwhelmed with thankfulness for being here with him again. Last night's stress over the future had disappeared. My time with him wasn't permanent, but being here with him was enough for now. I'd deal with the rest later.

Letting my mind return to the topic, I recalled a few times where I'd actually enjoyed my work and felt truly engaged. Unfortunately, those times had been brief. Yet, Jeff was telling me ninety-five-percent of the HRI people felt like that most of the time? I looked back at him and repeated myself, "That's astounding."

"Indeed." Jeff indicated the painting with a hand. "When Dad first started the company, he was running it on a shoestring budget, and as one would expect, intensely focused on building products to sell. But all the time he was doing that, he said he felt something was wrong, but couldn't figure out what it was or how to make it right."

I looked around the beautifully designed office and replied, "He obviously figured it out."

"Some might call it a miracle." Jeff shot me his teasing grin. "Pennsylvania had started a lottery not long before that, and for kicks, Dad bought a ticket. By the time taxes and everything were paid, he ended up winning a little over a million dollars. That is 1970's dollars."

I almost had to laugh as I thought back to my trash can experience. "He had better luck than you."

As he grinned widely at me, I wondered how winning had changed things for his father and thought back to when Jeff had talked about self-actualized lottery winners, which something told me was directly related to this bit of history.

"So that's how your father got rich? And..." I trailed off because I couldn't think of what I wanted to say. In his example of the lottery winners, I remembered Jeff saying something about if the self-actualized rich people lost their money they'd still be the wealthiest people around.

As usual, Jeff let me flounder a little while before coming to my aid. "This was before I entered their life, so I can only tell you what others have told me and from interviews my father gave after he won. In the first interview, the reporter asked him what he was going to do with his money. He matter-of-factly answered, 'Buy happiness.' And that's exactly what he did."

"How?"

"He changed the culture of his company to what you see today. He shifted the focus from the products being made, to focusing on the people working for him, and let the things they produced be a natural result of the growth of those people."

"What?" I asked, confused.

"Happy people work harder and smarter, and make more money for the company."

"Ah!" And how simple that philosophy was, and so rare that I bet it was almost unique.

"Happy employees are more creative, more innovative, and uphold the company's interest better, realizing that what's good for the company is good for them. Within months of getting the lottery check, Dad bought this building, moved the company here, and began working on changing the company's culture. It wasn't long before the company started making money hand-over-fist. And the more the company made, the more he was able to help others."

I smiled at Jeff. "So he did exactly what he said he was going to do with the money: he bought happiness. He did it by using the money he'd won to help other people."

Jeff nodded proudly. "A couple years after he made the first changes, he hired people to study the company, its people, and how they could help each other grow." As he was saying that, he went to the bookshelf, grabbed a book and tossed it to me.

I looked at it. *Now, Discover your Strengths* by Marcus Buckingham and Donald Clifton.

"Once they started looking for people's strengths," Jeff continued as he settled into his chair, "and changing people's jobs so they were working within their strengths, people began having such a good time being here, 'playing' with the new products, technologies and tasks, that a lot more got done than it ever had before."

He paused to let me absorb it.

It was brilliant and seemed obvious once I understood. I put the new book on top of the one Jane had given me. I'd look at it later; right now, I wanted to focus on what Jeff was talking about. Then I took another swig of my drink and summed up my understanding. "People who love what they do, do it more accurately, faster and with less downtime."

"Exactly. And because of the increased productivity, we're able to implement some programs that further increase the dynamics of the Institute. For example, free health insurance for employees who sign themselves — and their families — up for a healthy living program."

I smiled as I remembered Tom's statement. "Tom said you loved to talk about the health care program." Then sobered. Too bad it didn't apply to me, I thought, then forced myself to push that aside and continue. "But free health insurance? For a company this size, that's gotta be a huge expense."

He shrugged. "It depends on how it's being counted. If the only measure is the size of the line-item on the corporate balance sheet, then yes, it's a very big line-item. But once we start adding in things beyond the obvious, like our low number of paid sick-leave days, and the almost negligible amount of mental and physical disability payments we make, and so on, then add on top of it the increased productivity of a happy work-force, the number crunchers assure me that it pays for itself almost twice over."

I thought about it a moment. "Why don't other places do it?"

"They have different people who need to be kept happy. Here, since it's a privately-held company with no outside investors, the only people who have to be kept happy were my father, and now me. Whereas, most companies have stock holders or corporate investors to keep happy, and they want facts — line items and bottom lines in big, black numbers — not nebulous things like how happy the work-force is."

"Makes sense," I admitted.

"Yeah, and it's great insurance, too."

"But not for contractors," I said to myself, trying to not let the unfairness of the situation bug me too much. I was so grateful for the job that I wasn't going to complain about things I knew I couldn't change.

"Stanley," Jeff said.

I looked back to him, not really realizing that I'd been staring out the windows to the trees between his office and the parking lot.

"We'll take care of you for as long as you're here," Jeff said gently. "Tom knows I like to go over the insurance program with new hires, which is why he didn't mention it to you. He'll have you fill out the paperwork for the health insurance later. It'll take effect immediately, for you *and* your family. If your wife or kids need to see the doctor or need anything seen to, your coverage should be propagated to the various computer systems before the end of the week and if your wife wants to start making appointments for next week, she's welcome to do that."

Then he opened the drawer, pulled something out and tossed it to me.

Automatically, I caught it, identifying a box of tissues only after it was in my hands. "Thanks," I said as I pulled one out and wiped my eyes.

"Yeah, well, you can stop it now."

I gave a soggy chuckle. "I'll try. But it means a lot to me. I was scared."

Jeff shrugged. "It's not forever, but it's easy enough to do for now."

"Thanks, for now."

Then Jeff gave one of his Jeff-grins. "But there are strings!"

"Of course." There were always strings with Jeff.

"To qualify, the health program requires that each person in the program, employee and family members, get six or more hours a week of quality physical activity, all must be non-smokers, and either non-drinkers or moderate drinkers," Jeff listed, ticking the items off on his fingers. "Employees can do the physical activities during work hours or outside of work."

The light bulb went off on one tiny piece of the puzzle that this morning had been. "I'd thought it was strange that Sam rushed off to play racquetball during the workday."

"Did he ask you to play?"

"Yeah."

"Take him up on it," Jeff suggested. "Being humiliated by a seventy-five-year-old man is good for your ego."

"Seventy-five?" I asked, shocked. "The guy moves at light-speed, and my hand still hurts from shaking his."

Jeff laughed understandingly. "We can't get rid of him. I don't think he'll leave until we find him dead at his desk."

"Or on the racquetball court."

Jeff's look was one of total disbelief. "No way that'd happen! He wouldn't let death stop him from kicking anyone's butt on the court."

Then Jeff smiled, a smile that I knew wasn't good for me. "Wait until you've had your first real financial planning meeting with him. You'll spend a total of ten or fifteen frantic minutes with him and come away excited to be cutting your budget to the bone to pay off your debt. Then next month, you'll have your head spinning after a ten-minute meeting, excited to see what you thought was an unrealistic budget turn into reality, and the possibility of being debt-free."

In my ten fast-paced minutes with Sam, I could understand. "That should be interesting. Anyway, you were talking about the health care." Which I was much more interested in, now that I was going to be a part of it.

Jeff picked up where he had left off. "Have you been to the cafeteria?"

"Tom took me this morning and talked about how that fits into the health plan. It was good food."

He nodded. "Soon after we implemented the program, the money we spent for medical expenses dropped enough to cover the cost of the food."

As always, I was fascinated when Jeff spoke. "Amazing. That's great and it actually makes sense. Great to see a company care so much for its people."

"Some try and have some success, and others think they are but miss the point. I recently read about a company that offered unlimited vacations. At first, I thought that sounded great. We'd been doing it well before I was old enough to work here. I thought it'd be nice to see another company treating their people like we treat ours. But after I read the article about the other company, I felt sorry for the people who worked there. The article had statements like: 'Unlike many companies, adequate performance gets a generous severance package.' 'We're a team, not a family.' 'We have engineers who work pretty much around the clock because that's the way they work.' 'We only hire fully-formed humans.' and other stuff like that."

I shook my head at the unknown company. "Kind of takes the punch out of it, doesn't it?"

"Yeah. No wonder they offer unlimited vacation time, the people need it. At HRI, we don't want people working around the clock because we want *people* working here."

"I get that," I said and really appreciated the sentiment. "Far too many companies treat people like interchangeable pawns on a chess board. Experience doesn't matter; one tech writer can replace any other tech writer." Which is what had happened to me, more than once. I'd kept my ear to the gossip mill of my last job and found out I'd been replaced by a new college grad at half the price. Not that I think it's bad to give a kid a job, but you can't put a newbie into a job and expect the same throughput as an expert doing the job. "And morale doesn't matter anymore, either. Bosses don't care that everybody's afraid for their job, because they're pawns who can be easily replaced with another one." When I realized how *into* my rant I was getting, I stopped and said, "Sorry. Hot button, obviously."

"That's okay," Jeff said. "Completely understandable. Here, on the other hand, we want people who know we value them, and that we also value them having a life and a family. What we do here in the labs and cubes is exciting, what we do is great, and some of it can easily become an obsession for some of these folks, but people need to get out and have a life."

"How refreshing," I said sarcastically, thinking of a couple of the companies I'd worked at, where sixty-hour weeks were the norm.

Jeff laughed. "Indeed. And to go along with our policy of growing people, we reimburse almost every kind of training and schooling available. It doesn't have to be work-related."

"Cool!" Maybe I wasn't going to have to find a mountain top after all, the local community college might do just as well.

He continued, "The other great program that everyone is required to take part in is to volunteer for a charity one day a week, and that, too, is during business hours. They can choose who and how they volunteer."

"Jane had mentioned that. She said my boss—" I thought for a moment, then came up with the name "—Aaron, would be telling me about it."

Jeff beamed. "That's right! I'd forgotten you're going to be on Aaron's team. You're going to have a great experience this Friday."

I cringed. "When you say I'm going to have an 'experience,' I get nervous."

He just beamed at me, which didn't reassure me.

I decided to change the subject. "Between the gym and volunteering, you're cutting out a whole bunch of hours that people work, and yet the company is still making money. It seems counter-intuitive."

"It is absolutely counter-intuitive, if you're only looking at the normal business model. But the model of 'the beatings will continue until the morale improves' has proven for centuries to be counter-productive. They might turn out lots of cheap product, but they also turn out lousy people, which takes its toll on society in ways that are very hard to calculate on a balance sheet. Here, we lock the buildings after seven o'clock each night and keep them locked all weekend; otherwise I'd never get rid of some of these folks. And working from home after hours is severely frowned upon. After-work time is for family, friends and themselves."

"That should be fun to see." Every other place I'd worked, I'd spent most of the time counting down the minutes until I could go home.

"The people here are highly engaged in the projects they're working on, and by limiting the hours they can work, they come in each day ready to work. When you limit something people desire, it becomes more desirable."

I knew Jeff was Jeff, but still. "I find that really hard to believe."

He smiled a little wider at my skepticism but didn't comment. "That's a quick summary of the company, Stanley. I'll have someone show you around a little, and then you can head out, because I know you have a lot that needs to be done before tomorrow. I think you're going to enjoy it here. Any questions?"

I thought for a minute, the conversation I had with Beth back at home when I first heard about this job popped into my head. So, I asked Jeff, "What shape's the hole?"

With no knowledge of my conversation with Beth, he answered like he'd been part of it. "I can guarantee we have one that's Stanley-shaped. Part of the *experience*—" When he emphasized "experience," I winced, and he smiled wider. "—while you're here is to figure out what shape Stanley is. Once you figure it out, you can start actively looking for holes that fit you."

What a perfect answer. I sure hoped HRI had a hole my shape. Thinking "HRI" made me remember Alice's request for a T-shirt. "Hey, before I forget, do you guys have T-shirts? My daughter, Alice, wants one."

Jeff nodded. "Done. I'll have some sent for Beth and Cooper, too. Those are easy questions. Keep 'em coming while I'm on a role."

"Okay. What ex-presidents aren't buried in the United States?"

He stroked his chin and looked at the ceiling. "Hmmm... George W. Bush, Bill Clinton..."

Shaking my head, I stopped him. "Okay, okay, you got it. No one ever gets that one. Anyways, I always have questions with you, but I'm afraid to ask them. You answer them in very stressful ways." Even as I said it, I was again glad my trip with Jeff hadn't ended with me dropping him off yesterday. After a small pause I did ask, "So again, why me?"

"We needed a technical writer, and you seemed like a good fit," Jeff answered with a shrug.

"Come on, you know what I mean."

"That's the one question I won't answer. You're on this journey for a reason, but that reason is for you to figure out. For now, you're a technical writer at Havens Research Institute. Welcome aboard."

Chapter 21

Jeff stood and obviously our meeting was over.

"Thanks," I said, standing, too. "I'll do my best." I put the box of tissues on the desk and picked up the books.

"You can't fail here, friend. Not because of me, but because of what my father set up. And you'll learn a lot about yourself in the process. Much of that will overlap with our journey because my parents were great people." He came around the corner of the desk and stopped in front of me. "Now, I'd like to invite you to my house for dinner tonight."

Oh, that should be interesting. No way was I turning that invitation down. "Sure. What time and where?"

"How does six o'clock sound? I'll get you the address. It's informal, a relaxed time."

"I'll be there."

"Great. Now that my CEO business is done, I need to get back to my groundskeeper duties. I'll get Grace to show you around."

Jeff placed his hands on the handle of his cart, and I walked with him out the door and across the reception room to Summer's desk. "Summer, will you ask Grace to show Stanley around?" He then turned to me. "Stanley, did you get to talk to Summer at all? She's our Director of First Impressions, and she's the best there is."

Summer rolled her eyes. She'd obviously heard this many times before.

"We chatted briefly," I replied, "and I'd have to agree with you."

Summer laughed.

Jeff grinned. "I'm a figurehead. She's the driving force of the company. If anything happened to her, it'd be chaos here."

Summer smiled up at Jeff as she paged Grace.

Jeff shook my hand and then pushed his cart towards his next duty. As he was making his way through the left-side doorway, he turned back around. "Oh, Summer, would you tell Tom to get Stanley and his family on the health insurance program?"

"No problem, Mr. Havens."

"Great." As he was about to close the door, he stopped again and turned. "Oh, and sign him up for a grounds crew rotation." With that, he closed the door behind himself.

Summer smiled fondly after Jeff, and then looked at me while pointing over her shoulder to the mahogany doors to the right of her desk. "I don't know why he doesn't convert that office into some useful space. He spends a total of three hours a month in there, which, admittedly, is about three hours a month more than his father ever did." She then focused on her computer, clicked through some pages and then looked at me. "How about the week after next for the grounds crew?"

What was I supposed to say? "Sure."

She typed some on the keyboard and told me, "You're all set. I sent an email to Tom. He'll track you down and get the insurance taken care of."

I smiled big. "That's great. My wife will be thrilled."

Summer was about to say something else, when a young woman walked up. She looked to be barely twenty—if I was guessing on the old side—and very athletic, with a glow to her. I had heard people say you can see a person's soul in their eyes. I never really thought much about that until Grace walked up. Her dark brown eyes were easy to read. There was wisdom and peace in them which seemed too old for a woman this young. Her complexion was hard to place. She could have been middle-eastern, possibly American Indian or maybe Hispanic. Whatever it was, it added to her presence.

"Hi, Stanley. I'm Grace," the young woman said and extended her hand, smiling warmly at me.

As I shook Grace's hand, Summer said, "Grace will take good care of you. Bye for now, Stanley."

* * *

As I walked with Grace to the doors of the main area, I realized I was looking forward to seeing what the rest of the place looked like, and Grace graced me with just that. It turned out to be a guided tour with a very sweet young woman. She had an amazingly thorough working knowledge of all the projects she showed me, including all the research going on. Yet, I'd have judged her to be right out of high school.

The place was amazing. She took me to lab after lab, which were all buzzing with energy. On the way, we passed several more almost empty low-walled cube areas. After seeing the place, I could understand what Tom meant about people liking to be in the labs instead of cubes or offices with doors. Grace took me through small specialized computer labs and medical labs, and a huge machine shop that was equipped with every fancy fabricating machine I could imagine.

It took me a while to realize what was "off" compared to the other places I worked, but eventually I caught on: everything seemed to be set up for function instead of status. There weren't any desks fancier or bigger than others, or lab set-ups grander than others, or lab-coated people segregated from jeans-and-T-shirt people. The whole place seemed to be working toward efficiency instead of empire-building. The realization left me hoping that whatever lab I'd be working in would follow what seemed to be the norm, because that would be an extremely refreshing place to work.

After Grace introduced me to about the seventh or eighth group of people, I noticed that they eagerly explained the technical aspects of their projects, but never talked of planning or schedules. As a technical writer, project managers were usually the first people I talked to, to get an overview of the project, plans and schedules, then I'd talk to the technical professionals to get the details. So, as we walked to the next lab, I asked my tour guide, "Where do the project managers sit?"

She paused in the hallway and smiled a smile that was eerily like Jeff's. "At HRI, no one's only job title is 'Project Manager.' Sure," she said with a negligent shrug, then tugged me to the side of the hall so a group could pass, "we have folks who like to organize more than others, but everybody likes to have an active hand with their project. So, the organizer-types sort out amongst themselves who's keeping track of what aspects of which projects." She laughed. "Who better than the organizers to keep such things sorted out?"

I had to chuckle. It made sense.

"And it leaves them plenty of time to get their hands dirty. But one annoying thing they insist on," she made a face that I suspected was a truer indication of her youth than her astounding breadth of knowledge, "is for everybody to have the skills required to keep a project going in a coherent direction. So, we all have to take our turn at managing projects. I suspect they have a *list* for that, too."

It was said with such teenage loathing, it was really hard to not laugh, but I didn't want to hurt her feelings, so I only said, "I'm sure they do."

"But mostly," she said with another shrug, "projects just work. When we get a contract, a new core project group starts to form, people sign onto it as they have time available and applicable skill sets, or the desire to learn a new skill. Once the core project group is formed, the organizer-types and process-types get together with the techie-types and start laying out and designing the project, based on the contract's needs. The project's design and details are documented on our internal website, which after some web magic, allows the progress of the project to be tracked by our customer on our secure external website."

"Sounds very efficient."

"It is. One of the major drives here at HRI is to remove ambiguity; we want everything to be obvious to everybody. You can find any information you want on any project on our internal web site."

To me, it sounded like B.F. Skinner's *Walden II*, full of utopian processes and ideologies. But I was curious to see it in action. "So, what's a tech writer supposed to do if the group has documented the project so well?"

She grinned at me. "Don't worry. You'll have plenty to do. We're desperately short of writer-types at the moment. Some of the techie-types couldn't put two written words together if their life depended on it."

"Boy, do I know that," I said, and we laughed together.

Grace took me to her lab, introduced me to her team members and started showing the project to me. She worked on a team researching something called zero-point energy. She started explaining the project with great excitement and in great detail. Of which I understood a total of twelve words and those were the pronouns and conjunctions. But I gathered the goal was to generate electricity basically out of thin air, which sounded way too science-fiction to be real, so I occupied my mind with wondering how this kid, who looked to be just out of high school, knew this stuff?

When she started slowing down, I interrupted politely, "Grace, if you don't mind me asking, how old are you?"

Her pride showed as she answered the question, "I'll turn nineteen this month."

"So, you just finished high school?" I asked, astounded.

"Yep," she answered excitedly. "Graduated the end of May."

"What you're explaining to me sounds more like a Ph.D. dissertation than a high school kid that has a summer job before going off to college."

"Oh, I read my first book on Nikola Tesla when I was in junior high, and I was hooked. I've been studying physics ever since, and I got an internship here my freshman year."

Amazing! "You must've been really something in high school. Teachers don't get that many students with your motivation." I sure didn't have any when I did my student teaching. "When you graduated top of the class, it must have been hard dealing with the other kids' resentment."

She looked at me sort of confused. "I wasn't top of my class, I was sixth. But where I ranked didn't matter," she said matter-of-factly. "Grades aren't important in my family. My dad wouldn't even look at my report card."

That statement made me upset. To have a kid this brilliant and not care? That was cruel. Her father was probably interested in how many games she won instead of how good her grades were. So, I asked her, "Did he want you playing sports, instead?"

"Oh, he loved watching my basketball games," she answered enthusiastically. "We had a great team the last couple years and it was lots of fun. Cross country was harder for him to watch, so he sat and read when he took me to my meets."

At least he was an interested father, I thought. That counted for something. "Where are you going to college?"

"I don't think I am. At least not right now."

"You can't afford it?" I asked. If that was the case, I was astounded Jeff hadn't already fixed the situation for her. Her level of brilliance shouldn't be wasted from lack of money.

"No, it's not that. I've talked about it with my dad, and he doesn't think I need to go. He said," she changed her voice to try to imitate her father, "'I don't have a piece of paper to show how smart I am, and you don't need one either.'"

I was getting angry again, thinking about this brilliant, sweet girl with a father pushing her into sports and not even caring about her schooling or going to college. He was one of those guys, that if I ever met him, I'd probably want to punch him in the nose.

"Anyway," she said as she waved down the hall to more laboratory doors, "do you want to hear about more projects or eat lunch?"

"It's been a pleasure taking this tour with you, but we'd better eat lunch before my brain explodes."

Grace laughed, in the old-people-are-so-funny way that Alice was starting to get so good at.

"Great," she replied when she had her mirth under control. "Tell you what. Why don't we grab some lunch at the cafeteria? And Summer said you needed to talk to Tom again, then you can call it a day. By the way, Summer also told me to tell you this afternoon is paid time off. It's just part of our first day deal."

"I appreciate knowing that," I said, and I was. Every hour I was paid was money in the bank to get me dug out of the last few months of trouble. And if I was really going to be getting out early, it would give me time to deposit my check, run a few errands and then call Beth.

Grace was silent for a few moments as we walked down the hallway toward the cafeteria, then she said, "I've never worked anywhere else, but from what I understand, it's a culture shock coming here. People need time to adjust."

Tell me about it, I said sarcastically to myself. But aloud I said, "You're right about the culture shock."

The cafeteria was packed like it had been for breakfast and just as full of energy. The signs above the stations had changed from breakfast to lunch menus, but the pricing followed the same concept. The chili-cheese dog, my main staple, would take half my paycheck, but the Creole Red Snapper—228 calories—was free and sounded good, so I ordered that.

There was another menu with a big sign over it which read *Organically Grown Local Produce*. It looked like I was going to be eating pretty healthy for free while I was here.

Grace led us to a table with several people I'd met on the tour. The food was as fabulous as it looked, I enjoyed more conversation with Grace and my table-mates, and the kibitzing from the tables on either side of us was good-natured and informative.

Grace was absolutely right about the culture shock.

* * *

After talking with Tom to get health insurance forms filled out, I headed out and deposited the check, then did some shopping for staples that I'd forgotten yesterday.

Back at the hotel, I collapsed on the couch and called Beth. "Wow! What a day."

"I guess since Jeff is there you're okay now?"

"More than okay. I'm not even sure where to start." I was trying to think. "I guess the first thing is that Jeff is not a janitor; he's the CEO of the company."

She was definitely surprised. "Why was he pretending to be a janitor? That doesn't sound like him."

"No, he wasn't pretending. The company doesn't have a cleaning staff so all the employees take rotations to clean."

Through our conversations on the trip, I think she had developed her own relationship with Jeff even though she'd never actually talked to him. Her attitude toward him seemed to have gone from extremely skeptical, rightly so, to reserved admiration.

"You know, Stanley," she said hesitating some, "after we hung up last night, nothing fit and I couldn't sleep because it didn't make sense. He wasn't finished with you, so why was he leaving you hanging like that? But now I understand. You had to ask yourself the questions you asked last night: What did he want from you? And what more did you need to learn more from him?"

I took the phone away from my ear and looked at it, confused. Beth's an extremely smart woman, but grasping the whole situation and verbalizing it, in less than a minute was astounding. I'd had hours to think about it and couldn't have said it any better. The way Jeff left me hanging made me realize how much I still had to learn. "You're right. And it worked."

"That's wonderful."

"Oh, you won't believe everything else." I told her about the credit card loan, the prepayment of my paycheck, the health insurance and the check I deposited. And I learned, again, that the way to a woman's heart was to make sure her kids were taken care of.

"That's wonderful!" I could hear the tears of relief in her voice. After a moment she asked, "How's it looking as a workplace?"

I talked for over an hour, rambling on about the parking lot, the tour Grace had taken me on, the cafeteria, the work ethic philosophy, more about the credit card loan, the health care plan, and on and on. The only thing that saved her was a call for her portrait business she had to take. Before she hung up, I eagerly added that I was going to Jeff's house for dinner tonight, and Beth quickly made me promise I'd call her back and let her know all about it.

After talking with Beth, I was even more excited about being here with Jeff at HRI. And that scared me. I'd been excited before, and on too many of those occasions, reality had led to crushing disappointment. Sure, Jeff was here and apparently had a plan, but Jeff also liked to play games with people.

I heaved a deep sigh, then made a decision. I was here. Jeff seemed to have brought me here for a reason. And I'd probably handle it all better if I didn't let my innate pessimism ruin the show. I'd try for once to just let it play out as it wanted to.

That decided, I turned on the tube and watched it until it was time to leave for dinner at Jeff's, the whole time trying to balance the excitement and fear, but as I walked out the hotel room door, it was clear I wasn't terribly successful.

Chapter 22

Following the directions Summer had given me before I left work, I drove past a long, high stone fence to a big fancy gate whose post had the house number of the address indicated on Summer's note. As I rolled down the window so I could reach the intercom button, I looked through the gate to the house.

I guess you'd have to call it a mansion, but the word "mansion" carried so many connotations that this building didn't convey. It was big, but not big for the sake of impressing people with its size. Just like Jeff wasn't your normal kind of guy, the house wasn't your normal kind of house; it read differently than anything I'd seen before. In a way, it reminded me of Frank Lloyd Wright's masterpiece "Fallingwater," not that it resembled Wright's design in any way. Fallingwater had always impressed me with how it was integrated into the landscape, instead of being a monstrosity sticking out of the landscape. This house looked like it belonged here.

I sat there looking at the piece of architectural genius through the gate for a long while, before it occurred to me to hit the intercom button.

A male voice with a British accent answered, "May I help you?"

"Yes. This is Stanley Whitmore, and Mr. Havens invited me for dinner tonight." I'm not sure why I called him Mr. Havens instead of Jeff, but between the house, the intercom and the accent, formality seemed right.

Without a response, the gate swung open, and I drove up to the front of the house and parked beside the Rolls Royce I'd seen in the HRI parking lot. I couldn't help but admire it again. What a beautiful car.

As I walked up the polished granite stairs to the magnificently carved front door, a... butler?... opened the door, and all I could think was "Holy housekeeper, Batman, it's Alfred!" the caped crusader's butler.

He had silver hair and was fit, but taller than the latest Batman movie Alfred, and he wore a stereotypical butler outfit, dark suit and tie. The guy was maybe—*I was awful with ages*—a well-preserved sixty-five, with an expression almost as serene as Jeff's and an incredible depth to his gaze. "My name is Jonathan," he said in the same British accent that had answered the intercom. "Master Havens is expecting you. Please follow me."

Master Havens? Jeff had a butler?

A couple steps into the house, I stopped, caught off-guard to see it was a busy place, and my surprise forced me to realize that I'd expected to be the only guest, the only one eating dinner with Jeff, like we had on the trip. But the massive foyer held a good-sized group of young adults, adolescents and children gathered to one side, with several adults attentively watching. Two of the kids were in wheelchairs, but they all wore smiles, and the mix of skin tones made for a U.N. of people.

Several of them shot curious glances my way, but their attention was fleeting as it took me a moment to realize they were watching what appeared to be a contest to see who could slide the farthest in stocking feet on the marble floor. One contestant won cheers from the onlookers, then another, jeers as he leaned wrong and landed in a heap.

I glanced up at Jonathan, who was patiently waiting for me to take it all in. "Guess it keeps the floor polished."

"Indeed," Jonathan replied and even with his somber face I could see the affection in his eyes.

With effort, I took my attention off the people to look around more. On each side of the foyer were curved staircases carpeted in deep red. In the center of the ceiling was an enormous gold and crystal chandelier. The marble floor was done in an elaborate pattern that made you notice but didn't distract. The foyer was exactly what I'd have expected in a magnificent "mansion" like this, yet it wasn't. I couldn't figure out why.

I looked back to Jonathan, then smiled a little sheepishly when I realized I was standing in the way of him shutting the door. "Sorry."

"It happens frequently," Jonathan said as he closed the door. "If you'll follow me, I'll take you to the dining room."

I followed him through the astoundingly beautiful and

surprisingly busy house.

"Stanley!" a familiar voice exclaimed.

It wasn't until I was engulfed in a hug from Grace that I recognized the voice. Then she was off again, as quickly as she'd come, with a couple other young faces I'd been introduced to at HRI. It seemed that I wasn't the only one Jeff had invited from work.

Jonathan turned into an open pair of doors, and I followed into a large room that seemed to be a combination dining room and gathering room. Offset a little toward the right side of the room was a long antique table, that must have had place settings for thirty-five or forty people, with gaps where chairs were missing, which seemed on purpose, not random. Along the far right wall was a door and several buffets and china cabinets. The left side of the room and far corner contained several small sitting areas. In one, a pair of late-teens were playing chess, ignoring us completely.

As I paused to take it all in, I wondered why Jeff hadn't told me he was having a party. When he'd invited me to dinner, I'd assumed it'd give us some time to talk, and I found I was deeply disappointed. Then I gave a resigned sigh, knowing Jeff, he likely had a reason for the whole thing.

Jonathan led me to a richly colored couch and motioned for me to sit down. "May I offer you refreshments? Fresh lemonade?"

"That sounds great." I was at a loss, so lemonade would at least give me something to do until Jeff showed up.

Jonathan went through the door by the buffets, to the kitchen, I assumed, and returned in a couple minutes with two lemonades and handed me one. He kept the other, and to my surprise, sat beside me. "Master Havens has requested I entertain you until he is able," Jonathan said with calm confidence and a fond gleam in his eye that told me he deeply cared for Jeff. "He is otherwise occupied at the moment. Jeffery knows you have questions and felt you might want to ask someone other than him. You may ask what you will. I will answer the best I can, though I fear the answers will only lead to more questions."

"Oh, okay," was all I could think to say. This certainly wasn't what I'd expected to be hearing from somebody's English butler. In fact, it was so disconcerting that I couldn't come up with any of the questions I'd talked about with Beth last night. I took a drink of the lemonade to give me a moment to think, but when I finished, I still had nothing.

After an uncomfortable minute, Jonathan took pity on me and

began speaking. "Master Havens was grateful for the ride you gave him and has spoken highly of you."

"Do you think I had a choice?" I asked, half sarcastic, half really wondering.

My question brought the first hint of a smile from Jonathan. "No, I'm quite certain you did not." He then took a drink of his lemonade.

There was another pause as I tried to dig up a question to see if I could start trying to put some pieces together. "Have you worked for Jeff, Mr. Havens, long?"

"All of his life," Jonathan replied. "I was employed shortly after Jeffery came into his parents' lives."

That seemed a strange phrasing, but I wasn't sure why, so I pushed that thought aside. I had so many questions. Where should I start? Questions came to me, but none were ones I felt comfortable asking a stranger. Then I had to smile... a friend whom I haven't gotten to know yet. But that didn't help me figure out which questions to ask.

Jonathan again seemed to sense my unease and said, "Let me save you the trouble. I will start, and you may interrupt whenever you desire."

I nodded. "Thanks." This should be interesting, I thought.

"As I stated before," Jonathan began his story, "Jeffery's parents hired me shortly after he arrived into their lives. They were a splendid couple in every way. Mr. Havens was a business man with a genius for people. He started the company that Jeffery now runs, in which you are now employed. Mr. Havens' philosophy was to value, nurture and grow the people who worked for the Institute, and as a result of focusing on the employees, the Institute itself grew and became an asset for its employees, its customers and the community."

I interrupted, "That was obvious today. It's definitely different than a normal company."

Jonathan continued without taking much notice of my interruption, "Mr. Havens, Sr. always said that his primary product was his employees. When times were bad, he stood by the people who worked for him and by the community." He paused and circled his arm to encompass the room. "Many years ago, during a time when many people in the community were out of work, Mr. Havens commissioned the building of this house. Not simply to give people jobs, but also to give people skills, and to give people lives. If no member of the local community possessed a certain skill needed for the construction, he brought in the best of that trade and had them teach the local people the skills."

I was fascinated, and it seemed to fit what I'd seen around HRI.

"People did not build this house, this house built people," Jonathan said with obvious pride, "as it continues to do today. The majority of the craftsmen who built this house never lacked work again, because their skills are in great demand."

I looked around the room as he talked about the house. This room, like the foyer was much like I'd have expected in such a house — big, ornate, fancy wood, chandeliers over the table — yet it was different. From Jonathan's explanation of its origins, the difference became clear. I'd visited a couple houses this size, and now realized the whole purpose those other houses had been to impress visitors with the owner's wealth and status. Somehow, the people who designed and built this house did so in a way to erase the aura of arrogance; instead, this house had an aura of exceptional craftsmanship.

"Mrs. Havens was of the same mold as Mr. Havens," Jonathan continued. "She volunteered endlessly. Selflessly giving her time where it was needed. She worked a great deal at the local hospital, especially in the children's wards. Which is how they came to have Jeffery."

That got my full attention.

"Much to their disappointment, Mr. and Mrs. Havens could not have children. One day, while Mrs. Havens was working with the hospital's nursery supervisor, a newborn baby was brought in, apparently having been abandoned in the emergency room's restroom."

Surprise reverberated through me. It'd never occurred to me that Jeff had been adopted, and I realized Jonathan was right, the answers I was getting wouldn't do anything but create more questions.

Jonathan apparently sensed this. "Of course, a search for the parents was begun, newspaper advertising, television and so on. Mrs. Havens ensured that every attempt was made to find the infant's mother, to no avail. When all avenues had been exhausted, to their endless joy, Mr. and Mrs. Havens adopted the baby."

I could see it. After everything I'd learned of Clinton and Victoria Havens, I could just see it.

He gave me a moment to process this then gave the slightest smile. "As I'm sure you're beginning to realize, there are no coincidences."

I gave him a confused look.

"Jeffrey was meant to be the child of this extraordinary couple." He paused a moment, apparently reminiscing. "Those were happy years. He was a joyous child, but a challenge, because he questioned everything. If he had his mind set to learn something, one had best not get in his way."

That didn't surprise me in the least.

"When he was twelve, they removed him from school, which was the end of his formal education, and stopped taking him to church with them. Already, his knowledge had far surpassed his school teachers', and he argued endlessly with the church leaders."

I turned a laugh into a cough in an attempt to be polite. Jeff? Argue with the church? No. Never.

"You see, by that time, he had taught himself Hebrew, Greek, and Latin, among other languages. Not only had he read the Bible in the languages in which it was written, but he'd read many, many other ancient texts, which seemed to contradict much of which the church was attempting to teach him. Not surprisingly, churches do not like to be questioned, much less by a twelve-year-old boy."

"I bet." I laughed as I visualized Jeff, as a twelve-year-old, taking on the leaders of the church.

"Those were good years though," Jonathan continued. "Until— when Jeffery was sixteen—Mrs. Havens became very sick and died within four months. Mr. Havens never recovered."

I could tell from Jonathan's expression that he deeply cared for Jeff's parents and still grieved their death. Then I remembered being on the cliff with Harris when Jeff told the story of his parents, and I knew Jonathan wasn't the only one who the loss of these two people had affected deeply.

"After her death, Mr. Havens increasingly left the running the Institute to his top people, and if not for the great love these people had for him, it would have crumbled." Jonathan took a deep breath, as if reluctant to continue. "Mr. Havens died soon after Jeffery's eighteenth birthday, as if he waited until that event."

"I'm sorry," I said, not knowing what else I could say to the man's obviously painful memories.

Jonathan finished his lemonade and began again in a more neutral tone. "Jeffery was left everything, of course. The next day, he transferred everything to me with no stipulations, then loaded his bicycle's saddlebags and said 'Please understand, I need to find answers. I will return.'" Jonathan shook his head, apparently at the impulsiveness of youth. "He was a multi-millionaire the day before and left this house with one hundred dollars in his pocket."

A low-toned gong rang, startling me.

But Jonathan had apparently been expecting it and turned to face the hallway door.

Curious, I held my many questions and waited, too.

A few moments later, children, adolescents and young adults, along with a number of adults, some pushing kids in wheelchairs or helping them in other ways, started pouring into the dining room. As I watched, the wheelchairs filled the chairless spaces I'd noticed before.

Jonathan smiled fondly at the gathering, as he spoke again. "Jeffrey was away for eight years, and he returned a changed man. No longer a mourning youth, but a man with a vision and a mission. With him, he brought more love—" he tipped his head toward the quickly filling table "—as you can see. And in the ten years since his return, every molecule of this house has flowed with love."

To my surprise, Jeff entered through the kitchen door with a big tray full of steaming serving dishes. As he lowered the tray onto a holder that one of the kids had set there, Jeff started calling out orders, which with the smile on his face, the glow in his eyes and the love in his voice, did not sound like orders. As he called out names and directions, children and young adults all began moving to his commands in a well-coordinated fashion that spoke of much practice. Several more adults and young-adults came out of the kitchen with more trays and returned for a second trip, and food filled the table. Everybody but the butler was helping.

How strange, I thought, that the butler had to entertain me because Jeff had been making dinner for all these people.

As the others were getting the last of it arranged, Jeff came over to where I was sitting. "Hey, Stanley, glad you could make it." Then he grinned his grin that meant I was about to regret something. "You asked if I had kids, but you never asked how many."

You'd think I'd have quit being surprised, but at every turn Jeff had a new surprise for me. I'm sure my mouth hung open most unflatteringly.

He pointed to an empty chair about midway down the table. "Your seat's over there."

I stood and went to the chair he'd pointed to, between a boy and girl, both in the thirteen-ish range. Jeff and Jonathan took the chairs on opposite ends of the table.

Everyone settled in, quieted down, and held hands while Jeff led the prayer. Afterwards he announced, "Everyone, this is Stanley, a very special friend of mine. Stanley, this is my family, the Havens. You've met some of my kids at work already and this is the rest of them."

"Hello, Stanley," came the cheerful chorus from many throats, young and old.

"Hello back," I replied, not knowing what else to say.

They laughed and dug into the food.

As they did so, I looked around the table. There were boys and girls, young men and women, Blacks, Hispanics, Whites, Asians, and many I couldn't even guess where their genes had come from. Some were the ideal of beauty, some had obvious birth defects or Down Syndrome, and everything in between. One, who looked to be about ten, had old burn scars on his face. Three were severely handicapped, in expensive wheelchairs. Sprinkled in among the kids were adults, male and female, who were obviously well-loved caregivers, because the table was abuzz with laughter and friendly ribbing that was so familiar from my own table at home.

As I looked around, it was clear Jonathan was right. Every molecule of this house was filled with love.

The meal was loud and rowdy with lots of talking and laughing. My companions on either side had definite opinions as to which of the many dishes tasted the best, and between them, they insisted I try everything, which I did. It was all delicious. Jeff ate and talked to those he was near, but mostly he watched it all, glowing more than his normal glow.

Grace's profile halfway down the table caught my eye, and I remembered her describing her dad, the guy I'd wanted to punch in the nose for being a crappy dad. I replayed the conversation over in my head and realized it fit Jeff perfectly but not in the way I'd first envisioned. Her not being white, I guess, in my mind, removed the possibility of Jeff being her dad. I shook my head, amused at my misplaced assumptions, then shook my head again at Jeff's games. Why would I expect some employee of HRI to be his adopted daughter?

Once the chaos around the table settled a little, I started to interact more with the two children on either side of me. To my right was a girl who introduced herself as May, told me she was thirteen and had been adopted from China when she as an infant. To my left was the young boy. He looked to be about twelve or thirteen and wasn't especially attractive. It was hard to place his ethnicity. His hair was brown and curled in some places but stuck up in a frizzy, uncontrollable way in other places. He was in need of braces and I wondered why Jeff hadn't taken care of that. But, like all the people here, he had an expression of peace and happiness that overcame any physical limitations.

I extended my hand. "As you know, I'm Stanley. What's your name?"

He extended his hand and in a very dignified way replied, "My name is Dylan, but my friends and family just call me Dylan. I won't mention what my plethora of enemies call me, but why don't you call me Dylan."

As I equally solemnly shook his hand, I wanted to burst out laughing. The kid was a hoot. "I'm very pleased to meet you, Dylan."

He and I talked some more, with plenty of kibitzing from the girl on my other side and the kids across from us, and I couldn't help feeling a bond grow between me and this very unique boy.

Chapter 23

After dinner, Jeff playfully addressed the family, "Now that Stanley has met all you monsters, get started on your homework and leave us alone."

With Jonathan supervising, everyone pitched in, and soon, the table was transformed from a dining table to a study table. Some of the caregivers worked with the kids, others helped Jonathan, and some left, probably to complete other chores. Many of the older kids were paired with younger ones and everyone was focused on their tasks.

Considering the trouble I had getting Cooper to do his homework, I was positive I was witnessing a miracle.

Jeff waved me to the couch where Jonathan and I had sat earlier, and Jeff was still glowing.

"When I got back home from my search for answers," Jeff said, picking up the story from where Jonathan left off, "I realized it didn't seem right for this house to hold only Jonathan and me, so I started adopting kids who were 'unadoptable.'" He looked with fondness toward the busy table, then back to me. "Some were close to aging out of the system when I adopted them. A few of whom have moved on with their own lives, and others have stuck around to help with the younger kids and work at the Institute."

"I thought I recognized several faces."

He grinned. "Nepotism is the rule, not the exception, at HRI."

His comment startled me. Nepotism had a negative connotation for me, relatives mooching off other relatives and giving nothing in return. "You say that like it's a good thing."

"It's awesome, friend. If you can't take care of your family and friends, then what's the point of running a business?"

He had me there. If you can't help the ones you love, what's the point?

"And I'm sure you've already seen that HRI isn't the type of place where Uncle Ned wanders in at ten, takes a two-hour lunch and leaves at one."

"I gathered that," I replied sarcastically.

Jeff smiled and then continued, "Even if it starts that way with someone, it isn't long before they're so engrossed in a project that they're staying until the lights are being shut off in the evening, and as they're packing up their stuff to go home, they realize they'd completely missed lunch."

Already, I suspected that HRI was a place that sucked you in, twisted you into shapes you'd never thought you'd take on, and then spit you out a completely different person. As I contemplated what shape I'd end up at the end of my two months, I looked over at the table full of kids doing homework and it dawned on me. It was July. "Why are the kids doing homework?"

"Year-round school."

"Egads!" I again thought of my household homework battles. "How can you get them all doing homework like that in the summer?"

"Like HRI, the schools here are engaging."

"They'd have to be," I muttered.

"Once I started adopting kids with these kinds of challenges, it became clear how lacking the local public school district was. So that became my next area of work. With the help of the school district, we identified some schools. We looked at the schools with the worst performance records. Those became proving grounds for innovative instruction techniques and methods. Now, those schools are being held up as models, both in the district and rest of the state. The schools and town are better for the changes. And working so closely with them has made me a better person."

He was a miracle worker for sure, I joked to myself. As I did that I wondered, "Do they, I mean your family, know what you are?"

He looked at me with a wicked smile. "Do you?"

Exasperated, I looked at the floor as I thought back over the last week's conversations and then finally had to admit. "No, I guess I don't. I know you're something unique and special. Watching you at the Institute and here at your house, I know you're far beyond being merely a good person." I looked at him. "But having been sent from God or being a messiah? No. I still struggle with those." Then I looked at him more intensely. "But you know that."

"Sure. You need to say what you believe sometimes. Putting it into words helps you define it for yourself. When the time is right, when your heart is right, you'll believe the right thing."

"I hope so. I want to believe in you, in God, in Jesus —"

He stopped me. "Don't worry about it so much. If you're too focused on trying to believe something, you'll miss the message that goes with it. Focus on living the message and, in time, belief will come naturally."

I made a disbelieving sound.

"It will. I promise. As for my family knowing what I am, Jonathan's the only one who knows the whole of me. In fact, he knew before I did."

"Really?"

Jeff nodded. "When I walked out the door at eighteen, he waited patiently for my return, keeping the house in top shape and learning what was needed to properly take care of all the money I'd left him. When I returned, he tried to give the money back, but I didn't want the headaches that went along with maintaining it, so it's all still his, which leaves me free to do what I'm called to do."

Movement caught my eye, and I glanced up to see Jonathan approaching with two filled wine glasses. I took the one he handed me, and Jeff took the other. "And he still takes care of me like I was ten," he teased fondly as Jonathan returned to the kitchen.

"Cheers!" I replied, touching my glass gently to his.

"Cheers," he repeated. Then after he took a sip, he continued where he left off. "What I was put here on Earth to accomplish can't be about me as a person or even a figurehead. It has to be about the message."

"Which is?" I prompted.

"It's the same message that Jesus, Buddha, Mohammed, Moses, and everybody else has tried to communicate: Love. But I'm here to bring it to today's world. To take on the challenges that face people today. To communicate the changes that need to take place, *today*, in how humanity treats themselves, each other and our planet." He paused. "Getting the message out has to be done in a way which minimizes my part in it. If I become the focus, people will start taking sides as to who I am or am not. Am I a prophet or a charlatan? Is this the second coming? Am I the antichrist? And so on, endlessly, as has happened so many times before. And in that process, the message gets lost."

He watched his kids fondly for a moment as he took a drink of his wine. "I'm here to unite the world, not divide it. My message will be spread by others not me."

"How're you going to do that?"

"How do most messages get spread in modern times?"

I thought a moment. "I guess through the media. Or social media."

"Books, movies, music, news, Internet, TV, and so on. All of them will be used to teach the world. To *change* the world." He grinned at me. "Jesus had John the Baptist to spread the word; I have the media."

I didn't get it. Was he going to get a website, advertise with Google, get a Facebook or Twitter account, maybe start a band? Then a thought struck and I couldn't help myself. "Infomercials?"

Jeff laughed. "Only as a last resort."

I still couldn't make it make sense, but I knew I wasn't going to understand tonight, so I figured it was time to move to a different topic. As I looked around the room at the wheelchairs and the boy with burns, I asked, "I don't want this to come across wrong but, if you've got the power, why don't you heal these kids?"

He nodded, letting me know the intention of my question was understood. "Sure, I could, and I do. Just not in the way you're thinking. They have the best medical care money can buy, including full-time nursing care here at the house, and the most love a family can give."

I shook my head. "You're right, that isn't what I was thinking. Why let them suffer?"

He shrugged. "Would I be doing them any favors by healing them outright? After all, it's our struggles in life that define and build us." He looked around the room, proudly. "All of my children, with their physical defects and physical scars, will be better and stronger because of their perceived difficulties. The same with their emotional scars. It's the ones who don't have to struggle I worry most about."

I thought about that a moment. "'What does not kill me, makes me stronger'?"

"I love Nietzsche," Jeff said. "Wish people would take the time to really understand what he meant by 'God is dead.'"

And there was a topic that, after this roller-coaster day, I didn't have the heart to get into, so I went back to my own Nietzsche quote. "What made you strong?"

"Great question," he exclaimed. "My parents' love gave me one kind of strength. Their death gave me another. Their death was what pushed me to search for meaning; it pushed me into becoming who I am. If they were still alive, all these children would still be looking for homes, you'd be dead, and I'd be just a really smart, really rich, really nice person."

"Really crazy person," I muttered, and it took me a moment to process the me-being-dead part of the statement, then I remembered. "The motorcycle?"

He nodded and then stared off into space for a moment. "The Bible says Jesus drove out demons; today, we say those people are mentally ill. For *my* kids, in some cases, I have cast out demons of some truly horrific parenting. But for the most part, if it's something *my* children can overcome, I give them the chance to do that." He paused again and then, with a smiling glance at me, seemingly changed the subject. "You like to camp. Tell me about a camping trip with your family."

I finished my wine and set the glass on the table beside me as I thought back. Family camping trips were always a good time, but I knew the one he was talking about. "We went on a canoe trip a couple of years ago; Alice was four at the time. We weren't more than an hour down the river before we hit some swift water and low hanging branches, and we tipped over. Beth thought I'd tied the tent and cooler down, I thought she had, and it ended up that neither of us did. We lost the tent and most of the food from the cooler, and ended up splitting the last of the granola bars for dinner and slept on damp sleeping bags on the ground that evening. The kids never missed a beat and had a great time. I don't even think they noticed what went wrong."

He stopped me. "If I were to ask your family to tell me about a camping trip, which one would they tell me about?"

"We still talk about that trip. In spite of everything that went wrong, we all had a great time."

Jeff smiled. "It's all part of the experience."

There was that saying again, the one that kept echoing in my head. And boy, had I been having the experiences lately.

He seemed to know I was thinking and waited a moment before he continued. "It's what goes wrong in life that defines us and makes us grow. That's what makes life interesting. It also makes us realize what we have and who we are. The sorriest people on Earth are the ones who go through life with everything made easy for them. Those are the people who you can't wait to get away from, because after five minutes, they have nothing interesting to say."

"I know plenty of those people," I said and then reflected for a minute before the words hit me. "They're horizontal people, aren't they?"

"Exactly," he replied and then waited for me to continue.

"Your kids here." I looked around at them. "I'll bet they've spent a lot of time wondering why all these things happened to them. And since they're your kids, I'll also bet they've done some deep exploring of themselves. They've worked on their vertical growth, not just their horizontal growth of lessons and homework."

"Very good. They're working their way up to the top of Maslow's hierarchy," Jeff said referring back to our conversation on the trip out here. He continued, "You want to hear some scary statistics?"

"Sure."

"Fifty-eight percent of adults never read a book after high school, and forty-two percent never read one after college."

"That's mind-boggling."

"It gets worse. Eighty percent of families in America didn't buy or read a book last year, and seventy percent of adults haven't been in a bookstore in five years. When people do buy books, fifty-seven percent aren't read to completion."

"Really?" I had a hard time imagining that. "That *is* scary." Beth and I were in the bookstore almost every week, and we made sure we read to the kids almost every day.

After a pause, he continued, "Excluding the minority who can't read because of some physical or mental deficiency, what do these non-readers have to talk about? Or think about?"

"I can't even imagine." My dinnertime conversations with the kids were lively and diverse. Beth and I might avoid some topics for the sake of marital harmony, but we both had wide-ranging interests, and even after all this time, I still found her a fascinating person to talk to.

"Life is so interesting," Jeff said, "and the world wants nothing more than to be explored and discovered. Sure, people can get information from TV, but that's mostly surface knowledge, horizontal growth rather than vertical."

Jeff stopped talking, and we sat in silence for a minute. His phrase, "It is all part of the experience," kept echoing in my head. "All your kids have had a pretty bad life before they came here?"

"Very bad. Most of their stories would make you cry."

"So, the things your kids have gone through, and you losing your parents at a young age, all that kind of horrific stuff, it's all part of the experience?"

He looked at me matter-of-factly. "Absolutely. That doesn't mean it didn't hurt at the time and even later on, but it's absolutely all part of the experience of this life that we've been blessed with. It's all part of the experience that we use to learn and grow from." He paused a moment to let me absorb that. "With all the pain it caused me, all the heartache, sleepless nights and tears of grief, my parents' death was part of the experience of my life, and I'm a better person because of it."

He glanced around the room, not only at the people there, but as if he was trying to see all the people in the house. "All the pain *my* children have suffered is all part of their experiences of their lives. And my job is to help them use those experiences as catalysts for vertical growth. To help them discover the glowing essence of who they truly are and to help them find their place in the spiritual world."

We both fell silent. As much as I wanted him to be wrong, I couldn't make a case for it. I thought about the hard times in my life, and as painful as they'd been, they were also the times that kicked my butt in the direction I needed to go. I was now thankful my butt didn't need a stronger kick, and my parents, wife and kids were all still a beautiful, healthy part of my life.

Jeff looked over to the table, and I followed his gaze to see Dylan closing his book.

"You done, Dylan?" Jeff asked.

Dylan looked at Jeff and in fake Southern drawl answered, "Smoke comin' out ma ears done."

Jeff shook his head and laughed. "Gather up the gang and let's see if we can knock out some more of *The Hobbit*."

Dylan stood and saluted. "Roger that, commander. Out." And he was gone.

Now I laughed. That kid was a piece of work. "With him, why not at least get him braces?"

Jeff gave a full laugh. "You don't know Dylan yet. Ask me that question when you get to know him more. This family has paid for the local orthodontist's vacation home. Believe me, it isn't because the option isn't there."

For some strange reason, as little as I knew Dylan, what Jeff said made sense. There was something different about that boy.

Jeff stood, obviously getting ready to read to his kids. Which was fine with me, as I was exhausted and wanted to get back to the hotel.

We walked to the front door, and Jeff shook my hand. "Thanks for coming, friend. Hope it wasn't too much of a shock."

I smiled at him. "It's all part of the experience." The last thing I'd expected was for him to be a father of a massive family. Yet, watching him tonight, it fit. Whatever these kids' pasts were like before Jeff took them in, their current experience was beautiful.

As I was walking out, Dylan ran up and gave me a hug. This kid was definitely the part of the experience that I wanted to use to grow from.

I drove home with my mind overflowing from my unexpected day.

Chapter 24

That night I slept surprisingly well considering how chaotic my thoughts had been when I fell into bed. And, maybe for the first time in my life, I woke excited about going to work.

As I walked from the parking lot, I spotted Grace coming down the sidewalk, so I slowed to say good morning. We chatted until I got to Summer's desk.

"Good morning, Stanley," Summer said as she reached for the phone. "I'll call Aaron and have him come take you to the lab."

Grace interrupted her, "I can take him, if you want."

Summer hung up the phone. "If you don't mind. I'm sure Aaron would appreciate it."

"It's not a problem at all."

With that, Grace and I started down the hall together.

She turned to me as we walked. "You'll like Aaron and his group. They're working on a very cool project. You're going to love it." Before I could answer, she added, "Hope you enjoyed dinner last night. It's a crazy family, isn't it? More culture shock."

"I enjoyed it very much. It was great to see the love and energy of your family. I hope to see more of it," I replied honestly.

She laughed. "Oh, you will. Dad really likes you. Were we too much last night?"

"No, I wouldn't say 'too much.' But it definitely was impressive. I don't see how your dad does it. I mean, taking on that many unadoptable kids—" I stopped abruptly. How does one take back words already said? She was one of those kids.

But Grace was unfazed and seemed to know I regretted my word choice. "No problem, Stanley. I *was* unadoptable and for lots of very real reasons."

What a wonderful girl, I thought as we turned another corner, working our way to the rear of the building. She seemed so comfortable with her situation, and her acceptance of my stupidity made me feel like I could maybe go a little deeper. "Do you mind if I ask you a more personal question? 'No' is an okay answer." .

"I don't mind," she said with unusual openness for anyone, let alone someone her age, "and I'll even start so you don't have to ask. But let's go out there, where we won't be disturbed." As she said it, she pointed to a pair of doors.

Through their glass, I could see a highly manicured courtyard with an array of different colored flowers, and tables shaded by large trees. "Sure," I said, and followed her out to the warm, shaded area. I let her pick the table, and when she sat, I settled into the chair opposite her.

"I was nine," she began, "when Dad adopted me. I was the first kid he adopted. I have brothers and sisters who're older than me because, as Dad has obviously already told you," she rolled her eyes in loving annoyance, "he only adopts the—" she made air quotes " — 'unadoptable.' Which means older kids, broken kids like me, or kids with physical, mental or emotional handicaps. Some of my brothers and sisters were almost eighteen when he adopted them. Most of them were headed to homelessness or jail, because there wasn't anywhere else for them to go when they got too old for the child welfare system."

I cringed at the unfairness of life, but didn't say anything. The way Jeff had taken in all those kids elevated him in my eyes more than anything I'd heard him say or seen him do. If he wanted to call himself a messiah and followed through with doing things this loving and selfless, I wouldn't deny him.

Grace waved at some acquaintances through the window and continued with her story. "He gave us a home and a family, something most of us never had before. Certainly not me." She looked over at the raised flower bed next to the table, apparently reflecting for a moment, and then looked at me with a shrug. "When Dad took me in, I was a mess. I screamed, lied, hit, bit and acted out in every way you can imagine. The most astounding thing was he took me home with him, into *that* house. I went from a Hispanic ghetto to that house."

I had to agree with her it was astounding; I couldn't imagine bringing broken kids into a place like that. I'd thoroughly enjoyed looking at the paintings and antiques last night, but in my house with one normal boy, I didn't have expensive things because I knew they wouldn't last long.

"I broke stuff," she admitted, giving me a glance that was mixture of shame and sheepishness. "First thing when I walked in the door, right in front of Dad and Jonathan, I took a vase off a stand beside the door and threw it at the wall. I found out many years later, that vase had been worth over fifty-thousand dollars."

"Ouch," I said.

"Yeah, I know. But Dad, being Dad, walked over, grabbed the matching vase on the other side of the doorway and threw it against the wall, then turned to me and smiled his smile. He never quit smiling. He dropped to his knee and held out his arms. I ran over to his open arms, kicked him in—" She looked at me and blushed. "Well, you can probably guess where."

I could guess and winced in sympathy.

She grinned. "Yeah. There. Anyway, I did that, swore at him, then ran to the next breakable thing and broke it. He copied me, then dropped to one knee and held out his arms. I ran to him." She looked at me and grinned. "He kept his knees together that time, but let me hit him, swear and spit. This went on for a while, and he never quit smiling and never lost that look in his eyes." She looked at me. "You know the look, the one that says everything will be okay because you're his."

I smiled. "Yeah." I knew the look, even though the ones *I* usually got from him were the ones signaling I was about to get into big trouble.

"Finally, I ran to him and instead of the hitting, I fell into his arms and cried."

Her story made me remember Jeff's technique in the bar with Bear, and I now realized Bear hadn't been the first person Jeff had used the technique with. I suspected that a broken nine-year-old had been a tougher nut to crack than an old, angry biker.

Grace continued, "I cried for what must have been hours as he held me and told me he loved me and would love me no matter what. I'd broken lots of expensive stuff that day, and he did, too. But I didn't break him. Instead, he broke me." She paused for a moment. "Later, when I was a little older, I had a name for what he gave me that day and every day since—unconditional love—but even then, when he held me and let me cry, I knew how rare a thing it was." She had tears in her eyes as she said it.

I had tears, too.

"When I was thirteen," she said, looking past me to the opening between the wings of the building and the trees beyond, "my biological parents died. They'd accidentally overdosed themselves. Dad paid for the funeral, then made me go to it and helped me make peace with them in my mind. Forgive them. He, or, we tried to contact them, bring me back into their life but they wouldn't have me. Drugs were more important." She looked me in the eye. "He showed me they weren't bad people, that they were as much victims as I was."

We sat there in silence a few minutes as I absorbed the story she told.

"And now you're here," I said.

She grinned at me. "Quite the change, isn't it?"

"A miracle," I replied, in an attempt to lighten the mood some.

She laughed. "Don't discount those miracles. They happen with amazing frequency around that house."

"Yeah, I bet." Then I met her gaze. "Thank you," I said, trying to convey my gratitude for her trust.

"No problem." She stood. "We should get going; they'll be waiting for you."

"Okay," I replied as I stood. Then as I held the door for her, in an attempt to break the tension, I said, "Really, when I asked if I could ask a personal question, I was only going to ask what kind of music you liked."

She burst out laughing as she entered the building, which got smiles from several people in the hall, and then she composed herself. "That's easy. The Change."

That brought Cooper to mind. "My son likes him, too. He wants me to get a T-shirt from him while I'm out here."

"Shouldn't be a problem," she said as she stopped in front of a white metal door that read "Physical Lab #3."

I followed her in, and I instantly smiled at the feeling of the two-story tall bay with its steel trusses and industrial lighting, full of equipment and scattered with people. I was home.

I leaned against the steel-pipe railing and looked down at the lab floor ten feet below me, which struck me as odd since we'd been on the ground floor. I glanced over the rows of tall metal cylinders, towards the back of the lab at the large roll up doors, most likely a loading dock, and concluded that the building must be on the side of a hill that I hadn't noticed before. I quickly scanned the rest of the lab. I had no clue what all the equipment was or what all the people were doing, but I knew I wanted to be a part of it.

Chapter 25

"You must be Stanley," a vaguely familiar voice from my left exclaimed over the background noise, as a short, balding man in his mid-fifties wearing a white lab coat and prescription safety glasses hurried toward me on the wide concrete balcony that framed three sides of the room, with his hand extended in welcome. "I'm Aaron."

As I shook his hand, I realized he was the man who had interviewed me about the weather in California. Surprisingly, he looked almost how I'd envisioned him after talking to him on the phone. "It's good to finally meet you," I said. The lab's noise level was low enough that I could talk fairly normally.

"Wonderful! And, boy, are we glad to have you on the project. We really need a tech writer." He turned to Grace. "Thanks for bringing him."

"No problem, Aaron." She turned to me. "See you later, Stanley."

"Thank you," I replied, trying to let her know it was for more than bringing me here.

She smiled and excused herself, leaving me with my new temporary boss.

"Let me tell you about the project," Aaron said, "and introduce you to the team."

I followed him down the expanded-metal stairs and over to the closest of the—I did a quick count—ten shiny metal cylinders that looked to be about ten-feet high and three- or four-feet in diameter, each with a large bench, or two, full of computerized equipment with lots of wires running to the cylinders. When we got close enough, he introduced me to some of the people gathered there.

One very tall and broad-shouldered young man—maybe in his mid-twenties—I recognized from dinner last night as one of Jeff's older kids. The white lab coat he wore over his jeans and red T-shirt contrasted with his dark skin. He was introduced as Marcus.

Marcus shook my hand with a very firm grip and a warm, "Good seein' ya, again." Then returned to what he'd been doing, looking between several computer monitors that were apparently displaying things related to the big cylinders. As I watched, one middle-aged woman typed some stuff, and the graphs changed slightly, eliciting a moan from the watchers.

Aaron began speaking, so I turned to pay attention to him. "One of the biggest problems we have with energy is figuring out how to store it. Batteries are inefficient, plus they're made of all kinds of chemicals that are bad for the environment and rare earth minerals that are terribly destructive to mine. What we have here," he looked fondly at the big cylinder, "is a flywheel system. This system contains a two-thousand pound, carbon-fiber flywheel that rides on magnetic bearings inside this vacuum enclosure. The flywheel rotates —"

Aaron's phone rang interrupting him, and he answered it with a typical, "Wonderful," and followed with, "Oops! I forgot about that. I'll be right there." Then he directed his attention back at me. "Sorry, I forgot about a meeting, which is about normal for me. Let me get someone else to tell you about the project."

The first person who caught his eye was Marcus, who'd moved closer to our side of the cylinder to work on a keyboard below another monitor, so Aaron called to him, "Marcus, can you give Stanley an overview of the system? This may surprise you, but I forgot about a meeting."

Marcus looked up. "Give me a chance to talk about my favorite toy? Hmmm..." He put his hand to his chin and gave a thoughtful look, with an amused twinkle in his eye. "Guess I can do that."

"Wonderful. I just started, so you won't be repeating anything." Aaron turned to me as Marcus walked over. "You're in great hands now. Marcus will answer any questions you have." And he was gone.

With an ease of obvious familiarity, Marcus took over Aaron's role. He thumped his fist against the tall metal enclosure, which gave a dull thud indicating it had a pretty thick wall. "This is the containment vessel. Inside is the carbon-fiber flywheel spinning in a vacuum. When most people think of a flywheel, they think of wheel shaped piece of iron. The system we have here is light-years past that. This flywheel's a seven-foot tall, hollow cylinder that spins at roughly 16,000 RPM. Surface speed of the flywheel is over Mach two, which is over 1,500 miles-per-hour, which is why the containment vessels are reinforced. If the flywheel explodes—which they occasionally do, 'cause we work them a lot harder than any sane people would—everything is contained in the vessel."

I tried to imagine what would happen if the wheel came apart at that speed, and the word "bomb" came to mind. A little fearfully, I asked, "Are its walls thick enough to hold all of that in?"

Marcus grinned. "Sure. That's one of the beauties of modern material technologies. When a normal metal flywheel fails, it turns into supersonic bullets, which this shell wouldn't have a chance of containing. But when a carbon fiber flywheel fails, at that speed, it pretty much disintegrates and turns to a red-hot dust. So, yeah, it's contained."

I nodded in understanding. "That's cool."

Marcus continued, "The containment vessel is vacuum sealed so the flywheel spins with a very low drag coefficient."

I took the opportunity to show I knew something about something. "I guess the magnetic bearings Aaron was talking about also help to lower the drag coefficient."

He nodded and smiled at me. "You got it. Name of this game is drag. Because we're smart here at HRI, we've lowered the drag so much that our efficiency is around 90% and climbing."

"That's impressive," I replied. "Where would these be used?"

"Power plants mostly. You see, power plants have a sweet-spot where they run at peak efficiency, but unfortunately, people aren't kind enough to demand energy at a constant rate." He looked at me with a smile, inviting me to share his joke.

I smiled back. "How inconsiderate of us." I liked the humor, plus he was obviously super smart, and he carried himself with a confidence that wasn't accompanied by arrogance. It wasn't hard to tell he was one of Jeff's kids.

"You're tellin' me, man," Marcus continued with a grin. "People turn the lights off at night and use their A/C less because it's cooler, so the demand on the power plant is lower at night and higher during the day."

I chimed in, "Which means that the plant has to constantly adjust its production, based on demand."

"Exactly! Normal power plants spend very little time running at peak efficiency. Our goal with these flywheel systems is to have a plant be able to spin up these power-storage flywheels at times of low-power demand, while the plant runs at peak efficiency, and have the flywheels store enough power to handle the fluctuation in the demand so the plant can continue to run at peak efficiency."

"That makes sense," I said, thinking about all the implications. "I mean, that makes really great sense. What's the actual power savings?"

"That's part of what we're doing here," he replied, with a motion of his hand that encompassed the room and all its team members. "Trying to get enough numbers to figure out if it's a cost-effective solution at the scale a large power plant would need. We're also trying to find ways to lower the cost of production of the flywheel systems and increase their efficiency even more. For instance—" he began giving examples of different composites, formulas and speeds, and lost me very quickly.

I waved to stop him, and he laughed.

"Sorry, got caught up in it."

"You really like this stuff, don't you?"

"Oh, sure. It's great. Best thing is, it makes everything I'm learning in college have a purpose. My classmates are seeing this stuff for the first time in their lab classes and don't have any real-world application for it. I've been working with it for a while."

"So, you're going to college?" I asked. "After talking to Grace, I thought your dad wasn't into college."

"Man, Dad's a crazy dude! They need to lock him up," he said with a straight face.

I was taken aback and responded with a puzzled look.

Then Marcus cracked a smile; he knew he got me with that one. "He really is crazy, though. Must be crazy to take in the kids he does."

"I spent a week in a car with him and thought he was crazy. Going to your house last night removed all doubt. But at the same time, it wasn't crazy. It was, I don't know, controlled chaos." I held my hand out to him. "But having a calming force like you around must have been great for him over the years. I can imagine your younger brothers and sisters look up to you."

He paused and smiled at me as he thought. Then he pointed. "Let's go to a conference room; it's not so noisy and we can talk."

He led me to the side of the lab and up some more expanded-metal stairs to an area with a couple small, windowed, conference rooms. When the door shut behind us, it was suddenly much quieter. He sat down at the table, and I sat across from him.

He leaned back in his chair and gave a short laugh. "Calming force." He looked down at the table as he reflected on that. I wondered what memories were going through his head. He then looked up. "Let's answer your first question; how the crazy dude handles college."

"Sure. I'd like to hear that."

"Sometime, usually around the time a kid's in the tenth grade Dad sits each kid down and talks about their plans for after graduation. Together, they work out what they think they need and whatever they decide, Dad supports them. Grace would be wastin' her time in college; there isn't a professor who could keep up with her. And I don't mean with only computers or physics, I mean in every subject. She's a certified genius and could be teaching them. Plus, she writes poetry that makes me cry."

I smiled at that, but when he didn't return the smile, I realized he wasn't joking.

He gave me an expression that was a little embarrassed for having admitted such a thing, then continued, "So what sense does it make for her to go get a degree when she can do more, learn more, here? For me, it's different. I'm going to college 'cause, I've got something to prove."

"What do you mean?" I asked, baffled. "You're obviously very smart. What you just explained to me wasn't a walk in the park."

"No, not in that way. I can handle the coursework fine. In fact, I'm working on a double major right now, Mechanical Engineering and Music. Classical guitar."

He said it with a shrug, like that much work didn't mean anything special, and I suspected the attitude was something he'd learned from Jeff.

"But where I grew up," he continued, "no one valued education, so I have a point to make."

Just as with Grace, I was interested in how he'd become Jeff's son. "Where'd you grow up?"

"Bronx. Worst part."

"Ouch, not a great place," I replied.

He shrugged, again, like it was nothing. "Most kids don't grow up there, they die there. I was going to die there, too, soon as I got out of jail."

He grinned at my surprise, then I remembered Grace talking about her brothers and sisters and jail. But the young man in front of me was so different from the story he was telling me.

"I was in a gang, 'cause if you live there, you've gotta be in a gang, no choice for a big dude like me. At sixteen and with so many drive-by shootings happenin', I was picked up by the cops, and sitting in a cell. My court appointed lawyer, said with the case they had against me I was going to juvie until I was eighteen and then the Pen for a nice long stay. That was it. He was gone. Never saw him again. The court date was coming soon and the guard tells me I've got a visitor. Figured it was the lawyer 'cause no one else was gonna come see me. My mom died when I was fourteen, I don't know who my dad was, and no brothers or sisters." He looked at me with a smile. "Wasn't the lawyer. Wanna guess who?"

Because I knew the end of the story, it wasn't hard to guess. I chuckled. "That must've been an eye opener."

He smiled back. "You're tellin' me, man. Anyway, they led me in handcuffs to a room exactly like you see on TV, with the windows so the guard can watch, a metal table in the middle with a chair on either side, they shoved me into a chair and locked my hands to the table. In walks this white dude, with a big goofy smile, and he says he wants to adopt me."

Marcus shook his head and smiled as his mind went back to that moment in time. "A white dude! No brother wants to be rescued by a white dude. The Bronx are filled with the failed attempts of white people trying to come in and save us from ourselves. And here sits this puny white guy with a goofy smile telling this sixteen-year-old kid who grew up on the streets, gang wars, armed robberies, drugs, and all of that, he wants to adopt him."

He stopped and let me think. That was heavy. "I never thought of it that way."

"Believe me, I thought of it that way. The conversation was over. I called the guard and left his white butt sitting there. I didn't need him running in to save this poor misguided black kid." He ended the sentence with dripping sarcasm. "Let me tell you, spend some time sitting in a cell contemplating your future. It starts making you think. I wasn't getting out for a long time. My lawyer finally did come and was acting like a white guy should. He spent a couple minutes with me, told me I was going to be locked up for a minimum of fifteen years and he left. All I could think was, another black kid was off the street."

I was stunned. I didn't know what to think. Is that the way they really see whites? The ones that aren't trying to save them from themselves were trying to lock them up. I wanted to say something but had nothing helpful to say.

Marcus saved me. "He came back and was even more crazy. The dude lays a check in front of me and says if I read a book for him and write a book report, the check is mine. I leaned across the cold metal table with my hands fastened to it and looked at the check." He mimed the action, leaning across the conference table toward me with his hands firmly on the table, looking down at an imaginary check. "I didn't have much schooling at that point, but I knew my numbers good enough that I could see the crazy white man had put a five-hundred-thousand dollar check there."

Now I shook my head, but not in surprise, I had no problem imagining Jeff doing exactly that.

"I asked him which book," Marcus continued, as he leaned back in his chair, "because I was wondering what he would try to force down my throat. And he said I could pick any book I wanted, as long it was over two-hundred-fifty pages. Then he laid out a second five-hundred-thousand dollar check and said I could have it if I could beat him in a full contact sparring match."

At this point, I was shaking my head again. *Typical Jeff.*

Marcus' astonishment was almost as fresh all these years later, as I'm sure it must have been back then, "He was going to get me out of jail, give me a million bucks to read a book and knock the crap out of him."

Marcus leaned back in his chair and grinned at me. "Sure, he had stipulations like, no drugs, drinking, swearing, breaking stuff, stealing, and especially, no fighting with my 'new brothers and sisters' and to treat them with respect. He said if I needed to fight, to take care of my anger, I could spar with him anytime I wanted. As much as I hated it, I had made up my mind I was going to go with him before I sat down. But now, a million bucks, I was in. They loaded me in his Rolls, and his butler drove us to his house." He stopped, obviously thinking back, remembering.

"Well?" I prompted after a moment.

"Reading that book was hard. I mean, yeah I could read some but I'd never actually read a whole book," he admitted. "Writing the report was next to impossible. He wouldn't take it unless it was very good. But I was determined. I was gonna get that rich white man's money, and gonna get out of that crazy place."

"I bet that didn't happen like you planned."

He smirked, and he shook his head. "With Dad around? No way. But I didn't know that back then. Got my own room, and I pretty much locked myself up. Usin' books and stuff that I borrowed from the house's library, and the computer that was in the room, I taught myself how to do it."

Even having known this young man less than an hour, I wasn't surprised in the least.

"Dad offered me tutors and stuff. Offered to help me himself, but I was gonna prove I didn't need that fool for nothing."

"Which book did you pick to read?" I asked, because I was wondering if the book he read was part of what had made such a difference in him.

"Oh, it was nothing, some stupid trash novel. I've read so many books since then I don't even remember." Then he grinned. "'Til you said that, I hadn't thought about it in forever. I should find it, just for the memory. Anyway, I did exactly what any kid in my situation would do, I looked for a book that was two-hundred-fifty-one pages, with simple words and big print."

I grinned. "Of course." Then had to ask. "But the book must have been more than a trash novel. You stuck around."

He paused, thoughtfully. "It wasn't the book that changed me. I'd look out the window and watch the family out by the pool." He paused as he thought about what to say. "Wait. I'm going to go the long way to answer that if you don't mind. I think this story is important."

I shrugged. "That's fine. I'm guessing it will be a great story."

"It is. You'll love this. I'd been there only a few days when Dad took me to the gym to spar with him. I was *so* ready for it. Knew I had to keep my cool in the house to get the half million for the book, but at the gym I was gonna let loose on him. Wasn't going to hold back. Half million was mine for the takin'." Marcus chuckled. "Dad asked if I wanted any equipment, any head gear, hand protectors or anything like that? Heck no, I told him, but not in those exact words."

He grinned at me, and I shared his smile as I remembered Jeff asking Bear's table full of bikers to not cuss.

"The gym was full of people, and Dad explained to the gym's owner there wouldn't be any rules—everything was fair game— not to stop the match no matter what happened, and I wasn't to be held responsible for hurting him. He said that, in front of all those people. The owner was trying not to laugh, but the others weren't so restrained, and their laughter pissed me off even more. I was six inches taller than that goofy white dude, seventy pounds heavier, solid muscle and grew up fighting for my life. No one could even touch me. I'd never lost, I mean never lost, and these people were laughing at me."

I was totally absorbed in his story. I'd seen Jeff stand and let a man take his anger out on him, and I was waiting to hear how Jeff handled this kid.

"That man must've traveled to the East and learned all sorts of ninja monk stuff." Marcus shook his head, laughing at himself. "Took me a while to realize he was playing with me. I went after him with everything I had, he let me do it and never once let me land a punch. I've fought the biggest, meanest, best fighters on the street. I've fought multiple people at the same time. I can take a punch like nobody's business. I've been hit with bats and pipes by people trying to kill me. But dad finally quit playing with me. It was like a train carrying semi-trucks filled with TNT exploded. I've never been hit like that in my life. I remember the pain and then nothing until some muffled voices started becoming clear. I laid there with my eyes closed trying to figure out how to get up like it wasn't a big deal, like a scrawny white guy didn't just knock me out."

I nodded.

"But I heard something strange and opened my eyes to look around. Everyone who'd laughed at me, they weren't laughing any more, they were clapping. I was ready to rip some heads off... then realized they weren't clapping to make fun of me, it was out of respect. Ends up, that's the best anyone had ever done against Dad, and I hadn't even laid a hand on him." He smiled at the memory. "Afterwards, the owner told me that Dad actually had to try with me, and I had people asking to spar with me, to teach them how to fight like me." He gave a shallow laugh. "They were going to pay this young, stupid, kid from the streets to spar them? They were going to pay me to fight?"

"Wow. One punch." I shook my head.

"Yeah, one punch that was like nothing I ever felt before. He was as cool about it as can be. No bragging, gloating, nothing. Anyways, I tucked my tail between my legs and retreated to my room. It was clear I wasn't going to get that check but I could get the one for the report. At first, I spent most of my time in the room and only left to get food or use the bathroom. Knew if I acted out too much I'd lose my half million bucks, so I ignored everyone. I'd hear them at the meals, laughin' and having a great time. I'd look out the window of my room and see them playing in the yard or swimming in the pool.

Sometimes they'd be doing yard work, cutting up with each other, having a great time. It was so foreign to me. Never seen people be happy together like that. Where I grew up, you only watched out for yourself and used other people to get what you wanted. None of that in Dad's house. These people were nice to each other."

I tried to imagine what it had been like for him and realized I couldn't begin to comprehend it.

"One day I was watching them out the window. I watched him jumping rope, double Dutch in fact, with a Black girl, a White girl and boy, two Chinese girls and a Mexican boy. They were having a blast. Here was this guy, the most powerful guy I could ever imagine. He had tons of money. He took me to the mat like I was nothing. He was powerful in every way and he was jumping rope with a bunch of little kids. He was like that at dinner or helping with school. It dawned on me that he wasn't a rich white guy trying to make himself feel better. He was a man using his resources to help kids in need because that *is* who he is. I let it go. He wasn't a White guy saving a Black kid from himself. That was it. At that moment, he became my Dad. That was all there was to it."

"Wow." Was all I could think to respond with. That was a huge mental shift.

"Yeah," he nodded. "The book didn't change me, the fighting didn't change me... it was that family. Took me two months to learn to read and write well enough to read the book and write the report. During that time, I saw a different world, and by the end, I wanted to be part of it. And to my surprise, I was welcomed into it."

Marcus pulled out his wallet and laid the check in front of me on the conference room table.

There it was, a half million-dollar check with "Read book/Write book report" in the memo line and "VOID" written across the face of the check in big letters.

"I voided it," Marcus said. "Funny that 'void' carries so many meanings. I proved I didn't need him to learn to read and write, but I found out I needed him and my new family for so much more. Being part of that family made me realize it wasn't about me, I was part of something bigger than me. Then I started going to church with them, and Dad started talking to me about the church, about God, and I realized I was part of something even bigger than my family. It isn't even about us; it was so much bigger than us. I took the void from my life and left it on this check."

He drew in a deep breath, likely covering feelings he wasn't comfortable showing a stranger, then enthusiastically, he exclaimed, "But when I finally beat him in the ring, I'm not voiding *that* check!"

I grinned. "And I don't think you should."

"I'm training six days a week in boxing, Shotokan karate and Shaolin kung fu. Between the gym and Dad, they've hired some of the best teachers to train me. I'm fighting MMA matches and moving up. I'll beat him yet, and I'll cash that check, for sure."

Jokingly, I asked, "So you went from the bad parts of the Bronx to here, and now you work as a research scientist, working on a double-major, and train six days a week? What do you do with your free time?"

He took my question seriously. "I'm working on my career as a musician. I'm going to have my first CD out next month."

Flabbergasted, "Oh" was all I could say. This guy was as much a genius as he said Grace was, only in a completely different way.

He then tried to minimize it. "But, I'm only working here part-time. So, I have more time than it sounds like. They're really good about that here."

"It's good you have that flexibility."

Marcus shook his head. "Yeah, I'm thankful for that." He held up his hands beside him. "So that's my story. Any other questions?"

I snorted. "I'm in awe."

Marcus laughed. "You're only allowed that when I beat Dad."

"It's a deal."

"Then let's get back to work. Gotta leave pretty soon."

I followed him out of the room, down to the lab floor and we got to work.

Chapter 26

As the morning progressed, I became more amazed at the flywheel energy storage system and was eager to learn everything I could about it. A little before eleven, Aaron came back from his meeting and showed me to a desk in the open-cube area outside the lab, and gave me all my logins and other information I needed to get started.

After I got things settled at my new desk, I went back into the lab and Marcus showed me where the current documentation was stored and said I could either work at my desk or hop on a computer there in the lab and read it. I liked the energy in the lab, and it gave me people to answer my questions. I now understood why the cube areas were so empty, why work at a desk when you could be in the middle of all the excitement? I plopped into a chair at one of the computer stations on the balcony overlooking the lab floor and started reading with fascination.

As I read the documentation, it didn't take long before I was wondering why they needed a tech writer. As far as engineers or scientist go, they were doing a great job. I could clean it up some, but it wasn't two months' worth of work.

After about an hour of me digging through the documents, trying to find a reason to justify my time here, Aaron came over.

"How's it going?" he asked. "Sure hope you can help us get that in order."

I looked at him trying to not appear too confused, afraid I'd talk myself out of a job. "I'm not sure you need me. I mean, you guys are doing a great job with this. Yeah, I can do some, but there isn't a lot for me to do." I wished as soon as I said it I'd have just kept my mouth shut.

Aaron smiled broadly. "Wonderful! Then come over here with me."

Confused, I followed him as he led me further around the "U" of the balcony, over to some lockers and industrial gray metal shelves that were filled with boxes of supplies.

He turned, looked at me and then turned back to the shelves. He reached in a box and pulled out a white lab coat, handed it to me and then handed me some safety glasses. "What size shoe do you wear?"

"Ten and a half," I answered.

"Wonderful." He ran his fingers down a stack of boxes. Pulled one out and handed it to me. "See how those fit."

I opened it to see a pair of steel-toed safety boots, then sat in a nearby chair and put them on. "They fit fine."

"Wonderful. I'll put a request in to get name tags for your lab coats." He then led me down the stairs to the lab floor, and headed towards the back of the lab to one of the flywheels. He grabbed two wrenches off a cart and handed me one as he motioned me to go up the ladder beside his. Once at the top of the cylinder, he instructed me on the sequence to loosen the bolts to remove the top. When that was done, we started disassembling more of the unit as he explained what the parts were, how they worked, what the designers planned on changing, challenges they needed to overcome, and on and on. My mind whirled with all the information.

Back on the ground, as we positioned the overhead hoist over the cylinder to lift out the carbon fiber flywheel, a deafening alarm blared, scaring me out of my steel-toed boots. Everyone put down their tools and headed to the door. I was getting worried and looked around for smoke or a run-away flywheel but saw nothing.

"Wonderful!" Aaron exclaimed as he let go of the hoist controller and let it hang from the ceiling. "It's lunch time."

"That alarm was the lunch bell?" I asked, astounded, as I set my wrench on the cart.

He laughed as he headed toward the stairs, and we followed the others to the lab's door. "Sure was. A while back, management got mad at us because we'd been missing too many lunches. We were losing track of time and working straight through until the time-police," he smiled at the term, "came to kick us out of the lab at six o'clock. It took some work, but we finally negotiated a deal with them. If we took a half-hour lunch, they'd let us stay until six-thirty."

"Okay, but where'd the horn come into it?" I asked as we stepped into the hallway, still following the crowd toward the cafeteria.

He chuckled. "We tried normal alarms, watches, cell phones and such, but everyone ignored them like usual. Then some bright techie got the idea to hook up the horn."

"Can't ignore that one," I said with a slight laugh.

"That was the point." He grinned. "And to warn you, it goes off at six o'clock, too. That gives us a half-hour to wrap stuff up."

I was still laughing softly to myself as we entered the cafeteria. This was by far the strangest place I'd ever worked, but considering it was Jeff's company, it seemed just right.

* * *

The next couple days passed in a mind-boggling rush. To get up to speed, I shadowed my teammates, and they were unexpectedly patient as they explained every gory detail of their experiments with the various flywheel set-ups. That was fun, but when they took me to the machine shop and let me help make new parts, I was in Heaven.

Anything I didn't know or understand was patiently explained, even if it meant delaying a crucial part of an experiment. I asked Aaron about their unexpected openness, and he called it "removing the silos of knowledge." He said HRI was committed to ensuring everyone knew as much as they wanted to about any project they were interested in, which ensured there was never a shortage of helpers when extra hands were needed or if someone was called away for an emergency.

And because I was there to revise their documents, my team seemed committed to explaining everything, no matter how technical.

Wednesday morning, Aaron realized the complex mathematical equations being tossed around in one meeting stretched my simple algebra skills way past their limits, and before the day was over, I had a lunchtime tutor, who promised he'd have me up to speed in no time.

I'd never learned so much in such a short period of time. And I readily admitted that it was possible only because my teammates were so enthusiastic about explaining things, I couldn't help but learn it. Plus, because I got to turn right around and use my new knowledge on some aspect of the flywheel project, I was able to practice, and therefore retain, what I'd learned.

If that wasn't enough, Aaron hooked me up with the company's ride-share website, and before Wednesday afternoon was up, I had a ride to and from work. I'd also been instructed on the use of the electric cars that HRI owned—for use when people who shared rides or rode the bus needed to run out for something during the work day or had to go home in an emergency. The electric cars were way cool. And the lab team had given me lists of all the dollar theaters in the area, plus all the libraries and used bookstores. It looked like I was finally going to have a chance to catch up on my reading and movie watching.

On our evening Skype video calls, Beth patiently listened to me rattle on like a lunatic about all the stuff I was doing. The whole time I talked, trying hard to get the words out as fast as my brain was pushing them, I could see her smiling; she'd never seen me excited about a job before and was happy for me.

* * *

After Thursday's lunch, I had some time to sit down at one of the computers lining the railing above the lab and look again at the documents I was supposed to be updating. When I did, I was surprised to see how many changes needed to be made. What had looked fairly complete a couple days ago was now full of misinformation and obvious gaps. It seemed natural to begin fixing stuff.

Before I knew it, the alarm went off and scared the tar out of me.

It was six o'clock, a half-hour before they'd kick us out, and I'd been completely engrossed in fixing the documentation for almost six hours and hadn't realized it. Unreal!

Aaron appeared at my elbow. "How's it going, Stanley?"

"Oh, fine," I answered, my ears still ringing from the alarm. "Working on this manual."

"Wonderful! Mind if I look?"

"Sure, go ahead." I got up from the chair and let him sit down.

He started reading it, muttering his "wonderful" over and over. Then he looked up at me and teased, "I thought you'd said the documentation was pretty good and you wouldn't have much to do?"

It took me a moment to put my realizations into words. It was like the documentation had totally changed in the last two and a half days, but I knew it was my understanding that had changed. My teammates had taught me so much, that I wasn't a tech writer trying to drag information out of irritated engineers, I was an engineer with great writing skills trying to tell how this masterpiece of technology worked. "Well, once you guys rewrote my understanding, I had no choice but to rewrite this."

"Wonderful! This is what we needed. This is great. This is more than great. This is wonderful!" he exclaimed as he stood.

And I had to admit it to myself, it was pretty wonderful.

Then Aaron's expression changed to become even more excited. "Hey, what I came up here to tell you was that our team has started its own charity, and tomorrow's our charity day. And since you're now on the team, you're joining us." He paused. "I mean, that is, if you want. You are free to work with any charity group you want."

A feeling of disappointment flowed through me that surprised me. It took me a moment to realize that I didn't want to stop working on their manuals. I'd even had tomorrow's tasks all planned out; there were a couple sections that I was anxious to understand better, which would mean getting to work in the machine shop again, and that was really cool.

I looked at Aaron and realized he was waiting for an answer if I was going to help them with their charity. "Oh, sorry, got lost in some thoughts. Sure, I'd love to help you guys."

"Wonderful, can you meet us here at five?" Aaron asked. "The time police don't put limits on us for charity day, so we're starting early and working late."

"Five in the morning? Um... Sure, I guess."

"Wonderful! When you get here, pull around to the back of the lab, because the front will still be locked up. See you then."

I watched him walk back to his computer with a bounce in his step. The guy was way too happy about getting up that early. Shaking my head in confusion, I sat back down at my computer. If I wasn't going to get back to it until Monday, I wanted to get to a good stopping spot before I had to leave.

* * *

The next morning, I pulled into one of the few open parking spaces behind what I figured had to be the right loading dock because a large group of people were already gathered around two open bay doors, even though it wasn't even five yet. After I got out of my car, I stood beside it a moment, trying to figure out what was going on. I'd assumed only the flywheel research crew would be here, and yes, I spotted familiar faces, but Jeff was here, and some faces I recognized from the cafeteria and hallways, and there obviously were more people inside who I couldn't see. With a shrug, I headed toward the lab. The only way to find out what was going on was to ask.

Instead of lab coats, most people had coveralls with name tags on them, others were in jeans and T-shirts. They were eating donuts or bagels, happily chatting with each other, and greeted me cheerfully as I worked my way through them. When I finally reached the open door and glanced in, I saw the people inside were gathered around a mid-80's Pontiac Bonneville that had seen better days.

When Aaron saw me, he hurried over. "Wonderful! Glad you made it. Welcome to Flywheel Labs Charity," he said waving his hand happily at the dilapidated car, "where we help the elderly who can't afford to help themselves. Every Friday, we fix garage doors, leaky faucets, re-shingle houses, or anything that we can do to help."

"Very nice," I replied, more than a little confused. Helping was good, but why in the world did they need this many people for just one car?

"Today is even more wonderful than usual." He looked back at the Bonneville. "Here we have a piece of emotional history. This car was bought brand new, in 1983, by a couple to celebrate their thirtieth wedding anniversary. The owner has been a widow for about five years now, and every time she drives it, she relives all the happy miles they drove together. But as you can see, it needs a complete overhaul."

From what I could see of the rust and crappy paint job through the people milling around, "overhaul" was putting it mildly, but I was still confused.

"We've been planning this for a couple of weeks," Aaron continued, "and have everything in place. You're working with me and a few others on the engine crew. You ready?"

"Sure," I replied and decided to just play along. If nothing else, I was certain it would prove to be an entertaining day.

"Wonderful!"

Before he could continue, a cry of "Five!" went up from the gathered people.

I felt more than saw the scurry of people coming in from the outside.

"Four!"

I looked at Aaron in confusion, and he was grinning like a loon as he pointed up to the big clock over the hallway door. "Three!"

They were counting down the seconds to five o'clock.

"Two!"

"One!"

"Go!"

Like a gun had gone off at the beginning of a race, the group exploded. Floor jacks came out, the car was off the floor in moments, and the ceiling hoist positioned itself over the front of the car as several people unbolted the hood. Within minutes the tires were off, and the door and body panels were being swarmed by what looked like an army of ants attacking their prey. And everybody was laughing and joking and having the time of their lives.

Aaron pulled me into the middle of the fray, and shortly, I was working beside him as he instructed me in helping to remove the engine. I had done quite a bit of automotive work in my life but not at this pace, so I just let Aaron and the rest of the crew guide me.

These folks must have been reading the repair manuals for weeks, because car parts were being unhooked and removed at an alarming rate. Within an hour, the winch lifted the engine out of the car, and we maneuvered it to an engine stand and fastened the engine to the stand.

As I watched in wonder, the engine was dismantled at amazing speed, and I felt like I was a hindrance more than a help, because I kept getting distracted by everything that was going on around us.

"Stanley!" a male voice bellowed.

I turned around abruptly. "Sorry. What can I do?"

A guy I recognized from a few hallway encounters handed me a drawing of a complex mechanism, exploded to show how the various pieces fit together. "Would you head over to the machine shop and get these three guys?" Then pointed to three outer pieces. "They should have them ready by now."

I stood there a couple seconds staring dumbly at the drawing. "They're making new parts? Why not just buy them?"

Aaron must have heard my question, because he exclaimed, "Where's the fun in that?"

The group gathered around the gutted engine laughed.

The man who'd given me the drawing explained it to me. "You give a project like this to a bunch of over-eager engineers, who have unlimited resources and every tool imaginable, and what you end up with isn't a rebuild... it's a redesign. Our aim is to up the engine efficiency by thirty-percent and the transmission by twenty-percent. Plus, new wheel bearings, braking system, computerized cooling system and so on. By the time we're done, this car'll be in better shape than when she came off the assembly line."

"Oh," I said.

The guy patted me on the shoulder. "You'll get used to it."

I had to laugh at myself, as I turned to head for the machine shop. I keep being surprised by the way this place ran, and somehow, I didn't think I'd ever get used to it.

* * *

The controlled chaos continued until around one in the morning. Food was brought in at regular intervals, so the work never stopped. And I don't think I'd sat down for longer than it took to answer nature's call.

Finally, we stood in an awed ring around a car that looked show-room new. A sense of satisfaction and accomplishment permeated the room.

Jeff came over to me and put his arm around my shoulder as we looked at the car. "Twelve hours at time and a half for this. That should help your paycheck."

"What?" I asked. Now that the flurry had stopped, exhaustion was making its presence known.

He clarified, "You put in a twenty hour day, today. So, twelve of that is time-and-a-half. I told you, we only limit the hours you can put into work-work, charity hours get paid at the full rate."

I looked at the people standing around admiring their work with looks of satisfaction, and gently ribbing each other in friendly camaraderie. I suspected most were on salary, so they didn't get overtime, but even given that... "You do realize that HRI just spent more money on that car than it would have cost to buy a new one, don't you? Why not just buy the woman a new car?"

Sounding like Aaron, Jeff replied, "Where's the fun in that?"

I gave a tired laugh. "What could I *possibly* have been thinking?"

He grinned. "Besides, the car has huge sentimental value to its owner. And look around at these people. Did you see all that energy and excitement? They gave themselves a challenge to do it in one day, and they did! They loved the challenge. On top of that, they got to do something they loved, for someone who really needed and valued it. Can anyone pin a price on that?"

He paused a moment, but being used to his *ways*, I just waited.

"And I'm sure you noticed that there weren't any TV cameras here to document the challenge. No notoriety. The only ones who'll know about it are us, and the lady who owns the car."

Even as tired as I was, I caught his dig at all the pathetic reality shows with their staged enthusiasm. That sure hadn't been the case here, not a drop of today's enthusiasm had been staged by anybody.

I gazed at the car for a little while, admiring our awesome accomplishment, until Jeff interrupted, "And now it's time for bed."

Glancing around, I saw that the crowd had already started to thin, with a few stragglers finishing up cleaning and putting parts and tools away.

As Jeff and I walked out one of the large bay doors, he asked, "Would you join my family and me for church Sunday, friend?"

Maybe it was the exhaustion that made the question seem really funny. Should anyone really tell a messiah "no" when he invites you to church? I know I wasn't that brave. Who knew what dire consequence Jeff would call down upon my head if I refused? Besides, Beth had asked me to check out the local churches, and Jeff's church seemed like the perfect starting point. "Sure, let me know what time and where. Oh, and what to wear."

"Nine o'clock, I'll email you the address. And dress however you feel comfortable, it's casual."

"Can do." It took a monumental effort to open my car door, and even more to keep my eyes open on the drive back to the hotel. I debated taking a bath to loosen up, because I knew I was going to be sore in the morning, but instead, barely had the energy to shuck off my filthy clothes before I fell face-down on the bed.

Chapter 27

After my grueling but great Friday, I slept late Saturday, then thought I'd laze in bed and watch TV for the morning, since my hubby-do list was back home in California with my wife and kids.

After about fifteen minutes of flipping through channels, I landed on one show that was so bad that I couldn't help but pause and wonder how people watched this stuff. Maybe my months without cable had warped my perspective, but could there really be people who thought this insult-to-intelligence was entertaining? Then a thought struck and I had to laugh: the only TV shows where the people on the show actually watched TV were all shows about dysfunctional families.

Which seemed to answer my question about the people watching the crap on TV, so I switched to the Science Channel and spent a couple minutes watching before I had a revelation.

A lot of TV watchers sat around watching people on TV do stuff, and I was the first to admit that sometimes, watching people doing stuff was interesting. But if that was interesting, maybe the watchers should get off their couches, get out and do stuff themselves, instead of watching others do stuff.

Considering this epiphany, I decided to put my money where my mouth was and shut the tube off. As I got dressed and got myself breakfast, I wished my family was here to go explore the town with me; exploring by myself wouldn't be the same.

That got me thinking that I'd call Beth and the kids. As I was about to do that, I saw my wallet open with a credit card showing. I'd given the finance folks at HRI all my account information, and they'd promised to pay off the cards, but I'd never actually checked the balances. I logged onto one of my credit card accounts and was overjoyed to see its zero balance. I logged into another account and saw the same zero balance. The rest were the same.

I hadn't realized until that moment how heavy a burden those credit cards had been; I suddenly felt so light I could fly.

Haven's Research Institute had done what they'd promised, paid off my credit cards, so I figured now was a great time to hold up my end of the deal, get rid of all but one credit card.

After a little research, I found the one with the best interest rate and closed down all the other accounts. As I leaned back, I smiled at myself in the mirror above the desk. After all the stress of the last few months, this had to be one of the best feelings in my life.

As I dialed Beth's phone, I picked up the book Jane, the finance person, had given me and opened it.

"Hi, Stanley," Beth answered.

"Guess what I just did?"

I could hear the hesitation in her voice. "Lately, I hate to even guess."

"I closed all of our credit cards but one. We no longer have any credit card debt." My voice was ecstatic, and she could hear it. The burden that had been slowly killing us was now gone, instantly replaced by a very manageable loan.

"Wow!"

We talked a little longer, but how can you top that in a conversation? I talked to the kids and told them how much I missed them, we did some "Seussing' and we tossed around some ideas for things we could do when I got back home.

After I hung up, I made some sandwiches, then put my book in a backpack with the sandwiches and some drinks, and walked to a wooded park I had driven by a few times. One nice thing about this area was there were lots of trees. I hiked along a mulched path until I found a nice shady bench that looked out over the river and sat.

I'd planned to read, but my thoughts were so full that I couldn't concentrate on the page.

What a week it'd been. I don't think I'd ever experienced such wild swings of emotions. In some ways, this week had been worse than the trip out. From the desperation of Jeff leaving me, to the joy at discovering him in the restroom at work. From the revelation of his family, to the relief of having my credit card debt suddenly made manageable. From the dread of starting a new job, to the eager anticipation of returning to work on Monday morning.

I thought back to Beth's comment about finding the mountain top after work, and now, less than a week later, no mountain top was required. I was thrilled with work, we had health insurance, we had money in the bank, my time with Jeff wasn't over, and I was seeing a side of him I hadn't seen on the trip. I'd gotten to meet Jeff's extraordinary family, I was getting to work in the machine shop and helped rebuild a whole car in one day, and the tech writing itself was engaging, instead of drudgery. I was pretty much as close to Heaven as a guy like me could get.

As I thought that, my innate cynicism asked: *Why?*

Why was I here with Jeff? Why was I being teased with a place like HRI, knowing it was temporary and I would have to return to the real world in two months? Why had Jeff picked me? It was obvious that he'd brought me here to learn something, but why didn't he just tell me instead of putting me through all this?

Why did it feel like I was being set up for disappointment again?

That was the scariest question, because I knew exactly the disappointment that was coming, the disappointment of leaving HRI and Jeff, was going to be worse than any disappointment I'd felt before.

I thought about that for a long time as I watched the ducks on the river. After a while, not having come to any conclusions and tired of my depressing thoughts, I picked my book back up and read, the questions still rumbling around the back of my head.

When I got hungry, I marked my spot in the book and opened the backpack to grab lunch. As I did so, a cliché sprang to mind. One I'd always thought was kind of hokey, but maybe, just maybe, I finally understood. I popped the top of the Dew and considered: It's better to have loved and lost than to have never loved at all.

Maybe after these next two months, I'd never have a job like this again, but now, I had a direction to follow and a goal to aspire to. When I got home, I'd find a place like this to work, or maybe I'd make a place like this. Or, if necessary, I'd work from inside a company and turn it into a company like HRI. Because now that I'd seen what I wanted—now that I loved—sure, I'd be sad to see it go, but I knew I wouldn't regret a moment of my time here.

I bit into the sandwich and thought again that maybe, just maybe, Jeff would hire me as a permanent employee. I could move Beth and the kids here. Sure, it would be disruptive, moving always was, but to keep working at HRI would be worth it.

As a mother duck squawked loudly at a pair of mostly-grown offspring, reality returned. If Jeff had intended to hire me permanently, he'd have done that from the beginning and not messed with hiring me as a contractor. Which meant he was being his typical manipulative self, showing me a slice of Heaven and then making me leave it.

But... it was better to have loved and lost than to have never loved at all.

And blast it! I decided as I finished the last of the sandwich. I'd let the future take care of itself, because I was going to enjoy my time here, learn everything I could, and leave without a single regret.

Yeah. That's what I'd do. And I'd start that by going to church in the morning with Jeff. I grinned. That was bound to be a learning experience.

With a laugh, I drained the Dew, put the empty in the backpack and picked up the book again.

When the mid-afternoon heat became oppressive, I headed back to my room, read more, caught a SciFi movie and, in general, enjoyed a lazy evening. It was a day well spent.

* * *

Sunday morning, I pulled into the crowded parking lot of Jeff's church. It was a modest looking, mid-sized church, and its name didn't indicate a denomination, so I figured it was the denomination of "Nondenominational." As I smiled at my poor joke, I realized that I hadn't really thought about what kind of church Jeff's would be. Would a messiah go to a Catholic, Baptist, Methodist, or some other kind of church? I got out of the car, figuring I'd find out what kind of church it was in a few minutes, and if nothing else, since this was Jeff's church, I knew it'd be interesting.

Grace and Dylan saw me walking through the parking lot and Dylan ran up. "Want to come sit with us to hear the runic message?"

Confused, I looked down at him and asked, "Runic?"

He closed his eyes tightly and rattled off, "Runic. Definition number one: Having some secret or mysterious meaning. Number two: Consisting of or set down in runes. Number three: Referring to an interlaced form seen on ancient monuments, metalwork, etc., of the northern European peoples." He reopened his eyes and looked at me. "I used definition one in that sentence."

I looked over at Grace, who had caught up with Dylan and had her arm around his shoulder.

"That's his word of the week," she said, smiling proudly. "One of the first things he does every Sunday morning is find an interesting word, memorize the definitions and then annoy us all week as he works it into every sentence he can. Last week's word was plethora." She smiled down at Dylan and pulled him into a tight hug.

He looked up at her, returning the smile.

What an interesting kid. And then the memory of plethora hit me. "Your plethora of enemies?" I asked, highly amused, repeating his sentence from our dinner conversation.

He looked at me with an excited grin, but Grace playfully answered, "Every sentence he can."

That was simply awesome.

I looked Dylan in the eye and accepted his invitation. "Sure, I'll join you. And maybe you can help me understand the runic message."

We headed towards the church and entered a minimally decorated foyer. The inside of the church was as nondescript as the outside, white walls and ceiling, with wooden pews padded in beige.

Dylan slowly turned around, looking at all the walls. "There are no runic art pieces here." He looked over at me. "That's definition three."

I'd already forgotten what definition number three was, but the fact that there were no art pieces at all made his statement true. I looked down at the interesting boy. "So it seems."

The only thing that stood out to me was how the place was obviously designed to handle a large number of handicapped people due to the wide doorways and aisles, and some shorter pews to accommodate the wheelchairs currently occupying the spaces.

Before being seated, Grace tried to introduce me to the other Havens kids and members of the congregation, but ran out of time before the service started. Dylan excitedly sat next to me.

Some of Jeff's teens were in the front row with other church youth. Even so, the Havens took up three pews.

I asked Dylan, "Don't you want to sit with your friends up front?"

He shook his head. "Not today. There isn't enough Dylan for everyone, so they'll just have to understand."

I was impressed that the boy could say such a sentence and not sound conceited; I knew I couldn't have done it. But from him, it sounded natural. Amused, I leaned back in the pew as a middle-aged man approached the pulpit.

The service started out like any typical Protestant service: hymns, prayers and bible readings. As the sermon was about to start, to my surprise, Jeff snuck in and Grace made room for him to sit beside me.

"Sorry," he said quietly. "Had to take care of some stuff."

Obviously, I'd made the false assumption Jeff would be the preacher. So, who preaches to a messiah? I wondered. Just as I finished the thought, Marcus walked out from a door to the right of the pulpit. All I could do was shake my head. On top of everything else, this ex-gang member was a preacher?

Jeff was beaming. He leaned over to me. "I love hearing him preach."

I looked at Jeff in shock. "There is no way he has time to run a church."

"No. He just preaches whenever he can. We have a full-time minister, Pastor Jones. You'll like him. Great guy. He likes to see people involved. If people have something to say, he'll give them the platform."

I looked at Jeff with a questioning expression. "Something to say? Like you?"

He pointed to the pulpit. "Up there's not my place."

Jokingly, I added. "Biker bar is your place?"

In a rare serious moment, Jeff looked me dead in the eyes. "Yes, exactly."

I tried to think of how to respond but couldn't. I turned my attention to Marcus.

Marcus looked natural at the pulpit as he calmly scanned the congregation giving them a warm smile. "I love the story of Jonah," he began, "and all the messages we can glean from it. We have the clear message of God's mercy, when God spared the people of Nineveh once they gave up their wicked behavior. We have the message of the power of God..."

My mind started echoing, "Nineveh, Nineveh," until I remembered Cooper's music video, the impressive guitar piece by that rap guy, The Change. At the time I heard the song, I hadn't associated the name with the Bible, but now I remembered. In the book of "Jonah", Nineveh was the city God sent Jonah to save, which made it a very interesting title for a guitar instrumental. Not that I wasn't interested in hearing Marcus' sermon before, but now I was even more interested. Why would a rap artist name a song "Nineveh"?

I focused back on Marcus.

"The hearts of that great city were changed when they heard God's word. A great city, a great nation, not even a single heart changes quickly unless there is a great power behind that change. And God's power is assuredly great.

"But this morning, I want to approach the story from a different angle. Have you ever read the story and wondered why Jonah tried to run from God? Think about it.

"God talked to Jonah, ordered him to go to Nineveh, and Jonah said 'No!'" Marcus paused and looked around. "Jonah said, 'No!' to his destiny. That's what it is, isn't it? If God tells us to do something, then it's our destiny.

"We hear that story and wonder: why would Jonah run in the opposite direction of his destiny? We think: if God told me to do something, I'd do it. Don't we?"

Marcus was captivating to watch. He looked out at the people in the pews, and when he looked in your direction, you were sure he was looking directly at you, speaking directly to you. When his gaze seemed to meet mine, I felt the weight of it, the weight that might have been God speaking through him, and it made me pay even more attention to his words.

"For all you grown-ups out there, when you were little, what did you want to be when you grew up? What kind of hobbies excited you? What ideas made your mind race and your pulse explode? When you were about to graduate from high school, and a new world was going to open up for you, what where your dreams?

"Think back hard, and *then* think about what *stole* those dreams. Those dreams, hobbies and ideas, those were God speaking to you. Those were your destiny!"

The last word thundered, and I felt the congregation jump at his vehemence.

"Why didn't you listen to your destiny? Why did you say 'No!' to God? Were you afraid to fail? And—even worse—were you afraid you just might succeed?"

That one hit me hard. I hadn't thought about high school for years, but what came to me in a flash was notebook after notebook full of stories I'd written. Stories that I'd passionately read to anyone who would listen. I'm not sure when that changed, when I gave up on my dream to be a writer. Maybe it was when I went to college. Between classes and working, I didn't have time to write my own stories anymore, and the only stories I wrote were for class assignments.

I don't remember actually saying "No" to that passion. It seemed like it just faded away, unnoticed, as other things in life became more important.

Marcus took a drink of water to give people time to think back to their youth before continuing. "A brilliant psychiatrist, Abraham Maslow—some of you may know the name from Maslow's Hierarchy of Needs—took the story of Jonah and applied it to people afraid to follow their destiny, calling it the 'Jonah Complex.' He asked us many questions. Why do we run from our destiny? Why do we ignore our talents? Why are we afraid to succeed? Why don't we live up to our potential? And why do we choose the well-worn, safe path?"

I added my own why: Why was the sanctuary so hot? Wiping the sweat starting to form on my forehead, I looked around. Unlike when Beth's church was hot, I didn't see any women using bulletins as fans. Was it only me sweating?

Marcus turned his attention to the youth in the front rows.

I wonder if it's a universal truth that church youth get away from their parents by sitting together in the front. Then I let the thought pass and looked back up at Marcus.

"For the younger ones sitting here, write down your dreams and passions, and carry them in your wallet or purse. Then write out, don't just print it off from the computer, write out with a pen, Robert Frost's poem *The Road Not Taken* on the same paper as your list of dreams. And every day find a quiet time, pull the paper out, and read it. Then clear your mind and ask God to tell you what your destiny is... and listen carefully. Jonah tried to run from his destiny, but God didn't let him. Clear your mind of all the clutter the world is telling you that *you* need to do. Clear your mind and listen to God talk to you.

"And when Got talks to you, add to the list. Or cross things off. That's okay, *if* you *are* listening. As you grow, you'll change, so the list will change. But listen to that hard-to-hear voice telling you what your destiny is, not what the world is telling you what you *should* or shouldn't do."

As I thought more, I realized I wanted to find and re-read the stories I'd written in high school. I barely remembered who that boy was, but I did know that the idealistic boy had grown into a man afraid of failure, a man who'd taken the safe, over-used path, which had never led him to fulfillment.

I'd read Frost's poem countless times in various English classes, but never paid it much mind. Why was that?

Why, when I looked at the fork in the road, didn't I choose the road that *wanted wear* as Frost had told me so many times to do?

I quickly glanced around to see if others were as struck by the sermon as me, but it was hard to tell. People were engaged, but I couldn't tell what they were thinking.

Marcus then gave me hope. "The beautiful thing about the story of Jonah is that God did *not* give up on him. Jonah took the wrong path, but God didn't go find someone else to fulfill his command. Why? Because it was Jonah's destiny and no one else's.

"God didn't even make Jonah go back down to the fork Robert Frost was talking about and let him choose again. God took Jonah to his destiny. The same is true for us. When we miss one fork in the road, another one is up ahead for us to take another try at fulfilling our destiny.

"After the giant fish spat Jonah on the shore, he finally listened. At that fork in his road, he didn't say 'No' to God; he said 'Yes.' Which is a great metaphor for how we move forward.

"Granted, God isn't going to spell it out for you in great detail," Marcus said with a wry grin. "You're not going to be handed a to-do list so you can check off each item when it's complete."

"Too bad," I muttered to myself, and caught Jeff's quick grin in my direction. I could really use a to-do list right about now.

"As you learn to block out the distractions of this world," Marcus continued, "as you block out the outside messages coming at you from every direction, as you take time to listen to yourself, listen to your passions, push yourself up towards the top of Maslow's pyramid, you will start to see what your destiny is."

After all this talk of destiny, if I wasn't working at HRI right now, going to a job on Monday—a job that obviously *wasn't* my destiny— would have been tough. Which made me wonder how many people in the congregation felt the urge to quit their jobs and try to become artists, musicians, firemen or whatever their childhood dreams had been.

But Marcus was on top of that thought. "Now, all of you out there supporting your family, supporting our country with your taxes, I'm not telling you to quit your jobs. That's stupid."

A quiet laugh rippled through the congregation.

"What I'm telling you to do is to listen, and start bringing those dreams back into your life. Start bringing your passions to the job, and maybe transform your job into your destiny. But mainly, take some quiet time and start learning to listen.

"I recently read an interview with Francis Collins, Director of the Human Genome project, and liked what he said about prayer. 'Prayer for me is not a way to manipulate God into doing what we want him to do. Prayer for me is much more a sense of trying to get into fellowship with God. I'm trying to figure out what I should be doing rather than telling Almighty God what he should be doing.'"

He paused a moment to let that sink in. "So, learn how to pray in a manner that brings you into fellowship with God — pray for understanding, instead of stuff — and learn to listen so you can hear God's answers. And don't make God send a giant fish after you!"

I chuckled along with the rest of the congregation as Marcus stepped away from the pulpit, but the sermon had hit me hard in the gut. Marcus' sermon made it clear to me that I'd become a tech writer because it was the safest path, illuminating with startling clarity why I'd always been so unhappy with my career.

I'd never had a sermon hit me so hard and then keep hitting me. Suddenly, it was so obvious I wasn't just running and hiding from my destiny, I was sticking my fingers in my ears, closing my eyes tight, and humming loudly, so there wasn't any way I could hear any whispers God might have sent to me.

Feeling really stupid, I looked over at the big fish smiling beside me and wondered why he wasn't telling me in clear words what my destiny was. He didn't have to whisper, he was sitting right there, he could just tell me.

As I thought the thought, the big fish in question turned his head and gave me a mischievous grin, and I knew without a doubt that he had no intention of telling me anything. It was very hard to not groan aloud.

After Marcus stepped down, there was more of the usual church stuff, another song, announcements and the closing, but I was so absorbed in my own thoughts, I barely heard. In fact, Dylan was the one who found the page in the hymnal for the final song and nudged me to stand at the right time.

When church was over, as politely as I could — giving Jeff's kids polite good-byes and Dylan a hug, ignoring Jeff as best I could — I left to begin mentally licking my wounds.

Up to this point in my life, I'd given a really loud, resounding, "No!" to God. And to make matters worse, I'd become so good at it that I was blind to what my destiny, my calling, might have been.

The rest of the day was not a good day at all.

Chapter 28

I survived my miserable Sunday, and by the time I got into work Monday morning, my second week on the job, I was more determined than ever to learn whatever Jeff had brought me here to learn.

I flopped into my chair at my desk in the cube outside the lab and pulled up my email. Immediately, I was drawn to one marked "High Importance," and my mood lightened considerably as I read it. This coming Friday evening, HRI—meaning Jeff, as I couldn't see Jeff using company money for something like this—had rented a conference center and was having a party, to which all the employees, friends and family were invited, to celebrate the release of Marcus' album. And Marcus was giving us a concert, too.

I remembered Marcus saying last week that he was majoring in classical guitar and had a CD coming out, but I hadn't realized that it was coming out so soon. And the idea of a concert was cool! I loved watching classical guitarists play, especially the really good ones, because with all my years of guitar lessons—resulting in no real gain in skill—I was in utter awe of their ability.

Well, good for Marcus, I thought. And I'd be sure to attend the party and support him however I could.

It turned out that I wasn't the only one thrilled for the guy. After finishing up a few tasks at my desk, I went into the flywheel lab and most of the people were gathered in a group congratulating Marcus and giving him an outrageously hard time. I joined the group to add my well wishes, but didn't know him well enough to be comfortable teasing him as his teammates were doing. He laughed, taking it all good naturedly. After ribbing Marcus a little longer, the group broke up and headed to their testing stations.

My next project was documenting the flywheel braking system, and after a few questions, I was pointed to the right group. Within moments of meeting them, I was given a wrench and told to help dismantle the system, because they needed to inspect its guts after a stress test.

After about an hour, my brain was full enough I had to go empty it. I debated between using my cube or a computer on the balcony. It was a toss-up, as my cube was quieter so I could think better, but the balcony put me closer if I had questions. After a moment, I opted for close and went up the metal stairs and sat at the nearest unoccupied computer to work while it was fresh in my mind. The way the lab's guys pulled me into actually working on the project, both physically and mentally, made the documents' weak points totally obvious, so the writing part was practically painless.

As I was typing, Aaron came up the stairs and to my desk. "I was reading some of the improvements you made last week," he said, "and they're wonderful."

I saved the file, realizing how glad I was to hear him say that. In most of my past positions, I'd been left wondering if anyone cared even the slightest bit about anything I'd written, so to have anybody show a genuine interest was great, especially when it was my boss. "Thanks."

"You deserve it," he said. "Just let me know if you have any questions or need help in any way."

I smiled at him and said thanks again. Aaron seemed exceedingly smart, yet very approachable and likeable. I didn't know what the other groups were like at HRI, but I was glad I was in his group.

He was about to walk away when I remembered one of the questions I'd been meaning to ask. "Oh! You got a second, now? There *is* something I wanted some clarification on."

"Sure," he replied, turning back around to face me.

"I was looking over HRI standards and procedures, but it wasn't clear what quality management methodology you folks use. In my various jobs, I've worked with most of the common systems, and it'd help me to know how the documentation process works, so I can do it right the first time."

Aaron smiled and pulled up a chair beside the computer desk I was working at. This gave me the impression I wasn't going to get a one- or two-word answer.

He asked, "Did you read our standards?"

"I skimmed them, mostly looking for a clue as to which

methodology you guys use."

"Wonderful! Well, you'll have seen that we don't adhere to any of the formal quality processes such as CMMI, ISO-9000, or Six Sigma. Those are all wonderful, and process is extremely important to us. When we find a good idea, we explore how to incorporate it to improve our current methodology, but we don't force everyone to adhere to any one process. Over time, HRI has discovered there's a fine line between processes that benefit a project and processes that suck the life out of the project and the people."

"Been there, done that," I muttered.

Aaron smiled. "Me, too. But working on a project where no processes are in place, where nothing is documented or understood, has just as much sucking power. That isn't so wonderful"

"Oh yeah," I answered. "I've been on both ends and hated them both."

Aaron went on, "Long before my time, Mr. Havens, Sr. spent a lot of time and energy studying HRI's processes. He accumulated huge amounts of data on which systems and methodologies worked best for which kinds of projects and people. But he never controlled or mandated anything, leaving the process decisions to the people intimate with the project."

"That makes a lot of sense," I replied, remembering all the pain and agony I'd been forced to endure as one-process-fits-all systems were put into place at most of my old companies.

"I hate to use the word 'empowered,' because it's become overused and misunderstood, but Clinton Havens empowered everyone here," he said tapping my desk to emphasize his point.

"He certainly created a great place. And everybody seems to have a fondness towards him."

"And rightly so," Aaron replied forcefully. "He was a master with people. He brought out the best in everyone. What you see here in HRI is his genius made into reality. He took the time to look at people and figure what made them, as individuals, tick. For example, some people love to organize, and if you give them a job to organize and remove ambiguity, they're in Heaven. But others couldn't organize a single index card, not even if their lives depended on it."

I laughed. "I know several of those kinds of people."

He grinned back at me. "Me, too. So, as a manager here at HRI, my job is to find people's strengths, help them work within their strengths, and poof! they're happy campers... and wonderfully productive ones."

I looked out over the swarming mass of people on the lab floor and couldn't deny that it worked. Then remembered Jeff talking about finding people's strengths, too. "Yeah, Jeff said much the same thing on my first day — gave me a book, too — but seeing the concept at work this last week, it makes a whole lot more sense, now."

"Wonderful!" Aaron leaned toward me, obviously getting into a topic that he loved to talk about. "Discover what people's strengths and natural interests are and build from there. Don't try to force everybody into a title and a role, whether they fit or not." He mimed squashing two things together, then shook his finger at me once. "And! That doesn't mean anarchy. It means doing some work upfront."

It was fun watching Aaron. He was normally a high-energy guy and very positive, but I realized the more excited he got the more he used his hands and his body.

"When things go wrong, look at the people-situation first and try to fix that. If someone is failing, that means you aren't using them right. You can't get mad at a hammer for not screwing in a screw." He mimed the action again. "But in our society there are plenty of hammers who desperately need a job, and if someone's got an opening to drive screws they'll convince you they're a screwdriver."

Which lead to my long-standing question about what shape I was. I guess — using the tool metaphor — I wasn't really sure what tool I was, either. In the past, tech writing had had its moments, but in general, it was just something I did to get paid, and even working here for a week didn't convince me that it was my natural tool.

"I like that metaphor," I replied as he paused for a breath. "It reminds me about a quote, sometimes attributed to Einstein, saying that if you judge a fish by its ability to climb a tree, it's a pretty stupid animal."

Aaron clapped his hands together in glee, like I was an unexpectedly bright student. "Wonderful! Exactly right! A fish can't be forced to do something it doesn't have the ability to do. On the other hand, the hammer isn't doing anything *wrong* getting a job as a screwdriver. The hammer's trying to work, support his family, pay the bills, which is a wonderful thing. And, chances are, they don't even know they're a hammer."

I grinned at that. "Tell me about it."

I meant it sarcastically, but he took me literally, and with great enthusiasm, miming actions to go with his words, he explained,

"Their father may have been a screwdriver and their siblings may be screwdrivers, so they may think they are, too. Except they're throwbacks to dear old great-grand-dad who was the fastest hammer in the west."

"I get it, thanks." The guy was a hoot!

"Happy to help. But Mr. Havens and all his smart guys, you see, figured when the company hires someone it's to the company's benefit to work with the person to figure out who are the hammers and who are the screwdrivers. Which goes back to happy employees are more loyal and more productive employees."

I interrupted, "How's that work in reality? If a company needs a tech writer, they hire someone who has that skill set. If they need a machinist, they hire someone with that skill set. A company can't afford to just hire random people and then figure what tool they are."

His expression turned serious, and he leaned towards me, looking at me intently. "What tool are you, Stanley?"

I thought about giving him a joking answer, then realized that if I really wanted to find out what tool I was, what shape I was, honesty would work better. "I don't know. I mean, you guys hired me as a tech writer because that's the experience I have."

He leaned back away from me, reducing the intensity. "So, we hired a tech writer. What have you done since you've been here?"

I paused a moment to sum up last week and today. "I've been working on the documents, and I guess, working on the flywheels. Went to the machine shop a couple times. Helped take apart a car and put it back together."

Aaron smiled and nodded his head. "Wonderful. I've been here a while, and like osmosis, over the years I found I've started to notice what drives people, what people are drawn towards." He pointed at me. "Your first day here, we put a wrench in your hand, and obviously, that was part of who you are; you're a wrench. Then you sat down to the computer and began working on the documents, it was equally obvious that you're also a pen, a writer. But it's also clear that you wouldn't be happy just being a tech writer or just being a mechanic. You're both, and at the same time, much more than either alone."

"Huh," I replied, kind of reeling at his words. So simple, but true. I wasn't one tool or one shape. I enjoy doing too many things.

"During the hiring process, it's sometimes really hard to sort out the hammer from the screwdriver from the wrench from the pen.

And over the years, we've hired many hammers to put in screws, but once the mismatch is clear, we work with them to find a better fit. Or—" he paused dramatically "—we teach them a couple more skills and end up with an impact-driver, which is endlessly useful."

I couldn't help but laugh. "That's stretching the analogy a bit."

He laughed, too. "Anyway, we got off on one of my favorite topics, but I'm sure you have better things to do than listen to me ramble on."

"Actually, this is great." I thought back to Jeff saying there was a Stanley-shaped hole here, but maybe that's not what he meant, maybe Jeff meant that while I was here, I'd find out what combination of shapes I was, so I could return home and find my Stanley-shaped hole. I tried to put that into words. "I can see your skill at finding people's strengths. You didn't just point me to the computer and say 'write,' you let me explore the other kinds of things that were going on around here, like the machine shop and the hands-on flywheel research. People are involving me in their parts of the project to the depth that I find interesting. But nobody's pushing me in one direction or another."

Aaron nodded. "Pretty wonderful, isn't it?"

"Yeah." I leaned back in my chair and tried to put thoughts into words. "And even though being a pen might not be all I am, I'm finding that working on the project's documents is fascinating."

"Well, it shows," Aaron replied, with a friendly smile, having wound down from his soap box enthusiasm. "And it's some wonderful writing. Has a wonderful plot." He smiled at his own joke, and I repressed a groan, thinking that telling your boss he wasn't as funny as he thought he was, was a bad idea.

"And on that note, I'll leave you to it." Aaron stood and walked away.

What an interesting ... no ... what a wonderful guy.

* * *

I worked on the documentation some more, until Grace tapped on my shoulder, startling me out of my own little tech-writer world.

"You want to go out and grab some lunch?" she asked. "I've gotta get a newspaper for Dylan—he needs it for a school project—so I thought I'd hit the food stands in the park, and I don't feel like eating alone, but Marcus says he's too busy, none of these guys want to take that long for lunch, and Dad says he's got a lot more work to do—whatever that means—before he'll let me walk that far in this part of town without somebody with me, and I could drive, but it's gorgeous out and I want to walk, so you want to go along?"

She'd said it all in one breath, which impressed me, and at the same time, I had to hold back my amusement at being her last resort. "Sure. Sounds great." I looked at the clock on my computer. "If we hurry, we can beat the alarm. That's the worst part about working here so far."

Grace grinned at me. "My lab doesn't need an alarm. We're rational people."

Laughing, I saved my files and closed them all down. After lunch, I'd work from my cube where it was quieter.

As soon as I stood, she took me at my word and ran to the door. Feeling silly, in a good way, I followed. And as the white metal "Physical Lab #3" door banged closed behind me, I heard the sound of the alarm. "Just made it!"

A few minutes later, we were out the back of the building, beyond the open-air pavilion, and into the woods, following a crushed-stone path that I hadn't noticed before. As we strolled along the path, I realized that with this cheerful young woman walking beside me, I felt like a teenager skipping school. I smiled at my silliness, and put the feeling onto my tell-Beth list, because she'd get a kick out of it, too.

As we walked, we chatted about the latest goings-on in her lab. The thought of free energy was so cool that I was full of questions, and because it was her passion, she was full of answers. After maybe fifteen minutes, we came to the edge of the woods to find that they bordered a nicely kept park, with strips of stores across the streets on either side and office buildings on the far side. As she had said, there were a bunch of food vendors, all with people waiting in line.

Since I wasn't eating in the cafeteria, I got myself a chili dog, and even though it meant standing in a second line, I got a Mt. Dew, too. Grace had already claimed an empty park table, away from the Frisbee players and the groups of little kids screaming and playing tag, so I joined her and savored my treat.

As I ate, I thought about how interesting a place HRI was. When you were on the property, with its creek running through it and countless large old shade trees, you felt like you're off by yourself, removed from the city. Then you take a short walk through the trees and find yourself back in busy suburbia, surrounded by stores and offices.

Interrupting my thoughts, Grace asked, "So, how are things going?"

Since I'd just taken a bite, I had a moment to find an answer to a question that was simple but wasn't, all at the same time. "Really well. Exceptionally well, in fact. It's an impressive company. Be glad you've never worked anywhere else."

"Oh, Dad isn't going to let me off that easily," she answered with a smile.

I gave her a questioning look as I took a drink of my pop.

"You know my dad. Everything's a lesson," she remarked with a teenager's acceptance of the immovable mountain that was her father.

"I know that all too well." Yes, I thought, *all* too well. In fact, it was kind of a relief that I hadn't seen much of Jeff since we'd arrived, just dinner at his place my first day, then briefly during the charity day and at church on Sunday. It gave me a chance to gather all my scattered thoughts, which I valued, because I knew Jeff well enough to know my peace wouldn't last much longer. And—I had no qualms about admitting this to myself—I kind of dreaded the lessons Jeff no doubt had planned for me next.

"Does he have a lesson planned for you?" I asked, curious, then had to duck as a Frisbee nearly creamed me, followed by a pair of running hooligans, who, thankfully, went around the table, rather than over it, which it looked like they had considered for a moment.

But Grace didn't even miss a beat. "Oh, sure, I've got lessons. We've talked about it a bit, the fact that eventually I've gotta leave HRI, go try out new places, learn new things. He's exactly right." Grace shook her head in a teenaged annoyed way. "No big surprise there."

"Why would you have to leave?" I asked, surprised. "It seems like a really great company for you and your skills."

She shrugged as she took a swig of her own drink. "Yeah, it's great. I love what I do, and I'm good at it. And, of course, the people are great. But Dad's taught us all that in a perfect world nobody grows, because there aren't any challenges. And if a world is perfect, there's a limit to how much anybody can contribute to it, how much anybody can do to make it better."

"Huh," I said. "Guess I never thought about it that way. But it sounds about right."

"So, I finally had to admit," she replied, her exasperation clear, "that before too long, I'll have to see what the normal world is like.

Dad says I need to struggle if I want to grow. I told him that I'd struggled enough when I was young to last a lifetime. But Dad, you know Dad..."

"Yeah," I said, commiserating.

"He just looked at me with that highly annoying smile of his and said that I'd learned all I can learn from those struggles, and now I need new ones if I want to keep learning."

"Not fair at all," I said, hiding my grin behind the last bite of my chili dog.

"It's not. But he's right. And he's also right, that if I want to really, really help the world, I need to do that from a place that actually needs the help. Havens Research Institute is so perfect, there isn't anything for me to fix."

Grace's napkin blew off the table. She bent and picked it up and then continued her thought. "All I can do here is research. Which of course isn't bad, but I'm almost nineteen years old and need to learn how to deal with people who may not want to deal with me. I haven't had to worry about that since Dad took me in. I was broken, and he fixed me, and I haven't seen broken since. Before long, I'll need to see broken again, if I want to grow more as a person."

Chapter 29

"You need to be broken?" I asked, worried about this beautiful young girl being hurt.

She grinned. "No, Dad says I got that down pat."

"Good!" I exclaimed, relieved.

"But I gotta *see* broken, again. I have to be in a world that doesn't function right, a place that's broken, so I can learn and grow. Plus, I'll need to be there to have something I can do to make it a better place."

I let that concept percolate for a moment. Once Jeff rescued her and healed her, all she'd known was Jeff's house and HRI, and in order to be a whole person, she now had to learn how to function in a dysfunctional environment. Even though I'd only been at HRI a week, I could see it was very womb-like, warm and safe, which was good for people like me coming into it from the outside. But when it's the only thing Grace had known, it was easy to see how that wasn't good, how she needed to learn to live in the real world.

"Sucks," I finally said, not knowing what else to say.

"Nah," she replied as she threw the last of her sandwich at the gathered pigeons, then picked up her trash. "Sure, the work is fun, but Dad's right, it's getting boring. And I'm kinda looking forward to getting out of here for a while. He thinks I should wait a couple years, but he says he'll support my decision."

As I gathered my stuff, I squelched an unexpected bit of envy. Here she was, almost nineteen years old, and she had herself all figured out; she knew exactly what shape she was—what tool she was—because she'd been encouraged to be herself since the day Jeff had brought her home. But here I was, thirty-nine years old, and just beginning to figure out who I was, because I'd spent my whole life doing what I *should*, doing what others wanted and expected, and doing what I had to do to survive and provide for my family.

Without a word, Grace took my trash from me and took it to the garbage can, giving me a few more moments to follow the line of thought.

In order to find myself, I had to get away from the world and all its demands. I needed to be in an environment that *was* fixed, so that I could get my traction and figure out who I was. And Grace needed to leave the exact same place, for the exact opposite reasons; it was *too* fixed for her to stay.

No wonder I was going crazy, the world was a crazy place.

As she returned to the table, I was shaking my head. When she gave me an old-people-are-weird look, I just smiled back, as there wasn't any way I could explain my insight that didn't make me look like a complete idiot.

"The convenience store is over there," she said, pointing. "I figured we could kind of make a circle, and head back on the street in front of work."

"Sounds good," I replied and followed, my mind still whirling.

A few minutes later, I held the door for her to enter the small convenience store. Other than a guy back by the coolers, we were the only customers.

The tall, lanky young man behind the counter looked up from the cigarette rack he was straightening and cheerfully asked, "Help you find anything?"

My cynical self, still reeling from my revelation, thought the clerk seemed a little too happy to be working a minimum wage job. Especially when his slight southern accent indicated he was a long way from home.

"Just picking up a paper," Grace answered, much more politely than I would have, as she took one off the newspaper stand just inside the door.

"Well, looks like ya found 'em," he replied cheerfully.

She smiled at him as she walked up, put the paper on the counter and paid for it, then she said politely, "You have a great day."

"I will, for sure," he replied with another happy smile. "Have to stay up, else you'll be down, and I've been down and it ain't no fun. Up's more fun, so I am. You have a great day, too."

Grace grinned at him. "I will."

As we stepped away from the counter, I considered the clerk. His name tag read "Keith." He seemed to be in his late twenties, was working a minimum wage job and — from my snapshot assessment of his appearance and speech patterns — wasn't likely to get much further in life, yet he was "staying up." Then I considered myself, with so much more going for me, I was "down" and had been so for most of my life. Didn't take a great leap to see who was the better man.

Grace stopped part way through the open door, and in my distraction and annoyance at myself, I barely stopped myself from running into her. When she returned to the counter, I figured she must have forgotten something else she wanted, so I stepped back to wait.

After Keith rang up the other customer, he turned to Grace with a kind smile. "Did ya forget something? I do that sometimes, but I usually get home 'fore I remember. Lucky for you, you didn't even make it out the door 'fore you remembered."

She smiled up at him in an oddly intent fashion for a moment, then asked, "Do you like working here?"

"Oh, it ain't bad," he replied with a shrug. "Had worse. And I like the people. My other job's got no windows and I don't talk to nobody, so it's harder, but still, had worse." He shrugged again and then smiled at her. "So, no complaints. I gotta make money ta support my mama and my boy, you know. And I stay up, that makes everything okay."

This seemed really out of character for Grace, so I eased closer, both offering support if she wanted it, but also curious to see where she was going with this.

After looking at Keith for a long moment, in a way that would have made me uncomfortable, but he seemed to take in stride, she asked, "Would you like a different job? One job? One that would help you support your family better?"

He looked at me questioningly, but I was as clueless as he was, so I gave a shrug and a confused shake of my head to let him know I wasn't going to be any help.

After a moment, he answered, "Course I would." His confusion was clear on his face.

She pulled out her phone and dialed. "Jane, it's Grace. I'm sending someone to you. His name's Keith, and I want you to give him a job."

The clerk looked at me, and I'm sure I looked like an idiot with my mouth hanging open, so I snapped it shut. Not hard to tell she was Jeff's kid; a chip off the old block she was.

As both Keith and I returned our attention to Grace, she spoke again, "Thanks Jane," hung up the phone and stuck it back in her jeans pocket, then she pulled her wallet out, extracted a business card, and using a pen from the counter wrote something on it. When she'd finished, she looked up to him and held out the card. "Whenever you're ready, go to this address, it's through the trees there—" she briefly pointed toward HRI "—and give this to Summer, the receptionist. She'll get you right to Jane, the hiring manager. Call me—my number's on the card—if you have any questions."

As he took the card, looking at it questioningly, Keith wasn't smiling anymore. He turned to me for confirmation, and I gave him another confused shrug, then a nod, letting him know I hadn't a clue what was going on, but that she had the power to do what she'd said. She was Jeff's kid, if she said for Jane to hire this guy, Jane would. Heck, I suspected if anybody at HRI asked Jane to hire somebody, I was betting Jane would. And as I thought about it, I realized that was pretty darn cool.

"HRI?" the clerk asked hesitatingly as the door opened behind us, letting in a couple teen boys who headed straight back to the pop coolers. "You can get me a job there?"

Grace confidently answered, "You *have* a job there, if you want it."

He looked to me again, so I nodded encouragingly and said, "They're great people. If you want a job, it's yours."

Keith nervously scratched his head as he looked at the card again. "Some of them come in here sometimes. They're all real smart people." He looked at me and then back to Grace. "I'm not so smart, in fact, didn't finish high school."

She looked at him, her face an echo of her father's compassionate sincerity. "HRI hires all kinds of people. And when some of them started, they thought they weren't smart, either. But pretty soon, they all found out how smart they really were, and so will you."

The two teens approached the counter, so Grace and I stepped back as Keith automatically rang up their purchases and gave them their change, his mind clearly on Grace's offer and not the kids.

I could imagine what thoughts were battling in his head, and I had to admit that I'm not sure I'd have had the courage to take Grace up on her offer, to trust a stranger enough to take the chance.

After the door closed behind the kids, he looked back to meet Grace's eyes, clearly worried how she was going to react to his next words. "Need to finish my shift. Need to make sure they have someone to cover my other shifts. Need to give the other place my notice."

Grace smiled kindly. "However long it takes, the job will be there for you. And in the beginning, if you can work only part time, to make sure you're being fair to the companies you're working for, that's perfectly fine."

Still obviously trying to grasp what was happening, he looked to me. "This for real?"

I gave a rueful laugh. "Oh, yeah. And believe me, I know how you feel; I started there last week and I'm still astounded. For what it's worth, Grace's father runs the place, so her word is gold."

After a thoughtful pause, suddenly the guy grinned the hugest smile I'd ever seen. "Okay!" he declared. "Okay. Man! I'm up now! Wait'll I tell my mama and little boy. I got myself a real job!"

Grace laughed, and Keith laughed with her.

"Thank you," he said, still grinning. "Thank you very much."

"It was my pleasure," she said with kind sincerity far beyond her years, then turned to leave.

I gave the guy a shrug, then a thumbs up, and laughed with him as I followed Grace out the door.

We started down the sidewalk back towards work, and I was thinking about how many times I'd wished I could have done something like that. That was so very cool.

After a few minutes of walking in silence, Grace interrupted my thoughts. "I've never done that before, just to let you know. But he struck me as someone who deserved a break. Someone who'd appreciate it and take advantage of it." She was quiet for a minute and then smiled. "Isn't it funny? I want to send him to the Institute for exactly the same reason I need to leave."

No, I thought as we turned the corner into the driveway to HRI, no, it wasn't funny at all, but I didn't know what it was.

I thought more about Grace's comment, "... wasn't it funny ...", as we walked to the building, then parted ways, and I headed back to my desk alone. After I sat there a while staring at the blank computer screen, I decided it wasn't funny, it was sad. Sure, it was great Grace could do such a glorious thing for a guy who just needed a helping hand. But it was really sad the rest of us, back home in our real lives away from Utopia, were left with nothing we could do to help people like Keith. The rest of us, no matter how deserving, or how smart, or how educated, could barely keep ourselves employed, let alone gift someone else with gainful employment.

In most companies, people were interchangeable parts, cogs in the corporate wheel, toss them out one week when profits are down, hire more the next week when profits were up. Experience didn't matter, loyalty didn't matter, giving a person a chance didn't matter, nothing mattered but the bottom line.

It seemed like yet another example of the short-term thinking that seemed to be epidemic not only in corporate America, but in all of America. This week was all that mattered, next week could take care of itself. Me and my immediate circle were all that mattered, the rest of the world could take care of itself. Environmentalism and scientific research were fabrications of the left-wing devils meant to sway men from the truth of rabid individuality and Christian conservatism —

I took a calming breath and got down off my mental soap box. I'd heard it too many times from Beth's church's people, and it never failed to enrage me. But I didn't want to be angry now, so I took another breath to let the anger go, and tried to get back to the point of my thought.

Thinking short-term was all fine and dandy if you didn't have any intention of being alive a year from now, or if you didn't have any kids, so you weren't worried about what kind of world you were giving to them.

I sighed. It sure felt like the Iroquois had it right, that we'd be a whole lot smarter if we spent more time looking at the impact of our decisions on the seventh generation instead of just this week or next. And it seemed Jeff had it right, he and his father had kept HRI a private company, so they had the freedom to take the long-term into account, rather than pandering to the shareholders, who were only interested in today's profits and to heck with tomorrow.

But, I thought as I sighed again, I can't do anything about it today, so best get back to the work Jeff's paying me the big bucks to do.

Knowing I wasn't in a mood to be able to write coherently, I went to the lab and tracked down Marcus. He needed to mill some new parts, so I went to the machine shop with him and he showed me more about working the computer-controlled milling machine and explained what was wrong with the old design and how they were going to fix it.

It didn't take me long to shake off my blues and be glad that I had a job at HRI, and to appreciate that even if I couldn't help everybody, today Grace had had the courage to help one guy and that was a great start.

Chapter 30

After helping Marcus, I went back to working on the documents. About an hour before the quitting bell, I looked up to see Jeff walking towards me, and suddenly I remembered the way I'd fled from the church after Marcus' sermon, and I felt guilty that I hadn't even mentioned to Marcus what a great sermon it had been. Maybe I'd tell him after I finally figured out what my destiny was, after I figured out how to tell God "Yes" instead of telling him "No" all the time. That sounded like a better plan than telling Marcus how his sermon had made the last twenty years of my life seem like a complete waste of time.

"Sorry about leaving so quickly after church, yesterday," I said quickly as Jeff stopped at my desk.

"No problem, friend," he replied with his usual smile. "Marcus knows to take the fleeing masses as a great compliment."

I let out a short laugh. "I'll bet he does. And people keep coming back for more?"

"We have our biggest attendance when he preaches." Jeff pulled a nearby chair over and sat down. "Will you come back for more?"

I looked at Jeff seriously. I hadn't thought of that. The sermon was painful, but at the same time, it was profoundly moving. It was what I needed to hear even if I hurt afterwards, unlike Beth's church where there was little substance pushing people to grow. "Yeah, in fact, I'm look forward to next Sunday."

He winked at me. "There you go. The people who want to grow come back, and the people who want spoon-fed-religious-blah, don't. You have next week off from Marcus though. But you'll like it."

"You?"

He reached over and gently popped me on the side of the head. "Quit trying to make me a front man."

I started to respond, but he held up his hand prepared for the next strike. "This one's going to hurt." He cocked his head and looked up at me with a questioning look. "Done?"

Defeated, I slumped in my chair. "Yeah."

He grinned at me. "Good. But anyway, Grace told me the labs she took you to, and I was wondering if you'd like a tour through a few more."

Always up to looking at more toys, I said, "Sure."

"Great!" he said in his usual gleefulness. "Finish up here, so we can both leave for home after our tour."

"Sounds good." I quickly closed down my programs, then paused. "How long's it going to take? I carpooled in this morning and won't have a car if this runs late."

"You should be fine, but if not, I'll drop you at the hotel."

"In the Rolls?" I asked, hoping my eagerness didn't show too much. But how many times in my life would I get to ride in a Rolls?

Jeff laughed. "Yes, in the Rolls. You might as well call them now, I can tell you suddenly aren't in any hurry."

"Hey," I replied, pretending offense and gathering my stuff into my backpack, then slung it across my shoulder. "Given the choice between riding in a Rolls or in a Prius with three others, the decision isn't a hard one."

He shook his head at me. "Come on. We'll start with the engine lab, since you have cars on your mind."

I nodded approvingly. "Engines are always cool." As we walked, I let the carpool guy know I was catching another ride, then followed Jeff down another corridor to another white metal lab door. And even before he opened it, I could hear the noise of the engines.

Ear-muff-style hearing protectors hung on pegs right inside the door. We both grabbed a pair, and as soon as I put mine on, the relief was immediate. A quick glance around the lab showed me why it was so noisy. There were at least eight engines on stands, all wired up to computers and vented to the outside through flexible tubes that dropped down from the ceiling, and five of the engines were running, with people gathered around looking at each engine's monitoring equipment.

"They're working on a six-stroke engine design," Jeff said as he strode to an engine, most of whose pieces were spread across several wheeled-workbenches.

His voice was muffled by the ear-protectors, but I could hear him clearly enough. As I followed him, I could feel the slight vibration in the concrete floor from the running engines.

"Six-stroke?" I asked when he picked up what looked to be a cut-away piston prototype from a workbench. "What do you mean by that? I understand two- and four-stroke but have never heard of a six-stroke."

"That's why this is so interesting," he said, showing me the intricate metal mechanism. "The first four strokes are like a traditional four-stroke engine," he pointed to parts as he explained, "intake, compression, power, and exhaust. And then there are two more for a steam cycle. The steam cycles use the heat from the previous combustion cycle, recovering more of the combustion energy and improving the overall efficiency of the engine. This also removes the need for a cooling system."

"Steam cycles," I remarked, thinking over the implications of the two extra strokes. "It makes a lot of sense. Wonder why it hasn't been done before?"

"Actually, the concept was first explored in the 1880's and several times since, but now, with the push for higher mileage cars, there's renewed interest, and we're helping show its potential. And these folks—" he waved his hand to encompass the busy room "—are getting close to working out some of the kinks. They just need to clear a few more hurdles, and it'll be a production-ready technology."

"Cool."

He smiled at me as he put the demonstration piece back down on the cluttered workbench. "It's very cool. But they're about to start shutting down for the day, so we'll get out of their way."

We put our ear-protectors back on their hooks, and as he led me to another lab, possibilities swirled in my head. What would the implications be for the world if high-mileage cars were the norm rather than the exception?

I was still considering the question as Jeff opened the door into a lab that, like the flywheel lab, was two-stories tall, but considerably bigger. As I leaned over the metal railing for a moment, I looked around. The lab contained what seemed to be several houses, granted they couldn't be more than a couple rooms each, but they were almost normal single-story house-height. The lab's ceiling was cluttered with all kinds of various tubes and wires extending down to the little houses, with huge clear plastic curtains that presumably could be pulled around a house to close it off from the rest. Big banks of lights were over one house, and another had water jets over it. And the folks working here were obviously closing down for the day, not paying us any attention.

"We're working on some emerging building technologies here," Jeff explained as he walked down the stairs.

I followed him past some techie-types at computers and around the back of the closest house.

He leaned against the wall and crossed his arms. "So, I assume you've heard about super-insulated houses?"

"Sure. Wish more of that would have been happening when my house was built. My utility bill would be much easier to open up each month."

Jeff uncrossed his arms and put his hands in his pockets. "Yeah, it sounds like a great idea, doesn't it? But what problems does that introduce?"

I looked at the house he was leaning against and pondered. For a temporary, proof of concept house, it had a very nice paint job on it. It was a shade of blue I have always been partial too. Not sure I would paint my whole house this color, but it was nice. In fact, not sure I would want to repaint my whole house at all. What a pain painting is, and I hate the fumes. Painting outside isn't so bad but inside is awful at best. We have to open all the windows and have fans for fresh air. That brought to mind one problem with air-tight houses. I looked at Jeff and gave him my first thought. "Well, fresh air is one thing. I don't know the numbers but they say a house should have so many air exchanges per hour. If you seal up the house tight then you don't have that."

"Point number one. So, to remedy this we have large, expensive, energy sucking, forced air ventilation systems. And I assume you have heard of sick building syndrome?"

I nodded in affirmation.

"We seal up the house, lock in all the toxins from the out-gassing of the paints, glues, composite wood products, cleaning chemical and such. We lock in all the moisture and then put in a massive system to remove the toxins and moisture. If you don't the house becomes unlivable very quickly." He pushed himself off the wall and turned to face the house. "But this house we can lock-up, shut all the windows and doors, shut off all power, then come back in five hundred years and take a deep breath when you walk in."

I smiled. "Really?" Then I placed my hand on the blue siding.

"What's different? It looks pretty typical to me."

"That's one of the nice things about this is that it does look normal. This is a standard two by four frame but with magnesium oxide siding on the outside, magnesium oxide board on the inside instead of drywall and then rock wool insulation between them."

With a funny look I asked, "Magnesium? What if that catches on fire? From what I understand it is almost impossible to put out."

Jeff shook his head. "Magnesium burns like mad and produces magnesium oxide. So, in fact, it is non-flammable, which gives it one of its many beneficial properties as a building material."

"Hmm, that is interesting. What are the other properties?" I asked.

"So, we have non-flammable, waterproof, insect proof, impact-resistant, unlike drywall, it is structural, Magnesium Oxide is one of the most abundant minerals in the Earth's crust. When MgO is combined with the right non-toxic mineral catalysts and aggregates it will absorb CO_2. A city built with MgO could do what a forest does."

He was about to keep going but I put up my hand to stop him. "Come on, Jeff. If this stuff is so great why isn't it already being used?"

Jeff looked around suspiciously and leaned in close. "We need to be quiet or the black SUV's may show up. This is an ancient idea, in fact, one of the oldest building technologies out of Europe and Asia have been combining clay and MgO treated wood chips in blocks and boards for several centuries. But a more profitable product has kept it out of America."

I looked at him questioningly. "Really?"

He stood up and grinned at me. Back to his normal voice he said, "Well, I like that better than saying we have been using vastly inferior building technology for many, many decades for no good reason. I mean, this is great stuff. It breaths. You know, they sell the clothing now that they say are breathable. It doesn't trap moisture next to the skin." Jeff patted the wall. "These do that same thing. With traditional buildings we use moisture barriers to keep moisture out. But that also keeps moisture in, thus needing the air conditioning systems to remove the moisture from the house so it doesn't mildew. These walls will not trap moisture and they are mold proof."

I interjected, "So no sick building syndrome. Very nice."

"Yeah, and no need for forced air ventilation. We can do it all with radiant heating and cooling."

I looked on approvingly. "I like it."

Jeff walked into the house and I followed him. He smiled as he looked around. "I always like walking in here. It just feels different to me." He looked at me with an amused look. "Some friends of one of the guys who works in this lab were having a baby. They wanted to redo a room for the baby but didn't want all the toxic fumes from the paint in a room for a new born. So, one weekend we went in, tore out the drywall, reinsulated the walls, put up MgO board and painted it with a breathable, nontoxic paint. Well, they found themselves sleeping in that room with the baby. We ended up redoing their room also. It just feels different. There's an energy to it."

I agreed silently but wondered if it was psychological rather than physical.

We started to walk but Jeff stopped and raised his finger. "Oh, the hotel you're staying at? We own that, and it was built with this."

This struck me because I had used the 'energy' phrase this morning about the hotel room. "Really?" But I let it go at that. I wanted to think about it.

Jeff started walking and I followed him out the other door and back into the lab. He walked to a workbench full of window frames and windows. "You spend all this time and energy building walls to keep the inside conditions of your house inside and then you put big holes in the wall, so you can see out and get light in. Compared to the insulated wall, the window is a wide-open hole; heat and cold transfer through it easily. On top of that, the thermal gain from the sun can be impressive, depending where in the country you live."

"I know all about how quickly the sun can heat up a room, and the electric bills that go with it."

"Then you'll know that window technology is moving forward with glazes to block the sun without dampening the view," he picked up one prototype after another as he continued, "and automatic shades, when maintaining a view isn't critical. We also have automated systems to open and close windows and turn on vent fans to draw fresh air throughout the house when the outside temperatures are suitable."

I'd read a lot about some of this stuff and at first glance, the prototypes on the bench wasn't all that revolutionary, but I suspected that HRI was taking old concepts to new levels. Which lead me to a thought I hadn't considered before. "You guys must be making a fortune off the patents."

He looked at me and grinned. "You read much about Ben Franklin?"

I smiled back. "I try not to read about him. I feel like I'm wasting my life after I read all he did. He was an amazing guy, even if he did have his flaws."

"Do you know about the Franklin stove?"

"Ah! That's where you're going." I was excited that I actually knew what he was talking about. "Franklin refused to patent it. Does that mean you guys don't patent this stuff?"

Jeff leaned back against the workbench, resting his palms on the bench's edge. "I can't tell you how many times I heard my dad quote Ben Franklin. 'As we enjoy great advantages from the inventions of others, we should be glad of an opportunity to serve others by any invention of ours, and this we should do freely and generously.' My dad took that idea seriously, but in a modern way."

I looked at Jeff questioningly. "But that doesn't make sense. If you guys don't patent what HRI discovers or invents, then others could patent it and get all the credit for it. I mean, companies buy whole other companies just for their patents, so they don't have to pay patent licensing fees or fight patent infringement legal battles."

"You're a smart man, Stanley," Jeff said with an approving nod. "Dad's modern twist was to hire cut-throat patent lawyers and patent everything he could, no matter how trivial."

I knew that wasn't the whole story. "And?"

"As long as the technology is used for, as Franklin stated, 'an opportunity to serve others', then we license our patents 'freely and generously.'"

It took me a moment to translate that into terms I understood. "So, if people are using a patent for worthwhile things, they can use it for free?"

"Exactly."

"But what about everybody else, the ones who aren't doing worthwhile things, and want to use the patents?"

"We charge them out the wahzoo and funnel the money into a huge children's education trust my father set up."

All I could do was look at him in utter disbelief. "This place gets weirder and weirder by the minute."

"Normal is boring, Stanley, and only for under-achievers," he said with a grin, then pushed away from the workbench. "But enough on patents. You'll find this much more interesting." He waved me toward the back door of the building.

I opened the door and entered the room of the little building, and when Jeff closed the door behind us, I was surprised how dark the room was. No windows. After all the talk of windows a minute ago, it seemed strange to walk into a room without them.

"Hit the light switch."

Considering it was totally dark, that was a bit of a challenge. I groped for the door behind me, then found the switch beside it, and flipped it. And the room lit up, to show me it was empty, no furniture, no test equipment or anything.

"What do you think?" Jeff asked.

I looked at him strangely, looked back around at the room to see what I missed. After concluding I hadn't missed anything, I looked back at him. "I think it's an empty room."

He beamed. "Yes, it's empty. No lamps, no light fixtures, nothing."

He had me confused. I was missing something. No lamps... no light fixtures... nothing. I looked around more and then what I was missing struck me. I spun around quickly looking for it, but it wasn't there anywhere. The room was empty, the walls and ceiling were totally flat; there were no light fixtures anywhere, yet the room had lit up when I hit the switch. "That is so cool!" I exclaimed. "How does it work?"

"It's a light emitting paint. When a small electric charge is applied, it emits light. It can be applied to any surface just like regular paint."

Now this was something I hadn't read or heard about. Wow! "That's really, really something," I said as I did another turn. "I take it this is more energy efficient than other lights?"

"Vastly." Jeff just stood there, clearly enjoying my astonishment.

I tried to come up with something intelligent, beyond "this is so cool!," which it was. "Will I be able to paint my walls with it at home?"

"Not this year," Jeff said with a straight face, then he opened the door on the other side of the room and flicked off the lights... the paint... the whatever.

"Ha, ha," I replied as I followed him out, back into the lab, which was mostly deserted. Obviously, these folks didn't need the deafening alarm to tell them it was quitting time.

He walked over to the little house next to this one, and over the next half-hour, showed me photovoltaic windows, siding and shingles. Then water saving systems which recirculate water so when water comes out of the faucet it's immediately hot; no more wasting water waiting for it to get hot. Next was a dual-water system that used clean, but not potable, water for the toilets, showers, and other water systems that wouldn't be used for food or drinking. I'd always wondered why we flushed highly-processed water down the toilet or watered our lawns with it, so to see an alternative was exciting.

As we went from one little house to the next, as Jeff had said, there was a mix of new and old technology, but it was all pulled into highly efficient systems.

Seeing that I was beyond the point of absorbing any more, Jeff took pity on me, and we walked out of the — now deserted — lab and started down the hall toward an open stairwell.

In an attempt to recover from everything Jeff had shown me so far, I focused on the movement of my legs as I climbed the stairs. Still, other thoughts filled in the empty spaces between steps.

As Jeff reached the top of the stairs and turned right, I asked, "How do you guys get your projects? I mean, most companies focus on one thing and get new projects based on their expertise in that technology, but you guys seem to be doing some of everything. How do you convince people to invest in you when you're so diversified?"

Jeff paused and turned to me. "Good question." He turned back around, facing ahead of me down the hall, then pointed ahead to the right, where two sets of tall windows met at a corner. "Let's talk out there, it's a nice day."

I walked beside him as he began to explain.

"HRI has a long-standing reputation for producing results, because my father and other people created a culture of organization, cooperation and efficiency. Early in the formation of the company, they worked hard to figure out how to best use their people."

From what I'd seen, they had succeeded, but before I could get any further with that thought, we got to the windows, and I saw where Jeff was taking us and all other thoughts fled.

"Wow!" I exclaimed.

Jeff smiled as he opened the glass door outside to a second-floor, grass-covered patio, that had to be the roof of the front entrance. Potted trees shaded several tables, and flowers provided a colorful edging beneath the pipe railing that surrounded the two open sides of the patio.

As I followed him out, my mind quickly jumped to wondering how the weight of the grass and soil was supported; there must be columns in the entry way that I hadn't really noticed. I'd have to look next time I went into the room. And what happened to the water when it rained?

Jeff sat down at one of the white, painted metal tables, as I walked past a couple of large potted plants to the railing, trying to figure out what I was looking at. It wasn't until I looked down that I realized it was the beautiful skylight that ran the length of the entryway. I could see people walking below me leaving for the day. This was impressive.

I followed the rail around to the corner opposite the door, to the huge cedar rainwater harvesting tank that I saw from the ground on the way in every morning. Up close, it looked even bigger than I'd thought, more than twice as tall as I was.

Jeff patiently let me look around. When I'd taken in most of it, I joined him at the table, sitting across from him and dumping my backpack into the chair beside me. Once I was settled, he continued with his explanation.

"My father always said that HRI's most important product is its employees. And as I'm sure you've already seen, there are no cookie-cutter roles here. We look at each employee as an individual, as a person. For the more senior people here, it's second-nature to quickly spot an employee's strengths."

"Ah." I remembered the book he tossed to me in his office my first day, and that's what Aaron had talked about earlier, with his hammer and screwdriver analogy. "I haven't started *Now, Discover Your Strengths*, yet. But it looks interesting."

He nodded. "Once a company learns to spot people's strengths and puts people to work within their strengths, most of the work of delivering a quality product to the customer is done, because having the right people doing the right job is what gets the job done right."

Chapter 31

I laughed. "That's definitely deep, Jeff." Then I let a question come to the forefront of my mind, a question that I'd been afraid to ask, maybe because I was afraid of the answer. "What are my strengths? I know you must have chosen me for a reason, but I still don't get it. And being here? Yeah, I can write a decent manual, but surely you went to all this effort for more than that. What's *my* right job?"

"That, my friend, is for you to discover," Jeff replied with the gentle smile that let me know he understood the pain beneath my question.

"But you know!" I demanded, except it was more a question.

"Of course."

"But you aren't going to tell me?" I don't know why I even bothered to ask the question, because I knew how he would respond.

"In this case, it's better you discover it on your own."

"Not helpful," I muttered.

He grinned. "It's not my job to be helpful, friend. Call your local community police officer if you want helpful. Me? I'm here to make waves."

"Ain't that the truth," I grumbled. "Anyway..."

"Yes?" he asked politely, obviously having fun at my expense.

"We seem to have gotten off topic. Back to how HRI gets all its contracts."

"Okay. After HRI puts people into jobs that support their strengths, we find that we don't need to employ carrots-on-sticks as motivators, nor the-beatings-will-continue-until-moral-improves forms of punishments. While those approaches may have short-term positive effects for some companies, the long-term effects are profoundly negative, and HRI has always been a long-term-thinking kind of place."

I heartily agreed with the detrimental long-term effects of both carrots and beatings. But I'd worked for places that liberally used both and disagreed with Jeff, in that I wasn't sure if either carrots or beatings produced any short-term benefit. The morale in those companies had been consistently low, and their employee turnover was high.

Jeff went on before I could say anything, so I let the thought flow away and listened.

"If people want to work and they have a positive attitude, we can find a way to have them produce and feel like they aren't even 'working', because they're doing things within their natural strengths. However, the most important part of that paradigm is for the person to have a positive attitude."

"Really?" I asked, because I'd worked with a whole lot of grouchy people who still seemed to get a lot of work done, and I'd have thought the "want to work" part was more important than being happy about it.

"For example," Jeff said, leaning back more comfortably in his chair, "Keith, the guy you and Grace met today at the convenience store. He came in a little while ago, and we had a chat."

I let out a sigh of relief I hadn't even known I was holding. "I'm so glad he showed up. I'm not sure I would have. But I was glad to see Grace offer him the job. He seems like a guy who just needs a chance."

"Exactly. He's made some unwise choices that continued limiting his opportunities years later."

"I kind of figured that."

"But, unlike many people in similar situations, he's learned from his choices and taken responsibility for them. Even though the price has been heavy, he sees the value in tough times and is able to maintain a positive attitude. That's what prompted Grace to offer him the opportunity she did."

I thought about it a moment. "Yeah. Now that you say that, I see what you mean. He could have been the hardest worker in the world, but if he'd been grouchy and grumpy, Grace wouldn't have even given him a second thought."

Jeff nodded. "Watch what happens to him here."

"Will it be good or bad?" I was a little worried about Keith trying to fit in with the people here. It was pretty obvious his knowledge level was of a different caliber than theirs.

"Watch and see for yourself," Jeff said with his Jeff-grin. "Back to your original question. Because HRI has put the systems in place to value our people above our products, we actually produce results better than our competitors. HRI actually has the opposite problem of most companies, we have far more inquiries that we could ever possibly accept. Which is great because it means we can be choosy about the ones we pick."

I smiled. "Better than not having enough and having to make do with the choices of a bad project or no income. How do you pick which projects to accept?"

"My father set the criteria when he chose HRI's motto: 'making the world a better place through technology.'"

"Cool." I mentally sorted through all the research projects he and Grace had shown me and could see how each of them fit with HRI's motto, but a question still nagged. "For most research places I know of, the Defense Department is their bread and butter. I haven't seen any of that here."

"We will take military contracts," Jeff admitted, "but only for non-weaponizable projects. We're here to help, not hurt. And humanity needs all the help it can get, because if humanity continues the direction it's going, it risks killing itself, the Earth, or both. Most people know this, but change is difficult because it causes so much hardship. Plus, too many people stand to lose too much money if things change."

"How so?" I had my take on why, but was interested in hearing what he had to say.

"It's impossible to count the ways," he said with a shrug. "But given your love of cars, I'll use that as an example." He waved a hand toward the parking lot now about half empty of its many fuel-efficient cars. "Logically, it's easy to say a car that gets ninety miles-per-gallon makes more sense than a car that gets eighteen MPG, when all the other features are equal.

"But economically, more money changes hands with the eighteen-MPG car. Not only does it use more gas, which means bigger oil companies, it also employs more people in more gas stations —" Jeff ticked the list off on his fingers. " — which employ more construction people to build and maintain the gas stations. Plus, the car is bigger, so it takes more materials to make, so it employs more people in the material-handling and manufacturing industries, and so on. Which all boils down to, in an economy based on growth, there's no economic motivation to move toward more fuel-efficient cars, and every reason not to."

"I've never thought of it that way."

He nodded. "The core technology to build a ninety-MPG car, or even a truck, has been within reach for a long time, but the motivation hasn't, because economically, the eighteen-MPG car makes more sense."

"Wow," I said, as I leaned back in my chair, trying to absorb what he was saying. "Gas mileage has always been one of the first things I look at when I buy a car, but it doesn't seem like many other people consider it—at least until gas prices went up. And I've never understood why other people didn't think it's important. But now you're saying that high-mileage cars would cause economic problems. Interesting."

He shrugged. "On top of that, the low gas-mileage car's threat to the environment or to humanity's health is too nebulous, too far away, for most people to grasp. The gratification they receive when they drive a certain kind of car, or the inconvenience of a smaller car, or lack of features, or many other more immediate concerns are much easier to understand. The car's gas mileage is fairly far down on the list for most car shoppers."

I just stared at him for a moment. "I understand."

For the first time, I really understood; it wasn't as black and white as it had seemed from my point of view. If we forced manufacturers to make higher MPG cars, we'd put a whole lot of people out of work. And the most affected jobs would be tradesman-type jobs, which were already scarce to begin with.

Except, the long-term consequences were black and white! I leaned forward again, resting my arms on the table. "Except we're killing the Earth!"

"Nah. The Earth will be just fine. You may cause the sixth great extinction, but the Earth will keep moving right along without you guys."

I ignored him leaving himself out of the "we" and let my tree-hugger anger take over.

"Killing the Earth or just killing ourselves off has the same effect on us," I said to him fiercely, "All these holier-than-thou people at Beth's church—" I waved my arms in a wide circle. " —and all over, who're driving the huge SUVs getting six miles-per-gallon at the same time they're proclaiming how *saved* they are and how much better they are than me!" I abruptly stood, pacing as I spoke. "If they're driving the SUV 'cause they've got a heavy-duty job they need it for, that's one thing." I waved them off into their own category of justified working stiffs. "But to just drive a monster SUV to the mall and back, that makes me so angry. And it's so hypocritical that those better-than-everybody-else Christians couldn't care less about what they're doing to the environment!"

"Generalizing a little, Stanley?"

"All the blasted time!" I stalked back to the table and leaned on it with straight arms, challenging him to answer me. "And all of those blasted mega-churches and Christian TV channels. They talk about how it's a Christian's duty to be stewards of the Earth, but only because they want to pick a comfortable topic, and environmentalism is comfortable." I was waving my hand for emphasis, almost in Jeff's face, but I couldn't stop myself. "But, do any of the people actually do it? Or do they think that listening to the sermon is all that's required to make you a Christian and actions aren't necessary?" I threw up my hands. "Heavens no, they just sit on their smug little butts in church, and drive home in their huge SUVs that've never been worked harder than a trip to the mall, all while they vote for politicians who're doing their best to destroy God's creation!"

Fuming, and at the same time embarrassed at my explosion, I paced to the railing and leaned on it, looking out at the trees and beautiful landscaping to calm myself.

After a moment, I said, "How come they can't see their hypocrisy?"

Jeff stayed silent until I turned to look at him.

"Because, as humans, Stanley, you can't see your own hypocrisy until it bites you on the butt. Then you still have a hard time seeing it, because it's behind you. You don't think to look back to see what's causing the pain."

I gave a huge sigh, shook my head, and leaned back against the railing. "Mine's biting me on the butt, isn't it?"

"I'll let you determine that Mr. holier-than-thou."

I lowered my head and thought. He was right. "Okay, I hear you." I gave up my anger and ambled back to the table and sank into my chair. "But explain it to me. It seems like Christianity should be on the forefront of taking care of the Earth, on the forefront of researching new technologies to make our world a better place, yet most seem to just ignore it and many actively resist it."

"You're generalizing again, Stanley. There are millions of

Christians who feel just as strongly about saving the Earth as you do, if not more so. But to answer your question: if you were to do a survey and ask people to list the top characteristics of Christianity, environmentalism wouldn't top the list."

"But why?"

"The easiest way to explain it is that Christianity is based on the teachings of Jesus and Paul, and the Old Testament prophets before them. When Jesus walked the Earth, the world's population was less than two-hundred-million people. The people lived lives which had a much smaller impact on the Earth because material goods were relatively scarce since everything had to be handmade. Plus, they didn't have plastic.

"If Jesus would have stood upon a hilltop, with the crowds of peasants gathered around him and preached--" Jeff stood and raised his hands, and addressed an imaginary crowd in a deep authoritative voice. " —'Blessed are those who reduce, reuse and recycle, for they shall bring the Kingdom of Heaven unto us, and we shall all live lightly upon the land.' The crowd would have looked at him questioningly and said," Jeff cocked his head to the side imitating their confused look, "So ... We're good on that one, right?"

I had to laugh at the picture. "I get it. It wouldn't have meant anything to them."

"It wasn't a message for their time. Even eighteen-hundred years later, Thomas Malthus' theories on the issues of population growth got very little traction, because the common person couldn't feel the impact of his worries. You know much about him?"

I dug into my brain and brushed some spider webs off of a pile of college memories. "Vaguely. One of my classes talked about him. Something about how many people the Earth could support. Oh, its *carrying-capacity*."

Jeff nodded and let me continue.

"He warned of limits, but since then, new technology has increased the carrying-capacity of the Earth."

Jeff smiled. "Not bad, Stanley. You listened well in class."

I smiled at myself. Who'd have thought that some knowledge from a required class I had to take in college would be useful in a conversation with someone like Jeff so many years later.

He continued. "So, now with population growth at its current level, it's easy to see that there's a limit to how much new technology can help sustain more people. It's not just a matter of food, but also limits on how much gasoline, coal, and fresh water humans can produce.

"Even though it's impacting everybody negatively in their everyday lives, because so many people stand to lose significantly — in very real, short-term ways — there's a massive resistance to the idea of using technology to *conserve* resources."

Nodding, I said, "Global warming is a hoax and cigarettes aren't bad for you."

He smiled. "Exactly. The good news is that many people are starting to see the need to change their habits, and the technology has advanced to the point it can give people the comforts they want without burdening the Earth even more. People just need to demand it. Churches need to demand it. Buckminster Fuller was right on track with his idea of improving humanity through technology."

"So, can't you push that along? You've got this whole company full of brilliant people, can't you just fix it?"

Jeff shook his head, as if I'd totally missed the point. "Haven't you noticed I'm throttling this company back? If I let the Institute work as much as they wanted, we'd be producing technology that the world isn't ready for, which would cause far more problems than it solved. Change has to happen at the right pace. Nikolia Tesla is an example of that."

Tesla had always fascinated me. "Yeah, I hear you. His theories were too far beyond what people could accept."

"His technologies that survived — two of which were AC power and the radio, and those two alone changed the world — were only a small part of what he had to offer."

"But the world wasn't ready for the rest," I said, "and he died for it."

Jeff grinned. "Someone's been watching too many conspiracy-theory shows. But it's not much of a stretch so say that he did indeed die for messages he attempted to deliver that were too early for his time. It puts him in excellent company."

It took me a moment, but I did catch his meaning. "Jesus."

He laughed, then went on with the topic. "Technology takes off when the world is ready for the technology. All through history, you can see the same ground-breaking ideas being worked on by several people, at roughly the same time, in different parts of the world, and they had no knowledge of each other. For example, Newton and Leibnitz discovered calculus at the same time."

"Alexander Graham Bell and some Italian guy, who I forgot his name —"

"Antonio Meucci."

"Yes. That's it. They both invented the telephone."

"But if the world isn't ready, the ideas collect dust until the time is right. Blaise Pascal invented a mechanical calculator in 1642, but it wasn't until the nineteenth-century that a calculator became a commercial success. So sure, I could push the technology, I could make it happen, but it'd be a futile effort. The people need to change, the society needs to be ready, and then the technology will be embraced."

I just looked at him, trying to gather my thoughts. "The technology is available to fix our Earth?"

Jeff nodded. "With the technology available and with what you guys are on the cusp of, humans could live almost as gently on the Earth as the people of Jesus' time."

"I hear a 'but' on the end of that."

"But..." he said dramatically, and I grinned. "But you have to be willing to put up with the turmoil and uncertainty that change would require. Jobs will be lost, many of them. But new jobs will be born in industries that can't even be imagined today. Companies will go under. New ones born. Lives will be destroyed. Others will get rich."

"Hard times," I said softly, considering what he was saying.

Jeff shrugged. "The point I want to make is just because there's change and upheaval, it doesn't mean that the only outcome is a bad one."

I thought about that. "Grace said you have to see broke before you can fix it."

"She's a wise young woman."

I stared down at the table as I mentally agreed with him about her wisdom. Then Grace's statement took on a second meaning, and I looked up at Jeff. "You have to *see* broken before you can fix it." I thought for a moment, to put my insight into words. "Most people don't even *see* what's broken. Couldn't we just teach them to see it? It seems easy enough; just buy a hybrid instead of a gas-guzzler."

Jeff leaned in towards me. "There aren't any simple answers here. Even our fixes are broken. The rare earth minerals computers require are hellish to mine. The batteries hybrids require aren't that green."

"And on, and on," I said, waving my hand in despondent circles. I leaned forward again. "Then what's the answer? Earlier, I was thinking about the Iroquois' seventh-generation thinking strategy, but right now we can't predict what the world will be like in ten years, let alone seven generations from now."

"You were a Boy Scout, Stanley. What's the first part of the Boy Scout oath?"

I resisted the urge to hold up my fingers in the scout sign as I replied, "On my honor, I will do my best—"

He interrupted "There you go."

I gave him a puzzled look.

"It's what we do every day at HRI. It's what we do in every lab in this place, in every cubicle or office. We *do our best* with what we know today. We put saving the Earth before saving money and we work with what we know today... knowing that tomorrow, we'll know more. And when tomorrow comes, and we realize the need to make better decisions, we will."

Collapsing back into my chair, I heaved a long sigh. "Do my best? That's it? That's the answer?"

"Almost. The second part is: When you were on camping trips with your scout troop, what's the last thing you did before you left the campsite?"

I smiled as my mind's eye pictured myself as a kid and the gruff old scout master barking out the order, "Police line!" and we'd form a line spanning the campsite and march the length of it, picking up trash, whether it was ours or from previous campers.

I looked at Jeff and repeated what I heard time after time on scout camping trips, and the line I'd spoken on the couple camping trips I'd taken with Cooper's Cub Scouts. "Leave the campsite cleaner than you found it."

Jeff nodded. "Now take that thought bigger."

Wondering what he meant, I let the thought roll around in my mind—take it bigger. So... Not just the campsite. Not just on campouts. The world! All the time! Then it struck me and I looked at Jeff. "What a great metaphor for life. 'Leave the world a better place than you found it.'"

"It can be even bigger than that, Stanley, if you're willing to take it to its fullest potential."

"Huh?" I'd thought that the world was pretty big.

"Not just physical things." he said, gently. "Leave your work better than you found it. Leave your relationships better than you found them. That's the ideal, Stanley." He paused looking me straight in the eye. "Everything is better, Stanley, because you're part of it."

My mind tried really hard to reject that idea, because it was too big, too much responsibility.

"Whether you realize it or not, Stanley, 'do your best' and 'leave things better than you found them' are both very big parts of who you really are."

I interlocked my fingers and looked down at them. In my heart, I knew Jeff was wrong. I didn't do my best and things were rarely better because I was around. Heck, I wasn't even doing as much with Cooper's scouts as I should have been doing. Looking back up at Jeff and meeting his gaze, I said, "I can do better."

He responded with that never-ending smile and the perpetual look of acceptance, but at the same time I couldn't help but think he was waiting for me to catch onto something.

Except, he was telling me the answer was one I'd heard my whole life: "do your best." Cliché, to the point of being meaningless. So obviously that wasn't what I was missing, but I didn't have a clue what the heck it might be.

The silence stretched, not an uncomfortable silence, but I didn't have even the vaguest notion what he was waiting for, nor even a direction to start looking. So, I finally gave in and gave up. "I'm done, Jeff. Take me home."

He nodded. "It's a lot for anybody, Stanley. You're doing just fine."

I gave him a self-deprecating smile. "I'm doing my best."

He looked me straight in the eyes. "Yes. Yes, you are, friend."

I looked away and grabbed my backpack as I stood, making it clear I wasn't going to let him talk me into any more.

Chapter 32

A few minutes later, we were outside and walking toward his car. As we approached it, I thought about how the Rolls stood out among the mass of high-efficiency vehicles. It was a contradiction. A contradiction that I couldn't let pass after the conversation we'd just had.

"Jeff? You just took me through all the labs, talked about how we need to change, how we all need to do our best to save the Earth, and then you're going to drive home in that? I mean, what kind of mileage does it get?"

In typical Jeff fashion, he smiled and with his finger motioned for me to follow him to the front of the car. Without saying a word, he popped the hood, and I looked down at a stunning, beautifully polished, engine. The evening sun reflected off the metal adding to its elegance.

It took me a moment to recognize what I was seeing, which I wouldn't have known before a couple hours ago. It was a six-stroke engine and a work of art equal to the car itself.

"Seventy-five," he said with a wink.

I was puzzled. "Seventy-five miles-per-gallon? No way! Rolls' are built as heavy as tanks!"

He just smiled at me.

"No!" Surely he was pulling my leg, then I thought back to more of the things he said during the tour of the engine lab. "You said they're still working out the kinks?"

"You're right, 'they are.' I built this in my home shop."

I looked at him in amazement for a moment and then had to just laugh. In his home shop, he'd built the engine a whole team was trying to figure out, an engine that could save the planet, but the only version of it was in his tank of a Rolls. I knew without asking, that this would stay the only version of the engine until the world was ready for the technology. "It's beautiful." What else could I say?

He nodded, accepting the compliment as his due. "Doing the right thing doesn't mean the results have to be ugly. Nor does it mean one has to throw out the achievements of the past."

I threw my hands up; he'd officially blown my mind. "I'm done. I've had it. Take me home."

"Get in, Stanley. You can collapse at the hotel."

I did as he said, and he drove me home, and man! the car rode like a dream.

* * *

Up in my hotel suite, I did indeed collapse on the couch, my head whirling and swirling with all that I'd been through.

But pretty soon, hunger got me up, and I fired up Skype on my laptop as I made myself dinner. Beth and I had been leaving the Skype call open so we could interact in a semi-normal way throughout the evenings; I had it on my laptop, and she had it on the computer in the office at home. Most evenings, they'd be in and out of the office talking when they needed me for something, or just to say "hi," and I'd read bedtime stories to Thing 1 and 2. We'd even joked about putting the computer on the dining room table so I could eat dinner with them, but Beth wasn't sure she could get the computer back together after she moved it, so it hadn't happened.

Being alone in the hotel in the evening left me with a lot of time on my hands, since I didn't have the usual household chores or family obligations to fill my time. In the week I'd been here, I'd already developed a habit of lying on the couch reading. There hadn't been many times in my life when I'd been able to relax and enjoy reading, so this was nice.

But tonight, I couldn't focus, so I had the TV on, watching stupid, mindless people doing stupid, mindless things. It was all I was up to.

A couple hours later, Beth moved in front of the camera. "Someone wants to say good-night to you."

I glanced at the clock on the wall; with the time difference it was Alice's bed time. "Yeah?" I said, muting the TV, sitting up and turning the laptop so it was angled better. "Who might that be?"

Alice's voice came on but she was off-screen:

"This is little Thing 2 saying good-night.
I wish you were here to hold me tight.
But I got the next best thing money can buy,
An extra big T-shirt from HRI!"

She jumped in front of the camera with her arms flung out wide and a HRI T-shirt on, and I laughed. I'd forgotten about the T-shirts, but Jeff hadn't. I'd have to thank him tomorrow. "I'm glad they made it."

"Thanks for the shirt. I love you, and good-night, Daddy!" She blew me kisses as she backed away from the camera in the direction of her room.

A proud "dad" smile covered my face as I beamed at my little Suess-ling. "I love you, too." And blew her some kisses.

Beth came back into view and had her HRI T-shirt on. She put her elbows on the desk and rested her chin on her hands.

"Guess Jeff got you guys the T-shirts."

She tried to nod with her head supported by her hands. "Yup, everyone got one. But you know... Cooper wasn't too impressed with his. He's still waiting for his from The Dollar."

I had to laugh. "The Change." It was strange for me to correct anyone on current music, especially rap. If Grace hadn't said something about liking the band, I probably wouldn't have remembered. "'Fraid he's out of luck." The chance of me finding Cooper's shirt was pretty slim.

"You going to tell him that?"

"Let's go with the plan of not mentioning it and hope he forgets."

She laughed at me. "Great plan by any standards." She paused, looking at me across the thousands of miles that separated us, then said, "What's wrong, Stanley? You look down."

I shrugged. "Not down. Just a lot to think about." I paused, trying to put my feelings into words. "I'm glad my time with Jeff isn't over, but as much as I hate to admit it, it's been nice not seeing much of him lately. Until tonight, that is."

"What'd he do now?"

I thought for a minute as I looked away from the screen. What did he do? He unintentionally made me feel bad for not "doing my best." He made me want to do better. I looked back at Beth on the screen. "Can you sign Cooper back up for scouts? When I get home, I want to get more involved in that."

She looked at me confused. "That doesn't quite answer my

question."

"I don't know. Something Jeff said today made me think of that." Reaching out, I spun the TV remote on the coffee table beside the computer and watched it until it quit spinning. "Wish he'd just tell me what he wants from me."

"Do you?"

I changed my focus from the remote to her and smiled. "Don't you start. That's exactly what Jeff would say right now. I don't need two of you guys."

She smiled back. I loved her smile. "What should I say then?"

I shrugged and looked way from the screen. "I don't know."

"Can I make another 'Jeff' statement?"

I turned back to her with a grin. "Guess I'd better get used to it."

She didn't smile but looked at me intently. "You under-sell yourself, Stanley. Jeff sees something in you because there's so much to see. I married a guy who I think is a really great guy. I married a guy who asks important questions. I married a guy who doesn't take simple answers. I married a guy who always does his best."

If I wasn't listening before, I was now. I quickly replayed our conversation in my head. I don't think I'd said "do your best" to her. She'd joked about making a "Jeff" statement, and here she was, repeating Jeff's words.

She went on. "I married a great person, a great father, and a great husband. I'm a better person because of you."

Now I stared at her; I'm sure my mouth was gaping open in surprise. I might have said something about doing my best in our conversation and not remembered it, but I *knew* I hadn't said anything about things being better because I was around. It had to be a coincidence, didn't it?

I closed my mouth, trying to think of how to reply—

"Mom!" Cooper called from the kitchen. "Can you come here?"

Saved! I thought. "Thanks for saying that," I said quickly to Beth, "and go help the kid. I'm tired and going to bed soon, so we'll talk more tomorrow. Love you."

She looked at me strangely for a moment, then shrugged. "Okay. Love you, too. Talk with you tomorrow."

I signed off and slouched back in the couch, resting my head on the back of it and stared at the ceiling, thinking.

It was so strange Beth had said I always do my best and she was a better person because of me. Those were almost exactly the words Jeff had used.

What does "Do your best" even mean?

In my past jobs, I know I hadn't done my best. Sure, I'd tried to do good, and they'd all seemed happy with my work, but the jobs were just ways to make money, nothing special, none were worth enough to put any extraordinary effort into.

Then I thought about HRI. I was definitely putting in extraordinary effort in here, and I was engaged and excited. Did that mean I was doing my best here?

But what would happen when I leave? How would I do my best when I didn't have HRI to make it easy? What would "doing my best" mean then?

I got up to get a Dew from the fridge, and after I popped the top and took my first swig, leaned with my elbows on the counter as I thought about the clean camp metaphor.

I liked it a lot, "leave the world a better place," but just like "do your best," I wasn't sure what it meant in the reality of day-to-day life.

Beth had said she was a better person because of me.

I couldn't say that was true in all my relationships and other daily activities, but I could see some places were better because I was involved.

The next thing that came to mind was a little perplexing. Why was I drinking a Mountain Dew right before bed? I examined the can as I thought about that and the other things.

I don't know how to quantify "doing my best" or "leaving things in better shape than I found them" but it was sure something to think about as I moved forward in life. Right now, at HRI, it was easy because I felt I was doing my best and people seemed to feel I was making the documentation better. It's when I leave here I wondered what it would all mean.

I put the partially drunk can back in the fridge and headed to get ready for bed.

Standing in front of the mirror brushing my teeth, I studied my reflection and tried to look at myself with different eyes. With a mouth full of toothpaste, I said to the reflection, "So Stanley, what exactly does 'do your best' mean?"

My reflection, being much more polite than me, leaned over the sink and spat out the mouth full of toothpaste, rinsed, and then looked me square in the eyes. "Well, goofball, you're taking it way to seriously. It doesn't mean you have to be perfect. If you try to be perfect, you're setting yourself up for failure. If you try to be perfect at work, you'll fail at being a dad. If you try to be a perfect dad, you'll fail at work. You may succeed in one area but have a lifetime of regrets in the other areas."

Intently listening to the reflection speak, I started to respond, "But..." then stopped and looked down trying to figure out what to say and ran my fingers through my hair.

The reflection waited for me to look back at it before it responded, "'But' nothing. Quit trying to make it into something it's not. Sure, you could do better. Can't everyone? The key is to minimize your regrets."

"Minimize regrets?"

He nodded. "Sure. If you try to be perfect in only one area of your life, in later years, you'll look back and regret not being better in other areas. Living a full, but balanced, life is doing your best, numbskull."

I smiled at his bluntness, and he smiled back. As I stood there for a moment looking at my reflection in the mirror, I found a bond growing between us, one of respect. He was someone I'd seen my whole life but never really talked to. I'm not sure I even cared for him before, but now, as I looked at him, I saw someone who was a worthwhile person with some useful insight. With a look of gratitude I responded, "Thanks. That actually makes some sense. You're an alright guy."

He nodded in agreement. "I knew you'd see that someday. It's just taken you longer than it should have."

With a look of mild embarrassment, I apologized, "Sorry. But I think I'm catching on now." I pointed my toothbrush at him. "I think things will be different. Here it's easy, but I think even after I leave here, I think, as you say, 'I can minimize regrets.'"

He winked at me, and I smiled at him, put my toothbrush in the holder and then went off to bed thankful for a new friendship.

Chapter 33

The morning came, Tuesday morning, a work day, and I lay in bed looking at the ceiling, feeling strange and trying to figure out what the strangeness was. Some people aren't morning people until they'd had their cup of coffee. I'm not a morning person until it's the afternoon. But this morning wasn't like that. I was ready to get up and get going, and my mind and body were trying to reconcile the shock.

After a short time, I rolled out of bed and got ready for work. Grabbing the partially drank can of Dew from the fridge, I looked at the clock. It would be at least a half hour before the carpool guys got here, but I felt full of energy and didn't want to just sit around, so I texted the carpool driver and said to not stop by today. Work was a short drive, and the walk wasn't too bad. I headed out the door, wondering what the day would bring.

* * *

A couple of hours into the work day, Marcus came up to me at my computer in the lab. "Stanley, would you do me a big favor?"

"Does it involve killing anyone?"

He put his hand to his chin and thought a moment, then shook his head. "Think we can avoid it this time, but next time it may be required."

I nodded, trying to hide my smile. "Then I can help this time, but next time it won't be a favor. I'll want lots of money."

"It's a deal, and thanks." He continued with his request without missing a beat. "One of my older sisters is a fourth-grade teacher, and I've been volunteering in her class. I read to 'em. But with the concert and everything, I can't make it 'til things slow down. Could you read to them for me?"

I looked at him confused. "Read to a fourth-grade class? That's the favor you want from me?"

He gave me a worried look. Apparently afraid I'd say "no," he tried to sell the idea. "Really, it's fun. They're a neat group of kids."

"I don't mind doing it," I replied quickly, because I didn't like him thinking that I was offended or anything. "In fact, I'd be very happy to do it. It just wasn't what I expected. Let me check with Aaron. I just started my second week here, so I can't just run off."

Marcus replied with a smile. "Already done. Wanna guess what he said?"

"Wonderful?"

"You got it. He's all for it. Said the documentation's looking 'wonderful.' Everything's cool. Already explained it to my sister."

"So, the guy from the hood who could barely read is now volunteering to read to a fourth-grade class," I said in a friendly way while looking at him.

He handed me a piece of paper. "You got it, brother. Spreading the love." He smiled as he turned away.

I looked at the information on the paper which had the time and directions. He hadn't given me much warning; I was supposed to be there in an hour.

As I turned back to my computer to finish up a couple small things before I left, it dawned on me that I'd walked to work this morning. How was I going to get to the school?

Under my breath, I muttered, "Well, this is another fine mess you've gotten yourself into, Stanley!" and leaned back in my chair trying to figure out how I could get home quick enough to get my car to get to the school on time.

Movement caught my attention, and I looked over to see Aaron coming up the stairs.

He saw me looking at him, and as he headed over, he looked at his watch. Before I could say anything, he said, "Don't you need to get going?"

I raised one side of my mouth in self-disgust. "Aaron, I think I messed up. When Marcus asked me to do this, I'd forgotten I'd walked to work this morning."

He looked at me confused. "You can't take one of the electric cars?"

"What?"

"Didn't anyone explain that to you? That's exactly what they're for."

"Well, duh!" I said, thunking myself on the forehead, feeling like an idiot. "I forgot about them. That's perfect." I sat looking at him, thankful my dilemma was solved.

He looked at me still confused. "Well? Get out of here. Go do something wonderful with your time. And I don't want to see you rushing back to get work done. Helping out at the school is more important than anything we have going on here."

I smiled as I stood. "Thanks, Aaron." And patted him on his shoulder as I walked by.

* * *

I went to Summer to sign out an electric car, and she was thoughtful enough to print out directions for me. I quickly made my way to the solar panel covered charging area and was soon noiselessly zooming down the road.

Following the directions Summer had given me, I found I was getting into an area of Bethlehem I hadn't previously explored. Lawns disappeared as the unkempt houses got closer together, and graffiti was getting more prevalent.

I obviously lived in a better part of the city and didn't know there was this discrepancy. As I got closer to the school things started looking better.

The school itself was a large, nice looking building and contrasted the neighborhood with lot of trees, grass and greenery around it.

I walked toward the school, and was greeted by an official looking gentleman who politely asked if he could help me. He seemed pleased when I explained how I was drafted into reading to a classroom, and he eagerly escorted me to the office to register.

After I registered, one of the office staff accompanied me down a hall painted with colorful childhood art, to a classroom whose door was framed in a bright construction paper arch of grape vines, with large leaves and bunches of fruit. The leaves and fruit bunches bore names that I assumed were students in the classroom, and the arch, over the door declared "Ms. Havens" in rainbow text.

My escort opened the classroom door and waved me into the room.

As I stepped in, I glanced around. I'd been in my kids' classrooms only a handful of times, and in a lot of ways, this room was like any other elementary classroom, a wall of windows across from the door, whiteboards and posters on the walls, desks formed into pods and a reading area in one corner. But at the same time, this room was different. It had a peaceful feeling instead of the restrained chaos I'd felt when visiting my kids' rooms.

I took another step as my escort closed the door behind me, and my movement caught the attention of the teacher, presumably Jeff's daughter. She had straight, dark brown hair, cropped short but stylish, and wore brown pants with a hip-length white shirt. When she looked over from the long whiteboard on the right-hand wall, where she had apparently been watching some kids doing math problems, she smiled widely and exclaimed, "Stanley!" and started walking my way.

As she quickly made her way towards me, I glanced down towards her legs to see why she was limping so badly. She had pants on and had no obvious cast or brace, so I couldn't see what the cause was, but her limp didn't seem to slow her down. I quickly looked up, not wanting her to think I was staring.

After she weaved her way between the pods of desks in the middle of the room where students had been working in groups on some project with colored liquids in bottles, she held out her left hand. "I'm Rita, and I'm sorry I missed you the other night at dinner. I've heard great things about you." Her right hand was held close to her midsection and wasn't formed quite right. I quickly realized her limp wasn't from an injury but a birth defect or childhood disease.

I reached out and shook her hand, while I repeated her name to myself a couple times so I'd remember it. "To tell the truth, Rita, if you hadn't said anything I might not have noticed you weren't there. It was pretty overwhelming, and I only remember a few names." I returned her infectious smile.

She gave a quick laugh. "I understand that. I try to make it there a couple times a week, but it's nice to avoid the chaos with a quiet meal at home when I can." Rita turned and looked out over the room, then looked back at me, held her left hand to her mouth as if she was going to address me privately, but in a loud voice said, "Especially after dealing with these hooligans all day."

The class replied with a number of light-hearted comments, which showed a relaxed relationship with their teacher, but at the same time a deep respect.

Then in a normal voice, she addressed the class. "Mr. Havens is busy getting his CD ready and won't be able to read to us for a while."

The class let out a collective groan, as it took me a quick mental jump to associate Marcus with "Mr. Havens."

Rita, over-powering the groans, added, "But... when I asked him to find a replacement who you'd like, he said he had the perfect person. Class, say 'hello' to Mr. Whitmore."

A disorganized chorus of greetings was tossed my way.

As she turned from the doorway to lead me into the classroom, she said, "Thank you for coming on such short notice."

Following her, I replied, "It's not a problem. I'm looking forward to it." And I was. Rita's positive persona seemed to infect the room itself.

She led me to the far right-hand corner of the room to a reading area situated under the windows, with a group of kids relaxing on bean bags, reading. The kids watched me with curious smiles.

As we stood in front of a pair of well-stocked book shelves, with a sweeping gesture, Rita said, "Take your pick. Marcus just finished the book he was reading so you get to pick the next one."

Instantly, I felt the pressure of having to choose a book the class would like. I didn't know anything about books fourth-graders would enjoy. But luck was with me as I scanned the first row, and my hand automatically reached out and grabbed a book I was familiar with. Showing it to Rita, I asked, "Has your class read this?"

A look of approval came to her face. "No, they haven't, and it's one of my favorites. You have excellent taste."

I breathed a sigh of relief as Rita started towards the whiteboard at the front of the room. When we got there, she pointed towards a tall stool for me to sit on and then addressed the class. "Get comfortable for the story."

From behind us, I heard, "Ms. Havens?"

We both turned and looked. A girl who was at the whiteboard doing math problems when I first came in was looking at us.

Once the girl had Rita's attention, the child asked, "Can we finish the contest? We only have one more problem to break the tie."

Rita looked towards me as if it was my choice. I shrugged and said, "That's fine with me."

I was rewarded with a smile of approval. The girl and boy at the board each copied two five-digit numbers side-by-side, separated by a multiplication sign, from their book onto the whiteboard. Another boy and girl pair had their backs to the board waiting for the problems to be written.

The girl at the board said, "Ready!"

The pair with their backs to the board tensed up, ready for the contest to begin. The whole class watched.

The start sequence continued, "set, go!"

The contestants turned to face the board and began writing numbers under the left most number.

Things had obviously changed since I was in school. When I was a kid, five-digit multiplication meant five rows of numbers under the problem, which then had to be added up at the bottom. These kids quickly wrote numbers, from right to left, in one row, and the clunk of the girl's marker being set on the tray was instantly followed by the boy's. The two answers were the same, and the girl who gave the starting call looked at what was apparently the answer in the book and declared it correct. The girl who'd set her marker down first did a little happy dance to the approval of her classmates, and her opponent took it with good grace.

I nodded approvingly and looked at Rita. "Impressive."

She smiled with pride. "Ever see the Trachtenberg System in action?"

I shook my head. "Never even heard of it."

"They can do arithmetic as fast as they can write the numbers. It's amazing it isn't taught everywhere."

"Interesting, and impressive to watch."

As the children from the board started making their way to their desk, Rita once again told the kids to get ready for reading time.

Some students brought bean bags to sit in front of me, others just relaxed at their desks.

Rita gave me a look which let me know it was all in my hands as, surprisingly, she settled onto a bean bag also. Way back in my student teaching days, most of the teachers I knew used opportunities like this to exit the room for a break from the kids.

I chided myself for being so cynical. There were many hard working teachers, and maybe if I hadn't left the classroom every chance I got, I wouldn't have mingled so much with the teachers who'd lost their spark.

I looked down at Rita. Her spark was infectious. She looked on with an excited gaze, waiting for the story to start. Looking out over the children's faces I saw the same excited gaze modeled by their teacher.

With all the eyes focused on me, I realized I was actually a little nervous. I had looked out on a class of high school kids during my student teaching days, many years ago, but these fourth-grader faces were different. They were so young. Not so cynical and closed up. Smiling, I started to speak but a hand went up, and I nodded to let the girl know she could talk.

"Do you have kids?"

Thankful for the question which would help break the ice, I answered, "Yes, I have a six-year-old daughter named Alice."

A boy interrupted. "Does she live in Wonderland?"

That made me smile. "She probably doesn't think so."

That got a laugh from the class.

"And I have an eight-year-old son named Cooper. I can tell you, he's positive he doesn't live in Wonderland."

Which got another laugh.

Another hand went up. "Are you going to play guitar for us like Mr. Havens?"

Giving them a jokingly serious face, I answered, "Oh no, you wouldn't like that. You'd run from the room screaming."

The light-hearted question-and-answer period went on for a few minutes. As it did, I felt a connection grow with the children. When Marcus asked me to do this, I was doing him a favor and hadn't really thought about it. But now, I was enjoying being here, and the kids seemed to like having me here.

A boy near the front asked, "What are you going to read?"

I pointed at him. "Ah! A very good question. This is a book I've read to my kids. When I saw it on the shelf I knew it was exactly what I wanted to read to you." I held it up, showing the class the cover. "*Hatchet*, by Gary Paulsen."

Turning the book so I could see the cover again, I thought about why this book had jumped out at me so quickly. I voiced my thoughts. "It's about a boy who's in a plane crash. A two-seater plane. The pilot is killed, so the boy is stranded in the Canadian woods by himself. He has to learn to survive all by himself." Looking away from the cover to the faces listening to me, I added, "I guess what I found so interesting is how the boy adapted and grew. He was in a bad situation but kept moving forward. Kept doing what he needed to do to survive."

I paused, then repeated, more to myself than to the class, "The things that go wrong in his life end up building him, making him stronger, helping him reach his potential."

Feeling dazed, I turned to Rita sitting on a bean bag with her crippled hand resting on her leg. She had a wide smile on her face.

For a moment, it was like seeing Jeff's face looking back at me, saying, "I think you're finally starting to get it." A chill ran up my spine, and I turned away from her.

If the class noticed my shock, they didn't react to it. They eagerly looked on, waiting for me to continue.

I opened the book and began to read.

What seemed like only a short while later, a bell rang, startling me so much the book fell out of my hands, and a burst of laughter filled the class. Somewhat embarrassed, I picked the book up and tried to find the page I'd last read, to mark my stopping point, and discovered I was almost forty pages into the book.

With difficulty, Rita began to rise from the bean bag. As I watched her push up off the ground using only her left hand and then with effort get her right leg under her to stand, I admired her even more for including herself in the class instead of sitting aside, excluded, at her desk or leaving for the teacher's lounge.

She walked up and thanked me, and then invited me to eat lunch with them. There was a chorus of "please" from the kids.

Surprised at the invitation, I looked out at them and smiled. "Sure."

Chapter 34

Standing in what appeared to be a typical school lunch line, I chatted with the kids about the book and was happy to discover they'd actually listened to the story. Eventually, the line moved me through the doorway and into the serving area. I took a tray and placed it on the stainless-steel tray rails, exactly like at my kid's school. After looking up from my tray to the food and then to the cafeteria staff, I turned to Rita behind me in line. "Let me guess, training ground for the culinary school."

She grinned at me. "I see you noticed a similarity to HRI's cafeteria."

"Vaguely," I joked. "Guess this is the efficiency version."

"Exactly. We can't serve all the choices that HRI does, but it's good food and, as much as possible, from local farms."

I looked at my choices; none of which were the canned foods that had been plopped on my tray when I was in school years ago, or eaten with my kids at their school. This looked edible and smelled great. I paid the cashier at the end of the line a very reasonable sum and followed Rita and her class towards the tables.

Sitting at a long cafeteria table with the kids and Rita, I looked around at the other tables and realized there were quite a few adults eating with the students. One of the things I had noticed when eating with Thing 1 and Thing 2 was that most of the teachers used their lunch period as a time to be away from the students, but clearly, that wasn't the case here.

As we ate, I watched Rita talk with her students. She listened intently, as if what they said was important. It was clear the kids adored her.

Including me in their camaraderie, the kids and I talked about normal school stuff, but I wasn't getting the answers I'd expected. "What's your favorite subject?" was answered with actual subjects or "all of them," when I'd been expecting at least one kid to answer "recess," "lunch," or "summer vacation." Then I asked how their grades were and got blank stares.

Rita interrupted, "One thing about having Jeff Havens," saying her dad's name in a playfully low voice, "in the community is that he pumps a lot of money into it, which means he gets some say into how that money's used. At his suggestion, the district picked a couple of its lower performing schools as test beds for new teaching methods."

A bell went off as she was talking, and the kids started gathering their trays and standing. I quickly scooped up the last bite of green beans and followed.

Rita turned to me as we walked to the conveyor belt with our trays. "Do you need to get back? If not, you can hang out with us for recess, and I can tell you more about our school, if you're interested."

I was extremely interested, and I already had Aaron's order to not rush back, so the answer was easy. "Sure, that'd be great."

After we dropped off our trays, Rita and I followed the kids to the playground and found a bench facing a kickball field. Sitting, I looked around the playground and mentally compared it to my kids' school. I'd read that the trend in most schools was to minimize recess to gain more classroom time. The playground at my kids' school reflected that mentality with minimal space and equipment outside.

Over the years, I'd felt sorry for Cooper's various teachers. My kid was a little ball of energy stuck behind a desk all day. As far as I was concerned, it wasn't any wonder the schools were having so much trouble keeping boys interested in classroom activities and the Ritalin usage rates were skyrocketing. When the schools refused to give kids opportunity to burn off their energy and forced them to sit for unnaturally long periods and quietly listen, what did the schools expect would happen? Their attitude seemed the antithesis of a normal childhood.

But it was obvious this school hadn't bought into that mentality. Not only did they have an actual field for kickball—where a bunch of kids choosing up sides for an impromptu game much like baseball except with a big rubber ball that they'd kick—but the school also had plenty of other equipment to help kids burn off their energy.

We watched the game for a while as I thought about what I'd

seen so far in this school. It was so different. It was an exciting place to be, in much the same way that HRI was an exciting place to be. Jeff's handiwork was apparent in both situations. I looked over at Rita. "Your dad sure knows how to make things different, doesn't he?"

Her smile grew wide as she nodded. "Without a doubt." She paused and her expression changed to a more serious one. It appeared like a series of thoughts had been triggered by my question. I could only imagine what she'd experienced with him, or before him, and the memories seemed to be bouncing behind her eyes right now, which made me feel a little guilty for foolishly saying something which apparently carried so many emotions for her. But as she watched the kickball game, her smile gradually started coming back.

"Yes, everything he touches transforms." I followed her glance as she scanned the playground, then she continued, "Look at this place. When I was little, school was terrible for a girl with challenges like I had. But not here."

I didn't know what to say. Remembering how some of the physically and mentally disabled kids were taunted when I was in school, I could only imagine the cruelty she'd suffered.

Yet, the interesting thing was, as she watched the children play, I realized her thoughts were about them, not her. In a compassionate voice, she confirmed my realization. "They've been given a wonderful opportunity with this school. In turn, they'll go out into the world and give the same opportunity to others."

"How so?" I asked, curious for her take on the situation.

"Because of the money Dad puts into this school." Rita spoke as she looked out over the game, as the teams swapped positions. "He does it so wisely. We're a research facility, trying to discover how to really educate kids. The teachers here aren't simply teachers; they're researchers."

Surprised, I asked, "Researchers?"

She nodded. "Our day begins and ends with research staff meetings to go over results of ongoing studies. My class has two actual teachers; my teaching partner is off presenting an in-service in one of the neighboring districts today. Which is too bad, you'd like him." She glanced at me with a hopeful look. "But he'll be here next time you come read."

I understood her implied question of whether I was coming back or not. "I'll look forward to meeting him."

"Great. Each classroom shares a set of full time researchers, not teacher slash researchers, with other classes of the same grade, to try to eliminate teacher bias from the studies. We also have a variety of different types of psychologists and scientists on staff. And we regularly publish papers in peer-reviewed journals, so other educators can benefit from our research."

"It sounds like the kids are lab rats," I said, then instantly regretted my words.

But she only shrugged. "I guess you could say that, and some people do. That's why our processes are implemented in only some of the schools and not the whole district. Some parents and students don't feel comfortable with the changes here, so the district gave them the option to stay in normal school settings." While looking affectionately out at the kids playing, she added, "But these are the lucky lab rats. And they're cute and sweet."

With her left hand, she adjusted her right arm as she paused to think. "A lot of work and thought goes into what we do to ensure it's less destructive than the normal public school. That's our bar."

It sounded like a slam to typical public schools. "Do you see public schools as destructive?"

"Not intentionally, and I certainly am not discrediting those who've dedicated their lives to serving. But it's a flawed system, and most people know it. There are good schools and bad schools, but the balance isn't even and doesn't work in the favor of many kids. The homeschooling movement is growing for a reason. People are losing faith in the education system."

I reflected on my frustrations with my kids' school and could understand what she meant. "So, what are you folks actually doing differently?"

"Oh, where to start?" She thought for a moment. "Well, I do think that what we do here in the classroom is important, but I guess the two places we focus on that most schools can't are family and community. Everything starts and stops there. No matter how hard we try to improve the classroom, no matter how much we care for the kids, if we send a child home to be beaten, ridiculed, exposed to drugs, or even ignored, as teachers, we won't succeed. And... no matter how much a parent tries, no matter how much they care, if they send their child out into a community to be beaten, ridiculed, exposed to drugs, or even ignored, none of us will succeed."

A red kickball came bouncing toward my legs. I reached down, picked it up, and threw it to the child running towards me.

Rita waited and then turned to face me. "We have a massive volunteer base of parents, teachers, churches and community members who want to see these schools succeed. They work with community businesses to get their employees involved in the school and in their children's education. Next, we work with any parent who is unemployed, or under employed, to either get them a job or an education that fits their needs."

I watched the kickball game for a moment, thinking about her comments. As I thought, it really sank in, for the first time, how hard it would be for a kid to get an education if the family or community situation was a mess, and how really glad I was that I hadn't pursued teaching. I wasn't built to handle the kind of stress teachers today had to deal with. The teachers who could do it, like the one sitting beside me, were saints in my book.

Rita patiently waited until I turned back. "We work with community churches, of all faiths, to get families involved and to help families that need help."

I was impressed. "That's outstanding."

She smiled. "Drive around to businesses near this school and look at their windows. They'll have displays that support our sports teams, but most will also have displays that support our scholastic competitions as well, like UIL."

She looked at me questioningly, and I let her know I understood. "University Interscholastic League. Cooper, my son, has competed in some of their events. In my town, UIL doesn't get much notice from anyone other than the participants' parents."

"It's a big deal here just like the science fairs, art, theater arts, spelling bees, music, and chess matches. We're working with our community and families to change what they value. Sports in schools are great, but education is what's really important and exciting. It's also vital for America's future."

"How so?" I had my ideas, but wanted to hear hers.

She looked around at the kids for a moment, apparently thinking of how to start. "An ancient proverb says that a society's values can be judged by what it pays its professionals. If we look at America through that lens, we apparently value entertainment and sports the highest, because those are the professionals we pay the most, and education is very far down the list. Unfortunately, history has plenty of examples to show us that any society who values education so little is destined to fail. We," she emphasized the word and swung out a hand to embrace the whole of America, "are destined to fail, unless we change."

I nodded. "I've read a lot of news articles that talk about how far behind American students are, especially in the sciences."

"Exactly! Which isn't to say that sports and entertainment are bad, because obviously they're not, as long as they are valued less than education. The teachers in this school are some of the highest paid professionals in the community. All of our sports positions are volunteer."

"Interesting."

"What's really interesting is that under our system the whole dynamics of sports changes. The people who coach, do it because they love to coach and because they love the kids. The kids play, because they love to play, not because of the status associated with the game. And if I do say so myself, our sports teams are doing great, and the games are fun to watch. But our school's superstars are in our classrooms."

That was actually pretty exciting to hear. "I like it. I'll have to come to some of the scholastic events and sports events while I'm here."

She nodded approvingly, and we watched some more of the kickball game. The kicker gave a powerful kick but the ball went too high and was caught by an infielder. It must have been the third out because the teams changed positions.

We watched as I thought about our conversation in the lunchroom. "So, the lack of grades? Jeff, your dad, had something to do with that?"

She nodded. "He hates the concept of grades. I think 'hate' might even be too weak of a word for what he feels."

I had to laugh to myself at that. Of all the things in the world for a "messiah" to hate, grades seemed a strange thing. Yet, for a reason that I couldn't quite formulate into a thought, it fit with Jeff. But I was curious about Rita's thoughts. "Why would they bother him so much?"

Rita shrugged like the answer was obvious. "Grades are a distraction. When a student's goal is to get an 'A' or 'B', they learn just enough to get that 'A' or 'B'. Whereas, if their goal is to gain knowledge and understand the concepts enough to apply them, they'll learn in a different manner, one that means they will likely retain the knowledge for life. That's the mindset we're growing here. From a teaching standpoint, when we study about the discovery of America, our goal is for the students to learn about the discovery of

America. We really get into it. We read from many different sources—not just one approved textbook—we take field trips, we bring in guest speakers, we learn from everywhere we can, everything we can."

I repeated her earlier statement. "Grades are a distraction." I'd have to think more, because those words seemed to hold some meaning beyond just grades.

Turning the subject back to the school, I asked, "None of this fits with the current rhetoric I'm hearing about education. In most schools, there's a lot of focus on standardized tests. It seems to be all my kids' school worries about."

I prepared for a look of disgust since all the teachers I knew hated the standardized tests, but I was given a captivating smile. "We love standardized tests. There's a lot of controversy about teaching to the test, but we actually do that here and see the value."

Surprised, I motioned for her to continue.

"As researchers, we understand the need for quantitative data. Plus, test taking is a skill that needs to be learned, and it wouldn't be fair to not teach our students that skill. In the classroom, we spend about four hours a week preparing for standardized tests and the rest of the time is for real education." She gave me a conspiratorial look. "We blow the curve on the tests, and the kids are prepared so well they find the tests trivial most of the time."

I laughed. "I bet they do." I took a moment to admire the woman sitting beside me. She was fascinating, and I wondered more about her. "On a personal note, you went to college, right?"

"Sure."

"Where does your dad stand on that? Grace said he told her she didn't need college. And it's easy to see that Marcus is going because he feels he needs to prove something. How about you?"

She nodded, as if she'd been expecting the question. "For me, specifically, I couldn't teach if I didn't have a degree. But in general, if a kid in our family is a self-learner, like Grace, they can gain more by working at a job that caters to their interest, as long as they don't narrow their focus to exclude essential knowledge like history, math, writing, and so on. For some of my other siblings, college or trade school gives them the structure they need. The path we take is up to us, not Dad. As long as we can provide sound reasoning, he'll support us, unconditionally." She paused for emphasis. "And just as with grades, no one needs a degree, but they *do* need to be educated."

Nodding understandingly, I said, "Interesting."

A group of girls from her class ran by, taking a quick detour to give Rita a hug. Their affection for her was clear.

After they ran off again, I noted, "It seems like you picked the right field of study for yourself. Just in this short time in your class, I can tell how deeply you've touched these kids."

"I can't imagine doing anything else."

I glanced up and noticed the boy walking to the kickball plate had a limp reminding me of Rita's. His teammates shouted encouragement as the ball was thrown, and the boy succeeded in kicking the ball, but the ball only rolled a few feet. Even so, he started running as fast as he could, which wasn't very fast, towards first base.

As he ran, an unexpected thing happened, the members of both teams remained in place, and together started counting down. "10... 9..."

I looked at Rita, she just smiled and waved a hand for me to look back.

"3... 2... 1... 0!" Suddenly, the fielding team burst into action as the base runners sprinted to the next bases, and by the time the catcher retrieved the ball from where it'd rolled and heaved it to first base, the boy had made it safely.

I look at Rita, again. "What's that?"

She grinned. "He's new to the school, and soon after he arrived, the other players noticed him watching the games and invited him to play. He refused."

"Can understand why." As slow as the boy ran, he'd never make it to a base safely, but interestingly enough, he had.

"Yep. But the other players knew he wanted to play." Rita looked out at the boy on first base. "Peer-pressure can be a good thing. The other players pestered him until they found out what it would take to get him to play."

I was watching him, too. Standing on first base, leaning forward ready to run, he had a grin which only meant one thing, it wasn't peer-pressure that got him to play. "Acceptance is even better," I said interrupting her.

She stopped for a second to think about that. "You're a smart man. I can see why my dad and family like you. But back to the kids, you can see they worked out a deal. Anytime he kicks the ball, he has a ten-second head start to run to the base. And the greatest thing is that when they first came up with the plan, he needed fifteen seconds, but he's down to ten seconds and moving faster every day."

"That's just too cool," I replied still looking at the kid. "Too cool."

The next kid kicked the ball, right to the second baseman, and the limping boy got tagged out running to second, but the grin on his face wasn't dimmed in the least as the teams started switching positions. As he limped to the outfield, players from both teams patted him on the back as they ran by.

I turned and looked out towards the rest of the playground as I spoke, "You know, I still remember the feeling of recess and the groups I could and couldn't play with. I spent a lot of time by myself." I scanned, looking for a boy like me, one who didn't seem to fit, the one whose face showed his longing to be asked to play. "There was a group of boys I had to watch out for. Hide from. It was like they'd look for me every recess, and I'd be glad when I saw them picking on someone else, because it meant I was safe." I looked around for the kid nervously watching for the bully.

"When I was in school," Rita said softly, "I gave up on recess and found teachers who let me help them in the classroom, while the other kids went out to play."

Switching my focus from the playground to her, I knew she understood the feelings I was remembering. "The news has had some coverage on problems caused by bullying. Some of the school shootings seem to link back to it. Granted, I'm only sitting on a bench watching, but to me, there's a feeling of togetherness here, instead of exclusion."

She nodded. "That isn't by accident. We actively teach social skills. Sometimes, we line up at the slide and role play being a bully in the line. Or we role play striking out in kickball and being laughed at. Or we role play striking out in a game and being encouraged by our teammates."

"That works?"

"It isn't magic, but after a while the kids seem to get it. We don't have much of a problem here with bullying, because we've been doing social skills education for so long. But other schools do. That's where my teaching partner is right now. He's at a neighboring school teaching an in-service on role-playing social skills."

I gave an approving nod. "I like that idea."

She added, "In many public schools, so much of the teacher's time is spent on dealing with behavior problems they don't have time left over to teach state-mandated concepts. The classrooms' time on-task is alarmingly low. In my opinion, they'd be better off spending time at the beginning of the school year teaching social skills, so that by the end of the year, the time on-task in the classroom would be almost one-hundred-percent."

"Fascinating!" was all I could think to say.

The bell rang ending recess.

Some things, I thought with a smile, schools couldn't get away from.

After saying good-bye to the kids and promising to come back, I signed out at the office, and walked to the electric car.

As I got in, I caught my reflection in the rear view mirror, and my new friend from last night smiled back at me.

In that instant, I realized how much I'd enjoyed experiencing this awesome school. I needed to make sure to thank Marcus for the wonderful opportunity he'd given me.

* * *

As the electric car silently breezed down the road toward work, I thought about my kids' school. Beth and I had always been disappointed in it.

Our perspective had been poisoned by Cooper's kindergarten experience. Most nights, he'd come home with about two hours of homework, and many times, he'd had to stay after school to finish the work he hadn't been able to complete during class. Beth and I had considered that an awful situation for a kindergartner, and we'd complained to the teacher, to no avail. But the worst experience happened one of the last days of the school year. His class went on a field trip, but because Beth and I had forgotten to return his homework folder, he'd had to write sentences while he watched the other kids play. To us, kindergarten should've been a place to start a child's love of learning, not a year spent comforting a crying child. Since then, in our eyes, the school could do almost no right.

We'd talked about homeschooling our kids but hadn't made that move. With a full-time job, I didn't have the time to be their homeschooling teacher, and even as frustrated as we were by the school system, Beth was worried that she wouldn't be able to provide what the kids needed to get a thorough education.

As those thoughts crossed my mind, the flood gates of guilty realization opened. I'd let Cooper's kindergarten experience poison my perspective more than I'd thought. Other than the few times I had eaten lunch with my kids or went to parent-teacher conferences,

I'd rarely been to their school. The one thing Rita had made clear today was the reason her school, and the kids in it, were so successful was because the community was involved and volunteerism was the norm. Was I using that one year's bad experience as an excuse to limit my commitment to my kids' schooling?

What was Cooper's teacher's name last year? I couldn't remember. Alice's teacher was Mr. Wheeler or Mr. Welder or something like that. And as I thought about it, I wasn't even sure I'd actually met either teacher; I think Beth had gone to their student-teacher conferences. And now, school was about to start, and I hadn't even looked up their new teachers.

I'd met the principal once. Mr. Ham-something. He'd seemed like a decent enough guy. Maybe, all those years ago, we should have talked to him about our experience, instead of just complaining to the teacher.

When the next thought struck me, I had to pull over into a parking lot and lean my head against the steering wheel.

In a blinding flash of the obvious, I'd realized that for all these years, I'd been putting the entire responsibility for my kids' school experience on the school and taking no responsibility myself.

I sat up and looked in the rearview mirror and saw my friend from last night's bathroom mirror. His expression was one of gentle encouragement, inviting me to offer a solution.

I knew what he was thinking. "It's easy. When I got back home, even if I have a job, I can take a bigger part in the kids' school."

He nodded at me.

"I really enjoyed reading to those kids today. I could start with something like that."

He gave me an approving look and, as I pulled back on the road, I was feeling much better.

Chapter 35

I walked back into the building and waved at Summer. Even though Aaron had given me permission to spend as much time as I needed at Rita's school, I felt guilty having spent lunch there, too. Mostly because, I knew my time here at HRI was short, and I wanted to get enough work completed that they felt like I'd done a good job. So, taking an entire morning off to read to school kids, no matter how valuable, went against the grain.

I waved to a couple more people as I headed back to my desk, when a realization hit. I wasn't doing stuff just to look good and feeling guilty because I wasn't doing it. I *wanted* to get back to working on the documents because I had so many ideas rolling around in my head that if I didn't get them down on paper quickly I felt like my head was going to explode.

Sitting down at my desk and logging back into my computer, I admired the novelty of wanting, no *needing*, to get back to work on my documents... how strange. Good. But strange.

Within minutes, I was so into my task that when the lab alarm went off, I added a bunch of unintentional letters to my current document before I managed to lift my fingers from the keyboard and look around. *It was six already?*

Indeed it was, so I made some quick notes in the document so I could easily pick up the updating tomorrow, then checked my email. There were a bunch of usual work stuff, plus one of the guys I was carpooling with asked if I wanted to go to a rock climbing gym in a nearby town with a group from work. It sounded like grand fun and something I had always wanted to try, and thankfully, I'd been bringing gym clothes to work with me on the off-chance I'd get invited to play racquetball, so I accepted the offer enthusiastically.

Then I sent a quick text message to Beth so she wouldn't expect me on Skype that evening. A couple minutes later, I got back a reply from her with a smiley face and "have fun."

* * *

The next morning, I sincerely regretted my decision to go rock climbing. Every muscle in my body hurt just lying in bed, and I knew moving was going to hurt worse. After a long debate with myself, I worked up the courage to slowly sit up, biting my lower lip to endure the pain.

I'd thought I was in pretty good shape, but obviously not. And equally obvious, I should have taken it easier at the gym, but I'd been having too much fun, and now I was paying for it.

I grabbed my phone as I painfully made my way to the bathroom to run a hot bath. It didn't help my ego when my carpool buddy couldn't stop laughing as I told him why I'd be driving myself today. Grumbling at my own stupidity, I downed some pain pills and climbed into the tub, and yet, even with all the pain, I was looking forward to the next time I could go to the rock climbing gym.

Thankfully, the bath helped some, and once the pills kicked in and I started moving, my muscles started feeling better.

I made it into work, walking very slowly, and spent the day working at my desk in the cube area outside the lab, because it was closer, and I would be less tempted to take the stairs down to lab floor to work on a flywheel system.

By three o'clock, I decided I'd had enough. Whatever enthusiasm I'd had yesterday was overshadowed by the pain, which distracted me enough that I could barely form words into sentences. Given my relative incoherence, it was easy to rationalize my desire to go home and sleep. I told myself that since I'd come in late I'd make it up by leaving early.

As I slowly and painfully walked out the front of the building, a moment of dread filled me as I saw Jeff leaning against the wooden railing of the bridge over the entrance stream. "Busted!" I sputtered.

A look of amusement came to his face as he watched me drag my hurting body his way. "Rough night, friend?"

After making it to the bridge, I bent forward gradually letting my back muscles loosen up enough to lean my elbows on the railing beside him. "Nope. Feeling pretty good."

He laughed. "Want me to fix it?" he asked while looking at me with a devious smile.

Remembering the kiss in the hotel room on the trip out here, I replied, "I'll slug you again if you try." I gave him a weary look and said, "And I earned this pain so you aren't going to take it away."

His face switched from amusement to playful approval. "I like that philosophy."

It was hard to know how much he was joking with me, but I let it drop. I hadn't seen too much of Jeff since I'd been here, and I found myself glad to see him, even if he always stressed me out.

He straightened from the railing and asked, "You up for doing something or too sore?"

"What're you thinking about? I mean, I'm not going rock climbing for a few days or playing racquetball."

He gave an amused snort. "Na, nothing like that. Some leisurely walking at most."

Shrugging, I replied, "Sure, I think I can handle that."

Jeff turned and started making his way to the parking lot. "Great! Let's go shopping."

I gave him a look of horror as I slowly followed. "Jeff! Out of all the things you've said to me, out of all the things I've seen and been through with you, that's now at the top of my weirdest-things-ever list. Guys don't say that to each other. You may be on a quest to change the world, but that part of the world I really don't want to change."

"So? You'll go?"

"Sure, why not." If nothing else, shopping with Jeff was bound to be more interesting than watching TV back in my hotel room.

"Good, you're driving."

We got in my car, and for once I regretted getting a stick-shift car, but it didn't hurt as much as it had that morning, so I gritted my teeth and drove as he guided me to where he wanted to go. It was a typical strip mall exactly like thousands of others littering the country.

Thankfully, I found a parking spot near the front of one of the big box stores in the center of the complex so I didn't have to walk far. Getting out of the car was bad, but once I started moving I was okay again.

I followed Jeff to one of those stores where everything's a dollar. Jeff pulled open the glass door and held it for me. After the door closed behind us, I let him lead as we wandered down the first aisle.

He picked up a plastic soap dish, looked at it, then put it back and wandered a little further and picked up a rubber box that I didn't know what it was for, looked at it and put it back, then picked up more stuff I really couldn't even tell what they were and looked at them.

All the while, I wondered why we were here and what he could possibly be looking for. Why would Jeff—who owned a thriving business, a mansion, and a Rolls—want to shop in a store like this?

After about five minutes of going down aisles where a couple things looked like they might be good values, but the majority looked like junk, my patience expired. "What're you looking for, maybe we could ask somebody to help find it?"

"Oh, nothing really. Just looking around," he casually answered, as he picked up something else.

Fed up, I heaved a sigh and, hoping he would get the message, I went to the front of the store and stood by the door, waiting.

After an annoyingly long time, we left, and I followed him to a clothing store. Then we went into another clothing store, and then yet another clothing store. After about two minutes looking at dress pants, I'd had enough and walked outside to lean against the pillar holding up the awning that covered the walkway in front of the stores. Guys weren't made for this kind of shopping. If we wanted something, we knew what we wanted, we knew who sold it, and we went there and bought it; none of this browsing stuff.

Jeff soon joined me, and with my arms crossed in a way I knew was belligerent, I quietly exclaimed, "Enough already! What are you looking for? I'll help you find it!"

In a playful "Jeff" way he answered, "Oh, that would be great." He inquisitively tipped his head toward the doors of the store we just left. "Did you see 'contentment' on any of the racks in there?" He looked at me, smiling. "I was hoping to get a two-for-one deal on it."

I sighed in irritation at him, which he ignored.

"Which aisle do you think shelves 'happiness'? Which store do you think sells 'validation'? I don't see it here." He turned and pointed towards a large electronics store, which was much further than I wanted to walk, and said, "Bet they have it. Or there's a hardware store next to that, maybe it's there?"

My irritation bloomed into anger. Yeah, sure, the guy could be seriously frustrating at times, but in the end, he was fun to be around, but not this time.

We were partially blocking the sidewalk and some shoppers wanted by, so I held my tongue until they were out of hearing range, then I let loose. "So, you're torturing me to make a point I already understand? I don't come to places like this—" I waved my hand at the line of stores "—and look for validation or happiness, and my wife doesn't either. Why are you doing this to me? And in such a stupid way?"

"I know you don't, but look around. Look at all these people." He gestured to the next group of shoppers walking toward us, but I refused to give him the satisfaction of looking and kept my annoyed focus on him. He didn't seem to notice. "Many of them have closets full of clothes and are here to buy more. Then they'll go next door to the dollar store and buy stuff that'll go into the garbage in less than a week without ever serving a purpose."

Anger morphed to confusion. "Jeff, aren't you making a lot of gross generalizations? That isn't like you."

With a faux introspective expression, he said, "Huh? Am I?"

In a way, I was almost happy about this; Jeff hadn't lost his mind, he really hadn't wanted to go shopping, he'd dragged me here to prove some esoteric point.

I decided the quickest way to get this over with and get home to rest my aching body was to plow head-first into it. "Yeah, over-generalizing. But let's go with that, people buy stuff in an attempt to buy happiness or status. They go to stores that sell expensive status symbols they can't afford, where they whip out the credit card to pay for it and go even further into debt at a twenty-five percent interest rate." I shrugged at him. "This isn't a big shock, Jeff. I'm used to more from you. I usually can't sleep after I spend time with you because my head's spinning. Now, you're here telling me people spend too much money to try to feel better about their life? That's not a new concept to me."

He put his hand to his chin. "Hmmm... Not impressed? You're a bright guy. Okay, oh enlightened one, explain economics to me." He taunted me.

"What do you mean? People make stuff, so other people can make money, so they can buy stuff?"

"Sure, that's a good start, for a fifth grader. Look at our chain store over there." He pointed towards the building on the other side of the parking lot. "Explain how it works for them."

"The same, just a bigger scale. A lot of people go buy stuff, so the company can pay their employees a little and their top executives a lot. Then those employees go buy stuff from other businesses with their money. Around and around the money goes."

He nodded, then continued with the leading questions, "And what happens when people slow down their buying?"

"The economy slows down and we may go into a recession or, even worse, a depression. The stock market then tanks, company profits decrease, and top executives lay off people who live paycheck-to-paycheck so the executives don't have to cut their own salaries and bonuses." I was trying to stay ahead of him.

He looked at me with questioning eyes but still with his smile. "You really have something against the executives, don't you? Don't you like CEO's of companies?"

Returning his smile, I said, "I've met one I like. I'm sure if things got tough at the Institute, you'd be the first to cut your pay so people could keep their jobs."

He smiled some more. "No, I actually wouldn't do that."

I let a questioning look came across my face, but he said nothing. Then it hit me. "Don't tell me you don't get paid? How can you walk around with hundred dollar bills all the time?"

"I get paid, but my salary's the lowest in the company. I don't need more. My living expenses are almost nil, since I live in my parent's house — which is paid for — and I drive the 1966 car they left me."

I burst out laughing. "I love the way you spin that. You make it sound so meager. You have the most beautiful house I've ever seen, and the old car they left you is a vintage Rolls worth more than my house." I knew he was playing with me. "But your food bill has to be astronomical."

I loved seeing the smile in his eyes. It's always so warm and friendly. It lets you know you can't do anything wrong. "Well, I see your point, but food comes out of Jonathan's budget, and my point is still valid. I have no debt and very low living expenses relative to my family size. What my parents left Jonathan and me is more than I could ever spend or give away, so I don't need to make money, therefore why pay myself more than I need? But anyway, back to our discussion. So, a company announces its sales are down, and then their stock goes down, right?"

"Right."

"And when a company announces huge profits, then their stock, in most cases, goes up, right?"

"Jeff, this is still Economics 101. Where you going with this?" I was starting to lose my patience again, and the post I was leaning against was getting hard.

"In Jesus' day, there were roughly two-hundred-million people alive. And now we've topped seven billion." He stepped away and waved at me to follow. He walked as he talked. "How many times has the population doubled in those two thousand years?"

As I followed him, I started counting my fingers and carrying tens and finally said, "A lot."

"That's pretty darn close. How many more times can¯ the population double?" He sat on a bench in the shade of the awning, in front of one of the clothing stores, and waved for me to take the place beside him.

I thought about his question as I sat. If we doubled the current population, that would be over fourteen billion and then twenty-eight billion. "Man, one, maybe two more times? I hope not more than that."

"Right. And depending on who you talk to and their assumptions, future population estimates are all over the map. Some extremely pessimistic estimates put the current doubling time at about sixty-five years, with more growth after that. Neutral estimates say that population growth is slowing and will stabilize. With the best-case estimates saying we'll top out our growth at only a few billion more people than now, and then world population starts to decline.

"But—" he paused for emphasis "—for the sake of argument, let's say the stabilizing-population-people are wrong and the Earth's population growth doesn't slow, what'll happen then?"

"It seems pretty obvious. At some point there won't be enough resources for everybody, and the economy collapses."

He nodded. "So, back to our Economics 101 lesson. Let's look at the opposite case, the population stabilizes or even starts to decline, what'll happen then?"

"Well, I guess the number of consumers would eventually stabilize or actually decline?" I was grasping at straws to figure out where he was going.

"Exactly. Which is great, resource-wise. But bad, because the current world economy is based on growth. And if we believe the optimistic estimates, we're quickly running out of years of growth. What'll happen to the economy then?"

I thought a long moment, turning ideas over in my head. "I guess that the reduced demand for goods, from a stable or reduced population size, will force us to abandon our current growth-based economic model." I smiled to myself, because that sounded very profound.

Jeff nodded again. "Whether they like it or not, humankind is going to be forced to change, because the current economic model can't be sustained much longer. The question is whether they'll have the foresight to plan proactively or are they going to handle it reactively after disaster strikes."

I leaned back to think.

Jeff gave me a minute, and then added, "As in all history, the people who have the most to lose in the shift to a new system are going to fight the hardest to keep the status quo. And they'll obfuscate the facts, as much as they can, to make it easier for everyone to justify not changing."

I attempted to sum up some history. "From what I understand, even back in the beginning days of civilization, societies sought out new societies to trade with, so they could make more money. Which means that the growth-based economy has been around basically forever. How can an economy be anything but growth-based?"

"Let's look at a different perspective. Why is gold worth so much, but the rocks that make up the concrete—" he tapped his foot on the walkway "—are almost worthless?"

"Because gold is harder to come by. It's less available, therefore more valuable."

"Okay. Now, as an exercise, imagine anyone could walk into these stores and get whatever they want for free... gold, diamonds... anything."

"Huh." The possibilities boggled my mind.

"Let's take it a different way. Imagine you could go to the car dealership and hop in a car and drive it off, for free. Same thing with the electronics shop down the way. So, you could have the ultra-big screen, 3D, HD, surround sound TV and the BMW 7 Series, and all the other status symbols you've always wanted."

Jokingly, I asked, "Just a BMW? I've been eyeing an Aston Martin." But something was rolling around in my head that I couldn't quite grasp.

He looked up in the air thoughtfully. "Yeah, an Aston Martin would work too." Looking back at me, he went on, "But everyone else could have one, too. Now, in this hypothetical world, if everyone on your block had a BMW 7 Series in their drive," he held out his hand towards me, "or an Aston Martin, there wouldn't be any status associated with the car in anyone's driveway, would there?"

"No, I guess not. You can't have something be a status symbol if everyone can get it. Status is based on exclusivity."

"Exactly. And there's no validation with the big TV, big house or anything else because everyone can have anything they want. If we had a world like that, what would our economy be based on, how would it function?" He paused then added. "Meaning, what would we value? What would people use to validate themselves, to give themselves status among their peers?"

I looked out at the parking lot full of cars and the people walking around. "Okay, this is less elementary. Let me think." I watched a man walk past us and then out into the parking lot to his high-end Mercedes and that, in some weird fashion, finally triggered the memory that had been niggling at me. "A long time ago, I read a book..." I tried to dig up the name or the author, but I couldn't. "It was about a space colony where they didn't have money because all the people had been raised by robots."

"Hey, that's a great book! I loved it." He grinned at me. "*Voyage From Yesteryear,* by James P. Hogan. Tell me what struck you the most when you read it."

I dug into my memory of the book. "When the Earth people first went to the planet's version of a store and everything was free. The colonists could have anything they wanted, anytime they wanted it, as much as they wanted."

"Uh-huh. And what was valued in the resulting economy?"

It took me a moment to drag up that part of the plot. "Individual talent and creativity... I think."

"Oh, great memory."

I turned to Jeff quickly. "But we can't implement that here. The author had to work really hard to set up a situation which justified that economy and give the people a completely egalitarian power structure. We don't have any of that."

"Very true. So that's not a model we could use for an economic system replacement in the near future, but maybe someday. But don't fret, other economic models more sustainable than the current model are being proposed and investigated every day."

"Whew!" I leaned back again. For a minute there, I'd thought we were doomed.

"The trouble is, implementing any of them destabilizes the current structure, which will cause a lot of pain and agony all around."

"Ouch!" I said, as I thought about the situation he'd laid out and my part in it. "Beth and I are lousy consumers. We don't do much status buying and tend to wait for the old gadget to quit working before buying a new one." I paused, imagining the consequences if everyone did that. "The whole world economy would collapse."

"Indeed. But it's going to collapse sooner or later anyway." He slapped his knees. "Now, you ready to go home? I don't like these places," he said, smiling as he stood and started walking toward my car.

I wasn't happy, but had to laugh as I followed him. "So, you're doing it to me again? Going to leave me with my mind in knots?"

"Answers mean little when no work has gone into achieving them," he said as we approached my Jetta.

I shook my head as I realized tonight was going to be a long night, lying in bed thinking about economies. That triggered a memory of the pain I'd experienced getting out of bed this morning, and I realized I didn't hurt now. I laughed under my breath. Jeff had taken care of my pain without a kiss or at least he distracted me from it.

As I opened my car door, I noticed a Smart car parked a couple cars over. "Okay, mister-know-it-all, here's a question I've thought about a bunch and can't come up with an answer. Would you mind answering it for me?"

With his typical smile, he replied, "Sure."

"Why's that called a 'Smart' car? What's so darn smart about it? It's less than half the size of my car, has the get-up-and-go of a rabid sewing machine, and gets almost twenty-percent worse gas mileage. I could see it being a 'smart car' if it got sixty- or seventy-MPG but it doesn't."

He'd been about to get in my car, but he stopped and looked at the silly looking car. "Beats me."

"Thanks." I slid into my seat and fired up the car and the AC in one practiced movement, as he sat and closed his door. "I feel validated in my confusion now. If you can't answer that question then it can't be answered." I love this guy. He's an interesting guy to hang out with even if he did take me to a shopping mall.

* * *

That night, I sat on the edge of the bed, letting my mind wander. I was nearing the end of my second week—tomorrow would be my ninth business day—in utopia.

I'd meant the "utopia" thought to be sarcastic, but it didn't take me more than a couple more breaths to realize it was fearful, instead. HRI, so far, *was* utopia—I'd loved every minute working here—but realistically, I knew this was the honeymoon period; I'd liked working the first couple weeks at plenty of other places. Quickly, I chastised myself for being so pessimistic, but even then, I couldn't help but feel I was being set up for disappointment.

If disappointment was ahead of me, I thought as I lay down, at least the last few weeks had been the most interesting ones of my life. And, if I'd learned nothing else on this adventure, I knew this was *all part of the experience*. Then I laughed to myself at the thought. It was strange thinking of disappointment as being just "part of the experience" and not a huge devastating event, but like most of what Jeff had taught me, it made a weird sort of sense.

As I bunched the pillows exactly right and got settled in, my mind drifted back to the questions raised at the shopping mall with Jeff. What would an economic system look like that wasn't based on growth? Where was our global economy heading? What Jeff said about our economy being forced to change because of either an increase or decrease in population made sense since we were at the verge of an unprecedented change in human society. But what was that going to look like? How would it be handled?

My pessimism returned as I couldn't envision any pretty scenarios. Then I smiled to myself as I remembered what I'd said to Jeff early in the shopping trip discussion. I chastised him for stating the obvious, and not making my mind spin like most of our conversations do. Well, my head was indeed spinning, and there was a strange comfort in Jeff being his annoying self.

Chapter 36

The next morning was a bright and sunny Thursday. I'd slept surprisingly well considering my troubling thoughts going to bed. It didn't take me long to get dressed, and I was out the door just as my carpool arrived. We arrived at HRI, and seeing the nearly empty parking lot was still a strange sight for me after all the years of packed parking lots and empty bicycle racks. I was beginning to catch on that most things at HRI were reversed from normal companies.

As we walked through the front door of the building, two of the guys were giving the driver a hard time for parking crooked, and I laughed along with the driver. They sure were a fun group of guys.

Then as we passed the couch I'd sat on my first day here, the memory struck me of filling out the paperwork and looking up to see the groups of employees entering the building that day. I'd watched happy people entering, which had seemed so strange at the time, and now, here I was laughing with my carpool buddies. I was just like those people that first day. I hadn't entered the building today—or any day I'd worked here—with a feeling of dread, like I'd done at almost every other job I'd had. Instead, I was excited to be here. How cool was that?

Summer greeted us by name as we passed her desk, adding to my feeling of contentment. Each time I saw her, she'd smile, and somehow, her smile seemed to say "Everything's good, everything will always be good." HRI really was a utopia.

"See ya this evening, guys," the driver called as we passed through the doors to the left of Summer's desk, and the others answered as went our own directions.

"See ya!" I called, in response. As I went through the flywheel lab's door and set my backpack at one of the computers by the railing, all I could think of was how grateful I was to be here.

Then, before I could get the computer turned on, my stomach reminded me there was free food at the cafeteria. I grabbed the printout of the section I'd wanted to proof and headed there to get food and read.

* * *

The Greek yogurt with blueberries and bananas was pretty good, and I had my eyes focused on the flywheel magnetic bearing system description, when the chair across the table was pulled out, shaking me out of my trance.

I looked up as Grace placed her tray across from mine.

"Hope you don't mind me joining you."

"Not at all," I replied, smiling.

We made small talk as we ate, but the topic soon turned to Dylan. Surprisingly, schoolwork was giving him some trouble.

"I wouldn't have thought he'd be having trouble. He strikes me as a very bright kid. And your sister's school seems like the perfect place for him."

She looked at me confused. "Rita?"

"Yeah." Now I was confused. "Doesn't Dylan go to her school?"

"No. He's decided to go to the middle school closest to home, and he's having a hard time keeping up."

I smiled. "Well, whatever he lacks, he makes up in personality. He's really a neat kid."

She gave me a gentle gaze. "Dylan's really taken with you." She paused, and it was clear some thought was forming in her head. "Do you—" She stopped.

Looking at her questioningly, I said, "Go ahead."

She looked mildly embarrassed. "No, it's out of place. Never mind."

"Grace, let me decide what's out of place. What is it?"

She shrugged and hesitantly continued, "I don't know. Just a thought. I think he'd like working with you on his schoolwork. I think you could help him."

I was perplexed. "Why's that out of place? If I can help him, I will. Did you have something specific in mind?"

Her expression eased. "Just helping him with homework would be great." She smiled. "I can get you a free meal out of it." Then she switched to a playful look. "Oh, but that would mean eating with the chaos of my family."

I smiled. "When do you want me there? And do we need to check with your dad?"

She laughed. "Really, Stanley?" She put her finger under her chin and looked up at the ceiling thoughtfully as she mocked me. "Hmmm, would my dad have a problem with you coming over and eating with us and helping Dylan with his homework? Hmmm..."

"Okay, okay." I laughed. "That was a stupid question. When do you want me there?"

She looked at me, hopefully. "Tonight? Six-thirty?"

"I'll be there."

Her shoulders rose as she smiled excitedly. "Thanks."

We talked a little more before she left, then I went back to my reading.

* * *

A little while later, a group of people came by, and hearing a voice I thought I recognized, I looked up to see who it belonged to. It turned out to be Keith, the ex-convenience store clerk.

Jeff had said to watch him but our paths hadn't crossed until now. As they ate, I continued my reading and periodically, looked over at Keith just to satisfy my curiosity. I'd met some of the people he was eating with, and they struck me as pretty bright people. I was happy to see that they were making sure he was included in their conversation.

The group got up to leave, and as they passed my table, Keith looked down towards me. "Hey!" he exclaimed and reached out to shake my hand. The rest of his group continued on as I stood and grasped his extended hand.

As he eagerly shook, he said, "Glad I saw ya'. Been watching for you. Wanted to thank you for helpin' get me here."

I smiled, but shook my head. "That was Grace's doing. I was just a bystander. But regardless, I'm glad to see you here. How's it going?"

He gave an exasperated sigh. "I'm pretty nervous. I can tell you that much."

I motioned with my hand for him to sit down.

As Keith sat, he looked toward the group he'd been with as they exited the cafeteria. "They're being really good to me. Real patient.

But boy, are they smart."

I turned my gaze to follow his, then looked back to him. "I know how you feel; a couple of the guys on my team work with me at lunchtime to explain the math behind the flywheel equations that I need to use in the documentation. I'm picking it up, but slowly, and they just keep explaining it, as often as I need, without making me feel bad. And I don't think it's just my group who's so nice. I get the feeling the whole company's that way."

He gave me a look of agreement. "Yeah, that's how it is with my group. I feel like I'm asking the same questions over and over, and each time they answer like it's the first time I asked. They must be thinking I'm an idiot, but they never show it. Can only imagine what they say when I'm not there."

I recalled my first day here when Tom and I sat next to the table having the argument. They wouldn't continue their conversation until the person being talked about was there. I'd seen that happen repeatedly and couldn't think of a time when I'd heard people talking about other people without them present.

It took me a moment as I thought about how to respond. "You know, I bet they really, truly, don't think you're stupid, no matter how many times you ask something. I get the feeling they'd see that as shutting someone down, and they'd rather build people up. So, I bet they think if you don't know something, it's their job to teach it to you."

He looked at me for a moment, thinking about what I said. "Yeah, it seems that way. But still, it's like I don't even speak the same language."

"Yep, that's how it feels to me, too." I gave a little laugh. "And learning a new language is hard."

"Yeah. Don't I know it. Anyway, spent some time talkin' with the head guy, Mr. Havens. He's real encouraging. Said to just do what I can and learn what I can. He set it up so I'll be workin' with a bunch of different people. Says I'll just float around for a few weeks, to see what I like, and then he wants to talk again. Even more cool, he said if I wanted, he would help me get my GED, and then college if I want that, too. Won't that make my mama and my boy proud of me!"

Keith's good nature, the spark that Grace and I had seen when we first met him, was shining through. He was understandably nervous here, but it was clear that he was going to give it a good shot. "That's great. And I suspect it'll work out exactly that way. I've only been here a couple weeks, myself, and I can tell you this is a different kind of place."

"Sure hope so. I screwed up so many things in my life." He looked at me seriously for a few seconds, as if he was sizing me up. He wanted to say something but wasn't sure if he should.

I leaned back a little and relaxed, hoping he would relax some also.

He wet his lips with his tongue and then carefully started. "I'm not much of a religious man, but I prayed." He looked at me, like he was trying to read whether it was okay to continue.

If he didn't have my attention before, he had it now. I leaned forward to show my interest.

Keith's shoulders loosened up and lowered some, showing me he was feeling more comfortable. "I'm talkin' down on my knees type of prayin'. Never done that before. I prayed for just one more chance, just one more was all I asked for. I'd take it and I wouldn't screw it up." He shook his head smiling. "Strange thing, you an' Grace came in the following day and handed me that chance. What do ya make of that? I mean, it's kinda freaky."

I had no idea what to make of that.

A few weeks ago, I'd have flatly said it was a coincidence. But now, I wasn't sure. It was a weird feeling to find myself leaning towards believing in the power of prayer. I'd spent all my years in Beth's church mentally rejecting most of what they said, including totally rejecting the idea that prayer could change anything. As I thought about the shocking concept that prayer might have physical repercussions, I realized the cognitive dissonance—the echoes of disharmony between my old beliefs and what I was hearing now—was going to make it even harder to change anything, because it was so hard to admit I'd been so very wrong for so very long.

But, I thought as I pondered it more, after what I'd seen from Jeff over these last few weeks, in some strange way, it seemed almost reasonable to believe whatever vague image of God was starting to germinate in my head *could* answer Keith's prayer.

I looked at Keith and I simply answered, "I don't know. I'm coming more and more to believe..."

Something caught my attention, and I glanced past Keith towards the archway entrance of the cafeteria about fifty feet away. Jeff was leaning in the archway with his arms crossed, looking directly at me with his blasted smile, and my brain froze.

"What're you startin' to believe?" Keith asked, looking at me with curious intensity.

Still meeting Jeff's gaze, I made myself say the words. "I'm coming to believe things happen for a reason."

Jeff nodded, turned, and then walked away.

My mind was spinning. It couldn't be coincidence he happened to be there, right when I said that, could it?

"Sure hope so."

Shoving my disturbing thoughts aside, I turned back to Keith.

With a worried expression, he said, "But right now, I'm so nervous I'll screw up that I just *know* I'll screw up. Hope the reason for this great job isn't just so I can fail again."

What an awful outlook, I thought, but I totally understood. "This isn't that type of place." I was glad I was able to offer that comfort to him. "Relax, and be yourself," I paused for emphasis, "as long as yourself wants to learn."

He chuckled. "Yeah, I do."

"Then you're set. They're going to give you time to find what you're interested in, so take that time and explore. It may surprise you what you end up gravitating towards."

"Sure hope you're right. I'm tired of failin'. I'd sweep floors if they wanted."

I thought that was pretty funny. "I'm doing that next week, and cleaning toilets."

He laughed. "Maybe I'll join you. May end up gravitating towards that."

"It doesn't sound like you can make a career out of that here, so it'd just need to be a hobby."

He laughed at that even more. "Thanks for talkin'. It really makes me feel better. Everyone's been like that. I'm waiting for the hammer to hit, for somebody to tell me how bad I screwed things up again."

"I think you can quit waiting for that," I said, knowing exactly how he felt as I reflected back to my "utopia" thoughts from the morning. I looked towards the empty archway again. I repeated, "I think you can quit worrying." And wondered if I could take my own advice.

* * *

Six thirty on the dot that evening, I pushed the buzzer on Jeff's gate, to answer Grace's request to help Dylan. The dinner bell rang shortly after I walked in the door, so I sat beside Dylan at the meal, and he seemed excited to have me help him. The meal, just like last time, was loud, chaotic and wonderful.

After the clearing of the table ritual, the after dinner homework ritual began, without a word from anyone. Jeff, Grace, and several more older kids were either paired up helping a younger sibling, or doing their own personal studying.

Dylan finished the last of his chores and ran up to me, saying he was ready to start. "Let's go to the library. It's less cacophonous there."

Since a number of kids were already sitting at the massive dining table and some were on the couches and chair, I could understand his reasoning. It wasn't exactly noisy in the room, but it wasn't quiet, either. But cacophonous? "Is that your word of the week?"

"Two weeks ago," he admitted, "before plethora. This week's word is runic."

"Oh, that's right." I remembered him using "runic" at church several times.

"Cacophonous means..." He recited definitions and synonyms as he led me to the library.

I was laughing as I entered the big room, then had to smile at the room itself. This was definitely Jeff's library. The enormous room was decorated in what I'd call a Baroque style. The domed ceiling had an elaborate mural, the rooms' molding and pillars were ornately painted with rich colors. The bookshelves, all filled with books, were all carved wood. If Jeff had bought all these books from George—the bookseller I'd met on the trip out here—then George was a rich man.

The room already had some other kids in it, and Jonathan moved from person to person, obviously ready to help whoever needed it. Marcus sat at a table with a stack of his own books, deeply engrossed.

Dylan led me to the most remote table, I assumed so that he would have fewer distractions.

"Let's start with math," he said as he pulled a book out of the stack on the table. "That gives me the most trouble. I think my chances of being a quantum physicist are remote."

I smiled at him. What an interesting kid.

He opened his book and turned it around toward me so I could see what he was working on.

As I looked, I hid my frown. He wasn't underselling himself; for his age, he was doing very basic math. I mentally told Grace I was sorry for doubting her estimation of his abilities and buckled down to see what I could do to help.

We spent a lot of time reviewing basic math facts, because that was stopping him from moving on to the lesson's concepts.

As we worked, I realized that I hadn't been prepared for this level of intervention. After meeting Grace, Marcus, Rita and some of Jeff's other kids, I'd assumed they were all at the top of their learning systems. But Dylan obviously wasn't, and it wasn't only math troubling him. We struggled through every subject he had, but it wasn't for lack of trying on his part or from any unwillingness to learn. He had a great attitude but was clearly frustrated at how hard he had to work. Yet somehow, he managed to maintain his unfailing wit the whole time, which made the clearly difficult task bearable and even enjoyable for both of us.

We kept at the work until Jonathan came by to tell us it was time for Dylan to head to bed.

As Jonathan walked away, Dylan turned to me with a grin. "You see what I mean about my chances of being a quantum physicist? A career as a rocket scientist is probably out of the question, too." Then he paused mischievously. "I'm really good at talking, though. I've often thought that I needed a job where math and reading, and general intelligence, aren't important, but talking is." In mock sincerity, he scratched his head and pretended to think, then his eyes lit up and looked at me. "I've got it! I could be a politician."

I burst out laughing. I don't know what his learning disability was, but he wasn't lacking in intelligence. "Don't limit yourself Dylan. You need to set your goals higher. I'll bet you could be a talk show host."

Dylan smiled large and laughed. "Thanks for the encouragement. It's nice to have someone behind me, pushing me forward, so I don't waste my life in some meaningless job."

As I laughed more, it occurred to me that spending this time with Dylan made me really miss Cooper. The two of them would get along splendid. Cooper and I had a great time razzing each other in a loving way and Dylan would fit right in. It made me want to talk to Cooper tonight. With the time difference I would still have time when I got home.

Jeff came into the library as Dylan was cleaning up his study area. "Dylan, the gang's winding down, getting ready for *The Hobbit*. Tell them I'll be there in a little bit."

Dylan acknowledged Jeff with a nod and turned towards me. In a rare, sincere tone for him, he said, "Thanks, I really appreciate you doing this for me." He then gave me a hug, ran to Jeff, jumping to give the highest five possible, and was gone before I could respond.

Jeff's expression clearly conveyed his profound gratitude. "It's a beautiful thing you've done here tonight, Stanley."

I was confused. "What? Helping him with his homework? Why wouldn't I?"

Jeff continued his intense look; it was hard for me to keep eye contact. "Don't minimize what you have to offer the world."

I was still confused. I'd only helped Dylan with his homework.

Then Jeff broke the intense eye contact and waved an arm to encompass the library. "Help yourself to anything here."

Looking around the room full of packed, floor-to-ceiling bookcases, I didn't even know where to start. "I'll come back when I've got more time. Besides, I've a couple books at the hotel room I'm reading."

He sat down at the table and pushed Dylan's books to one side, which made me think about the kid again.

"What's up with Dylan? I mean, he doesn't make sense to me. He seems bright, but considering how much he struggled with the work tonight, he obviously has some learning problems."

Starting with a soft sigh, Jeff answered, "Dylan has a heart breaking story. His parents had severe substance abuse problems— which left him severely compromised at birth—plus atrocious parenting skills, on top of a knack for taking the worst possible choice at every given opportunity." Jeff paused for a moment, looking toward the door Dylan had exited. "He has some great coping skills, but has a tough road ahead of him."

"I guess after meeting Grace, Marcus and Rita, I expected all your kids to be high achievers."

He shook his head. "No, most of them will never be high achievers, and some will have to work really hard to be average. Grace, Marcus, Rita and some of my other kids have the aptitude. Simply put, Dylan doesn't. IQ tests are not the greatest measuring tool, but they do give some useful information. Dylan's IQ was measured at about seventy-five. If I told you Grace's or Marcus', it'd scare you. But what all my kids have is the right attitude."

"How so?" I asked, curious as to what Jeff considered a "right attitude."

"Did he ever compare himself to any of his siblings?"

I thought back. "No, he didn't."

Jeff nodded. "I think self-discipline is a better predictor of ability than someone's IQ score. If you were to compare him to other children with the same IQ measurement, his self-discipline is far above theirs. But even more unique, Dylan's bar for achievement is himself. He knows he has to work hard, and he knows he'll never be the best there is at anything, except for being Dylan. And that boy does an outstanding job of being himself."

I nodded in total agreement. "Man! Is he ever good at that!"

Jeff continued, "To watch someone work and work and work, like he does, knowing he'll likely never get past what others consider mediocrity, is inspiring in itself. In many ways, I find Dylan to be far more impressive than Marcus and Grace. They *can* be the best there is in almost anything they decide to do, so it's easy to understand why they push themselves."

Looking to the far side of the library, I watched Marcus surrounded by his textbooks, leaning over a book and then writing in his notebook. He was impressive, and I knew he worked hard to push beyond his talents. But Jeff was right, what Dylan was doing was much more impressive.

Jeff watched me watch Marcus and then continued. "It's the people in this world who push themselves, despite knowing they'll only ever achieve mediocrity, who are truly impressive. I've never seen Dylan roll over and give up."

I nodded. For once I knew exactly what Jeff meant. "As hard as he struggled, he never backed down. It was amazing to watch."

Jeff grinned. "Grace said you heard his word of the week."

"Yes. He used 'cacophonous' tonight, but 'runic' is this week's word. It's impressive to watch him rattle off the definitions. But after hearing him read tonight, I don't know how he memorized it so thoroughly."

"Every Sunday morning at five o'clock, he comes to the back patio carrying his dictionary and waits for me to finish meditating—or praying if you like that word better. When I'm done, we open up the dictionary to a random place and with his eyes closed, he picks a word. Then I help him until he can read and understand the entry. He spends the time until breakfast memorizing it and asking the others for help using it in sentences. If I happen to be gone, Jonathan helps him."

Thinking back to Grace's playful comment, I added, "And then he spends the rest of the week annoying everyone with the word."

"Yep, and they absolutely love it." He smiled fondly as he said it.

"We all know how hard it is for him, so they hassle him, just as Dylan would expect. That's how he works. His sense of humor makes it all possible for him."

Shaking my head, I said, "He's definitely got that going for him."

Jeff's expression turned a little serious. "You may think Marcus is my poster child for humanity, but you'd be wrong. It's Dylan. Humanity will only ever produce a small number of Marcuses, but we have a world full of Dylans."

The obviousness of that statement made me wonder why I hadn't thought of it before, which made me feel bad. But Jeff didn't give me time to berate myself for my closed-mindedness.

"And as limited as his abilities are, Dylan uses every bit of them. Plus, he understands himself well enough to know how he works, so there're no delusions in his psyche that will cause him pain when real-world experiences bump up against them. But best of all, he doesn't compare himself to others, nor does he make excuses for why he can't do something, even though he might be justified in doing so. Nor does he blame his past for why he can't do something, even though he'd be justified in doing that, too."

I knew a lot of people who'd had lives far easier than Dylan's, who spent all their time blaming their past for their problems. It was definitely another mark in the "Awesome Dylan" column that he, who actually had a reason for blaming his past, didn't.

"He's on his middle school football team, and he's the best third-string quarterback they've ever had."

That made me laugh.

"He's rarely asked to play, but he practices with just as much gusto as the first-string players."

"That doesn't surprise me at all." Then some of Jeff's comments from our trip started floating to the surface of my brain, and I looked at him questioningly. "Vertical growth? Exercising our modern brain?"

A satisfied expression came across his face. "Starting to make some sense?"

I nodded as I thought more about Dylan, but couldn't put what I was trying to say into words.

Jeff helped clear up my thoughts. "There are a couple of aspects to vertical growth. One is a deeper relationship with yourself and understanding of yourself. The other is a deeper relationship with God and understanding of God — by whatever name you want to call it — and the deeper connection to God's creation."

The word "connection" struck me. Dylan had made a connection with me from the moment I met him, and I'd enjoyed helping him and the time I spent with him. In a strange way, I felt like I got more out of it than Dylan did.

The next thought I had, I said out loud, while gazing unfocused at the table top. "The campsite is cleaner than he found it." Referring to the Boy Scout analogy Jeff used on the HRI roof top patio.

"And..." Jeff paused, and I lifted my gaze to his. "He isn't the only one leaving the campsite cleaner. Thanks for being so willing to help him."

I protested slightly. "Jeff, it was nothing. I'm glad I was given the chance."

Jeff repeated his earlier statement. "Don't minimize what you have to offer the world."

Looking at him, I said nothing, because I knew if I said something it would minimize what I'd done tonight. It bothered me I didn't know any other way to respond. Logic implied there should be another way, but at the moment, I didn't know what it was.

"But now," Jeff said, standing, "I have a group waiting for *The Hobbit*."

I stood too, and he walked me to the front door, then handed me something. It took a moment to register that it was a remote for the gate.

"Thanks again, Stanley. Dylan really seems to have taken a liking to you, and you taking the time to help him will raise his own bar. You're always welcome to come help him. In fact, you're always welcome just to come here."

By any standards, getting a remote to the gate for Jeff's house ranked up there in life's great moments. With a voice of sincere gratitude I said, "Thanks. See you tomorrow."

He gave a slight shake of his head. "Not until Marcus' release party. I won't be with your charity tomorrow. I'm working with another group."

"Ah, then I'll see you at the party. I'm really looking forward to it. I love watching a talented guitarist."

Jeff gave an approving smile. "Me too, and Marcus is one of the best I've ever seen. You'll be blown away."

Smiling, I turned and walked down the granite steps to my car. I drove away feeling pretty good, and was pleased to realize I felt best about making a difference to Dylan.

Chapter 37

Our team's Friday charity started late, not until seven in the morning. We met at work, and Aaron had groups formed and task lists for each. I was assigned to a group with a couple guys and a woman from the flywheel team who I didn't know very well.

We were assigned to an elderly widow's house. Together, we studied the list: mow lawn, fix squeaky doors, fix leaky faucet, replace broken garbage disposal, weeding, fix fences, etc. It was a list of all those little things that build up, but the elderly have trouble getting fixed. Thankfully, HRI's charity teams were well prepared for work like this. And from a storeroom that rivaled a small hardware store, we loaded a truck belonging to one of the group members with most of the tools and parts we needed. We might need a trip to the hardware store after we figured out specifics of what we were working on, but we were starting with most of what we needed.

By noon, I was under the kitchen sink pulling the garbage disposal to the accompanying smell of cookies baking in the oven.

The widow glowed with excitement as she made us lunch. I got the feeling she liked having us here, having the company, even more than the work we were doing. Shortly, she had everything ready, and we all sat around her dining room table chatting.

Eating the delicious food, I reflected on what a beautiful thing this was. Her gratitude was overflowing due to our simple help. And helping her in the way she most needed was such an easy way to bring joy to someone who truly appreciated it.

After lunch, while I was weeding the flowerbed out front, a wave of guilt swept through me as I remembered, years ago, Beth's church had attempted to start a program like this. But it had dwindled away because so few people had volunteered to help... and I was one of those who'd contributed to its failure.

Why was that? I asked myself as I pulled more weeds. Was I too busy? Or did I let my irritation with the church's doctrines stop me from doing something so obviously good?

This triggered a whole new set of thoughts.

Before I left home to come east for this job, Beth had mentioned the possibility of finding a new church and I'd promised her that I would explore some new ones here. But as strange as it was for me to admit to myself, not only had I truly enjoyed going to Jeff's church last Sunday, but I was looking forward to going this Sunday and I had no interest in exploring any other churches.

Shaking my head, I realized I was in a place I'd never expected to be, looking forward to the next church service. I pulled more weeds and thought some more.

With the minister of Beth's church dead, the only person in the church with whom I felt any real connection, I couldn't see myself staying there, not even to make Beth happy. And with Beth, for the first time, mentioning the possibility of going to a different church, maybe we could find one more like Jeff's. I smiled at the thought. It would be really nice to find a church where I felt welcomed and at home.

My thoughts were interrupted when the woman whose house we were working on brought me a glass of lemonade. I brushed the dirt off my hand from the weeding and took the glass. She thanked me again for helping her and went back inside, I assumed to get drinks for the rest of the workers. I stood and drank the glass down and admired my work on the flower bed.

Jeff's analogy came to my mind: the campsite is cleaner than I found it.

I had missed the chance with Beth's church to make a difference, but I wouldn't miss it again. Wherever we ended up worshiping, I would help make a difference. Even if I had differences with the church's theology, I would do my part to help others.

I put the glass on the porch step and returned to my weeding, and it felt good to have made that commitment.

We got our to-do list finished in record time, which left us plenty of time to get ready for Marcus' HRI release party tonight. We all piled into the trucks with dozens of homemade cookies as thank you presents. After unloading and cleaning up at work, I went home, cleaned up and lay down to take a nap.

As I lay there, resting my tired body, I wondered how many other elderly people's houses were being neglected for the same reason; they didn't have any relatives nearby who could perform needed maintenance. And I felt a surge of gratitude to HRI for giving me the opportunity to help a woman so deserving; it solidified my commitment to help in similar ways when I got home. I drifted off into a content sleep.

* * *

I woke from my nap a little later than I'd planned, but I was refreshed and excited to see Marcus's concert.

An hour later, when I pulled into the convention center's parking lot—ten minutes before the concert was supposed to start—I was a bit surprised. This was an HRI event, but unlike HRI's parking lot, this one was actually packed with cars, and more arriving every minute. Even more surprising were the news vans parked off to the side of the main entrance. Then it occurred to me, convention centers usually hosted multiple events at the same time, so the news vans were probably there for another event.

I parked as close as I could, then followed several families to the main entrance in the center of the building and through the glass entrance doors. I was pleased to see Summer and a couple other familiar faces sitting behind tables near the entrance to one of the convention rooms. The families went to one of the tables, and Summer saw me and waved me to hers.

I walked over as I surveyed the activity in the entrance area. "Hey, Summer. Looks like a lot's happening here today."

She nodded and said, "Your timing's great. It's been a madhouse, but the line, just now, died down." She turned to the shelves behind her and pulled out a box with a big "W" on the front. From it she pulled a name tag and handed it to me.

"What else is happening here today? Seems pretty busy."

She looked confused. "Nothing. HRI rented the whole thing."

"Huh." That seemed strange. This place must cost a fortune to rent all of it. Why was HRI springing for an event which wasn't directly HRI related?

But it wasn't my job to police Jeff's budget, so I smiled to Summer and pinned on the badge after saying good-bye to her.

I went to the door to the right of her table. A man glanced at my name badge and opened the door for me.

Having a door attendant seemed a little odd, but as I entered I was even more surprised.

This was a much bigger deal than I had originally envisioned. I couldn't even begin to count the number of people in the huge room. A thousand? Maybe two thousand? I knew families had been invited, but it still seemed like way too many people were here for just HRI employees and their families.

At the far end of the room was a large raised stage mostly obscured by a white screen that had colored lights being projected on it in interesting patterns. The back of the room was partially-filled with round tables, about half full of people, with more milling around chatting.

"Huh," I thought again. I guess I'd expected a more intimate setting, with Marcus on a stool performing to a small crowd.

To add to the confusion, I looked to my left and saw news crews setting up their equipment along the back wall. "I must have missed the cultural shift when classical guitar became a big deal," I said to myself.

Then I looked to my right and saw what was really important, the sign marking the food area, which reminded me I was hungry. I headed that way.

The caterers were obviously ready for this crowd, because the buffet-style serving area was big enough I didn't have to wait, and it had a wide range of selections.

I helped myself to some cocktail shrimp and other hors d'oeuvres and found an empty table near the back of the room. I watched the crowd as I ate and wondered about all of this.

I knew I shouldn't be surprised, because nothing ever was what you'd expect when Jeff was involved, but still, I was shocked.

The first plate of food didn't last long, so I filled my plate a second time, and spotting some people I knew, I mingled. Since this was only the end of my second week of work, I didn't know very many people, but I got invited to go rock climbing again, which was very cool, and kayaking which was even better. But nobody could tell me what was going on. I suspected a couple of people knew, but they'd gotten a look in their eyes that told me they weren't about to share the secret.

At seven o'clock, the colored lights being projected on the screen in front of the stage were replaced with a huge projected display of what looked like a talk-show studio, set up for an interview of some sort, and the crowd quieted. On the screen, an attractive, blonde reporter sat in a chair with a small table separating her from an empty chair. A live audience could be seen to her side. The ticker tape at the bottom of the screen read, "This pre-recorded interview will be followed by a live concert. You can also watch it online at ..." and gave a URL.

I moved past several groups of people and toward the center of the room away from the tables, to get a better view. Thankful for the blessing of Southern cuisine, I put a bacon-wrapped jalapeno in my mouth and watched the screen. None of this was making any sense, but now, maybe, I'd find out what was happening.

The reporter began speaking. "Rap music is obsessed with money. The big names like to flaunt their wealth with big mansions, big cars, expensive jewelry and lives of excess. Their music is sometimes violent, angry and often glorifies life in the gang.

"But there's a new rapper rising fast in Pennsylvania who's very different from the norm. His YouTube videos have gone viral, giving him worldwide attention and a lucrative recording contract. His first CD, titled *It's Not About Me*, will be released in two weeks and the recording company says they've never had this much anticipation over an artist's first record. So, I'm pleased to introduce the newest rapper on the scene, very appropriately named, The Change!"

Rap music poured through the sound system, as a man bounded on screen onto the studio's stage with back flips, front flips and landed in full splits. He then rose in a movement of effortless grace like a well-trained gymnast.

When I recognized him, my mind quickly placed the puzzle pieces into place, and I gave myself a mental dope-slap for not seeing this coming.

As I tried to figure out what to do with my plate so I could call Beth to get Cooper to watch, to my annoyance and relief, Jeff came up beside me, and I quickly handed him my plate as I gave him a dirty look and pulled out my phone. "You could've told me Marcus was *The Change*!"

He grinned. "And ruin a surprise?"

I punched Beth's number on my phone and impatiently waited for her to answer. "Beth, get Cooper, get him on the computer, and go to—" I gave her the URL scrolling across the bottom of the screen. Thankfully, she didn't ask any questions.

As I waited for her to get Cooper and pull up the website, I turned my attention back to the screen. Marcus' back was to the camera as he greeted the reporter. He was wearing a black skin-tight tank top which accented his massive muscles and dark skin.

As I watched Marcus walk towards the studio's audience to greet them, bits of conversation over the last couple weeks raced through my head. How could I have not put this all together before now? Grace's favorite musician, and the one Cooper wanted a T-shirt from, was a man I'd been working side-by-side with and didn't even know it.

I gave Jeff another dirty look, but he was watching the screen and holding my plate. Why didn't he just—

Beth came back on the phone, and I covered my other ear to block out the noise and tried to talk quietly so I didn't disturb others.

Beth said, "That URL shows some guy out shaking hands with people and a rap song playing. Did I mistype it?"

"That's it! Put Coop on the phone."

"He's still coming."

As we waited, I explained what was happening to Beth. Separated by over two thousand miles, we both watched Marcus greeting the studio's energized audience. When he got near people, they all leaned towards him with hands extended trying to touch him, like he was a huge celebrity. Which was a very weird way to think about the guy I worked beside, listened to him preach and had eaten dinner with.

Beth asked, "Is that where you are? Are you in the audience?"

"No, I'm at a convention center in Bethlehem, watching it on a big screen. The ticker at the bottom of the screen says the interview was pre-recorded, but I'm not sure where. I'd guess Philadelphia."

The studio's audience sang and moved to the song playing through the speakers, a song I recognized from listening to Cooper's music.

The camera zoomed in on Marcus as he shook hands and waved at the people. His impressive arm muscles flexed as he moved.

Beth commented, "He's huge."

"Yeah. The lab coat sure hides a lot. I knew he was big, but not built like that."

Cooper finally got to the phone and his exclamation of delight made the hassle to get him worthwhile. "Hey, Dad! That's cool! You're there? Did ya find out where to get me a T-shirt?"

I smiled. "I don't think a T-shirt will be a problem. I've been working with him since I got here and didn't even know he was The Change."

Cooper's excitement shot up. "You know him? You've actually

talked to him? What's he like? I can't wait to tell the kids at school!"

"He's an awesome guy," I answered softly. "But, Coop, I'll call you after this."

"Sure, Dad! This is great! Thanks for letting me know. Bye!"

As Marcus finally made his way back to the studio's stage, I put the phone in my pocket and took my plate back from Jeff, then glared at him when I saw he'd eaten all the bacon wrapped jalapenos. Not only did the guy not bother to tell me his kid was one of the biggest up-and-coming rap stars, the guy was also a jalapeno thief.

He wiped his mouth with a napkin and grinned unrepentantly.

The music softened and the studio audience settled as Marcus sat in the chair next to the reporter.

She smiled and said, "Thanks for coming. You're making quite a stir on the local scene." She looked out at the audience and the camera followed her glance. "They seem excited."

The crowd stood and cheered.

The camera panned back to her, and she waited patiently for the cheering to stop. "And now it looks like the excitement is spreading to a worldwide audience because of your videos."

Marcus smiled at her. "The wonders of the internet age." He paused briefly before continuing. "It's great though, because my message can reach more people than anyone before me."

She asked a few more questions, then said, "Let's get back to what you call 'your message.' Change. You say, that it's your message, enough so that it's your name, too... The Change..." She paused. "But what, exactly, are you wanting to change?"

Marcus' expression turned serious. "I'm out to make sure that nobody ever again has to grow up like I did."

"And how was that," she asked compassionately.

Marcus looked down to his clinched fists resting on the arms of the chair he sat in. "Bad." He paused, then looked at the reporter. "The worst of the New York streets. My mom died when I was fourteen and my dad was MIA. I grew up with abuse, drugs, gangs, and more. That landed me in jail when I was sixteen. I've seen it all, and I've done most of it."

"And now you're here."

His delight in that fact was obvious. "I *am* here." He waved an arm to encompass the studio, and the audience cheered. When they quieted, he continued. "And I'm aiming for my message to get everywhere, so nobody—no matter the color of their skin, the amount of money in their pockets, or the place they grew up—has to endure what I did."

"That sounds like a huge undertaking." The reporter looked skeptical. "How are you going to do that?"

"I'm going to do it by understanding them, and helping those who want to be helped, in the ways they want to be helped. 'Cause I understand their anger. I understand their hopelessness. I lived on their streets. But I got lucky, 'cause I was taken from there and given something better. And now, I'm giving that back to them."

The TV camera closed in on the reporter on the large screen. "And you have plans for that?"

The camera returned to Marcus to get his response. He looked at her with a knowing grin. "Everything's changing." Emphasizing each word, he said, "*The Change is here.*"

The word play got a laugh from the crowd around me but, like me, I don't think they quite knew how to interpret it. Was he, himself, going to make all the changes? I glanced over at Jeff, but he was focused on the interview with his ever-present smile. I thought, "What's changing, Jeff?"

The camera turned to the studio's live audience who were cheering with their hands in the air.

The reporter also smiled at the word play but, unlike the audience, she got to ask the question. "What do you mean by that?"

"Exactly what I said." Again he pronounced each word with intensity. "The Change is here!" He looked out at the camera. "You'll see what I mean. Change like this can't come from the outside. People have to want change. But before they can want change, they have to know what is available; they have to believe change is possible. That's what I'm doing. I'm here to show them change is possible, if they invite it." With a tone of complete confidence and lack of arrogance he strongly asserted, "I'm starting a revolution. I'm starting a new age."

The crowd in the convention center murmured at that. I looked over at Jeff for some type of response, but he just watched the screen straight ahead with fascination. I tried to get his attention. "Jeff."

Without turning to me, he responded, "Shh, I'm listening."

Guess I'd ask later. I turned back to the large screen.

"A revolution? A new age? How are you doing that?"

Marcus leaned forward in his chair brought his hands forward towards her, like he was offering her something. "By sayin' what needs to be said. By sayin' what's ready to be heard. By givin' hope to the hopeless and unleashing their potential. When a society is ready for change, the message is ready to be heard. Now is the time for the message to be heard with new ears and new hearts." He looked out at the audience. "Are you ready?"

She had to wait longer this time for the audience to settle. Still with the questioning look she asked, "And what exactly is your message?"

Marcus leaned back and gave her a secretive smile. "That's what you're all going to have to wait to find out. But I can give you a hint."

"Please, do," she said with a laugh in her voice.

"It's the same message that's been told many times before, but I'm tellin' it in a new way. It's Martin Luther King, Jr.'s message. It's Gandhi's message. It's Mohammed's message. It's Buddha's message. It's Jesus' message. It's the title of my CD. It is a message that says we're not here to stand alone in the world. We're here to help and grow each other."

She reached and took a CD case off the table between them and read the title, *"It's Not About Me."* She then opened the case and took out the cover art insert. "Your song's lyrics are very unusual for a rapper." She opened the insert and started to read:

> *"The hesitation*
> *of an unsyncopated nation"*

The studio audience took it from there and added the rhythm of the song. She smiled, sat back and listened.

> *"stops the creation*
> *of an unbreakable relation.*
>
> *The rich and the poor*
> *of the ditch and the store*
> *destroy the horror*
> *that's working no more.*
>
> *The words of the King*
> *are wanting to ring*
> *removing the sting*
> *proving a nation can sing."*

She lowered the paper and looked at him. "The ditch and the

store?"

"Right. The people living in the gutters and the ones running our commerce systems. We're all part of the change."

She looked back at the paper and read, "The words of the King?"

"Yep. I think that's self-explanatory. I'm a big Elvis fan."

The crowd here around me erupted into laughter, as did the studio audience.

She laughed and added, "Well, I wish you and Elvis the best in changing the world." She put the CD insert down on the table and looked back at Marcus. "I hear there's a big event planned."

Marcus leaned forward. "Yes! Right after this interview airs, I'm doing a small concert for my friends and family which will be televised live. That's a preview for the big event. Tickets go on sale tomorrow for an event that's gonna be something the world's never seen. I've made my way up the mixed martial arts—MMA ranks and now will fight for the heavyweight title. We've worked for several months now, with MMA promoters to make this event something different. Before the title match, I'll—" he paused and flexed his impressive arms, to cheers from both crowds "—be taking on anyone from any hood in America, no weight classes, who thinks he can beat me in a full contact, no-holds-barred match. For months, we've been searching for the best street fighters in America. The promoters are narrowing it down to the top four."

I was dumbfounded and turned to Jeff. "Are you nuts? You trying to get him killed?"

Jeff raised one side of his mouth in irritation at me interrupting him. "Trust me. He'll be fine." With that he turned back to the screen.

The reporter asked with trepidation, "So, you'll fight four fights and *then* you're going to fight the current MMA champion?" The studio flashed a picture of a guy holding up a championship belt.

"Looking forward to it." Marcus paused as the studio crowd erupted in cheers again. "This way everyone knows it's not a gimmick. The champion isn't gonna give up his title for a gimmick."

"And it just gets better." She had a tone of skepticism in her voice. "After five fights, you're so sure you're going to win, you've planned a concert afterwards."

Marcus shrugged off her skepticism and answered matter-of-factly. "There's only one person alive who can beat me, and I won't be fighting him. I won't even be breathing heavy for the concert."

Normally, a statement like that sounds cocky, but from Marcus, it sounded as egoless as ordering a dinner salad. He wasn't bragging. He was just stating the facts as he saw them.

The reporter let the obvious question slide of who could beat him, but I knew who it was and looked over at Jeff. He was about the same size as me and wouldn't frighten anyone in a dark alley, or anyone in any place, for that matter. Yet, Marcus still hadn't won the check.

She moved on. "There's also a substantial amount of prize money for the fights, and another twist."

"Right. Four million dollars in prize money. A million for each hood fight. If they beat me, they win a million dollars, free and clear; they'll get the check that night. The amount for the fifth fight is controlled by fight promoters. I don't have details on that."

She interjected, "So you'll get at least four million if you win all the fights?"

Marcus drew his head back and looked at her like she was nuts. "No. I don't need that money. When I win, the money is going to fund the beginning of 'the change.'"

Her body stiffened on hearing this. "Interesting. You don't want four million dollars?"

He shook his head. "It's not important."

A few people standing around us turned, looked at Jeff and smiled. The reporter may not understand Marcus, but the people who knew Jeff understood his son.

"Okay, then tell us about the twist," the reporter continued. "If the people who challenge you lose, what happens?"

He grinned large. "This is important. They sign a contract committing them to earning a college degree. Everything will be paid for, and they'll get any help they need. I'll even go to class with them, if that's what they need. But they'll be committed to finishing it off. And once they get the degree, they'll be guaranteed a good paying job, in the field they studied for."

I smiled at this. There wasn't any doubt who his dad was.

Marcus raised his shoulders and held up his hands beside him as if balancing the options. "They actually win either way. If I win, they get a way out of a bad situation and the money goes to 'the change.' And no, I don't mean me or my band, because it's not about me. If I lose, they get the money. But I will tell you now, no one can beat me, so 'the change' will get four million dollars, and change will start to happen."

She looked at Marcus for a short moment like she was trying to read him. I understood what she was doing. With a statement like that you wanted to judge the speaker as egotistical but Marcus didn't read that way.

She moved on. "I also hear you won't make any money from the ticket sales for the event."

He affirmed what she said with a nod. "Right. Absolutely every dollar of profit from ticket sales and record sales goes to building a better world."

"Why?"

He stood from his chair and looked out at the live audience. "Because they want change." The audience responded accordingly with shouts and applause. "We will change things!" He raised his hands above his head and looked up. "'The Change!' is here!"

The camera panned to the audience as they exploded in cheers and clapping, which showed no signs of stopping. The image on the screen started to fade as the screen was raised, revealing a stage full of concert equipment.

I thought, "So much for a classical guitar concert."

A man walked out on stage and came to one of the microphones. "What a great interview that was. I'm glad we were able to present that for you. And now, for your viewing pleasure, a preview to what you will see in just over a month, we give you... The Change!"

I turned and looked in the back of the room. The news cameras I'd seen when I first came in were focused on the stage.

As people I assumed were Marcus' band members started coming on stage and picking up instruments, I quickly called Beth and got Cooper on the line. "Coop, are they showing the concert?"

"Yeah," he replied.

"Look for me in the audience, because I'm here."

"That's so cool, Dad. You're so lucky!"

The music started, and we couldn't hear each other, so we hung up.

I turned to Jeff with a grin and yelled over the music, "I'm at a rap concert, and my son's jealous. Who'd have ever seen that coming?"

He just smiled and patted me on the back, then pointed to the stage.

Much like Marcus entered the interview, he came bounding onto the stage. But unlike the interview stage, this one was set up for him. There was a system of poles, beams and platforms built all over the stage. Marcus leaped to a horizontal pole over his head. Whereas I can't even do a chin-up, Marcus pulled himself effortlessly past his chin and to his waist. From there he went into a handstand on the bar and then slowly lowered his feet back down to stand on the bar. He then leaped to the next bar above him and repeated what he just did. From there he jumped to a beam which was about twenty feet over the band.

I watched this with amazement. Cooper and I had watched countless videos on YouTube of people doing what appeared like superhero feats of strength and agility. To me, this was like watching a live Spiderman show with music.

Marcus, or I should say, 'The Change,' stood above the band on a clear platform and the music stopped. He brought his extended arm slowly from one side of his body to the other as if he was acknowledging the whole crowd. He adjusted his wireless headset and from there the music started again, and Marcus went right into the song.

> *In the past we had the mega follower.*
> *It won't last, no more lie swallower.*
> *The lie of the image, the lust of the power*
> *Dies like the passage of seeds that won't flower.*

The words "mega follower" caught my attention. Jeff had used that phrase at the gas station with the guys who wouldn't shut off their radio. He'd said he had plans to help them, just not at the gas station right then.

I'm not a rap music fan at all, but as the songs switched from one to another, I caught myself fighting the urge to like it. I'm sure Cooper's excitement about The Change helped with that. But I had to admit, the lyrics were good, positive and sometimes really funny.

During one of the songs, I got thinking about the five fights Marcus would have before his big concert. How could he do that? When the music quieted as a song ended, I leaned over to Jeff. "How can he be so confident that he can win the fights?"

Calmly Jeff replied, "Because he'll win."

I smiled knowingly. "You're rigging the fights, aren't you? Divine intervention?"

He shook his head. "Not in the least. I know how skilled Marcus is. No one can touch him unless he wants them to."

I added, "Except you."

He shrugged. "I get lucky."

"Yeah, right." I thought back to the biker bar where he just stood there taking hits. "So, you could've beaten Bear? You took a pounding, but you could've beaten him?"

Still—or always—smiling, he said, "Bear didn't need me to beat him. That wouldn't have fixed anything. I gave him what he needed."

I turned my attention back to The Change. The music was just a low rhythmic beat and he was standing silently on the edge of the beam about twenty feet above the stage. He spread his arms out beside him and calmly leaned forward as the crowd apprehensively watched him fall. He caught a horizontal bar about seven feet below him and used the momentum from that to spin twice in the air and land back on the stage, level with the band. The music picked up the instant he landed, and The Change went into the next song.

As I watched Marcus' power, Jeff's plan became clear to me. He's going to change the hood with their own values. They respected money, power, fame and image. All the primitive brain drives. The Change had more of that than any of them, but it wasn't what drove him. In my time with Marcus, I'd only seen the profound ability of his modern brain. But, in his "The Change" persona, he would reject all of what the fans were used to respecting and change it so they'd end up respecting something vertical, without them even knowing they'd changed.

I turned my thoughts back to the concert and had to admit Marcus had an impressive stage show to accompany his music. As I watched him in awe, I looked back at Jeff. "You have nothing to do with this?"

"Only that I chose him and taught him. He was a special person in a bad situation. But that bad situation is part of why he's a special person. He's so driven that he's going to pull a whole culture up onto the chair with him, and no one can pull him down."

That brought me back to the gas station with the goofy mobile. Pulling people up onto a chair was the analogy Jeff had used when he said he had plans, just not that day. Obviously, this "The Change" phenomena had been in the works for years.

He looked back at Marcus. "Don't tell him, but I'm struggling pretty hard when we spar to make it look like I'm playing with him. He's going to get that second check soon, and I'm going to have some broken bones. I don't look forward to getting hit by him." He cringed.

And I winced in sympathy. I didn't want to get anywhere near

Marcus' fists.

The Change and his band did a few more songs and then the stage lights went dark, leaving only one spot light in the center stage. Marcus walked out with a stool and a classical guitar. "I call this song "Nineveh"."

There it was again, "Nineveh."

He started playing, and the world around me seemed to vanish as I watched a true guitar master play a song that transported me like none ever had before. I've heard people talk about a song transporting them, but I'd never known what they meant until now.

Clearly, the song had a message, and I felt like I was on the verge of understanding it when the song ended. For a brief moment, disappointment consumed me. I loved where the song took me, but now I was back at the convention center. I looked around at the people with dazed faces who seemed to have gone on the same trip as me.

Then I looked at Jeff, who was just Jeff. I don't think he was transported anywhere because that's where he lived all the time.

Chapter 38

Monday morning, the start of week three, was my week on the facilities crew, which I really wasn't sure about.

But, regardless of my reservations for the week, I woke up in a good mood. I'd had a great weekend. In addition to the awesome concert Friday night, I went rock climbing Saturday and kayaking Sunday afternoon, and was just sore enough to feel like I used muscles which needed using. I've always liked that feeling.

Church with the Havens clan had been wonderful. Pastor Jones' sermon was powerful but didn't have me running to the door like last Sunday. Dylan and I planned a couple evenings this week to help with his schoolwork. Other than missing my family, it had been an excellent weekend, and I was energized for whatever the grounds crew week brought.

The carpool group and I parted ways in the parking lot, because I was to report to the facilities office behind the main building. Sam, the financial adviser, was there already. I exchanged casual greetings with a couple the others, but most I didn't recognize.

I walked towards Sam. I couldn't get through my head that he was seventy-five. "Glad to see you here, Sam."

He gave me his light speed, vice-grip hand shake. "Good to see you too, Stanley. This is going to be a great week." Then with a grin covering his face. "You gonna take me up on the racquetball game?"

Thinking back to what Jeff said, I replied, "Sure. Jeff said the humiliation would be good for me."

He laughed hard at that and said, "Great, we'll be hanging out this week, so it won't be hard to set that up."

I looked around. "I've never seen a company do anything remotely like this. I don't even know what to expect."

Or why they did it. It seemed bizarre HRI would hire a short-term tech writer and then put him on a facilities crew for a week. It didn't make sense, but nothing about this gig made sense. They could have gotten other tech writers to do what I was doing and paid them half as much. I was sure tech writing wasn't the reason I was here, but I still had no clue why Jeff had brought me here, or why Jeff did anything.

Sam's enthusiastic response pulled me out of my questions. "Expect a good week. I always look forward to this. I'm running it this week, also, so gotta go."

After Sam hurried to the front of the room, he checked his roster against who was there and seemed satisfied that they matched, he called out, "Okay, everybody sit down and let's get this started." As we settled into our seats, he continued. "I hope all of you did a better job than me coming up with a list of things to do. I'd gotten started on a good list, but the crew from last week already did most of them. So, what do we have?"

He went to a white board and started writing down tasks that people from the crew called out. Things like: a hand rail that needed to be repainted, stains in the carpet (which Sam jokingly accused the person of doing himself because the stains rarely lasted long enough for the facilities crew to get to), some flower beds needed mulch, and so on. The list wasn't very long.

He looked at it skeptically. "Well, let's start with the daily stuff and see if we can add to this list. We can't let last week's crew show us up."

With that, we divided the window washing, vacuuming, trash pickup, recycling, bathrooms, grounds-keeping and other daily tasks between us. Most of the people already had coveralls, and I was given my own pair to keep.

I spent the day with Sam, and as we vacuumed, he kept a close look-out for anything to add to the list. He inspected walls for smudges or chipped paint, looked for molding that was coming off, broken chairs, dirt buildup in corners where it's hard to clean. He was looking for anything, the kind of things most people would never notice or would just overlook. But given the size of the building, his list stayed surprisingly short.

We even went to the kitchen to see if we could help the kitchen crew in any way, and I was surprised to see that everything there looked like it just came from the showroom. I hadn't even paid attention to that before. All the stainless steel was perfectly cleaned and there wasn't even any buildup of grime in any corners or underneath.

Sam was getting frustrated, so I followed him up to the roof, to inspect it for leaks and such. He'd said that we'd be checking out the multitude of solar panels later in the week. Then we checked the painting of the parking lot lines. The only thing he really found to add to the list were some cabinets that needed to be cleaned and organized better, and they were in a less frequently used area. I was getting worn out just trying to keep up with the old guy.

After lunch, the cleaning crews gathered back at the office and a few more minor things were added to the white board list, and Sam was looking depressed. "Come on, guys, we have to be able to find something others have overlooked." Off we went again, working on the normal maintenance tasks while trying to find things that needed work done.

Through the week, I developed an in-depth understanding of the building and property.

The creek running under the sidewalk in front of the building was man-made. A gigantic rainwater harvesting system provided water for both the creek and any irrigation. The massive rustic cedar water tank was only a small part of the water storage system. Solar powered pumps circulated the water between a tank at the end of the creek back to a tank at the start of the creek, resulting in a babbling creek flowing pleasantly, and aesthetically, in front of the building. It was only after I asked that I discovered HRI had a connection to the city water as a backup for the creek, but the only time it was used was for precautionary testing to verify the connections worked.

We tested the wind turbines and solar arrays to verify their output and to see if any maintenance was needed. Like the water system, HRI was hooked to the city's utility grid but rarely took power from it. But unlike the water, HRI was able to put power back into the grid and get revenue. Also, some earlier prototypes of the flywheel system I was working on helped store energy for times when HRI was producing more than they were using, further reducing the need to use the city's electricity.

That's how the week went and the white board list didn't get much longer, but not due to lack of effort.

Walking through the building was never the same after that first day, and I knew that, from then on, walking through other buildings would never be the same. I was forever going to notice all the things other people casually overlooked and turn my nose up in disgust. Havens Research Institute was spotless, and I think if the cleaning crews stopped cleaning it would stay that way. Since everybody in the company had spent time on the facilities crew for so long, it had become a subconscious act for everyone to pick up the paper on the floor, wipe off a counter, clean up a spill, or to simply not bang chairs on the wall chipping the paint. At HRI, it wasn't someone else's job to clean the building, it was ours.

It was also a great equalizing force. I mean, the first week I was here, Jeff, the CEO, was on the crew. If you've cleaned toilets with the CEO, you quickly got the idea that it's everybody's job.

By the end of my facilities crew week, I had to admit Jeff's dad was a genius to implement a plan like this.

Since I spent most of the week working with Sam, I played racquetball with him a couple times and, as Jeff predicted, the seventy-five year old man stomped me, and I enjoyed every minute of it.

* * *

The following Monday, I was in my own world as I walked with my carpool group through the parking lot. This was the start of my fourth week. The end of this week would mark the halfway-point of the contract, and the thought brought me no joy.

I let the group move on as I stopped on the bridge over the creek and leaned over with my forearms resting on the railing. My mind was just bouncing from one fragmented idea to the next as I watched the water ripple over some of the bigger rocks in the stream.

A voice came from beside me. "Hey, Stanley."

I looked over to see Keith walking onto the bridge. "Hey, Keith. Good to see you. How's it going?" Last time he and I talked in the cafeteria, he'd said he was hoping this job wasn't just another chance to screw up. I was wondering if, since that time, he was relaxing and finding his way better.

He came up and leaned on the railing with me. "I guess okay. Stayin' positive, you know," he replied in an unsure tone. "How 'bout you?"

I thought, "How 'bout me?" Happy? Nervous? Excited? Scared? Afraid the dream-bubble would burst, and I'd be back in the real world.

I gave him a half-smile and a shrug. "Probably much like you.

This place is a lot to take in."

He nodded and looked down at the stream as we quietly reflected on our own thoughts.

Other people arriving at work passed us, but I was so wrapped up in my thoughts I barely noticed them.

After a couple minutes, Keith said, "This is nice. The fish and all. Kinda relaxing."

"It's a nice touch."

"I hadn't really stopped and looked before." He paused for a minute before thoughtfully continuing. "Seems like my life story. Can't think of many times I've stopped and looked at things."

Thinking back to the first time Grace and I met him at the convenience store, I wondered if that was really true. "I don't know about that. I think you need to give yourself more credit."

He watched a fish swim upstream under the bridge and reflected. "Thanks. Nice to hear someone support me. Didn't get much of that growin' up." He looked towards the entrance of the building. "Seems like the usual thing here, though. Yet, every day now, I wake up afraid. Almost want to run back to the convenience store.

"I mean, there at the store, the worst I could do is give the wrong change or stock the shelves wrong. Here, I'm getting paid so much, and every day they have me messin' with things—who knows how many thousands of dollars-worth—that they just shown me how to run and they leave me to it, like they think I can do it. If I screw up and lose this job..." He paused. "I mean, I didn't have much to lose before. It was an okay job. It was pretty easy, so it didn't cause me to think too much, not like this one does. If I lost that one, I could get another one just like it."

At this point, I went from watching him speak to watching the water. I wasn't sure how to respond to fears like he had. They were real fears. His risk had shot up exponentially in a short amount of time, and he was having problems adjusting. I looked back at him. "I don't think you need to worry here. They may be raising you up fast, but I don't think they'll let you fall hard. Here, you can climb to something better, whereas before, you may have felt some safety, but you'd always be at the same level."

Then my brain exploded, and I quietly said out loud to myself, "If you try to grow vertically, expand upwards, the risk of falling back down causes fear. If you grow horizontally, there's almost no risk, because there's nowhere to fall, therefore almost no fear."

Keith looked at me with a blank stare.

I smiled to myself as the thought matured a little more, then I tried to explain it, because I wanted it to make sense to Keith. "Like most people, we're afraid of heights. If we're growing vertically, it's like we're climbing a tower. The higher up we go, the farther there is to fall. But the higher up we go, the more we can see.

"You and I are used to being on the ground because we're afraid of heights. We've taken safe jobs on the ground, the horizontal jobs. Like you said, you didn't have much to lose before with your old job. But we were safe on the ground even though we couldn't see much, wouldn't grow much, and didn't find any fulfillment."

He continued his blank stare. "A tower?"

Excitedly, I answered, "Yes, we're climbing a tower here, and everyone around us—the people on the tower with us—have safety lines hooked to us. That's what you were just saying. The people here are supporting you." I noticed several people smiling at my animation as they crossed the bridge behind us, but I couldn't help myself. "As long as we keep climbing with them, we don't risk falling, because they're holding us up until we get used to the new heights."

I looked at Keith and there was a small light of understanding in his eyes, but the bulb was still trying to come on. I couldn't fault him for that. This was what Jeff had been trying to tell me, and I was just now beginning to get it and it was a cool feeling.

There hadn't been very many times in life when my brain finally made such a huge connection. There were those few times I'd heard something over and over, then suddenly, when all the right neural pathways had formed, the message instantly took on a new, profound meaning. This was one of those moments. I'd heard Jeff talking about vertical growth but only understood a shadow of his meaning.

Suddenly, another chunk fell into place—The Jonah Complex sermon and me being afraid of my calling—which explained more about my fear of falling from vertical growth. I was afraid to follow my calling, because if I failed, I was terrified at how far I'd fall. But with my new insight, I knew that, while it felt like a real fear, it was a fake one. When you grew vertically, you couldn't fall because there wasn't any way to go but up. Any so-called failing was just another aspect of the growing process. It is just part of the experience. Wow!

I looked over at Keith. "Thanks for this talk. It was amazingly helpful."

He gave me an unsure smile, and I could tell he was wondering what the heck I was talking about, but after a long moment he shrugged and said, "Happy to help, Stanley."

I laughed and he joined me. We rose up from our leaning position on the bridge railing and started walking into the building, talking about lighter topics.

Knowing Keith was rotating around different labs, I asked where he was going to be this week.

"Somethin' to do with a flywheel. Not sure what that is but guess I'll find out."

"Hey, that's cool. That's the project I'm on, so I guess we'll be seeing each other this week."

His face lit up. "Really? That's awesome."

Chapter 39

Over the next few days, I wasn't working directly with Keith, but from my vantage point looking down over the lab floor, I worried as I watched him. Despite the acceptance everyone showed him and the relaxed environment, Keith was a nervous wreck.

Wednesday afternoon, he came up the stairs and over to where I was sitting at my computer.

I looked up at him. "You okay, Keith?"

Solemnly, he told me, "I just don't think I'm cut out for this. I don't understand a lot of what they are tellin' me to do, and I'm scared to death I'm gonna mess up something expensive. Everyone's super patient, but I'm so nervous I can barely listen to what they're explainin' to me."

Looking out over the floor at the equipment and the massive flywheel containment chambers, I tried to see it from his point of view. All the profoundly intelligent people in white lab coats running around, writing complex equations on rolling white boards near the flywheels, working like maniacs on multiple-monitored computers, or gleefully gutting large pieces of machinery. I was intimidated, too, so I could only imagine how hard it must be for him. I turned back to him and offered hollow words, but they were the best I had, "Just relax. You'll be fine."

His shoulders dropped even more. After our conversation Monday on the bridge, I think he had higher expectations from me. He gave a small attempt at a smile and left.

I spent the next thirty minutes just watching him, wondering what to do.

Then I had a thought that made me burst out into a grin as I had a WWJD moment, "What Would Jeff Do?" Turning back to my computer, I pulled up my instant messenger and asked Jeff to come to the lab.

Like he'd been waiting for my message, "On my way" immediately popped up in reply.

Ignoring my work tasks, I watched Keith standing nervously at the control panel of one of the flywheels.

In a remarkably short time, Jeff pulled up a chair beside me. "What's up?"

"I'm worried about Keith. He's too overwhelmed, too frustrated."

"Go on."

I looked at Jeff, a little bothered. I wanted him here, to fix things, not make me explain it; if I could've explained it, I probably could have fixed it myself. But I tried. "It's like he's almost paralyzed with fear, fear of messing up. To the point that I think it's going to be a self-fulfilling prophecy really soon."

Jeff turned back to Keith. "And..."

I was irritated by Jeff not taking care of this and the high pitch hum of the shop I was usually able to tune out was starting to get on my nerves, adding to the irritation. Showing my frustration, I huffed. "I don't know, Jeff! That's why I called you. I don't know! He's frustrated and scared he'll fail. I've told him this isn't that type of place, but he can't let go of that fear. Until he lets go of that fear, he won't be able to do anything here."

The humming was starting to drive me nuts. This lab was always noisy, but this was different than normal and it was getting louder.

"So, what you're saying," Jeff said, turning to me, "is until he has permission to fail, he'll never succeed?"

With the simple clarity of that statement, my anger dissipated, and I smiled at Jeff, the master of situations. "Yes, that's exactly what I'm saying."

The humming continued getting louder, and I looked out at the floor as people started scurrying around, and then congregated at the control panel Keith was manning. Oh, this wasn't good, the noise was coming from Keith's flywheel.

Voices started rising, orders were shouted over the noise, but within moments the order was given to clear the area and take cover. I started to get up, but Jeff calmly placed his hand on my leg, and we watched.

Less than a minute later, a horrendous noise echoed throughout the lab, shaking the walls and floor, and the humming stopped.

Now, I could hear the talking on the floor as everyone made their way back to the silent flywheel. "The containment chamber held. Wonder what the inside looks like?"

Jeff got up, and I followed.

When we got close to the gathered horde, it was easy to see that Keith's eyes were red, and he was trying hard not to shake.

Jeff calmly looked at him. "What happened?"

Keith could barely talk. "Was just foll... followin' instructions they... they gave me ta... ta test this. I swear I followed them step by step. I... I'm really sorry. I sh... shouldn't have been workin' on this. I'm really sorry. I..."

Jeff held up his hand to stop Keith. "Do you have the instructions?"

Keith's trembling hand held them out for Jeff, who gently took them and motioned for Keith to follow.

They stopped at the next flywheel control station, which I knew was the other one testing the same configuration as the now dead one.

Jeff set the paper down on the panel and matter-of-factly said to Keith, "So, let's walk through this." He started following the instructions and asking Keith questions about what he'd done at each step.

Then came the moment Keith had dreaded, Jeff asked him about one of the steps, and Keith turned white and almost went to the floor, but Jeff steadied him and asked, "You missed that one?"

Keith nodded in dooming affirmation.

Jeff skipped it and continued with the rest of the instructions, and soon the humming started again. Jeff began working at the control panel, trying to stop what had gone wrong, then he called Aaron over and some other engineers.

It was quickly apparent that there wasn't a fix, and as the noise grew, everyone backed away until the horrendous noise was heard for a second time.

Again, everyone gathered around, and Keith was more pale than before and more confused.

"You see that?" Jeff asked Aaron, pointing at the pair of now dead cylinders. "Looks like Keith just saved us buckets of money. If that configuration had gotten out into production, who knows what would have happened." He then turned to Keith. "Great job. You know we give bonuses when people do stuff like this, don't you? With as much as you've saved us, yours should be nice." Jeff handed Keith the instructions, patted him on the shoulder and headed for the stairs.

I quickly followed Jeff, in awe of what had just happened. All the time he'd been pushing me to explain the situation, he was busy fixing things and guiding me to my own answers about Keith.

We got to the top of the stairs, and I looked back to the two out of commission flywheels. "How much did that lesson cost?"

As Jeff opened the lab door, he turned to look back towards the lab floor and located Keith. "Our product wasn't damaged at all. In fact, we made a major upgrade to it, today."

All I could do was smile.

Back at my computer about twenty minutes later, Keith came up and sat beside me. I instantly saw the light bulb from this morning's bridge talk had finally been turned on.

"The fall didn't hurt." He smiled with a confidence I hadn't seen before. "I think I can start climbing that tower now."

Over the rest of his week with the flywheel group, I watched Keith. His whole demeanor had changed. He was indeed free. He now had permission to mess up, to fail, and as a result, he also had permission to take chances and learn.

Chapter 40

My calendar had an appointment for Thursday morning of my fourth week to meet with Sam to pick up my first official paycheck. The check Jane had given me had held us over nicely, but I was anxious to get this one.

When I got to Sam's office, I took a deep breath and tried to relax, because I knew once I went through that door an energy force I couldn't control would hit me. Yet, I found myself looking forward to this meeting.

I knocked and was beckoned in. Sam stood and about broke my hand with his handshake. Before I could get seated, a folder was placed in front of me, opened and the papers spread out.

Sam started. "So, here's what I got." Then he stopped, paused and looked at me. In slow motion for him, he asked, "Sorry, I forgot to check. Would you rather work with someone on my staff? Some people find me overwhelming. So, I don't mind at all. This meeting is totally for you, so my feelings won't be hurt."

I grinned at him. "No, Sam. I was looking forward to talking to you. I took my moment to relax before I walked in."

"Ha!" he exclaimed with a massive smile. "Then let's go. Pulled your credit report and this paper—" he pointed to one "—has all we can do to get that improved. Sign those papers—" he pointed to three more "—and put them in the envelopes under them and send them off."

He paused again, looked at me, then like a race horse being held back at the start of a race, he said, "Oh, also forgot to say, everything is optional. If you want, I'll give you your paycheck, and we're done. I've done some stuff here for you that I think will help your financial situation, but none of it's set in stone. So just slap me up-side the head to get my attention, and we will make any changes you want." He looked at me questioningly.

I raised my shoulders and cocked my head sideways. "Let's see what you got."

The race horse was let go. "Got some checks for some medical bills that are in collections. Took that out of your paycheck. But it all works into the budget, but we'll get to that, but we can change it if you want. Here are papers for a refinance on your house. We work with a great company and can beat any market interest rate. We guarantee the loan with them, so credit score isn't an issue. Fifteen year loan shortens what you have now, and because of the low interest rate and the price I found for your insurance, your payment is a little lower. Car insurance is lower, too, with more coverage." He moved those papers and grabbed the next stack. "Here's a—"

"Stop!" I exclaimed with a laugh.

He sat back and looked at me with mild worry on his face.

"You set up a refinance for my house and found me cheaper insurance? And got checks to pay off my medical bills?"

His eye brows lifted as his worried expression increased. "Yeah?"

Those were all things I'd tried to do, but couldn't get done. Another one of the dopey situations where you couldn't fix your finances because your credit rating had tanked, but you couldn't fix your credit rating because your finances were hosed. A smile came to my face and I fought a tear away. "Carry on."

He looked at me questioningly for a second just to verify I was okay.

I nodded.

"You have 401-K's in four different places. I've listed out what I think are your three best options." He shoved two more papers at me. "You just need to fill in the blanks with what option you want and send them off. Of course, future income and the economy are variables we can't predict, but I think I have a plan in place that can get you retired at a comfortable level before you're too old to enjoy it." He set those papers aside and showed me the next set. "Here is a first stab at a budget. It's a little painful this month, but we can take care of a bunch of your biggest pain-points right away, if you follow it. We don't need to review it right now. I want you and Beth to look at it and go over it together. And last, but not least, here's your paycheck." He slid all the papers together, closed the folder and looked at me as he held it toward me.

Jeff's words came back to me from my first day, when he'd said to wait for my first frantic ten-minute meeting with Sam, where I'd walk away excited to cut my budget to the bone. Jeff had certainly nailed it. I was pumped.

I took the folder and stood. "Beth and I will look it over. But I have a feeling we won't be changing much. My guess is I have just witnessed a true master."

He slapped the desk and let out a loud laugh. "I gave up a chance for a professional racquetball career to do this, because this is more fun. So, I'd better be one of the best there ever was."

That statement elevated Sam to a new level for me and truly made me want to be more like him when I grew up. I wanted to be able to make a statement like that and not have to feel like I should minimize my accomplishments.

* * *

The next two weeks passed quickly at the Institute. I was always engaged in something interesting. Coworkers invited me to do stuff with them all the time. I went rock climbing, kayaking, hiking, tennis, picnics, and of course, played racquetball with Sam and actually started scoring some points.

Excitement grew at work about Marcus' release concert and fight. As the event got closer, Marcus was making appearances on all sorts of talk shows, and the process of deciding which four men would fight Marcus was going on across America. National news stations were picking up on the excitement, and it was turning into a media circus, but that's what Marcus and Jeff apparently wanted. Marcus would need massive attention to get enough support for the changes he wanted to make.

I'd asked Marcus for a T-shirt for Cooper, and Marcus sent a signed one out to Cooper right away. Then Marcus went beyond that favor. He got the address to Cooper's school and sent a shirt (unsigned) for every kid in the school, after verifying it was okay with the school. The school's principal had seen Marcus on the talk shows and liked what he was hearing, so was happy to have the shirts. Cooper was riding high on the attention.

I also read to Rita's class three times a week and ate lunch with them. And I ate many meals with Jeff's family and helped Dylan with his schoolwork.

Dylan made some progress, and he kept pushing forward, never making excuses. After what Jeff had said about Dylan being the poster-child for humanity, I watched him more closely, and I watched others more closely. It isn't like I'd ever had grounds to doubt Jeff, but as I watched Dylan, I knew Jeff was right.

The mass of men who Thoreau talked about living lives of quiet desperation were probably typical everyday people, people who'd never excel at anything big-time, but if they chose to, they could awesomely excel at being themselves. Yet from what I could see, most of that mass of people wasted their lives attempting to impress others by being someone they weren't.

Whereas, Dylan—who wasn't a smart or good looking kid, and didn't bother following any trends—was Dylan through and through, and no one was going to stop him from being the best Dylan he could be.

Whenever I went over there, we'd talk about his school day. One day, he told me about the bullies who picked on him. When I asked him why he didn't go to Rita's school—which seemed a much safer, kinder place for him to be—he looked at me with an expression that was a mix of confusion and worry.

"What can I do for them from Rita's school?" he asked, in all his Dylan seriousness. "I can't help them if I leave." He sighed. "I kind of feel sorry for them. They just want to feel better about themselves, and picking on me is the only way they know how to do that. If I leave, how can I help them find a better way to feel better about themselves?"

I couldn't help but agree with him, and at the same time, admire his courage. I knew I wouldn't have had his courage when I was his age, and doubted I had that kind of courage now.

"Besides," he continued with his usual enthusiasm, "some of the guys who used to pick on me are now my friends. Imagine if I'd have left before that happened, how would they have learned a better way?"

My mind went back to Grace talking about leaving HRI. Dylan wanted to be at a broken school because he could make a difference, make it better. Yet, unlike Grace, this didn't sound like his dad's idea; it sounded like Dylan had come to this decision on his own, out of compassion for the bullies.

How cool was it for a thirteen-year-old boy to have such profound insight into such a painful situation and the compassion to endure the pain in an attempt to help others? Jeff had chosen a great poster child.

That evening after I was done tutoring Dylan, and while Jeff was reading to "the gang," as he called them, I sat on his back patio in his sinfully comfortable patio chairs, looking up at the stars in the clear night sky, thankful for my time here. I'd grown so much.

When I'd first arrived at HRI, Jeff had said the employees were the main product of the company and that was obvious in every action the company took. And personally, I felt valued as a person in a way that I never had in any company I'd ever worked for.

With Keith, after he blew up the flywheels, we talked often and I could see his metamorphosis. He'd discovered he loved the building technologies lab, and he'd found a person to shadow and learn from. Before my eyes, he was changing from an undereducated, nice person without any real future, into an engaged, contributing, nice person, who was taking night courses to get his GED and looking for colleges with building technologies degrees.

And Keith wasn't the only one HRI was changing in unexpected ways. The math equations my lab-buddies had taken the painstaking time to explain made total sense now, and when it came time to reformulate equations, I was doing them by myself. The effort the team had spent on me meant I didn't have to wait for someone else to do things for me in the documentation or on the product itself. Plus, I was redesigning and re-milling pieces for the flywheel system without the safety net of any of the team supervising. In a short time, I'd become more deeply involved in this job than I'd ever been in any job before. More importantly, my confidence in my abilities and myself were growing from the experience.

Without a doubt, Jeff, his dad, and the others at the Institute had built something magnificent.

As Jeff sat down in the patio chair beside mine, I turned to him and said, "It's an interesting thing the Institute does by saying their product is their employees."

"It's more than interesting." He looked up at the stars for a minute. "What most companies call their products are what we consider our by-products. For us, the by-products we supply to our customers are made by our main product, our employees. Since we produce such high-quality products—the employees—our by-products are high quality, too. And the effort required to produce our by-products is much less than other companies."

I nodded. "I've seen some of it, but tell me more."

"Because we spend so much time spreading knowledge and skills between employees, we can take almost anyone from the institute and drop them into almost any project, and they'll be a high-functioning team member almost immediately, which greatly cuts down on the training overhead that is usually spent bringing a new person onto a project. And, because we don't push people into areas they're not interested in, we find that the more engaged people are, the more engaged they want to become. HRI's culture is one that causes people to want to step out of their comfort zone and grow in new ways. Which benefits HRI all the more."

"If you want a testimonial for your website, I'll give you one," I replied with a smile. "I can't think of a job here I wouldn't want to do." I went through a quick inventory of what I'd seen people doing. I wouldn't even mind cooking for a while, that might be interesting. But then one popped in my head. "Well, I can't see myself doing Summer's job, mostly because HRI wouldn't seem like HRI without her there at the front desk to greet everybody every morning. And I know she does much more than that."

Jeff adjusted his patio chair from the reclining position to sitting up straighter, then returned my smile. "I told you when you first got here that she's the brains of the operation. Yet, you should see Summer run the CNC equipment. A bunch of years ago, she asked to learn, so we put her back there working with a team and got someone else up to be Director of First Impressions while she did that."

"I'll bet she was great running the milling machine."

"She was, and she's done many other jobs, both before and since. But she's decided she likes being Director of First Impressions the most, so she always returns."

I sat for a minute and thought about what he'd said, and Jeff let me do so. Then I looked over to him. "So, because your products are so well built, the by-products are well built. Once I start thinking about it that way, it seems pretty obvious."

He smiled as he saw me really starting to understand what he was talking about. "You're right; it's obvious when you have the right foundation. Now apply the concept to some other things. As Rita has informed you, I'm not fond of the idea of grades. Let's play with that idea. Other than the student, what's the product of a school?"

I thought about it a moment. "Knowledge?"

"Right. The product should be knowledge. Yet when you get out of school, what's the first thing people want to know about your education?"

That one seemed clear. "Your GPA."

"The product of the school has become the grades. As long as a student gets the right grades, what they actually learned isn't of much interest to anyone; education and knowledge aren't the product anymore. What we're doing at Rita's school is trying to move the school towards having the students and parents seeing knowledge as the product. Knowledge, education, understanding and the ability to learn how to self-learn, so the kids won't have to rely on teachers as they get older."

I repeated for my understanding, "So if knowledge and education were to actually be the product in a school, then grades would be the by-product."

"Exactly, friend. If students are studying Shakespeare's *Hamlet*, they should be doing their best to learn *Hamlet*. Once they do, their by-product will be a good grade. If, however, their product is the grade, chances are, they're only going to learn enough to get that grade, and then, most likely, will miss the deeper essence of *Hamlet*, its time, culture, meaning, current implications and so forth."

He paused again, so I said the next logical thing that came to mind. "'I am but mad north-north-west: when the wind is southerly I know a hawk from a handsaw.'"

Jeff looked over at me with a big smile. "'Well be with you, gentlemen!'"

I don't know why I was surprised Jeff knew the next line in Hamlet, but I wasn't going to let him out do me. "'Hark you, Guildenstern; and you too: at each ear a hearer: that great baby you see there is not yet out of his swaddling-clouts.'"

Still with his smile and in the new characters voice, he recited, "'Happily he's the second time come to them; for they say an old man is twice a child.'"

I was astounded. "You know the whole thing?"

"I should ask the same of you. That was impressive. My guess is that you got an 'A' on *Hamlet*."

"My high school literature teacher was great. And yes, now that I think about it, I did get an 'A.'"

And now that I was thinking about it, I realized Jeff hadn't taken his example of *Hamlet* out of thin air. Grades hadn't mattered to my English Lit teacher. She'd loved the subject, she'd loved to teach, and she'd made her classes so enjoyable it was easy to learn about *Hamlet*. Her not caring about the grades, certainly, didn't mean the tests she gave were trivial; you couldn't pass them if you didn't know *Hamlet* backwards and forwards, but because of her, I did. She was a wonderful teacher.

He watched with his typical smile as these realizations came to me. He then went on, "Religion suffers the same problem. They're selling the wrong product."

"Heaven? Salvation?" I wondered how that was the wrong product.

"Heaven and salvation should be by-products of living life in a way that would naturally bring you to Heaven. But when your product is Heaven, you don't look for the best way to live your life here on Earth, you look for the shortcuts to make sure you get into Heaven."

"In what way?"

"Let's say that a church has rules that say do 'A', 'B' and 'C', and they promise you that if you follow those rules, you'll go to Heaven. So, as a good church-person, focused on your afterlife product, you do 'A', 'B', and 'C'. Which may be great, but by being so focused on that product, they totally miss the opportunities to do 'D', 'E' and 'F' that would make their life on Earth happier and profoundly fulfilling."

Jokingly I added, "I can see people doing 'A' and 'E', but are you sure you want people doing 'D'?"

He gave me a wide grin. "Depends on the context." He paused and then added. "You want specifics? Would that help?"

I waved my hand in front of me. "No, I get it. Every church or religion has their own list. I know Beth's church does, and they focus heavily on those things. But if you try to bring up anything outside that list, like environmentalism, they won't get it. The people in her church tell me, 'It's not a salvation issue.'" I looked at him as the idea started to solidify in my mind. "You're right. The church's product is Heaven, and anything that doesn't lead directly to that isn't important, no matter how good or right."

"Not all churches, Stanley, and not all church people, not by any means. But, yes, there are many church people who feel everything else is a distraction from the end-goal. It's as if they are students who've been told what will be on the test, so that's all they're going to study."

I realized my head was nodding in agreement. Summing up my understanding, I said, "So, just like school, if your goal is a good grade on the test, you'll miss the point of the class. And if your only goal is to get into Heaven, you've missed the point of the teachings."

"Exactly. Heaven isn't a reward for checking things off a list. The people who live their lives checking that list miss so many ways to be more loving and compassionate people and to build a better life and better world right here and now."

I stood and walked towards the edge of the patio and leaned on the railing to think. This talk was triggering some uneasy thoughts that for a long time had seemed to float right below the surface of my mind, but were now bubbling to the surface, along with memories of our conversation of Heaven and Hell as we drove through the cornfields of Illinois. I turned and sat on the railing. "Fear." I looked at Jeff. "I've heard people in Beth's church say they don't want to go to Hell so they follow the rules: don't drink, gamble, sleep around, etc. Fear is what drives them."

Jeff looked at me with unconditional approval, waiting for me to continue.

"But like you said on the trip here, if emotions are amplified in the next realm—after we die—then if they live and die in fear, they're in trouble." I stood from the railing and paced with my crossed arms in front of me and looked down as I thought. "And they've missed the point."

Jeff got up and casually walked in my direction. "That's what's bothered you all along, friend. You know Heaven's in your heart. Yet you've been told differently by church authority figures. You want to believe what they say, since they're the experts and you think they should know what's real. But what they say doesn't fit with what you know, and you can't reconcile the two, so you've shoved the whole conflict to the back of your mind and lived an uneasy life."

I continued to look down and gave a nervous chuckle as the need to discount my knowing and trust in something that felt wrong permanently vacated my brain. "Heaven's not a selfish reward for following the rules while I'm alive; it's here in my heart, right now." I fought the urge to cry as the simple statement released a lifetime of confusion.

I looked at Jeff as he raised his hand and placed it on my shoulder. With a look of infinite peace he said, "Your heart is just where Jesus said it should be to enter the gates."

My knees grew weak, so I quickly sat in the nearest chair, leaned back and looked up at the stars.

Why hadn't someone said this to me long ago?

I'd fought the message that Beth's church had tried to teach me for so long, because it never made sense to me. But as I listened to

Jeff, what he said all sounded so right.

Watching TV news and seeing religions tear the world apart had done so much damage to me. Watching Christians — people who were supposed to spread love — protest various causes, using anger, fear and hate, had pushed me even farther away.

Back in my college days, I'd watched a man preaching on campus. He'd worn the sandwich board proclaiming, "God hates, gays, prostitutes, drug addicts, drunks, etc." And the words he spewed had been filled with anger and vile. I'd watched him, knowing the guy was wrong, but not knowing how to verbalize why I thought that. One day, one of the professors had come along and, visibly bothered by this man's message, had walked away, only to come storming back a few minutes later. He'd yelled at the man with the sandwich boards, "God does *not* hate those people! God *loves* those people! How can you stand up there and preach a message of hate in God's name?"

As I combined that memory with Jeff's example, I had to conclude that some churches weren't even teaching "A", "B" and "C", but instead, they'd developed their own hate-filled alphabet, and their by-product was going to come as a huge shock to them when they transitioned to a realm where all their emotions were unfiltered and amplified.

Giving Jeff a serious look, I said, "Thanks for taking me on this journey."

He winked at me. "It's all part of the experience, friend."

Chapter 41

The next week passed quickly, and suddenly, it was the end of my sixth week at HRI, and that Saturday a large group of HRI folks gathered in its parking lot to load onto rented buses to be taken to The Change's fight and concert. As I had no desire to drive in traffic, find the stadium, or try to find parking in Philadelphia, I locked my car and headed to the nearest bus with a book in hand and looked forward to some time to read.

Walking down the bus aisle, I saw Keith and Aaron sitting together, so I sat in the row across from them. During the trip to the concert, I got to read a little, but the group on the bus was in a very social mood, anticipating the event. Everyone speculated how the fights would go, but if anyone on the bus doubted Marcus would win, they didn't voice that concern.

In the week before, the media hadn't hesitated to air its doubt. I'd seen some news coverage showing the musical groups who'd been hired to perform if The Change was incapacitated. If Jeff's confidence was misplaced and Marcus was too hurt to play, I decided I'd go out to the bus and read since I had my doubts I could stomach any other rapper.

Strangely enough, considering my opinion of most rappers, I was looking forward to seeing Marcus and his band. They'd had a great stage show at the convention center and his music was growing on me. HRI had sold some pre-release copies of Marcus' CD, so I'd bought one to support him, and figured I'd listen to it once just to say I had. I'd put it in my car's CD player one morning as I drove in to work because I had to read to Rita's class, and interestingly enough, it hadn't left the player yet. I skipped the "Nineveh" track when I drove, because I got so distracted, but the rest of the songs were rapidly growing on me, to the point—I was almost embarrassed to admit—I actually knew most of the lyrics.

After an energetic trip, we unloaded from the buses in front of the stadium and started a journey through multiple security check points and multiple metal detectors, and I was vastly amused to watch men with sagging pants have to reach to their knees to empty their pockets. Thankfully, we'd gotten an email warning us ahead of time, so I hadn't brought my ever-present pocketknife Beth had given me the first Christmas we were married. Looking at the containers filled with prohibited artifacts, I figured some concert attendees hadn't gotten the memo.

Jeff, Jonathan, and most of Jeff's kids had driven up hours earlier with Marcus and had their own seating.

As the HRI group made our way to our seats, I scoped out the crowd. The stadium was packed and the crowd was highly energized. I mentally replayed Beth's words of caution as, given the expected audience, she suggested I not come to the concert. Actually, I was surprised at the diversity of the crowd. There were the expected thug personas but there were also a surprising number of people somewhat closer to my norm. And, under normal conditions I'd have rather done what she wanted and stayed home to watch in the comfort of my home, like Beth and Cooper were. But with Jeff and The Change, these weren't normal conditions. Besides, with all the check points and metal detectors, I was confident there weren't any weapons here, or at least not any metal ones.

As I followed Aaron and Keith through the crowd, we saw a couple of fights start, but security was there immediately and took the participants away.

The HRI group had seats together, so once we got to our area, I felt a little more relaxed and settled into my seat between Keith and Aaron. We had great ringside seats, right by the gate where the fighters would enter the cage. We could also see the huge monitors giving close-ups of the cage.

We talked amongst ourselves, but mostly waited anxiously for the event to begin.

Right on time, the announcer walked past us and climbed the steps to enter the cage followed by a plethora of camera people.

Once the exuberant crowd quieted, the announcer explained how the fights would work and the other arrangements for the evening. Then, once the formalities were out of the way, he introduced the first opponent, a guy named Tyrone, from LA; he was 6'2" and 240 pounds.

As he was being introduced, Tyrone and a number of men, I assume trainers and such, strutted past us to the entrance of the cage. He was stopped there and asked to remove his warm-up jacket. An official of some type patted him down.

Tyrone, wearing only baggy red athletic-type shorts and minimally padded red gloves, stood less than ten feet from me and I could easily see a number of tattoos of novice quality with some professional work mixed in. A trainer rubbed some Vaseline on Tyrone's face as Tyrone shook his arms to loosen them up and ran his gloved hand over his short cropped black hair. We were close enough to hear the conversation between Tyrone and his entourage, but because their vernacular was so different I had problems understanding them.

When he was released by the officials, Tyrone quickly climbed the stairs and entered the ring to be greeted by heavy cheering from the crowd, as he attempted to look cool and calm.

The camera zoomed in on him, and we could see a close-up on the huge monitors. To me, he was one mean looking guy. Then when he moved away from the announcer and paced around the inside of the fight cage, playing to the crowd, giving the typical hand gestures and arm movements that I'd seen on TV associated with gangs. To me, he looked like an idiot. Yeah, he was huge and had lots of muscles, but I wasn't impressed by his display.

The announcer then introduced The Change, 6'3" and 230 pounds.

Marcus nodded at us as he walked by, surrounded by his trainers and support team. He was stopped by the cage entrance and subjected to the same routine as Tyrone. Marcus had on skin tight white shorts with a black stipe on the outer thigh. He alternately pulled each arm across his chest by grabbing the elbow with his black-gloved hand. When the officials released him, he turned, gave our section a Marcus-type smile and as he turned back towards the cage, his persona change was remarkable. He strutted into the cage much like his opponent had, to some cheering, but not the overwhelming approval I'd expected, and the cheers were accompanied by a fair amount of booing and profanity by a vocal crowd.

I looked around the stadium wondering why, then looked towards Keith. He was in the age-group who listened to rap, and I thought he might have some youthful insight. "I thought The

Change was popular."

He shrugged. "I don't know. He's liked in some groups. Not too liked in the hardcore scene." He took a moment to look around more. "He wants to change things." Then he looked at me and gave a hesitant laugh. "Guess you could figure that from his name."

Jokingly, I nodded as if the meaning of the name had just become clear and said, "Ahhh."

Keith looked at me for a minute, as if he was wondering why I didn't know this before.

Immediately, I felt bad and made a mental note to watch my sarcasm. I really respected Keith and wanted to make sure I didn't belittle him.

Keith slowly started again, paying attention to my reaction. I hoped he didn't feel I was making fun of him. "Talked ta some guys 'bout him. They don't want change. Where would that leave 'em?"

I looked at him questioningly. "Better off?"

He shrugged. "Don't know. Losin' the only way you know isn't easy. Change ain't easy."

I thought, "But you jumped right into it." And I was about to say it, but my attention was drawn back to the cage.

Marcus's strut and exaggerated hand gestures annoyed me. I was disappointed to see Marcus trying to look cool. I would have put him above that. But then he stopped, looked at his opponent, then at the crowd, and started in again. It suddenly occurred to me what he was doing... Marcus was mocking the guy. As if to confirm my guess, Marcus bent over laughing, and then started up again and pointed at Tyrone. The camera guys in the ring were catching all this and displaying it on the big screens.

Tyrone apparently didn't see the humor in this and started yelling and trying to look even tougher.

Our seats were great. We could hear everything during the brief periods the crowd wasn't yelling.

The announcer started speaking again, and the crowds quieted. After the announcer finished, the referee entered the cage and called the two fighters to the center. The announcer held his microphone in front of the referee so he could explain to the fighters and audience the rules of the fight, which were pretty limited: no biting, eye gouging and other stuff like that. Each match was five rounds, each of five minutes in length, or the fight could end with a knock out, technical knockout (TKO), or submission. A submission, also called a "tap out", was where one of the fighters tapped on the mat or verbally ended the fight.

At this point, the announcer and all the TV guys left the cage, leaving only the ref and the fighters. I'd watched a couple of these types of fights on TV before I'd come today, so I was at least a little familiar with what was happening.

Tyrone reached up, took out his mouth guard and spoke, in a fake sugary tone, loud enough we could hear from our vantage point. "Gonna like stompin' your pampered, rich behind into the mat."

Marcus reached up and removed his mouth piece. "I wish you the best of luck. But have you thought about what college you're going to attend?"

Tyrone gave Marcus a cocky smile and put his mouth guard back in, and Marcus followed suit.

The referee told them to touch gloves. They did so, backed away and waited for the signal to begin.

The referee gave the signal.

As the crowd roared its approval of the fight, The Change dropped to his knees, holding his arms outstretched.

Tyrone had started a charge toward him, but then stopped with a confused look.

Marcus didn't flinch.

Tyrone eased up to him, waiting for The Change's trap to be sprung.

The Change didn't flinch, and when the large screens projecting the fight zoomed in on Marcus, you could see him close his eyes.

Gradually, the stadium went silent. They were as surprised as Tyrone.

Tyrone raised a fist and The Change, still on his knees, eyes closed, arms spread, didn't move.

Keith leaned over to me. "I like watching these fights. Watch lots of 'em. But never seen this before."

I didn't reply, but thought, "I have. Like father, like son." I wondered if Marcus was going to let five guys beat the crap out of him until they gave up.

Tyrone looked around nervously, not knowing what to do. He had a nation of eyes watching him, and he knew he was supposed to look cool and in control, but it was obvious he didn't know what to do with an opponent kneeling before him. Tyrone yelled, "Get up!"

Marcus didn't move or open his eyes.

Tyrone tested Marcus with a few jerky movements like he was

going to punch, but Marcus was a statue. Then Tyrone followed through and landed a solid punch.

The Change fell to the mat, hard, as the stadium full of people held their breath.

Tyrone watched Marcus as he slowly got back onto his knees, resumed his previous kneeling position with blood dripping out of his mouth. Marcus then smiled at Tyrone, closed his eyes, and spread his arms again, as the crowd started rumbling, clearly as confused as Tyrone.

Tyrone, obviously furious, yelled and whipped down another punch.

Not wanting to see what was coming, I closed my eyes. I remembered, all too well, watching his dad do this, and didn't want to see it again.

The crowd screamed and roared, joined by the HRI people surrounding me.

I was afraid to open my eyes, but after a moment, I realized the screams around me were excited, not horrified, and I gathered my courage.

Tyrone was on the mat struggling to get up, and The Change was doing back flips around the cage.

The Change then leaned against the chain link and waited for Tyrone to get up and shake it off.

I shook my head and smiled. That was classic. Marcus was a piece of work. The mental battle had begun, and I knew Tyrone couldn't match Marcus.

After Tyrone was up and moving, Marcus walked up to him and put up his gloved fists and settled into a fighting stance.

Tyrone obviously liked this better; it was what he was used to. He swung.

Marcus blocked the punch, spun Tyrone around, and then picked him up overhead by the back of his neck and waist of his shorts and threw him against the fence, which rattled loudly. The crowd roared as Tyrone slid to the cage floor in a heap.

Keith leaned over to me again. "Man! Didn't know he was that strong."

I smiled at Keith. "That's the truth."

We watched Marcus wait for Tyrone to get up, and Keith gave me his next observation. "Funny The Change isn't goin' for him on the ground. Most of these fights turn into grabbling matches."

The camera focused in on Tyrone as he stood. His anger was clear and hatred burned in his eyes.

Tyrone charged, and Marcus jumped into the air, wrapped his legs around Tyrone's neck, twisted in midair, and slammed Tyrone to the cage floor. Tyrone's body bounced and hit a second time. Marcus removed his legs from around Tyrone's head and stood as his opponent lay there.

From the enthusiastic reaction of the crowd, they were as impressed with the move as I was.

I said to Aaron and Keith, "That's going to be something to watch in slow motion."

Tyrone struggled to stand, and once he was finally on his feet, staggered.

Marcus walked calmly over and grabbed Tyrone by the neck to steady him. Then Marcus pulled his fist back, as Tyrone, with a dazed look in his eyes attempted to raise his hands to defend himself. Marcus's fist swiftly moved to Tyrone's face, stopping with great control just as it made skin contact with Tyrone's eye. The Change then pushed Tyrone back and one of the unsteady man's legs buckled under him.

There was a murmur through the crowd, and it was hard to tell what they were thinking. My guess was they'd expected to see a brutal match and this was not what they'd hoped for.

Down on one knee, Tyrone, with effort, stood again.

Marcus' first opponent of the evening, then turned and walked toward the door of the cage. He knew he'd been beaten.

The crowd rumbled loudly, not sure what was going on.

The referee ran to Tyrone to find out what was happening.

When he got to Tyrone, Tyrone placed his hand in the middle of the ref's chest and shoved him back. Someone opened the cage door, and Tyrone held onto the door as he carefully descended, supported by his trainers, who were arguing with him, trying to convince him to return to the ring.

The camera men swarmed.

The crowd's rumbles turned into loud boo's. The fight was over after only a couple moves, and they weren't satisfied.

From my seat so close to the aisle, I watched Tyrone's face as he pushed away from his people, threw his mouth guard to the side, and started peeling off his gloves as he carefully moved our direction, trying not to stagger with each step, and I was surprised by my reaction. I felt sorry for Tyrone. The man leaving the cage wasn't the same one who'd entered; Marcus had taken that man away. Gone was the cockiness and arrogance; replaced with humility. I wondered what the future looked like in his head at that moment.

Right then, the memory of Jeff walking away from me in the parking lot when we'd first arrived in Bethlehem came to my mind, and I was struck with a blinding flash of insight. The man who'd watched Jeff walk away wasn't the same man who'd picked him up at the stoplight in Bakersfield. Jeff had taken that first man away and left a new one in his place; I had changed so much. Granted, pseudo-arrogance wasn't one of my faults, but I had plenty of others, and in a strange way, Tyrone and I were kindred spirits. Men remade by Jeff.

As Tyrone got even with us, The Change ran out of the cage and placed his gloved hand on Tyrone's shoulder. "Please, forgive me."

Tyrone stopped with his back to Marcus and looked at the concrete floor for a few seconds. He then turned, looked Marcus in the eye, and shoved him back. Tyrone clinched his teeth and angrily exclaimed, "Forgive you!? How can I forgive you? You've just taken away everything I know, everything I was. I can't ever go home again. They'd kill me." He turned from Marcus, facing the long aisle again. "No! I don't forgive you!" Then after a long pause, he looked over his shoulder to Marcus. "You made me into nothing. Hope you got something for me."

The Change smiled and placed his gloved hand on Tyrone's shoulder. "Let's build something beautiful together."

Tyrone gave a half smile, nodded and walked out, ignoring the angry crowd, the camera guys and his trainers.

Beside me, I heard a soft, "Wonderful," and looked over at Aaron who had a slight smile on his face.

I quickly looked back to see Tyrone head to the changing rooms where Jeff was waiting. They walked off together with the trainers, and the rest hurried back toward the cage.

With a bit of humorous envy, I thought, "You know, Jeff never asked for me to forgive him after he ripped my world apart. Marcus has one up on him."

Marcus climbed back into the cage followed by some of his support team, and the official held up Marcus' hand and announced, to a very loud and very mixed—the boo's about even with the cheers—reaction from the crowd, the match's official time was two minutes and twenty-one seconds.

Marcus calmly walked to his side of the cage where his team was waiting for him. They gave him water as they waited for his next opponent.

The announcer introduced Andre at 6'8" and 320 pounds. Andre strutted down the aisle, and when he stopped at the stairs to the cage, he towered over the officials who were patting him down before letting him in the ring. When he removed his jacket, I heard a gasp beside me.

I looked at Aaron.

In an astonished tone he said, "I think there was a mistake when he was created. Those look more like legs than arms."

I turned back to Andre and took a closer look. Yeah, his biceps were bigger than my thighs and his dark blue shorts seemed to be overtaxed trying to contain his massively muscular thighs.

One of Andre's team reached out and gave Andre his mouth guard.

With a hand encased in a dark blue glove, Andre reached out, taking the mouth guard. The contrast in size of the two hands was shocking.

Andre coolly entered the ring like he owned it. He calmly walked to the center and was joined by the announcer, referee and Marcus. The TV guys swarmed, again.

The announcer did his job and then held the microphone in front of the referee so he could repeat the rules to the new fighter.

Before the ref could start, Marcus gave Andre a quick grin and spoke loud enough that the mic could pick it up. "Sure you want to do this? It'd be easier to just go sign the papers."

I expected the ref to stop it or at least remove the mic, but he did neither.

Andre reached up, shoved Marcus back, and started ranting.

He was as difficult for me to understand as Tyrone had been and was obviously from a different part of the country than Tyrone, but I gathered he said, "Whatever, fool. Don't know where you got that last clown, but none of that'll work with me. You let me hit you once, and you won't get a second chance."

Marcus calmly shook his head. "No, this'll be a different fight. Can't let you hit me. And to bring you down, I'll have to hit you."

Andre smirked. "Hit me all you want. Won't be nothing. Been hit by guys twice your size."

The ref forcefully started talking over them so they both stopped. He explained the rules and told them to touch gloves and get into their positions. Everyone left the cage, leaving only the referee and two fighters.

As the referee prepared to start the fight, Marcus's expression turned serious, and his hands went up protecting his face.

The ref gave the signal, and each man approached the other and threw a few test punches before Andre took a mighty swing.

The crowd approved, loudly.

I assumed they were probably hoping Andre would provide the kind of fight they wanted, unlike the first one.

Marcus side-stepped the punch and drove his fist into Andre's mid-section.

Andre doubled over, fell to his knees.

Marcus stepped back and waited.

Andre staggered up, still trying to get his breath back and trying to look like he wasn't really hurt. His face was twisted with anger. He charged Marcus, and as Marcus jumped to get out of the way, Andre's massive hand grabbed Marcus's arm which enabled Andre to get his other hand on him. He threw Marcus like a rag doll high into the chain link of the cage right in front of us.

In unison, we all put up our hands before us, as if Marcus was going to land in our seats.

There were multiple clanks as the metal mesh absorbed the force of Marcus' back, and he slid down to the mat landing on his side.

Judging by the crowd's loud reaction, this was more in line with what they were expecting. They wanted the action and the blood. Now it was being delivered.

And Andre wasn't waiting around like Marcus had. When your enemy is down you keep going after him.

From our close proximity, we watched Marcus start to get up, saw the blood begin to seep from the cuts on his back, and Andre's hand wrap around our co-worker's neck.

Marcus was jerked up off the mat as Andre's other hand went to Marcus' shorts and raised him over Andre's head, just like Marcus had done with Tyrone in the previous match. With all his power, Andre threw The Change as far as he could, and then watched in amazement as The Change twisted agilely in mid-air, landed on his feet, and rushed back towards him.

The crowd loved it.

In a full sprint Marcus jumped high into the air, sailing feet-first towards Andre.

There was a surprised look on Andre's face as he took a few steps back to avoid the impact of Marcus' feet in his chest.

Consequently, Marcus went for his opponent's knees, and there was a massive thud as Andre hit the floor. Marcus was up again and took a step towards Andre.

Andre pushed himself off the mat with one hand and swung the other as a counter-balance to quicken his turn toward Marcus.

Marcus grabbed the extended limb and in one motion twisted it behind the man's back while wrapping his legs around Andre's head in a scissor-lock.

I could sense Keith and Aaron tense up as we all winced, and I unconsciously moved my own arm in front of me in reaction to seeing the unnatural hold Andre was being subjected to.

There was a mixed reaction from the crowd. I heard, "Break his arm," called out nearby, along with calls for Andre to free himself.

Andre's face was set in an angry grimace—he was in pain and couldn't hold it back—but I could see his muscles straining, trying to throw Marcus off. After a long moment, while everyone in the crowd yelled encouragement to their favorite, he screamed and thumped the mat with this free hand, tapping out.

Marcus let go immediately, as the referee rushed over and called the match.

As Marcus walked away, Andre stood, rage covering his face. He shoved the ref out of the way, took three or four giant steps towards Marcus and brought his massive fist hard onto Marcus's back.

Marcus went down.

The crowd gasped.

In one motion, everyone in the stadium stood to try to see better.

I looked up at the monitors which showed Marcus laying there, not moving.

According to almost any standard, by hitting a man who'd been walking away, Andre just became the lowest of the low.

Boo's and profanity came from the crowd, loud and long, and growing with every moment that passed.

Andre looked around angrily, dismissed the crowd with a wave of his arm, and pushed his way past the people rushing in to check out Marcus.

As Andre walked through the cage door, Jeff was waiting for him with a calm look covering his face, oblivious of the TV cameras and people swarming around the two of them.

I'd been paying so much attention to the ring that I hadn't seen Jeff come up. And at first, I thought it was strange Jeff hadn't been the first one in the ring, but then I figured Jeff would know if Marcus needed him.

Jeff said something to Andre, which we couldn't hear over the angry roar of the crowd.

Just like Andre had done to the ref, Andre put his mighty hand on Jeff's chest and shoved him off the walkway and right onto Keith's, Aaron's and my laps.

With his head in Aaron's lap, Jeff looked up at us, and grinned, apparently excited to see familiar faces. "Hey! You guys enjoying the fights? That last move of Marcus' looked painful, didn't it?"

None of us said anything; I sure didn't know how to respond to the nut case.

We all helped push Jeff to his feet, and he was gone, following Andre to the locker rooms.

When I looked back to the cage, it was filled with doctors, medics and others. There were so many people around Marcus that, even on the big screens, no one outside the cage could see what was happening.

Over the angry noise of the crowd, I heard Keith's voice beside me. "Kinda feel for Andre, you know."

Confused, I looked at him. "Why?"

He shrugged. "I mean, what's he got now? He just got whooped. Just got booed out of the cage. Guessin' Jeff was giving him the way out. You know, that college part of the deal. And he shoved Jeff into us, which gives me the idea he ain't going to follow that one through. So, what's he got?"

I smiled at Keith. "You're really something. You know that?"

His expression turned worried.

I realized how that might have sounded and quickly held my hand up. "No, I mean that in a good way. I didn't even think of that. What does he have in front of him?"

His worry eased. "Yeah. Don't see much."

We both looked over as some people started leaving the cage.

In the ring, Marcus was walking around, moving his arms to stretch out his muscles.

The crowd started applauding and screaming, and I realized I was doing that right along with the crowd. I knew Marcus was fine but all the drama added an amazing energy to the night.

While Keith clapped, he leaned over to me again and expounded his wisdom. "They couldn't have done this any better if they planned it."

Over the noise, I yelled, "Why's that?"

"Think about it. The Change was gettin' booed when he first came out. Now they're cheerin' him. He's winning 'em over."

I looked around, and even the gang members were standing and cheering. Then I looked back towards Jeff, who was leaning against the wall going into the changing rooms, smiling like the Cheshire cat. Obviously, everything was following his plan exactly; the tides of change were in motion.

I looked back at Keith and wondered if he shouldn't be the one with Jeff. He'd see Jeff's plan long before I ever would. But I pushed that thought aside and returned my attention to the cage.

After a few minutes, only Marcus, the announcer and the referee were in the cage with the TV guys, and Marcus was just walking around trying to work the pain out.

The crowd quieted as the next opponent bounded into the cage and was announced as Raul, only 5'9" and 170 pounds. He was doing acrobatics much like Marcus had done before his concert at the convention center. Raul's flips and handsprings looked as natural as walking for him. Raul was tiny compared to Marcus' last opponent but his body reminded me of Bruce Lee. It was tuned for the task at hand.

Marcus looked at him and smiled.

Both walked up to the referee and with the announcer holding the microphone for the ref, the ref repeated the rules. He asked if the two fighters were ready.

Marcus extended his gloves and asked, "You ready?"

Raul was hopping around to keep loose. In a scoffing tone, he said, "Man, just shut up and let's fight. Let me just take you out, and I'll be on my way."

He was, obviously, a cocky guy.

The announcer kept the microphone there. I guess it was part of the entertainment.

Marcus grinned at him. "Just like that? You're going to take me out?"

The noise from the crowd egged Raul on. "I saw you fight those other two losers. They ain't fighters. This is what I do for a living. I fight. It's all I do, it's all I train for, and it's all I know, and I never lose." He addressed the last to the TV camera, and it played well on the big screens, and the crowd cheered for him.

"That's too bad that's all you know," Marcus said as the cameras zoomed in on him and the announcer leaned the mic to pick up what he said. "It's going to make the next phase of your life harder. Have you thought about what your degree is going to be in?"

I knew Marcus was playing with him now.

Raul pointed at him harshly. "It ain't entered my mind. All I've thought 'bout is what I'm going to do with the money. Now shut up and let's fight." He put in his mouth guard, as the crowd roared its approval.

The announcer and TV guys left the cage. The referee had them touch gloves, and they backed away from each other and got into ready positions.

The instant the referee gave the signal, Raul attacked and there was a flurry of fists and kicks flying from both fighters. It was hard to tell what was happening because they were in close quarters and moving so fast.

Marcus stepped back out of range, and Raul took the opportunity to rest.

Aaron leaned over and said, "They're fast."

"Amazingly fast."

As Raul tried to catch his breath, he stood there and looked at Marcus with a confused expression. After a few deep breaths, he went on the attack again.

Things weren't as fast this time, and it was easier to make out what was happening. Marcus was just dodging and blocking while Raul was attacking. Marcus wasn't returning punches or kicks, except for the few times he slapped Raul, just to show he could.

Raul was the next one to back off, and he was breathing much heavier, while Marcus just stood and waited.

Marcus asked loud enough, so we could hear over the noise of the crowd. "What's wrong Raul? Don't you have to hit me to take me out?"

"Man! Shut up!" Raul yelled. "Don't you have to hit me to take me out?"

Marcus replied without breathing heavy, "No in fact, I don't. You'll defeat yourself. So, come on and give me what you got, and when you figure out you can't beat me, just walk to the door of the cage. There's a guy waiting for you with some papers to sign."

"Man! Shut up! You can't beat me! Now take a punch this time, fight like a man!" Raul's face was red and he attacked again.

Marcus played with him more obviously this time, dodging and tapping Raul's face or stomach just to annoy him.

Raul started getting wilder and more frantic trying to land a punch or a kick. Then he suddenly backed off, visibly very angry.

"Hit me! If you want to win, you *hit* me!"

Then he attacked, and Marcus rose into the air spun around and landed his foot on the side of Raul's head. Raul's mouth guard flew out, hit the cage wall, and fell to the mat followed by Raul.

There was a collective wince from the stadium and a moment of anticipation as everyone waited to see if Raul would get up.

The referee stepped between Marcus and Raul, but it was only a formality because Marcus was slowly backing away and intently watching his downed opponent with concern.

Raul worked himself up to his hands and knees, and stayed there for a minute. Slowly, he moved one knee forward and put his foot on the mat. He wobbled as he stood and shook his head in an attempt to clear it.

The ref watched intently with one hand back towards Marcus, letting him know to stay back. Once Raul was up, the referee dropped his hand and looked over at Marcus, giving him permission to continue the fight.

Marcus simply stood as Raul took two staggering steps.

Raul gained some stability as he got closer to Marcus.

Marcus' gloved hands were at his side as Raul approached, stopping a couple feet from his opponent.

The crowd was almost silent in anticipation of more fighting.

Raul reached up and rubbed the side of his head. "I have some papers to sign. Hope this means you can teach me to fight like you, too."

As he said it, I realized I'd been holding my breath in anticipation of where this was going, and I slowly let it out and glanced around the stadium. There was a lot of background noise as the confused people talked quietly.

Marcus placed his hand on Raul's shoulder. "There's nothing I'd like better."

Raul looked at the ref. "Fight's over."

The referee looked at Raul questioningly, and Raul confirmed with a nod. As the cameras rushed in, the referee positioned each man beside him and held a hand of each. "The winner by submission, Marcus Havens, The Change." And he held up Marcus' hand.

There was a hesitant cheering from the crowd at the ending of an anti-climactic fight. Marcus' kick had been impressive, but having Raul concede wasn't making the crowd happy.

When the ref let loose of them, Raul turned and walked to the door of the cage, where Jeff was waiting for him. And together with Raul's team, they walked past us, down the aisle toward the changing room.

The announcer came into the cage, and in a serious tone said the fourth opponent had forfeited his match.

There was a loud murmur in the crowd, as they all turned to each other, talking amongst themselves. I couldn't judge what they were thinking.

Aaron looked over at us. "Isn't that something?"

Keith leaned forward to look at Aaron. "Yeah. Can't imagine what that guy's thinking right now. Seen Marcus, knows he can't win, so just avoid the embarrassment. Gotta be a tough spot."

Aaron laughed. "I sure wouldn't go in the ring."

I grinned at the mental image of Aaron, a short, balding, past-his-prime man, barefoot, in boxing shorts and gloves, out in the cage. I looked at him. "I don't know. I think you could take him, Aaron."

Aaron nodded eagerly. "I could beat him with two arms tied behind my back." He elbowed me. "As long as they were Marcus' arms and they weren't still attached to him." He burst out laughing, and I couldn't help but join in.

All that was left now was the championship fight, and as the announcer went into his spiel, the guy walked down the aisle like he was leading a parade. He paused at the bottom of the stairs to get inspected by the officials, and I had a chance to get a good look at him. He was a tough looking guy named Craig, about the same size as Marcus. It was clear Craig and his crew had done this before. His group was all dressed in team type clothing with Craig's name prominently displayed. As a professional, Craig was a brand and played the audience like a showman, greeting them with hand slaps and waves.

Craig entered the cage and joined the announcer, referee, and Marcus in the middle. Craig extended his hand and smiled. "Buddy, those fights were amazing." He paused, looked around at the crowd and smiled, "But you're not getting my title." He looked out in the crowd and playfully yelled. "You guys ready for a real fight?"

The crowd erupted into a cheer.

I liked the way Craig came across. He seemed like a good-natured guy who was confident but not cocky. That wasn't an easy attitude to pull off, but Craig did it.

Marcus played along. "I know I'm in for a challenge." He circled looking at the crowd. "Think he can do it?"

The stadium gave a mixed reaction to this, and I couldn't help but feel the mood of the place had changed. When the first fight started the boo's and slurs towards Marcus had made it clear he wasn't revered. But now, as Keith had pointed out, Marcus was winning them over.

All the extra people left the cage, and referee told the two fighters to touch gloves and get into position. The signal was given and the fight started.

Marcus put up his fists and got into a fighting stance.

Craig attacked with a lightning-fast roundhouse kick into Marcus' ribs.

The kick moved Marcus to the side a couple steps, then Marcus went into his dad's fighting style of just absorbing the impact of Craig's punches and kicks, not returning any of them. I can't even really say he was blocking. He moved with some of the punches and kicks to lessen the blow but was still taking a beating.

It was astounding to watch him take the abuse. And it made me think of one of the *Rocky* movie lines. "It ain't about how hard you hit, it's about how hard you can get hit and keep moving forward." Marcus was showing he could take a hit.

Craig paused and smiled at The Change. He removed his mouth piece. "I'm impressed. You can take some punches, but come on. Let's make this a fight. Show me what you got."

Marcus removed his mouth guard. "Okay, you ready?"

"That's why I'm here, and that's why they're here." He pointed out to the audience.

The crowd gave an approving cheer.

The fighters returned to their stances, and Marcus said, "I'm coming with a front snap-kick to your solar plexus." And put his mouth piece back in.

Craig motioned with his hands saying, "Bring it on." His expression became intensely focused.

Everyone was leaning forward in their seats watching with an equally intense focus.

I found myself having to remember to breathe as I watched Jeff's plan unfold.

Marcus covered the distance between them before anyone, including Craig, realized what was happening.

Craig tried to dodge and block, but before he could do more than barely move, he was on the mat holding his stomach gasping for breath.

Marcus walked over to him, to help him up, while Craig got his breath back.

As Craig started straightening, he brought an uppercut aimed at Marcus' jaw.

Marcus sprang back as the punch was coming and kicked Craig in the jaw as he flipped into a back handspring.

Craig went down again, and with blood dripping from his mouth, got up more slowly, and looked at Marcus with obvious confusion, probably wondering what had just happened. Then he shook his head and focused again on Marcus.

After a few test punches and low kicks were exchanged, Craig saw an opening and came at Marcus with a back fist.

Marcus grabbed Craig's arm as it passed his face, twisted the arm into a position that made the audience cringe as they waited for a snapping sound of the bone breaking.

The sound didn't come, but Craig went to the mat, let out a loud scream and pounded on the mat to end the match.

The referee jumped forward, and Marcus immediately let go and backed up.

As Craig stood, with his good arm, he cradled the arm Marcus had twisted. Craig grimaced with his eyes closed as he let the pain subside.

Marcus watched with concern but kept his distance.

Craig bent forward holding his arm but then stood, let go of the bad arm and started trying to straighten it. Once the look of pain started to leave his face he looked toward Marcus and shook his head. Craig's expression seemed to bestow respect onto Marcus.

As that happened, the announcer and crews started coming into the cage and the ref moved between Marcus and Craig, reached down and grabbed their hands, ready to declare the winner.

The crowd quieted slightly until Marcus' hand was raised and the announcer declared the winner. As the championship belt was laid over Marcus' shoulder, I found myself on my feet with my hands in the air cheering like a madman with the rest of the crowd.

Marcus had won the fight, and more importantly Marcus had won the crowd.

He took his gloves off, ran to one side of the cage and threw a glove into the crowd. He then ran to the other side of the cage and threw the other glove into a different section. There was an explosion of people in each section trying to get the glove.

One of Marcus' team handed him a black tank top, and he put it on as he walked back to the center and raised the championship belt above his head. He then pointed out at the audience and slowly started turning to acknowledge the whole stadium. As he pointed to each section, the cheering from that area ignited.

Music I recognized from Marcus' album started playing over the stadium's speakers and the chain link walls of the cage began to rise into the air, hoisted up by cables I hadn't noticed before. The people in the cage cleared out and Marcus jumped down off the platform and ran out into the audience.

This crowd reacted the same way as the crowd at his televised interview. As he circled the area around the fighting ring, each section erupted in excitement, clamoring for his attention.

I looked up to watch the cage rise and saw a platform was being lowered as the cage was raised. From my vantage point, I could only see the bottom, until it was almost on the cage platform mat. On the platform being lowered was Marcus' band, playing the song that I'd assumed had been recorded.

In addition to the band and their equipment, the stage held an impressive system of bars and poles, for Marcus' acrobatics, plus a number of clear platforms at different heights.

Marcus made his way around to our section on his way back to the stage. We all held out our hands as he passed, and he greeted each with a firm slap of the palm, before he tossed the championship belt to the head of his support team. Then he jumped onto the stage and grabbed his wireless headset, and stood there putting it on, with every eye in the deafening stadium focused on him.

Marcus was the champion, and the crowd was ecstatic. I scanned over the crowd and marveled at their transformation. They'd changed from booing The Change into a supporting frenzy. It had all happened so quickly that I don't think anyone had time to fully comprehend what happened. I'm not sure I understood what had happened.

I watched Marcus on stage, about twenty feet away from me. The band quieted for a few seconds as Marcus looked out into the stadium; who responded by quieting down.

Then he pumped his fist into the air and counted off, "One, two, three."

The band started a song I recognized from the CD and, like Spiderman, Marcus used the bars and polls to get up to one of the clear platforms unhindered by the fatigue of four fights.

Standing above the band, who again quieted, Marcus addressed the audience. "Thank you for being with me tonight! I am The Change and together, *we are The Change.*"

Marcus waited for the crowd noise to die down some but had to start talking over it. "It is time for a message to be heard. It is time for a message to be lived. You've seen power tonight but it isn't my power. I am a tool for the power. I'm a tool called The Change. I challenge you, and I dare you to join with me in hearing a message, spreading a message and living a message."

He paused and looked around. Again, he had to wait for the screaming and cheers to die down.

I looked around also. There was a diverse crowd. There were a fair number of people who looked like I'd expect to be at an MMA fight and then a fair number I would expect at a rap concert. From the negative reaction the rap audience bestowed on Marcus when he first came out I think they came here tonight to watch Marcus get beat; hoping to see him hurt badly. But Marcus had not only won all the fights in the ring, he'd also won the most important one, outside the ring, the one for the respect of this very tough segment of the audience. I wondered what the other segment had wanted.

As Marcus started talking again I recalled some of the other fighters standing beside me when they were getting ready to enter the cage. Because of their heavy street lingo I had problems understanding them. I was curious if Marcus would have reverted to that lingo if it wasn't for the mixed audience. For whatever reason I was glad I didn't have to decipher or have Keith translate for me.

In a loud, powerful voice Marcus addressed the whole stadium with the music behind accenting and adding to the excitement of the crowd. "It's a message about change, but it's not a message of The Change." He thumped his chest. "I only deliver it. *It's not about me* and it's not about you. We're all part of something bigger. It's time for my brothers and sisters to stop dying on the streets for someone else's misplaced arrogance. If there are to be fights, let the fight be like you saw tonight, in the rings where fights belong." He jumped to a platform a couple feet higher than the one he was currently on. "If there is to be anger, let it be a righteous anger, not an anger based in hatred of the unknown. Let it be an anger that gives us power to change things that need to be changed."

The way he spoke now made me think of how in church Marcus had an unparalleled ability to draw the congregation into his sermons. No one slept when he preached and people talked about the sermons in the aisles afterwards. But at this moment, it was striking how Marcus was able to scale his ability to capture the attention of an entire stadium and make it work with such a diverse audience, leaving us all hanging onto every word Marcus spoke. I would have laid big money against the odds of this ever happening, but I was seeing it with my own eyes, and still not sure I believed it.

He jumped to another platform and turned in a slow circle, making sure he was talking to everyone. The monitors switched perspectives as Marcus turned so everyone could always see his face. With the band playing music as a background, Marcus continued in an energetic tone, "It's time for us to stop giving money to the people who destroy our lives. It's time to start building a community who helps each other, instead of hurting and killing each other."

He stopped again and the music stopped. There was an eerie silence as the crowd waited for him to continue. Slowly the music started again, providing intensity to his words. "Each and every one of us grants power to someone. When we buy drugs, we grant power to people who wish us nothing but harm." The music stopped. "Who will you grant power to?"

I heard Keith beside me. "Huh, never thought of it that way before." I looked over at him, and he said to me, "I gave some power to some pretty bad people in my life."

The music started again and we both looked back towards the stage. "When we buy stolen property, we grant power to people who mean nothing but harm to our community!" The music stopped. "Who will you grant power to?" The music started again. "When we live life in a bottle of cheap wine, whiskey or beer, we are granting power to people that don't care about us!" The music stopped. "Who will you grant power to?"

The eerie silence continued.

Keith quietly spoke, "Least I haven't given them that kind of power in the last few years. Man, that was a hard thing to give up."

I smiled at him approvingly and was thankful I'd never had to fight that battle.

The music started. "When we listen to music that glorifies the destruction of our communities, we grant power to some of the most unworthy people walking around, because they think of only their gains at our expense." The music stopped. "Who will you grant power to?"

The music stayed quiet. The Change turned slowly around the platform with his arms outstretched, looking at people. "The change has started. You have a chance to be part of the change and let go of the bonds that hold you back. Today is a new day. Today is a good day. And if you want, tomorrow can be even better. Does anybody here want a better tomorrow?"

People stood and cheered, and I joined them. As I cheered, I scanned the crowd and didn't see anyone sitting. Marcus had the stadium activated.

Marcus' expression was approving as he turned and observed the crowd. Intensely, he then invited the people to action. "Join me in giving power to the people who deserve the power and taking the power from those who don't. Tomorrow will be a good day, but it won't be an easy day. When we take power away from those who aren't worthy of it, they will fight. When they fight, you'll see just how unworthy they are. Tomorrow will not be an easy day, but tomorrow will be a good day. Grant your power to the people helping your community!"

This was followed by an even louder cheer. Marcus seemed to be connecting with repressed frustrations of many of the audience and they were reacting.

"Healing your community!"

Another loud cheer.

"And then join in helping your community! Join in healing your community! Each of you hates seeing what's happening in your community, but feels powerless to change it." The Change upped his intensity. "I give you the power!!! I give you permission!!!" He yelled, well articulating each word. "Quit *trying* to be somebody and start *being* somebody!!!" Marcus raised both hands in the air and the crowd thundered.

The music moved into a fast thumping beat and The Change launched into his title song:

> *To be free to see*
> *what you want to be*
> *is a gift from me,*
> *but it's not free.*
> *Beat back the bondage,*
> *payback the homage,*
> *throw out the garbage,*
> *it's the start of a new age.*
> *Today is a new start,*
> *today I am free,*
> *to love with a new heart*
> *be the best me I can be.*

> But as I do, I see
> it's not about me.

I'd memorized the song's words from the CD that played in my car, so I softly sang along, and as I did, I looked around at the energized crowd and wondered what kind of day tomorrow would be.

As the concert continued, I found myself sucked into the music and excitement and, like the rest of the stadium, dancing as much as I could in the limited space.

There was a scream of, "Wonderful!" next to me every so often, and I'd look over at Aaron with his hands in the air moving enthusiastically to the music.

After a number of fast paced songs, the stage lights went dark, with one spotlight on Marcus as he worked his way down to the stage level, grabbed his classical guitar and moved to a stool and sat.

Picking up in the mood change, the crowd sat and quietly waited for Marcus to begin.

Into his headset he only said, "Nineveh" and started playing.

As the song started, I noticed Keith shiver and I looked over at him questioningly.

He gave me a half-smile. "Can't explain why but this song freaks me out. Makes me shake every time I hear it."

"In a good or bad way?"

He shrugged his insecure shrug. "Don't know. Guess good."

I nodded and turned back to the stage. I agreed with Keith. It was unnerving how the song drew me in. The stadium disappeared from my senses and I was consumed by the song. As I listened, I was taken back to the first sermon of Marcus' I heard. I relived his words: "A great city has changed its sinful ways" and "A great city, a great nation does not change quickly unless there is a great power behind the change." Marcus played the last few notes and let them fade, as I came back to the stadium.

As I did, I smiled to myself, because I finally knew what the song meant. A great power was behind 'The Change,' and the world was at a turning point. I wasn't sure what the turning point meant for the future, but after seven weeks with Jeff, I was excited about the coming change.

The stage lights came up slowly, and I looked around the stadium at the still tranquil people watching Marcus put his classical guitar up and calmly start walking around the outer edge of the stage just looking out into the audience.

I looked over at Keith to see how he was doing.

He looked at me with a little less insecurity in his smile. "Yeah, in a good way. It's all real good."

I wondered if he heard the same message I heard, but I didn't ask him.

Marcus got to our section, looked towards us, gave a friendly smile and then moved on. As he circled, he quoted a line from one of his songs, "The words of the King continue to ring." He stopped and looked around.

Right now, he was just calmly talking and moving slowly around, and it was such a contrast to the previous high-energy show, that it accented the moment, and I felt drawn into what he was saying. I looked around, and people were focused in on Marcus, waiting to hear what he was going to say.

"'I have a dream.'" He paused for a moment to let people recall where those words came from. "'That my four little children will one day live in a nation where they will not be judged by the color of their skin but by the content of their character.'" He cocked his head sideways and held his palms facing upwards next to his shoulders. "We aren't there yet. We've made progress, but we still have a long ways to go. But join me for a minute and pretend King's dream has come true. If you were to be judged only on the content of your character, how would you be judged?" Marcus looked down towards the stage as he thoughtfully strolled around it, giving time for his question to sink in.

From the silence, I assumed the audience was thinking about the question.

I looked down at the floor and thought. With all that had happened with Jeff in the last two months, I had a lot to think about, but Marcus' question made me look at things from a different angle. I'd been reflecting on how I saw myself, but thinking about being judged by others based on the content of my character put everything in a different perspective, and it worried me. How did other people judge me? As harshly as I judged myself?

I looked over at Aaron and then to Keith and tried to imagine how they saw me, and to my surprise, I realized they were safe people. Aaron would look only for the good in me, and Keith always seemed to value talking to me.

I glanced up into the stadium's stands, at the people who lived in a totally different world than me. How would they judge me?

My thoughts were interrupted by Marcus pointedly repeating his lyrics. "The words of the King continue to ring." I looked back towards him as he spoke to the audience. "Blessed is the peace maker. Love your neighbor as yourself. Turn the other cheek." He paused and then questioningly added, "Content of character?"

The cameras zoomed in on The Change, and the monitors showed him pointing out towards the camera. "And what about all of you watching out there? What is the content of your character and how can you be part of the change?" Marcus looked back at the stadium crowd. "I invite all of you here tonight, and all of you watching, to be part of the change. Change will only happen when you want it. We know what we're doing now doesn't work, so let's find something that does. Communities who need help need to start inviting churches, businesses and civic organizations to work with them and build something different, build something beautiful together. Build something that is yours. Build something that shows the content of your character." Marcus in a rhythm, half preacher, half rapper, emphasized the invitation. "Realize there is a better way and then invite the change!" He paused, then yelled, "Are you ready to invite the change?"

The audience erupted.

As Marcus waited for them to quiet, the big monitors switched from showing a close up of The Change standing on the stage with his band, to showing a website with the words *Invite The Change*.

Marcus continued, "With the help of many people, organizations, civic-minded businesses, local governments, community leaders, churches, and schools, we've put into place a system to start this change. This system has the resources it needs. It has the money it needs. The four million dollars from tonight is coins under the cushions. This new system is lacking only one thing. It's lacking a voice to tell it where the change will take place. That is you." He pointed out to the crowd. "You are that voice." He paused. "Are you tired of the violence?"

There was a resounding, "Yes!"

"The hopelessness?"

"Yes!"

"The broken promises?"

"Yes!"

The Change nodded in agreement. "Then you have a voice that needs to be heard. Invite the change into your community, and if you can gather enough voices with yours, we have put in place the people and resources ready to listen to you and fuel the change. You have a voice. And if your community doesn't want change, that's okay. I know, at one point in my life, this wouldn't have been right for me. I understand that and accept it. So, if you want change and those around you aren't ready, we'll help you find a community that does want to change, and we'll move you to that community. You're not forgotten anymore. You're not trapped anymore. Go to *Invite The Change's website* and be heard, find out what is happening and get involved."

Marcus paused, with the band playing some quiet, slower music in the background, to let people think about what he'd said.

I took that moment to wondering about this, too. He had said his group had the resources and the money already, which sounded like a lot of planning had already been done, except I'd been around Marcus for almost two months and this was the first I'd heard of it. I looked over at Aaron as he watched the stage with his normal eager-for-life expression, then gave him a slight nudge with my elbow to get his attention.

He turned his gaze from Marcus to me, with no diminishment in his eagerness. Just like at work, if I wanted his attention, I had his undivided attention.

"You know anything about this?"

His eyes glowed as he started to speak. "Oh, yes! It's wonderful, isn't it?"

I looked at him with curiosity, waiting for him to let me in on it.

Aaron leaned towards me. "Imagine a bunch of micro-HRIs all over the country, in communities that have nothing now. Just try to imagine that." He then leaned back to give me time to fulfill his request.

My mind filled with visions but strangely, not only of HRI. Rita and her school were part of the images flashing around in my head, and it only took me a moment to understand that her school was just another version of HRI. I reflected back on these last weeks at HRI and how its environment had stimulated my growth.

Then I snuck a look at Keith, who was intently focused on the stage, deep in his own thoughts. And I was almost overwhelmed with a flash, imagining a country filled with places where people where taken in, at face value, and offered the chance to grow from there. What a vision.

I looked back at Aaron. "You guys can do that?"

He gave me a mischievous grin. "We can try."

I returned his smile, then my attention was drawn back to the stage as the music picked up quickly and then stopped, leaving a sudden silence.

The lights focused down on The Change as he started to speak again. "We are planning a concert tour to promote this. We wish we could be everywhere at once, but we can't, so we'll listen to you, and we'll come to where we're the most wanted. The cities who have the most people inviting us to come to them, will be where we start. While we're there in the cities who've invited us, we'll organize with the people of the communities to listen to their needs and desires to change the status quo.

"But you don't have to wait for us before you start your own changes. We have people in place in most major cities to start the process right now. Go to the website to learn more, and then invite the change! If you don't have internet, don't worry, churches, schools, libraries and businesses all over the nation will be helping get you connected to The Change."

With that the band started back up and Marcus, in his Spiderman way, quickly made his way to the platforms above the band and performed a couple more songs before saying good night.

Chapter 42

The concert ended at about eleven, and as the HRI group filed through the electrified crowds, I watched the people around us, to see their reaction to Marcus and his grand plans. I wanted to see if it was anything close to mine; I was almost in a manic state. And compared to the uncertainty and uneasiness I'd felt when we entered the stadium, there seemed to be lots of smiles and laughing in the crowds around me, and the level of arrogance seemed to have dropped significantly. But I was rational enough in my euphoria to realize my perceptions were not trustworthy.

Plus, there was free stuff; free stuff always changes the mood. As we walked out, there were tables near all the exits giving out bumper stickers, window decals, bookmarks, and pamphlets. I'm not a big bumper sticker fan, but there was a window decal I thought looked kind of cool. It wasn't too bold and in nice lettering simply read, *Invite The Change*. I got a blue one of those that would match my car and some bookmarks and pamphlets. They had some T-shirts that weren't priced at robbery prices like most other concerts, so I got four. I knew Cooper would want one and I didn't want to leave out Beth or Alice.

On the bus ride home with Aaron, Keith and all the HRI folk, we carried the concert's energy with us, and I talked with Aaron more about the idea of micro-HRIs spread all over the country.

Of course, the micro-HRI concept wouldn't work everywhere, but that was part of the beauty of Marcus' plan. The places that wanted it, would be asking for it, "inviting the change." It wouldn't be a program that arrived at a place and, once there, attempted to attract community support. Instead, Marcus' plan was to have the support in place before they even got to the community.

The hour-and-a-half trip home was over before I got my fill of answers and wasn't even close to long enough for me to wind down.

When I entered my home-away-from-home hotel room, I didn't think I'd be able to sleep that night, but I ended up asleep in my clothes, barely remembering lying down.

* * *

Before I collapsed, I must have set the alarm, because it went off, getting me up in time for church. I was glad I'd been cognizant enough to set the alarm, because I'd really wanted to go to church. Then I had to laugh at myself. Beth would be shaking her head in disbelief if she ever saw me worrying about getting to church on time.

I arrived at the church parking lot and saw Dylan leaning against the outside wall by the front door, waiting for me. As I finally got to him, he held out his fist, so I greeted him with a knuckle bump.

I asked, "You like the show last night?"

He stuck out his lower lip in an approving expression. "It was superlative."

"Superlative? That the word of the week?" I hadn't expected him to have a new word today, but wasn't sure why I'd thought that.

He switched to a more serious face. "Affirmative." Then went back to his classic, playful Dylan expression. "I don't think anyone can say 'affirmative' without acting like they're on a military mission."

"Yeah, I think you're right. I know I can't say it in regular conversation." Then I realized why his new word struck me as strange. "You got up early enough this morning to learn the word, even after getting to bed so late?"

He waited for a couple people to go by us, into the church, and then followed them. "Yeah, pretty much a habit now. Also gives me some one-on-one time with Dad. You can imagine that's kinda hard."

Following him, I gave an amused huff. "I'd think one-on-one time with anyone would be next to impossible in that house."

We made our way to the Haven's section. Jeff looked up from the aisle at the other end of the pew, where he was wiping the drool from the mouth of one of his most severely handicapped kids. Jeff gave a wave to acknowledge me and then returned his attention to someone much more important than me.

Dylan and I sat and chatted more while we waited for the service to begin.

During the announcements, they said Marcus wouldn't be at church this morning, which I'd halfway expected, since I figured he'd be worn out after last night. But when the guy gave the reason, I was surprised and saddened. Marcus was with the family of Andre—the second fighter of the night—the one who'd hit Marcus in the back. In the early hours of the morning, Andre had been found dead on the sidewalk in front of his apartment, beaten and shot. The sad news reminded me of the first fighter, Tyrone, saying he'd be killed if he went back to his old home. Too bad Andre hadn't listened to him.

When the sermon started, Pastor Jones stood at the pulpit, and with a sad smile, surveyed the congregation. "I think we all heard Marcus' invitation to change last night, which has turned bittersweet with the news of what he's doing right now, mourning with the family of a man who refused to embrace Marcus' message." He paused and assessed the congregation. "That portion of last night's events greatly saddens me, and I will get into more of my thoughts on it in a moment. But the rest of the night's events, the rest of Marcus' change, that excites me!" He almost shouted the words, and his sad demeanor changed to one of strength and power. "I'm excited by the change that's coming, and I hope you are, too."

He looked to the paper in front of him and then back up. "In John 13:34-35, Jesus says, 'I give you a new commandment: love one another. As I have loved you, so you also should love one another. This is how all will know that you are my disciples, if you have love for one another.'

"In this commandment Jesus wasn't telling his disciples to only love the other disciples. Or in our modern equivalent, to only love the people of our individual church or community. No! Jesus was commanding the disciples to love everyone. And I praise this congregation for how truly and faithfully you have lived up to that commandment as you work tirelessly to better yourselves and support the many charity activities this church sponsors.

"And now, we are being given another opportunity to work with others, to amplify the power of our love. Bethlehem—" he swept out his hand to encompass the surrounding area "—is our home, yet we know so few people it in. But that's about to change."

I felt a nudge in my side and looked down to Dylan, who whispered, "Marcus has some superlative things planned." It was only with great effort I kept my laugh to myself.

"I hope you've gone to Marcus' website and registered to be a part of *Invite The Change*," Pastor Jones continued. "This church has already registered and we are working with community leaders and members to get them registered. And as part of the process, the city is inviting us to be part of the solution. Holy places of every faith are responding to the city's request for assistance in this. Businesses and schools are responding, too. The invitation to change is being accepted."

This reminded me that I needed to go to the website. I'd fallen asleep too fast last night to do it then, and rushed here this morning, so I made a promise to myself to look as soon as I got home.

Pastor Jones walked from behind the podium and towards the front of the stage. "I, as an individual, have accepted the invitation, and I hope many of you will also. I have also accepted the invitation on behalf of this congregation, with the intention that, while the ability of an individual to change things is great, the ability of a large group of focused individuals is much greater."

A murmur of approval ran through the congregation.

"This is a very exciting time for us."

My mind echoed that thought. "Very exciting."

His expression changed to a more solemn one, and he clasped his hands together before him. "But it's also a scary time."

I muttered, "You're telling me," to myself.

"Change is a scary thing, especially big changes. The status quo, whether of an individual or a group, doesn't like to be disturbed."

I thought about examples of cultural changes like slavery, segregation, women's rights, dependence on oil, and so on. All had been very tough changes, scary changes, and many people had died in the fight to resist each change. But if any of those cultural situations had persisted, or continued to persist in the case of our dependence on oil, then humanity would suffer for its myopic vision.

The pastor moved back to the pulpit and leaned on it a moment before he continued. "I received Marcus' call late last night, telling me the news. Andre's death weighs heavy on Marcus' conscience, and we talked a long time, but I don't think I helped Marcus much.

"As I lay in bed afterward, thinking about change and praying for Andre's family, I remembered Marcus' sermon from a couple months ago. And I think we just witnessed a clear example of what happens when we try to run away from the changes God has planned for us." He sighed. "Change comes at a cost. Small changes come at a small cost. And large changes come with much larger price tags. Tyrone and Raul, two of the men Marcus fought last night, and Leon, the man who forfeited his fight, have a difficult path ahead of them, and the cost of their change will be very high, but their journey is a positive one, a fulfilling one, with a bright future at its end."

He paused again. "But what most of us don't consider is the cost of *not* changing, the cost of fighting against a good, a necessary, and maybe an inevitable change."

That thought shocked me, in one of those blinding-flash-of-the-obvious ways. I'd always counted up the cost of change and almost always found the price too high or the effort too great. But I don't know if I had ever considered the price of *not* changing. That was something I needed to think more about, later.

"When Jonah ran from God's demands, he paid the price in loss of family and home, and he almost paid with his life. Andre, may God rest his soul, in his flight from God's demands, did pay that ultimate cost last night."

Dylan nudged me again.

I looked down.

"I'm very sad the man died," said Dylan.

"Me, too," I replied.

We shared a moment of empathy, then together, looked back to the pulpit when Pastor Jones began speaking again.

"Not being willing to grow or change has a cost. And that cost is charged against our spiritual, emotional, and physical selves, until such time as we take up God's plan and the demanded changes are embraced. But if change isn't embraced, the tally continues to mount against our various selves, just like interest is charged against a credit card account. If you don't pay your credit cards, the interest and fees keep growing, until you don't have any credit limit left and the creditors come after you. In the case of people who are in the terminal-stages of refusing to change, the price is often death of those selves, be it spiritual, emotional or physical death."

What did that mean for me? I wondered. I'd resisted change most of my life. What price had I paid by refusing to change? And if I resisted the changes that the big fish down at the other end of the pew was pressuring me to embrace, would I die?

Then an understanding finally kicked in. If I went back home and stayed the same old Stanley, feeling sorry for myself because life wasn't going the direction I wanted, and remained one of Thoreau's mass of men leading lives of quiet desperation, wasn't that a kind of death? A death of the spirit?

But if I did change, if I did do what Jeff wanted me to do, if I did pick up the task he seemed to have put before me, wasn't that a form of death, too? A death of the old me?

Right then, something strange happened. I don't really think it was a thought, but more of a vision or a vivid dream.

From a vantage point off to the side and above, I saw what looked like my body being lowered into a grave. Except I wasn't dead, my eyes were open, and I was obviously afraid, reaching out for help towards the people who lined the sides of the grave. But, as what appeared to be my body being lowered to the bottom, no one helped me, or even seemed to notice I was alive. Instead, they started shoveling dirt on the terrified body, beginning to bury it.

I tried to get a better look at the people around the grave, the people burying me, but they were somehow obscured from my view. Yet I got a feeling that I knew all of them.

Then the vision continued as one by one, the people surrounding the grave laid down their shovels and left, until just two people were shoveling dirt into the grave.

As I focused intently on one of the two, finally, I could make out that it was Jeff. Jeff was burying me, or burying something that looked like me.

That was such a strange situation, I peered intently at the other figure, only to be shocked when suddenly it was clear, and I could see it was me. I was shoveling dirt down, burying myself.

Snapping out of the vision, I quickly looked at Jeff at the other side of the pew. He was intently listening to the sermon.

What had he done to me? What was I doing to myself? What did the vision mean?

Thankfully, it didn't take long for my frantic mind to start understanding. The part of me who was terrified of change, and refusing to change, had to die—however unwillingly—before the new me, the new Stanley, could start taking shape. Jeff had begun systematically killing that old-fearful-Stanley on the day we left Bakersfield.

As that understanding came, so did the realization of who the people had been around the grave. They were all the HRI folk I'd met while I'd been here. People who, with shovelful after shovelful of acceptance and love, had buried my fears and let the new Stanley take root and begin to thrive.

I was standing over the grave; the new Stanley, not the old fearful one. That new Stanley was thankful for what had happened, thankful for all the changes that had taken place in the last two months. Even if one of the changes required of me was to help bury the old fearful, foolish Stanley, who was too afraid to be himself.

I looked down to Dylan and had to smile. The old fearful Stanley had been too afraid to be the best Stanley he could be. Would the new Stanley be any better at it? I didn't know, but if Dylan could do it, maybe I could, too.

I looked back at Jeff. He turned his attention from the sermon and gave me a slight nod.

My thoughts were interrupted by Pastor Jones walking off the podium, and everyone standing to sing. I instantly felt bad, because I'd missed much of the sermon. I'd really enjoyed his sermons on previous Sundays and regretted missing this one. But maybe the vision I'd had, the understanding I'd gained, had been worth missing the sermon.

As I stood for the song, the image of Stanley leaning on a shovel and laughing at me entered my mind.

When I realized what he was laughing at, I laughed too, which made Dylan look at me strangely. But I shrugged and began singing from the page in the hymnal Dylan held.

Who would have ever thought I'd get so mentally caught up in thinking about a sermon topic that I missed the rest of the sermon, and then felt bad because I'd missed the sermon? After spending years at Beth's church, fighting to keep my eyes open, this change bordered on the miraculous.

While I sang, I glanced Jeff's way.

He winked at me.

* * *

When church was over, Dylan said, "I have to write a paper for history. It's due Friday. Do you think you could help me?"

I had helped Dylan enough to know what this meant. I would be helping him read and comprehend the topic. Then I would have to start helping him organize his thoughts. I found Dylan worked best when we formed an outline together. Then we would have to get the rough draft and I know it would be rough. I looked down at him. "We had better get started on that Monday night. Is that good with you?"

"Yeah. I'll work on reading it. See what I can get through before you come Monday."

"Sounds good, Dylan." As much as I helped Dylan, normally I might have felt he was using me as a crutch, but that wasn't the case with him. He always did as much as he could by himself. This was not easy for him and he needed people to help him climb the ladder. I gave him a one-armed hug. "See you Monday."

I said my good-byes to the others and headed home. Once there, I warmed up some leftovers and went to the couch setting the plate next to my laptop. Then I pulled up Marcus' website.

A multi-colored map of the US was the focal point of the home page. It reminded me of some demographic maps I'd seen that showed distributions of a population's characteristics. The map was constantly active with blue, green, red and purple dots popping out of, and fading back into specific areas of the map. Beside the map was a key that made the meaning of this clear; a dot was added for each person or organization that signed up. Green dots were for the community members, blue were volunteers, red were businesses, and purple were religious or other organizations. When I hovered over the color keys on the side the map changed to show the data for that group. It was a cool website.

I browsed the site for a little while, just looking around, and then clicked the registration button. I was given the option to sign up as an individual or search for organizations nearby. I briefly considered which address to use, the one here or my home address. Jeff's church would obviously be very active in Marcus' change, but my time here was short. So, I looked up organizations in Bakersfield and was actually surprised to see Beth's church on the list. I knew I was being cynical, but from my past experience, they hadn't reached very far outside their walls. Wondering what had caused such a change in her church, I finished my registration, putting Beth's church as my organization, figuring I could change it later if I wanted. I clicked "Submit" and watched a blue dot pop out of Bakersfield and then settle back into it. Maybe when I got home, if we stayed at that church, maybe I could help them reach past their walls better.

That got me thinking about calling Beth, but with the time difference, she'd still be in church. I pulled up Skype and left her a message. We hadn't talked much about her church since I'd been here, and I wondered how the minister search was going. My skin grew cold as I thought of the preacher we'd listened to right before I left. Not that I wanted the man to be unemployed, but I hoped he found employment somewhere else and not as a minister.

Grabbing one of the books I'd been reading, I put my fingers behind the book mark and opened it. Holding the bookmark out, I reflected on it with a grin because it was part of the death of the old Stanley. For some reason I had started using the lottery ticket Jeff had given me on the trip out here. The book mark had a cash value of ten dollars and an emotional value of the death of self. I reflected on that for a bit and then found the place I left off, but was asleep within minutes.

The sound of a Skype call woke me.

After I clicked the accept button, Beth's face appeared on my screen.

She was still dressed from church and looked beautiful. "You rang?"

I sat for a brief moment and just enjoyed seeing her before I responded. "Yeah, I was just wondering about your church. Wondering how it was doing?"

Her eye-brows lowered in a confused expression. "Really? What brought this on?"

"I went to Marcus' website after the minister here talked about it. When I registered, I was surprised to see your church listed on the website. It just doesn't seem like them."

Her confused expression remained, as she answered. "Yeah, I guess I'm a little surprised, too. They finally hired a new minister, and this was his first Sunday. During the sermon, he talked about The Change and Marcus' website, and how the church needs to expand its work helping others. He said he'd signed the church up and encouraged us to join in."

I was watching her on screen as she talked. She was acting reserved. "You don't like the idea, or don't like him?"

A faint smile came to her face. "No, it's not that. It all sounds like a good idea, and I'll sign up after we talk. And he seems good, too. But this was his first sermon here, and he came across as a little pushy." She looked to the side and thought about that a second. "Maybe a little confrontational. I don't know. Definitely different than Reverend Allen." She looked towards me and her smile grew. "I actually think you may like him."

"Well, since he signed the church up to help Marcus' change, my impression of him is starting out on the right foot."

She leaned in towards the screen, resting her elbows on the table.

"Just two more weeks. It'll be nice to have you home."

That thought brought a big grin to my face. "Yeah. I'm looking forward to it." I carefully didn't mention my hesitation about leaving the job and having nothing job-wise lined up at home.

We were interrupted by the kids, so I chatted with them for a bit. Cooper was stoked about the concert and me knowing The Change. Alice was just my beautiful princess. By the time our call ended, my hesitation about leaving the job subsided, and I longed to be home again.

Chapter 43

Monday of my last week at HRI, I was in the cube area outside the lab. I loved being in the lab, but it was too easy to get distracted and start helping with the flywheels. This area had fewer people and distractions, so I could focus better on the documents. But I wasn't writing. I was thinking.

My time at HRI was drawing to a close, and I was trying to not think about it, but sometimes, despite my best efforts, reality intruded. I missed Beth and the kids, but whenever I let my mind wander in the direction of leaving HRI and finding "just another job," I got sick to my stomach. So, I didn't let it wander there very often. Beth had even stayed away from the subject, fearing for my mental health. I was rather fond of the big river in Egypt.

Interrupting my attempt to re-establish my façade of denial, Jeff pulled up a nearby desk chair and flopped in. "Hey, you remember Sally, the waitress we met on our trip here?"

Grateful for the distraction, I played along, and looking to the ceiling as if I was thinking, I tapped my index finger on my chin. "The one who looked like she would collapse any minute? The one you happened to greatly over-tip the exact amount she needed to pay her electric bill? Had the daughter with asthma? The one you gave some random book, because she only read English? No, I'm not sure I remember her?"

He smiled at my sarcasm and patted me on the shoulder. "We've been invited to her wedding. She called me and wanted to make sure we could come. She said she wanted us there so badly that she'd reschedule the wedding if we couldn't attend on that date."

I briefly wondered who she was marrying, but a different question came out. "She called you? You have a phone?" I was partly joking and partly serious. As far as I knew, he'd only given her my number, and I hadn't gotten a call from her or anyone else from the trip out here. Here's a guy, who owned a company that wanted to save the world though technology, and I'd never seen him with a cell phone.

Jeff laughed but didn't answer the question. "It just so happens that the weekend she was planning on having the wedding will be roughly the time you'd hit there on your way back home, anyway. So, I was thinking I'd ride with you, keep you company, and we could stop at the wedding on the way."

The thought of riding back with Jeff brought crashing down all my flimsy delusions of permanently staying in utopia.

I was going home. I was leaving HRI.

The true end of my denial hit me hard, and my mind started racing. This had been the most incredible working experience of my life. For the first time, I was contributing, I was valued, I was appreciated, and I was learning more than I'd ever thought possible.

Sure, from my first day here, Jeff had made it clear I wasn't going to stay, because my purpose was something outside the Institute—even though I had no idea of what that was. But some hope that I'd somehow find a way to stay had lived in the back of my thoughts.

But here was Jeff, talking about riding with me on the way home, and the idea of leaving the institute almost brought tears to my eyes.

Yet, I missed my family too much to not want to be home with them. No matter how much I loved the Institute, I loved my family more, and my place was with them.

On top of that emotional burden was the thought of traveling with Jeff again. The trip here had been so stressful that I had to wonder what the trip back would be like. At least this time, I'd be more prepared to handle the situation.

Then it dawned on me again that I'd been so busy here and preoccupied with everything—aka: living in denial—I hadn't even started looking for another job. Beth and I had been able to get caught up on bills because the credit cards were paid off and I was getting paid well—not to mention the time-and-a-half overtime I got from the charity work—but that wouldn't last long with no income coming in.

"Stanley?"

I don't know how long I actually sat there thinking before he'd said that, bringing me back. "Oh, sorry. I really zoned out there. You just triggered a bunch of thoughts." I waited for Jeff to respond, but he just looked back at me with his normal gaze that seemed so piercing.

It was always like he was looking into my soul. I wondered if he was.

He didn't say anything.

I lowered my voice so the woman a couple cubes away couldn't hear me. "So much has happened to me since I picked you up that day. The me who's going back is a different me than the one who drove out here two months ago."

Again, I waited for him, but he just continued his penetrating stare.

My mind started racing again, my heart rate went up, and all the reality of the situation began flooding my mind.

I'd finally found a place to work that I loved but couldn't stay! I'd never have a place like this again! I had no job lined up! The world was going to change, and I was somehow supposed to be part of that change, but I had no idea how! It was hard enough explaining what I was seeing, hearing and learning to Beth, yet Jeff seemed to want me to tell the world? Plus, I wasn't going to have Jeff with me to explain anything!

My head was spinning out of control trying to comprehend the reality of going back home and not having Jeff to help me though this.

I could understand him using Marcus to implement his plans. Marcus was like Superman. But I wasn't even a Clark Kent. What could I possibly do, compared to Marcus or Grace? Jeff would be better off finding more people like them, instead of a guy who's never really gotten the hang of life.

As I tried to slow down my breathing, I realized I was about to lose it right here in the office, which caused me to panic more.

There were people around and I had to control myself. I had to control myself! I had to control myself!

But the sudden realization of my time here ending was overloading my brain. It was more than I could handle, tears began forming in my eyes as I started to lose control.

Closing my eyes tightly, I tried to regain control, but it was no use.

I screamed, "No Jeff! I can't handle this! You picked the wrong person! I can't handle this!" I fell into the ground on my hands and knees, crying uncontrollably and screaming over and over that I wasn't the one to do this, that he'd picked the wrong person.

Through all of it, Jeff knelt beside me, holding my head, and after a very long time, I began to regain some of my composure.

When I did, I started wondering how my fit had looked to the other people in the cube area. I kept my eyes closed as I imagined people gathering around after hearing me scream. I didn't want to face them.

I clenched my fist as I prepared to push myself up and exit with as much dignity as I could muster. Except, as my fingers formed into fists, they didn't drag against carpet... the surface moved with my fingers. I opened my eyes and saw my fingers had made tracks in reddish tinted dirt. I jerked my head up and looked around.

We were at the cliff over the river, where Jeff had stopped Harris, the high school kid, from jumping. We were in Zion National Park.

In shock, I quickly looked at Jeff.

He was starting to stand from his kneeling position beside me, with a tangible, calm air of peace about him.

My head darted around as I tried to convince myself I was mistaken about being over a thousand miles from where I'd been seconds ago. When I couldn't find an explanation, I looked at him and tried to form a question. "How? ... What?"

He held up his hand to stop me and proceeded to ignore my present question. "Stanley, I will always be with you."

"But..."

He slowly shook his head letting me know this question wouldn't be answered. "Your path forward will be a challenge, I grant you that, but when you have questions they *will* be answered."

"I have one question right now!"

The corners of his mouth curled up. "Do you really think I could explain it to you in a way that would make sense?"

I started to say "Yes," but "No" came out. He was right. Nothing he said could explain the reality I'd just experienced.

"Good. So, we can move on to what's important?"

I simply nodded in response, as I climbed to my feet, then dusted my hand against my pant legs to get the dirt off.

"I have plans for you. The path you take isn't a path I can guide you on and still have it fulfill what needs to be done. If you have questions, they will be answered. They may not be answered directly, but your questions will be answered. I'll always be with you. You never have to be afraid. I will always protect you." He looked at me with his smile.

Man, I loved his smile. It's so calming, so reassuring, so deep. It's so infinite. His smile meant everything was good.

Slowly, I started walking towards the edge of the cliff. "Thanks for saving me from embarrassing myself. I never thought I could lose it like that. I didn't even see it coming."

I looked down at the river and then out to the setting sun. Not only had he brought me over a thousand miles away, it was also now dusk instead of three o'clock in the afternoon.

I looked over at Jeff, again questioning who and what he was. On the trip out east with Jeff, he'd released me from having to figure out what he was, and I'd taken full advantage of that for my own sanity. I mean, I'd watched enough episodes of *Ancient Aliens* to wonder if he was from Sirius rather than sent from God. And at the Institute, it was easier to ignore the question of what he was, because it wasn't just him who was magnificent. Plus, he continually attributed the marvels of HRI to his dad or the people around him, always minimizing his role. Now standing here, transported through time and space, I had to start asking again what he was.

I looked back over the cliff as a cool evening breeze rustled the shrubs beside me. The setting sun was a truly majestic sight as it turned sky and clouds fire red. I wished I had a camera to capture this moment. It was magnificent.

He walked up beside me and put his arm over my shoulder, joining me looking out at the sun setting over the river. "You're the right person. Be sure of that."

"How can that be? I have no idea what to do next. Can you give me some idea? Am I supposed to go home and start a church? Go stand on a street corner yelling out your message? Can you give me some idea?"

"If that's what you feel called to do, then do it. Though, I'd prefer you not do the street-corner-thing. That always comes across as kind of weird," he said to my relief on that point.

"Jeff, I don't feel any calling. I only feel confused; I can't make sense of anything that's happened. In fact, I'm standing here with a guy who may be the messiah, who just took me through space and time, and I still haven't come to terms with my disbelief in God, or what you say you are, for that matter." I was surprised to hear the last sentence come out of my mouth.

"You're a great man, Stanley."

A puff of air passed between my closed lips to proclaim my doubt. "But I really don't think I believe."

"And an honest one. Most of all, you're honest with yourself. I've told you before, what you see as disbelief is just confusion about how other people have tried to define God. As for what I am, call me whatever you want. That won't change the message." Jeff patted me gently on the shoulder. "Try to organize your thoughts. Once you start doing that, you'll start to see what you can't see right now. Have faith in yourself and have faith in God. You're part of God's plan for a new message to be heard."

Frustrated, I exclaimed, "What sense does that make? What am I going to do? Go around saying, 'If there is a God this is what he wants you to know. And you should trust me, because I heard it from a guy who's either an alien, a messiah or... or...'" I tried to come up with one of my other theories.

Jeff inserted, "Fourth-dimensional being? Mutant?"

I pointed at him. "Right." Then I continued my rant. "'But don't worry about what he is, because that isn't important; his message is what's important.'"

His eyebrows came closer together in a thoughtful look. "Yeah, yeah! I can see that working. Go with that approach." Then a smile returned to his face, and he reached up and gently bopped me on the side of the head.

I gave a soft laugh at his humor, but then we were quiet for a while as I tried to grasp what he was saying. But no matter how hard I tried, I still wasn't able to see how I was a great man. I was just me, as average as they came.

"You ready to go back?" he asked with a caring look.

I turned back towards the sunset which was starting to fade, and again wished I had a way to remember this moment. "I guess I've calmed down now. Thanks for letting me lose my sanity away from everyone."

As I spoke the last word, I was in my desk chair and Jeff was back in the chair he'd flopped into originally.

I looked around quickly. No one looked curious or shocked. What had happened to me seemed to have gone unnoticed by everyone.

Jeff looked at me with genuine concern. "You good?"

I didn't answer right away. Instead, I took the question very seriously and did my computer impression of an internal diagnostic. A mechanical sounding voice in my head replied, "All systems performing within acceptable parameters." Which, in itself, might have been a reason to call the mental health number on the back of my insurance card, but instead I answered, "You know, Jeff, I actually think I might be. I know after what just happened — your *Star Trek* impersonation and all — that I really shouldn't be, but I think I am. Maybe I'm just in shock."

I expected Jeff to respond with a typical "Well, just wait for the trip back," or something else with a smart-aleck flavor. But, instead he continued his compassionate tone. "Good. I know I've taken you through a lot."

In some ways, the smart-aleck answer would have been easier to deal with. I could have just given it right back and camouflaged much of what I was feeling. But with him dealing directly with my condition, I wasn't sure how to respond. So, I took the next most useful approach. I changed the subject. "What's the plan for the trip back? You said Sally's wedding is coming up soon."

Thankfully, he went along with my redirection. "Yeah. Not this Saturday, but the following one. I figured we could leave Monday or Tuesday, and just take a leisurely trip back home." His eyebrows rose up. "That is, if it's okay with Beth. I'm sure she would like you home sooner rather than later. If that's the case, I'll fly you back and ship your car, and I'll pass along to Sally your regret for not being able to attend."

I started to ask why he didn't just teleport me like he'd done a few minutes ago, but then I worried he might just do it. Being transported home might be cool, but deep down I knew I needed this trip with him. Leaving HRI and Jeff at the same time wasn't the closure I needed; I felt there was still something for me to learn and our time wasn't over. "No, Beth will understand. We can take a 'leisurely' trip back."

As he stood, he reached forward and caringly patted me on the side of my upper arm. "Good. I'll let you get back to work."

I nodded, and he headed back down the hall.

Chapter 44

There wasn't any working after that. How could there be? I told my carpool buddies I was walking home and then took a slow-paced stroll to the hotel as I continually replayed what had just happened. HRI one minute, Zion National Park the next and then back. How is that even possible and how is it I was the one experiencing it? It was overwhelming.

I got home, looked at the computer and debated making a Skype call to Beth. As I played the conversation in my head it sounded more and more absurd and I started questioning if it had really happened. But, it did happen. I was absolutely sure it did. I had to tell someone, and Beth was the only one who I could talk to about it. I made the call and almost dreaded my choice as I started talking.

She was quiet for an uncomfortable moment, reinforcing my regret. It sounded insane to me as I told her so there was no way for her to fit it into our concept of reality.

I started to blurt out a feeble retraction, but she interrupted me. "Stanley, stop."

My mind said, "Here it comes." This was just too much, and I watched her expression on the computer screen for some clue as to what was coming.

Her face stayed surprisingly calm. "You've been telling me crazy stories for over two months now. I've had no reason to doubt you up until now, so I have no reason to doubt you now."

I felt the tension leave my body. "Really? You aren't going to change the locks and have the padded van waiting for me when I get home?"

She smiled gently at me. "I've felt like calling that van to come get you almost every day of our marriage. Nothing's changed."

I found out putting your arms around a computer screen lacks any resemblance to a real hug. I backed away. "Oh, and I got some great news. You're going to get to meet him. He's going to come with me on the ride back."

The smile disappeared as the blood drained from her face.

I should have known better. My wife panics whenever she hears company's coming over, then she starts cleaning the house from top to bottom. To have Jeff coming added a whole new twist. I was afraid Thing 1 and 2 would be forced to live up to their namesakes. I had to laugh. "You're okay with all my crazy talk, but it's the thought of meeting him that freaks you out?"

"Of course. I believe you and all, but they're still just your stories. Now if I meet him, I'm no longer separated. I have to put a face to the stories, and maybe rationalize my own stories."

I tried to think about it from her point of view, and realized that's something I'd rarely done. The conflict in her mind must be overwhelming. If even a small part of what I was telling her was true, it would rock her religious foundations. So, the fact that she was supporting and listening to me gave me a glimpse of how much faith she had in me. If the situation had been reversed, I think I would have demanded she exit the situation, but she hadn't done that. She'd voiced her concerns and trusted me to make the best choice.

It was only right that I give her the out. "Sorry, I should have talked to you. Trust me, Jeff will understand. I'll..."

Beth cut me off. "No, you won't." She looked at me as deeply as Skype would allow. "Sure, the thought of meeting him scares me, but the thought of not meeting him, of not seeing the person you've brought into our life, that's something I'd regret forever."

Her saying that brought back the conversation I'd had with myself in the mirror, where I so wisely told myself to minimize regrets. Beth was willing to face her fear and challenge her faith, because the regret of not doing so would be worse. Which made me think of Pastor Jones' words, the cost of facing the change was less than the price of hiding from the change.

I couldn't help but nod with admiration.

Her face changed to a more questioning expression. "What do you think he is, Stanley?" She was obviously anxious about the impending arrival of our extraordinary guest and wanted to know more about him. "You've used the word 'messiah,' yet you say it with reservation instead of confidence. After all the things you've seen and heard, you should have some idea of who he is. I mean, when he gets here, I want some idea of who I'm letting into my house."

I understood what she wanted, but I couldn't give her the answer. "That's just it, Beth, I don't know. I've told him I don't know what he is, and he knows my hesitations and doesn't seem to mind in the least. But what's even more frustrating is my inability to believe." I looked away from the monitor for a minute to think. "What I've seen him do should be enough. I mean, I've traveled through space and time with him, I've seen him predict the future, all his bruises were gone on my first day at the Institute, so he healed himself overnight, and I watched him take a beating that should have killed him and transform a man's life instead." I stopped as my mind replayed more events of the last couple months.

"That's your M-O, 'I don't believe easily.'" Beth smirked. "Don't you think he knows that?"

Giving a short laugh under my breath, I lowered my gaze to the floor. "What I hear him say should be enough; no one has ever explained things to me like he has. It's like he knows exactly what questions I have and knows exactly what to say to make them make sense. I mean, once he explained Heaven and Hell as a realm with amplified emotions, it made sense." I looked back at her with tears starting to fill my eyes. "If I'd heard that at the beginning of my church experience, maybe things would have been different now. Maybe I could've believed. But I don't know if I can believe anything anymore."

In a quieter voice, more to myself than her, I repeated, "I don't know if I can believe." I focused on Beth's video image. "But he doesn't seem to care if I can believe. He seems to be fine doing what he's doing, telling me what he's telling me, showing me what he's showing me, and not ever directly trying to convince me of anything. He says I can call him whatever I want; he says what I call him isn't important to him."

We were both quiet for a moment until Beth broke the silence. "What about when he's here? What should I do?"

That was an easy question for me. "I know exactly what he'd say: 'Be Beth.' When he meets you, he wants to meet you, the real you, not someone else. And really, don't try to do anything other than what you'd do for any normal guest. He'd never ask to be treated special."

She looked skeptical.

"He'll like you just as you are, I swear." When that didn't help, I added, "Good grief, the guy seems to like *me*, you're so much better than me that you've got it made!"

Laughing at that, she finally began to relax. "Okay, I'll do my best to relax."

"Perfect!" I breathed a sigh of relief. I didn't want her stressing out over Jeff's visit, because I wanted her to be able to like him as much as I did. "Do your best. That's exactly right."

We locked eyes and had a moment together, then relaxed and chatted a bit longer. I told her I was going to Jeff's tonight to help Dylan with a paper.

"That's great you do that. You have really made a bond with him."

"Oh, he's a neat kid. It's weird because he really struggles with school but there is something much deeper to him than even Marcus or Grace, or even Jeff for that matter. He isn't smart but yet; he is. If I really knew what people meant by emotional intelligence I would go with saying he's a genius there but I'm not sure that's what it is. Anyways, I need to get going. Thanks for …" I paused, "… thanks for believing me. I'm not sure I would do the same if the situation was reversed."

She laughed. "I know you wouldn't. Have a good evening."

* * *

The dinner with the Havens felt different. It felt final. There would only be a few more times I'd experience this. After this week it would only be reflections. I was quieter than normal and simply watched and listened, trying to be in the moment and be thankful for this moment.

After Dylan helped clean up dinner we went to the library where he had made his study area. We waved at Marcus who was at his own spot typing on a computer. I wasn't sure if he was studying, writing or what. I would think he would be too busy for school right now. Dylan handed me a book and I looked at it. "Your need to do a paper on the Civil War?"

"Yeah," he answered.

I was a little disappointed. It isn't my favorite time of American history. I don't watch war movies because I'd rather not fill my mind with the depths of human cruelty. I looked at the index and, just from that, was reminded of what a bad time it was. That didn't change the fact Dylan had a paper due and my personal feelings about war didn't mean we shouldn't learn about the past of America. "How much have you read?"

"Jonathon helped me read most of it. I think if we talk some and start planning what to say in the paper, we can go back and look up information later. I think best when I talk."

I smiled at him because it was a very accurate self-evaluation. So, we talked and wrote and read and talked more. A lot of the conversation was uncomfortable for me. We read about the underground railroad and lynching of slaves. He looked up at Marcus as he spoke. "It doesn't make sense people ever thought that way. Why would people ever think some people aren't as good as other people just because of their skin color?"

I looked over at Marcus. I couldn't answer Dylan's question but thought about it silently.

Dylan kept his eye on Marcus as he spoke. "He has to be one of the most amazing people who ever lived."

"I really can't explain it, Dylan. I really can't. I've worked side-by-side with him and can't keep up. He's a brilliant engineer and it's not just me saying that. He's very well respected by everyone on the flywheel team."

Dylan shook his head sadly. "It's killing him not being there. He loves working there." Dylan looked at me seriously. "He and I are best friends. We talk a lot. He tells me everything."

With Dylan, it was sometimes hard to read him. He had a very dry sense of humor and it wasn't always clear if he was joking. I didn't think he was joking this time. "I'll bet you guys are. You're easy to talk to."

"Yeah, I am. I told you, that's what I'm good at, talking, well, and listening. I think I listen pretty good, too. And I like listening to Marcus. He needs someone like me around. He doesn't like becoming what he's becoming. He talks to me about that a lot. He said he just wants to be an engineer at HRI."

I looked at him confused. "Really? He's so much more than that. Not that being an engineer at HRI isn't enough for anyone but, he's an amazing athlete and musician."

Dylan shook his head. "I thought Marcus was wrong when he said that. But you repeated what he said."

I increased my confused look. "What? I don't get what you mean."

"Blacks are good at being athletes and entertainers."

"No, I didn't say that. Or I didn't mean it that way. What I meant was ..." I stopped to think about how to clarify what I meant. "I mean, he's good at those but he's so much more. I mean ..."

Dylan called out, "Marcus? Can you come here?"

I wanted to crawl under the table.

Marcus looked up from his computer and then stood up. He came up to Dylan and held out his fist. Dylan give him a fist bump. "What's up, my little man?"

"Stanley just said exactly what you were telling me the other day, that white people see blacks as athletes and entertainers and not engineers."

Now Marcus got a cross look on his face and then looked at me apologetically. "Dylan, you need to work on your tact a little bit. You threw this man under the bus." He sat down at the table and looked at me. "I'm sorry Dylan did this, Stanley. Let me explain." He scratched his head as he thought. "He and I were talking about role models. I told him I'd much rather be a role model for what I do at HRI. Then I said something about becoming known for being an athlete and a musician. That's what all the kids in the hood see and want to become. I want those kids to want to become scientists, engineers, teachers, doctors. The part about white people only seeing blacks as athletes and entertainers, well ..."

I stopped him. "No, I get what you're saying. Now that Mr. Tactless has pointed out the elephant in the room, I can see where the perception comes from."

Dylan looked at me funny. "I didn't say anything about an elephant."

"It's just a saying, Dylan. It means there are big, obvious ideas people don't want to talk about because they are uncomfortable. You just made me confront the elephant."

Dylan shrugged. "I still don't get it."

I smiled at him. "I'll explain later but now that we're talking about it, I have a question." I looked at Marcus. "Why don't you tell your dad you don't want to do this? Tell him you just want to work at HRI. I'm sure he'd understand."

Marcus burst out laughing. When he stopped he started working words in. "I really thought you knew my dad better. You think he's pushing me to do this? Really?"

He's reaction was almost hurtful. "Well, I'd have guessed that. He wants to change the world. You have the chance to make a difference."

Marcus shook his head in disbelief. "Man, that's not how he works. He doesn't push people. He releases people. Yeah, he's *going* to change the world, but he isn't going to do that by getting people to do what he wants. He's releasing people to do what they want. If I grew old and retired from HRI or any place else as an engineer, he'd be extremely proud of me, but that isn't who I am." He put his finger in my chest. "And, my friend, he's releasing you. You aren't here to be a tech writer. You are here to become who you are.

* * *

I walked out of the Haven's house in a major funk. I stood on the porch in a state of, maybe emptiness, maybe shock, maybe overload. There was a healthy dose of fear, that was clear. I wasn't looking at anything or waiting for anything as I stood. It was simply my chaotic brain being too occupied to worry about maneuvering the stairs. So, I stood. I tried to slow my brain down to focus on one thing at a time. I attempted to latch onto the feeling of finality at the house tonight and tried to focus on that. I know that scared me, but I knew I was trying to focus on that to avoid what Marcus had said.

"It isn't easy, is it, sir?"

I didn't jump or even look back. The voice didn't register until I saw Jonathan walk past me and sit on a first granite stair with a yellow glow from the porch light on his back.

"I was a butler in England in my younger days. It was a fine life with a proper family. And I was very good at my job." He paused. "Then it was gone."

The chaos started to dissipate as I looked at his back and replayed his words. He and I had talked some, but I was never alone with him. We had never talked at a personal level, other than the first day we met, and he was always, using his word, a proper butler. Now, here he was, sitting on the step like a regular guy. I went up and sat beside him.

"It was over thirty-five years ago when they fired me. I was homeless, wandering the streets of England. It didn't make sense." He looked over at me.

This brought up some mental images as I tried to invasion Jonathan much younger and wandering the streets in some English town. "Must have been scary."

"It was a very strange time in my life. Very strange." He stopped and thought. "But there was a plan for me. I was meant to be here, not there. The hands of destiny rigged the game to take me here." He held his hand out behind him towards the house.

This brought back Marcus's Jonah Complex sermon. It seems I wasn't the only one who was a victim to destiny.

I was going to respond but Jonathon looked over. "You are going to be okay, Stanley."

Him calling me by my name was sounded strange. He always called me 'sir' when he addressed me.

"You have been under a lot since you left California. Now that is ending, and you are standing on the front porch staring out into nothing. I understand."

We sat there quietly with a cool breeze going by. "Released. Marcus said Jeff is releasing me. Thirty-five years ago, Jeff wasn't here to release you." I looked over at him.

Jonathan gave a knowing smile. "No, he wasn't. One problem we humans have is we think in temporal terms. Jeff always existed. You have always existed. I have always existed. You, me and Jeff, are simply sharing this moment in time on this plane to realize who we are. Jeff has done a much better job of realizing who he is than most others."

"Released?"

"Very much so."

"And you?"

"Me? That is hard to explain. It is not my purpose, to become what Jeff is. It is my purpose to be of service to him. That is what I have been released to do."

As I was talking to Jonathan, I was regretting not talking to him before. Jeff had said Jonathan knew what Jeff was before Jeff did. That should have been a clue to me that Jonathan had some insight which could help me. Now I was at the end of my time in Bethlehem having a conversation I should have had much earlier. Yet, as I looked back, I'm not sure I ever had the opportunity. My time at this house was mostly with Dylan or Jeff. "I wish we would have talked before tonight."

He shook his head in a disappointed way. "Have you learned so little on this journey? Regret is the undoing of many great people. Take this moment for what it is and let the past be what it was."

Maybe I should have been hurt at his disappointment, but I smiled. "You know, you're exactly right. I have learned that over and over but still need reminders. Thank you."

"You are very welcome, sir."

"I'm guessing asking what I'm being released to do would be pointless?"

"All actions have a point, it simply isn't always the expected one." I saw a hint of a smile on his face. "But, to be truthful, I don't know what Jeff is releasing you to do and I think you are doing yourself a disservice trying to answer that question."

"Why? I mean, wouldn't it be easier if I know what was expected of me?"

He shook his head slowly. "You are understanding it wrong, sir. If you do something for him, you are doing something for him. Instead, live your life and grow. Bring joy and peace to what you touch. Only on that journey will you be able to accomplish what he already knows you will do." He stood. "Now, sir, I have duties to attend to. If it pleases you, I would like to bid you good-night."

Standing with him I replied, "There is a lot in what you just said. Thank you, Jonathan. You helped me a lot tonight."

"Have a good evening, sir." He turned and left.

With most of the mental chaos gone, I made it down the stairs and to my car. My mind was spinning and full, but in some ways, it felt like pieces of the puzzle were falling in place. It was a good feeling.

* * *

On Thursday of my last week at HRI, I went to Sam's office to pick up my final paycheck.

Sam, as always, was wonderfully overwhelming. Within minutes of sitting down, we finalized the refinance of the house, verified the transfer of all my 401-K's to the account Sam had researched and suggested, checked the status of my credit report to see if the payments I'd made and the letters I'd sent had taken effect. Next, we went over the personal budget report Beth and I worked out with Sam's guidance.

Sam looked at it with his finger quickly running over every item. Then he looked up at me. "You two have done a great job, and I see some sacrifices here. Is it a do-able plan? If not, we'll fix it now. Better to go slowly with a realistic plan, than to rush into something and then fail when it can't be implemented."

"Yeah, it's do-able. Tight, but we've talked, and it'll be worth it, so we're determined." Then I looked at the paycheck that was sitting on the corner of his desk. "Plus, look at the size of that check. Even with the money taken out to pay back the advance you guys gave me my first day, I'll have plenty left over."

He leaned over the desk and slapped me on the shoulder. My shoulder told my brain he wasn't seventy-five. "Great job. Going to miss you, Stanley. Your game has really picked up."

I was about to make a comment about my racquetball game, which was improving quickly, then as I looked at him and thought about how he'd said it, I don't think he was talking about that game. But I avoided asking the question, because I wasn't sure I wanted the answer. "I'm going to miss you, too. And thanks for your help with my game." Both of my games, all of my games. In that moment, I realized that in these two months, Sam had become almost as much a mentor to me as Jeff, and I'd really miss the guy.

As if Sam went into slow motion, he paused and looked me square in the eyes before saying, "It was an honor to serve you, Stanley. Please feel free to continue to let me serve you. HRI will let you use this service as long as you want." With that he stood and extended his hand.

This would be one of the last times I'd feel his vice-like grip. The thought hurt, but at the same time, I was truly thankful for having had this time with Sam.

* * *

Friday after work, my last day at HRI, my co-workers—now more friends than co-workers—had a big going-away party for me in the open-air pavilion behind HRI. I walked out of the building with some other guys from the lab, and as we made our way to the back of HRI, I commented on the weather. It was in the low seventies with a very gentle breeze; one of those days that demands you comment on it several times.

We reached the pavilion area, and as I looked around, I was glad to see it wasn't only HRI people who'd been invited. Jeff's family was there, church members, and others who I'd grown close to in this short time. I would get to say good-bye to everyone.

My thoughts were interrupted by some music starting. I looked to the stage, and smiled at what I saw. The Change was playing. How many people could say they had the current best-selling band play at their going away party? That was exceptionally cool.

I'd gotten to know many of the HRI chefs pretty well, too, and they had a special treat for me in the open-air dining area. Because of the price, I hadn't had a cafeteria chili cheese dog since I'd been here, but today the chili dogs were free and the Mountain Dew flowed in abundance. As I was handed mine, I felt like Heaven had descended to Earth.

Not ready for the emotional good-byes, I skirted the crowd and made my way to the stage. People hadn't started gathering there, so I was able to enjoy the music without distraction.

With chili dripping on one hand and the condensation of the Dew dripping on the other, I stood and watched my great friend Marcus and his band play. His music had really been growing on me. Even cooler, when Marcus noticed me standing there, he stopped the song they'd been playing, picked up the electric guitar from a stand beside him, turned and said something to the band. The drummer yelled out a very fast, "1-2-3-4," and Marcus started pounding out a driving three chord progression on his guitar that I recognized immediately and automatically started singing to. Jeff must have told him I liked the Ramones.

The song lasted about two minutes, so it was one of the Ramones longer songs. When the band finished, I set my cup and plate down, and gave them an energetic round of applause not caring I was the only one clapping. The few others who'd made their way to the stage must not have shared my taste in music. But I shrugged it off as Marcus and the band gave me a playful bow, it was my going away party after all. I couldn't wait 'til I told Cooper that The Change had played the Ramones for me; he'd be so jealous.

I turned from the stage and looked at this huge gathering of friends and acquaintances, more than I'd ever had at any time in my life, and maybe more than I'd had in the whole of my life. It was sad to think I'd never see most of these people again.

Despite the pain of being away from my family, this had been the greatest time of my life, and I was dealing with leaving much better now, than I might have even a week ago. I think that when I buried my fears last Sunday during the sermon, it gave me permission to begin to look forward to the changes that were obviously headed my way. Yeah, those changes would carry a cost, but the biggest gift that these two months had given me was the understanding how much *not* changing had cost me, and I wasn't willing to pay that price any longer.

I scanned the gathering, looking for Jeff but didn't see him. As I thought about it more, I was glad he wasn't here right now. If he'd been here, I'd have gravitated towards him and not appreciated my time with all these people as fully as I should.

I took a deep breath and walked into the crowds.

Everyone seemed genuinely sad I was leaving, and all the sincere good-byes were a heartwarming experience which meant I spent a great deal of energy trying not to lose control like I had back in my office the other day.

It didn't take long for Dylan to find me. He was clearly upset I wouldn't be around anymore and he remained my constant companion throughout the party, which was just fine with me. I wondered if Jeff would let him come to visit California sometime. He and Cooper would get along great.

Grace came up to me and hugged me with tears in her eyes. But she wouldn't stick around and talk except to apologize for not sticking around and talking, because she knew she'd cry.

I'd thought many times about her saying she needed to see broken again if she wanted to grow. And as I watched her make her way through the crowd, I realized at a deep level what she meant when she'd said that. I'd come to HRI a very broken man, and after these two months, I'd felt like I'd finally gotten some traction in life. I felt like I belonged and was an okay person. As that thought sat for a moment, I finally acknowledged to myself for the first time in my life, I felt unbroken, fixed. And now that I was fixed, I felt like I could go out into the world again, where I could see broken and still be okay. As the amazing young woman walked away, I knew to the core of my being I was okay with going home and facing what was ahead of me. I wasn't afraid.

My thoughts were interrupted by Aaron. He gave me a hug and told me what a *wonderful* experience it was working with me, and what a *wonderful* job I did with some of the design work on the flywheel, and how I had set the bar *wonderfully* high for the next person. He didn't even mention my work as a tech writer, which I knew he thought was *wonderful*, too. I smiled as I realized the quality of the tech writing was a by-product of my knowing the product so well, which Aaron had fostered as my manager. Aaron really and truly was a wonderful man.

Aaron triggered a whole new set of thoughts. Our conversation about what tool people were, started replaying in my mind, and my conversation with Beth about what shape I was. I wondered for a moment whether I'd figured out what tool I was or what shape I was, then came to the conclusion that the concept was stupid. I was having a great time, loved what I was doing and wasn't defined by one role. I was as many shapes and many tools as I wanted to be, and very happy to not be limited by my, or others', expectations.

Rita came with a stack of good-bye notes from the kids in her class. After reading some of the notes, I had to work even harder to control myself. They'd been such a joy to read to; I'd miss her kids terribly. But the experience of reading to them had opened my eyes as to how little I was involved in my own kids' school. That would change. That would most definitely change.

Even Jonathan, Jeff's butler, walked up and uncharacteristically of him, initiated a hug. As we hugged, I couldn't help but wish I'd gotten to know him better. My time at the Havens' house had been mostly taken up with Dylan or Jeff. But as I said good-bye to Jonathan, I got the feeling I missed out on something that could have been special, there was a lot more to him than just being a butler. I attributed that feeling to a nagging statement Jeff made that hadn't surfaced until just now. On my first visit to Jeff's house, he'd said Jonathan knew what Jeff was before Jeff did. What did that mean? And what did that say about Jonathan? But now it was too late to get that answer. To add to the discomfort of the moment, Jonathan gave me an eerie knowing smile, that seemed to say, "You're catching on." Then he was gone before I could get a question formed.

Looking down at Dylan, I said, "He's an interesting guy."

"Indubitably," was Dylan's reply, which made us both laugh.

As the evening wore down and the good-byes slowed down, I saw Keith sitting on a picnic bench by himself. Dylan and I went over and sat on the bench opposite him.

"Keith, you ever meet Dylan? He's one of Jeff's kids."

Keith gave a faint smile and extended his hand across the table. "Nice to meet ya, Dylan."

Dylan reached over the table and made a fist instead of shaking hands. "Don't worry about me being the boss' kid. Let's you and me cause some trouble."

Keith gave me a quick questioning glance but then looked right back at Dylan. Keith's faint smile grew bigger. "Right on." He made a fist and connected with Dylan's.

I playfully elbowed Dylan. It was clear Keith was burdened, and Dylan had a way of helping people relax and let their burdens go, even if only for a short time.

I started to ask what was on Keith's mind, but with the reprieve Dylan had just given him, it didn't seem fair to bring his burdens back in focus. "How's your mom and son?"

His smile showed I'd made the right choice. He clearly had much affection for them. "Oh, man. They're on cloud nine. We got a little money saved up now, you know. Never had that before. Went and saw some guy here about money. Other than needing some valium after leaving his office, it had to be one of the best experiences in my life."

"Ah, you met Sam. I can relate to needing something to calm down afterwards."

Keith gave a quick laugh. "Yeah, Sam. Man, he's almost magic. Got my money doing magic stuff. Wasn't none of it going nowhere good before him."

I had to replay that sentence a few times to realize it was a positive thing. "He has you on a budget?"

"Yeah, now I see things different. Didn't notice how much I was wastin' before, and I didn't even think I had money to waste before. I'm making tons more money now, and ain't none of it going to stupid stuff. Mama's actually looking at some schooling for her." His face showed his excitement about that as he turned from me to Dylan. "She had me young and couldn't do that before. She's super excited. And got my boy in karate. Oh, he's lovin' that."

I interjected. "That's great. My son loves karate too."

"Sam's even got a college fund started for him." Keith shook his head in amazement. "My boy's gonna get a chance."

Keith was one of those people you met and liked instantly. Somehow, Grace had seen that in the convenience store and acted on it, and in doing so, she'd changed everything not only in Keith's life, but his mother's life and his son's, too. Sure, he talked different than most people at HRI, but he was a perfect HRI employee, someone who didn't have all the answers and wanted to find them.

I recalled my vision from last Sunday where I was unwillingly being lowered into a grave. I think Keith had taken a running jump into his own grave and was one of the busiest people above it, burying his old fearful self so his new self could flourish.

We were quiet for a minute, and as I looked towards the stage and watched Marcus play. I noticed Keith look at me and felt his mood regress back to the point when we first came to the table. Now seemed like a good time to find out what was bothering him. "Why were you over here by yourself instead of mingling?"

He shrugged. "I don't know. Didn't really want to be here, but couldn't really not be here."

The response surprised me. "Why's that?"

He looked at me with a serious expression. Just like many times before, he paused as if he was deciding to say what was really on his mind. He started slowly. "It's funny." He looked out at all the people enjoying themselves. "They're some great people. They've all treated me better than I deserve." He looked at me with reservation. "But I almost feel like you're takin' HRI with you. Even though we didn't always work together, you magically seemed to be around when I need someone to set my mind straight. You always said things that made sense. You always made me understand things I didn't think I could understand." He grinned. "You're a word man. You make words mean something." Then he frowned again. "Won't be right here without you."

I tried to think of words to live up to being a 'word man.' But I was blank.

Dylan didn't let the uncomfortable silence last. "*That!*" he said with strong emphasis on the word, "is exactly what I wish I'd said." He grinned at Keith. "Well, not the HRI part, because I don't work here." He turned to me. "But making things make sense. I live in a house where anyone would give me their heart for a heart transplant if I needed it. When I need help with school, someone always helps. But with you helping, I was getting somewhere. Things make sense when you explain them." Dylan's expression mimicked Keith's frown; the first time I'd ever seen that expression on his face. "And now, you're leaving."

Dylan's statement didn't help words come to me, and all I could force out was feeble. "I hate leaving, too, but I have to." Then I attempted to brighten it up. "But we live in a world of instant communication: phone, Skype, IM, email. Contact me anytime about anything—"

Keith interrupted. "Anyway, that's why I've been sittin' over here. Didn't want to talk to you. I mean, I know you have ta leave, and I know you miss your family and want to see them. But I've been sittin' here, selfishly trying to figure out how to keep you here. But can't come up with a way." He glanced at me, then away. "I'm glad you were here, but not happy you're leaving."

Dylan interjected. "As Charles Dickens said, 'It was the best of times. It was the worst of times.'"

Both Keith and I looked at Dylan.

"I guess that sums it up pretty good, Dylan," I said. "And isn't that the way most of life is?" Thinking back to the grave scene. "You have to bury the old before the new can come into being." Then to lighten the mood, I said, "Yeah, it was fun being with both of you, but neither of you need me. You're both smart dudes. You'll find your way."

I tried to think of something else to say, but couldn't come up with anything, so figured distraction was my best alternative. "Have you guys had a chili cheese dog yet? I had one and am dying for another."

Keith's smile grew. "Ya see what I mean 'bout you making everything okay? Like a good chili cheese dog don't just make everything alright."

Dylan laughed and popped up from the bench. "I'm going to go ask Marcus somethin'. Don't eat without me."

"Sure." I watched him race toward the stage and demand his brother's attention in the way little brothers have done since the dawn of time.

Even from as far away as I was, I could see Marcus roll his eyes as he stopped the song he was singing and knelt at the edge of the stage. Words were exchanged, and it was obvious Marcus was exasperated for a moment, then he laughed and nodded.

Clearly thrilled, Dylan ran back to us as Marcus stopped the music and talked to his bandmates. Winded, Dylan halted in front of me. "This will make us all feel better, I promise."

"Looking forward to it," I said as I stood.

As the three of us made our way to my friends with the tall white hats, Marcus started playing, and we all laughed.

"*John Jacob Jingleheimer Schmidt*?" I asked, recognizing the song from my Boy Scouting days.

"Just wait!" Dylan exclaimed, giving me a knowing grin, holding my hand as we walked.

The band and Marcus stopped. Marcus addressed the crowd. "Come on. This is a sing along. We'll keep playing it until I see everyone singing." The band started again so.

The crowd bought into it, and we sang as Marcus and the band started changing it up, first a jazzy version, then they flowed into a bluegrass version, and into a rap version. The band ended the song to thunderous applause.

As the three of us turned and continued on our way to the food, Dylan said, "See! That helped. Everybody feels better now."

I held up my hand in his favorite knuckle-bump. "You're the dude, man."

We were still laughing as we ordered our food, and standing

beside Keith and Dylan as we ate, I surveyed the gathering with mixed emotions, far happier emotions than before Dylan's song, but still mixed.

As I looked around, a vision of my old gruff scoutmaster came to mind, and he was smiling approvingly at me. I was leaving the campsite cleaner than I found it.

Good-bye HRI and thanks for the experience. Hello future.

93316558R00157

Made in the USA
San Bernardino, CA
07 November 2018